D1096375

CATHERINE'S
INTRIGUE

CATHERINE'S INTRIGUE

a suspense novel

PAIGE EDWARDS

Covenant Communications, Inc.

Cover image: *Red Brush Strokes* © zoom-zoom, courtesy of istock.com. *Studio Shot of Young Beautiful Woman* © CoffeeAndMilk, courtesy of istock.com.

Cover design copyright © 2019 by Covenant Communications, Inc.

Published by Covenant Communications, Inc.
American Fork, Utah

Copyright © 2019 by Paige Edwards
All rights reserved. No part of this book may be reproduced in any format or in any medium without the written permission of the publisher, Covenant Communications, Inc., P.O. Box 416, American Fork, UT 84003. The views expressed within this work are the sole responsibility of the author and do not necessarily reflect the position of Covenant Communications, Inc., or any other entity.

This is a work of fiction. The characters, names, incidents, places, and dialogue are either products of the author's imagination, and are not to be construed as real, or are used fictitiously.

Printed in the United States of America
First Printing: March 2019

25 24 23 22 21 20 19   10 9 8 7 6 5 4 3 2 1

978-1-52440-673-8

For Loretta

ACKNOWLEDGMENTS

WITHOUT TRACI HUNTER ABRAMSON, THIS book would still be swimming around inside my head. She, along with the rest of my critique group—Ellie Whitney and Jen Leigh—nudged and encouraged me toward publication. Thank you to my beta readers: Emily Clark, Kanani Cox, and Renae Mackley; your suggestions made all the difference.

Thank you to Kathy Jenkins, not only for listening to my frightened pitch and requesting the manuscript but also for her Christlike example. A special thanks to Samantha Millburn; I was thrilled when I found out she was my editor. We met way back at my first writers' conference. She took a lump of sand and turned it into a pearl. Toree Douglas, thank you for the intriguing cover design. It was so hard to choose just one of your comps. And to all the rest of the Covenant family, I couldn't work with kinder individuals.

Thank you to my grandson Crew for liking Grandma's story from the very beginning, and to my husband, Ladd, who encourages me to spread my wings. Lastly, thank you to my Heavenly Father for giving me the words and placing the right people along the way.

CHAPTER ONE

THIS WAS A BAD IDEA. Catherine should not be driving. The lines on the center divider blurred as rain dotted the windshield, then turned into a downpour. She fiddled with the wipers, but the blinker came on instead.

Her brother Jack had picked her up at Heathrow in his newly restored 1966 fire-engine-red MGB, insisting she take the wheel once they reached the Cotswolds. So, four hours after landing on British soil, she was sitting on the wrong side of the car, driving on the wrong side of the road, and trying not to annihilate them in the process.

The lush, rolling countryside distorted through the windshield. She lifted her hand from the steering wheel and rubbed her sleep-deprived eyes.

"Catherine, you're going to get us both killed! The English drive on the left."

Jack's warning came just in time. A horn blared. Catherine swerved back into their lane with a hiss of tires on wet blacktop, barely missing a head-on collision. Her hands shook, and her heart thundered in her ears. The afternoon rain pattered against the windshield like the tick of a thousand clocks in the brief silence that followed.

"I wish I hadn't insisted you drive," Jack grumbled, though this was the car he intended her to use during her stay.

You'll regret more than my driving once you find out why I came.

Between derisive laughter and loud objections, her two oldest brothers, Ben and James, had voiced their opinions about her English "quest." Unfortunately, Jack, her next oldest brother, had a similar mind-set. She hoped the extenuating circumstances behind her visit would soften his attitude because she needed his help. Asking him without receiving a flat refusal would be tricky. She had a hard enough time opening herself up as it was, and Jack's antagonistic views on researching Mom's lineage could fill a sinkhole.

Traffic slowed to a crawl in front of her, and she downshifted, accidentally grinding the gears.

"Was that payback for making you drive?" Jack's chocolate-brown eyes flashed.

"No, but thanks for the idea on how to get you back."

"I spent almost eight months restoring this vehicle." Jack twisted in his seat and stared at her for a full seven seconds.

She knew it was seven seconds because she counted. It usually took seven to ten seconds for Jack to cool down when he was upset. He'd learned that little trick when they were kids, and it had kept him out of a lot of trouble. Catherine couldn't say the same for the twins.

Growing up with three older brothers, she had learned much about self-preservation. Rarely did she share personal feelings or opinions with others, preferring to keep them to herself. Now, at twenty-four, Catherine got scrappy with her brothers only when they pushed her too far.

The rain stopped as quickly as the turn of a faucet. Jack fiddled with the radio, selecting British pop rock.

"Okay, sis. What's going on? I know you love me, but no sister spends five months hanging out with her brother. Why are you waiting until September to start with that Washington D.C. design firm? I thought you were excited about your job." He laid his forearm across the back of her seat.

Catherine let out a sigh. So much for trying to postpone the inevitable. "There's a baggie inside my purse you need to see."

Jack rummaged inside her Burberry tote and retrieved a gallon-sized plastic bag containing a small, tattered book. He opened the seal.

"Whew. That's rank." He fanned the air and closed it quickly. "It's a smelly old book. So what?"

"Mom found that before she . . ." Catherine's throat tightened. Just the thought of Mom made speaking difficult.

Jack dropped the offending book inside Catherine's purse and looked out the passenger window.

Catherine cleared her throat, trying to get past the lump. "When you were offered that engineering position at Davis, Mom was over the moon."

"I remember." Jack's voice sounded like he had swallowed gravel. "She went on and on about me renting a house in the village Glorianne was from. What does that have to do with this book?"

Catherine said before she lost her nerve, "That's Glorianne's diary. Mom found it before her last round of chemo. When hospice took over, she asked me to use it to locate her family."

"Turn right." Jack scowled at her and drummed his fingers on the dashboard. "Do you know how many generations have tried to find Glorianne's family?"

"A few," she muttered and turned down the street Jack indicated.

"A few?" Jack's voice warmed with passion. "Try four. Four generations, Catherine. With all the money Dad has blown hiring professional genealogists, he could have invested more heavily in Coombes Enterprises or donated it to charity. Instead, he's squandered it on a dead-end cause." Jack drummed his fingers again, his eyes boring into her. "What makes you think you can find what doesn't exist?"

"I don't know if I can, but . . ." Unwanted tears burned her eyes. She blinked them away.

The tension drained from his face. "Sucker," he said gently.

"Come on, Jack. Help me. It'll be like hunting for buried treasure," she said, referring to their childhood obsession.

"I'll make you walk the plank if you ask me again." Though Jack's words were playful, she knew he meant them.

Her heart sank. On occasion, Jack could be every bit as maddening as the twins. She had hoped his attitude would soften after Mom had passed, but there was no budging him. She was on her own.

"Fine," she huffed. "Forget I asked."

"Now you're pouting."

"I don't pout."

"Then why is your bottom lip sticking out like that?"

Catherine glanced in the rearview mirror and sucked in her lower lip. She tried not to smile but couldn't help herself. She could never stay angry with Jack for long.

They crossed a medieval arched bridge over the River Rue, the tires humming over the cobbles. Catherine eased the car onto Bascombe's High Street. The honey-colored stone shops and cafés were smothered in wisteria's purple blooms. At one end of the village green stood the parish church of St. Sebastian, with its twelfth-century tower and ancient graveyard. At the other was Bascombe Hall, a former manor house converted into a B&B.

Jack motioned with his chin to continue straight. They reached a roundabout. Bascombe's only pub, the Slurping Monkey, sat on one corner.

Catherine was a big fan of British pub names, but this one's moniker took pride of place—though for a modern-day eatery, the title did not entice.

"This road will take us out of the village," Jack said.

Following his directions, Catherine continued on the two-lane highway, where shallow ditches filled with rainwater flowed on either side. The hedgerows disappeared, replaced by vistas of green pasture dotted with sheep. An Elizabethan manor house topped a steep hill.

"What a beautiful place," Catherine said as they passed the estate's elaborate stone pillars and wrought-iron gate.

"That's Ashford Priory. It belongs to an English aristocrat."

Distracted by the property's splendor, Catherine took her eyes off the road for a better look. The car veered off course as the highway curved around the base of the hill. She yanked the wheel to correct her error, but the rainwater covering the road sent them into a hydroplane.

"Pump the brakes," Jack spat.

Catherine tapped the pad beneath her foot in a desperate attempt to gain traction. The brakes were useless. She gasped as the MGB shot across the pavement. Water spewed out from under its wheels. Time slowed to a crawl. The car reached the edge of the road and dove straight into the ditch.

* * *

Nick Davidson, Viscount Ainsley, grandson and heir to the Earl of Rivendon, downshifted. With a bone-jarring bounce, the tractor's gear engaged, and the machine crept through the mud toward the burn pile, dragging a fallen tree. British Weather Services predicted rain for the next week, but rain or shine, he needed to clear the priory fields of debris in preparation for spring plowing.

Reaching the burn pile, Nick detached the tree and made a wide turn. The flash of hazard lights on the motorway caught his attention. Some poor soul had gone into the ditch. He hoped they were all right. The southern fields would have to wait. He turned the tractor and chugged across the uneven terrain to offer his assistance.

A young woman with a smudge of dirt on her cheek leaned against the rear wing of a vintage MGB, checking her mobile, no doubt, for service. His mouth went dry. She had the face of an angel, and her long legs in a pair of slim-fitting jeans had him biting his tongue to keep it from lolling outside his mouth.

A man not much older than she was bent under the bonnet.

The woman's eyes flashed up, connecting with his through the cab's windscreen. Air left his lungs as though someone had punched him in the gut.

He cut the tractor engine and climbed out of the cab. Pulling his Ascot cap low, he approached the couple. The man appeared about his height, standing an inch the other side of six feet, but he seemed a few years younger than his own twenty-eight. The woman was younger still and shivering violently.

"Is everyone all right?" Nick asked.

"Just stuck in mud," the man said.

A blush started up the woman's neck. Her long, golden-brown curls swung forward, hiding her face. She must be the culprit that had landed them in this predicament.

"I can give you a tow after I gather chains from the barn," Nick said, trying to hold back a grin.

The woman emerged from behind her tumble of curls and answered through chattering teeth, "That's very kind of you."

"Do you have a rug in the car?" Nick frowned.

"A rug?" She gave him a blank look.

"American?" At her nod, he translated, "A blanket. Do you have one in your boot?"

The woman glanced at her companion.

"No. I don't," the man said.

Another batch of shudders shook the woman's slender shoulders.

"She needs to get warm." Nick looked pointedly at her soaked boots and said to the man, "There's a pub down the road. I could drop her off before collecting the chains. A warm fire and something hot to drink will chase away her shakes."

The man took the woman by the arm and conferred with her in whispers. Her gaze shifted and met Nick's. "If you don't mind, I'll take you up on your offer."

"Very good." Extending his hand to the man, Nick introduced himself. "Nick Davidson."

"Jack Pressley-Coombes." Jack jerked his chin toward the woman. "My sister, Catherine."

A sister. His mood brightened considerably, and he took charge of the situation. "Miss, do you need anything from your motorcar before we go?"

"My bag." Catherine squelched through the mud to retrieve her purse. Her brother followed, handing her several pound notes.

"Don't worry. Everything's going to be fine." Jack patted her shoulder.

Catherine pocketed the bills and glanced in Nick's direction.

"My chariot awaits, Miss Pressley-Coombes. We'll have you thawed out and on your way in no time." Nick gestured toward his blue New Holland tractor.

Catherine followed Nick to the tractor and climbed inside, sitting on the folding auxiliary seat. She glanced around the cab's interior as Nick took his place behind the wheel.

"This is very high-tech." A note of surprise laced her words.

"Do you like her?" Nick asked with pride.

"Yes," she said through chattering teeth.

Turning the key, he fired up the tractor and cranked the heat on high. He contemplated her for a moment, then removed his anorak and draped it about her shoulders. Even though she was tallish for a woman, his jacket dwarfed her.

Her wide-flashing smile of thanks was so filled with sweetness he caught himself staring. His tongue tied in knots as he put the tractor in motion. She made him feel like a small boy who'd spilled his pudding down the front of his jumper.

He asked the first thing that came to mind. "Are you here visiting your brother?"

"How did you know?" Catherine's eyes grew round.

He laughed at her expression, his nerves settling. "I recognized his motor-car. In a village the size of Bascombe, it's hard to miss."

"Cars are Jack's passion. He works for Davis Racing."

"Formula One."

"He's an engineer." Her chin quivered, and she wrapped her arms about herself.

"I imagine you have amusements planned for your stay?"

"I've officially been on English soil for"—she checked her watch—"five hours. After wrecking my brother's car, I'd say I'm off to a good start, wouldn't you?"

"You are to be congratulated." He touched his cap.

Catherine's smile lit her aquamarine eyes this time. Nick forgot to breathe. *Get a grip, Ainsley.*

The tractor hit a pothole, causing Catherine to bounce high on the cushion. Nick grabbed her arm to steady her.

"Thanks." She tucked a long curl behind her ear and confessed, "I'm not the most popular person with my brother right now."

"If it helps, I doubt his motorcar's damaged. No rocks or debris litter the verges on that carriageway. I tow any number of vehicles out of that ditch on a fairly regular basis. They usually just need tidying up."

"I'm sorry we took you away from your work."

"I'm not sorry," he said and meant it. "What brings you across the pond?"

"I'm doing some research this summer."

"Are you at university, then?" With the heater running at full, he noticed her shivering had begun to diminish.

"Graduated. I start my new job this fall."

"Brilliant. As what?"

"I'm an interior designer with a master's in historic homes."

"Ah. Hence the distraction on that particular stretch of motorway?" He motioned toward the priory with his arm.

She nodded. "Most Elizabethan manors aren't so well preserved. Do you know if it's open to the public?"

"It's privately owned. As it happens, I know someone who could give you a tour." He bit back a grin.

"Really? That would be incredible." Her eyes sparkled like gemstones.

"I'll give you my number. Text me your availability, and I'll arrange a tour."

Catherine pulled her mobile out of her handbag and entered his number into her contacts.

Nick wondered briefly how she would respond when she realized he'd be giving the tour.

Within minutes, the Slurping Monkey came into view. He wasn't surprised to see Charlie's car in the lot. Nick should have known his farmhand would stop by the pub on his way home from his dental appointment. He steered the tractor into the graveled car park and set the brake.

Nick went around to the passenger side and reached up, taking Catherine by the waist and swinging her to the ground. A tangible zing of awareness shot through him when their eyes connected, and she blushed a delightful pink.

"Thank you, Nick." Catherine's voice sounded a little breathless.

"My pleasure." His own response came out winded as well.

Catherine removed his anorak and handed it over. Then, with a crunch of gravel, she headed for the pub.

"Miss Pressley-Coombes?" he called after her, trying to prolong their interaction.

She spun on her heel, a question in her eyes.

"Could you send Charlie out?"

"Charlie?"

"He'll be playing darts. Tell him Nick's in need of his assistance." He fought back a laugh. Charlie wasn't going to like this one little bit.

"Of course."

With open admiration, he watched her cross the lot and enter the pub, her graceful movements reminding him of a classical dancer. Climbing back inside the tractor, he waited for his delinquent employee.

* * *

Heads turned when Catherine entered the Slurping Monkey. As she approached the counter, her mud-splattered jeans and soaked boots left a trail on the wide-plank floors. A telltale blush burned up her neck as the patrons followed her progress across the room.

The black-and-white building was pure, authentic Tudor, complete with dark, low beams and hand-carved linenfold paneling. A fire crackled invitingly inside a massive stone fireplace.

While she waited her turn at the counter, Catherine watched two men in work clothes play a game of darts. A rugby match blared from a flat screen at the bar, where a trio of young men sipped their drafts and gave an occasional cheer.

"What'll it be, miss?" The proprietor, a man with gray eyes and grizzled brows, asked. By the gray streaking his brown hair, Catherine judged him to be in his late forties.

She lowered her voice as a few diners continued to stare. "My car went off the road about a half mile back. Nick asked me to send Charlie out to help him."

"That's a bad curve, that." The man shook his head. "You aren't the first to wind up in Ainsley's ditch. If Nick hadn't already offered, I would have rung him."

"He's very kind." And interesting, she thought, remembering the sudden tingles that had nothing to do with her frozen feet when he lifted her from the cab.

"Hey, Charlie," the man yelled at the dart players.

A young man with tousled hair the color of ripened wheat glanced over. "Ainsley's outside and needs your assistance."

"I told you he'd find out." The other player laughed and slapped Charlie on the back.

Charlie grunted, grabbed his jacket off a hook and headed out into the afternoon, the door slamming behind him.

"I hope he's not angry about towing my car," Catherine said with a twinge of worry.

"It doesn't matter if he is. The lad's been here all afternoon when he should have been working. Nick's his employer."

Remembering Nick's secret amusement when he'd asked her to send Charlie out, she giggled, liking the farmer even more.

"Charlie's all right. He needs something besides darts to occupy his mind." The man wiped the counter with a cloth.

"Nick won't fire him, will he?"

"I doubt it. Charlie's a good worker. But Nick will dock his pay." The proprietor took another swipe at the counter. "He's a savvy businessman, our Nick. I doubt he'll be upset. He's been aching to have a go at that new-fangled tractor of his."

She glanced at the menu above the counter. "Could I order a hot chocolate?"

"Absolutely. Are you traveling through, or have you lost your way?" He rang up her order.

"I'm a temporary resident."

"You've caused a regular to-do." He indicated the roomful of customers glued to their conversation.

Catherine glanced over her shoulder at the unabashed eavesdroppers. "So I see."

Catherine raised her dirty hands. "Is there a bathroom where I can wash up?"

The man's bushy brows twitched. "Loo's around the corner."

Loo? She found their expressions charming. "I'll be right back."

In the bathroom, Catherine cringed at her reflection: cold, wet, and curly; she couldn't look worse if she tried. It was just her luck to meet someone interesting when she was looking her worst.

When she emerged from the bathroom, her hot chocolate waited on the counter. "Thank you," she said to the man with the bushy brows.

"Marcus Johnston."

"Catherine Pressley-Coombes." She wrapped her hands around the warm mug and took a sip. "Marcus, this is delicious."

"My special recipe."

Running another gambit of stares, Catherine took her drink to a fireside table. Too embarrassed to slip out of her wet boots to warm her feet, she picked at a dried piece of mud on her sleeve and worried about Jack's car. She hoped her monthly stipend from her trust fund would cover the repairs.

Taking another sip, she removed Glorianne's diary from her tote and attempted for the dozenth time to read the first entry. The few visible squiggles blurred and ran together on the page. This would not be easy.

Her cell buzzed with a text from Gillian.

Welcome to the UK. Will call Sunday. Hugs.

Thanks. Can't wait to chat. XO, Catherine shot back.

Gillian Buchanan was the closest thing she had to a sister. Her former college roommate and best friend was currently enrolled in graduate studies at the University of Edinburgh. Catherine planned to visit her as part of her trip and spend time with her in the Highlands of Scotland.

Catherine finished her hot chocolate and debated whether to order another when her phone rang. "Jack. How's the car?"

"Muddy, but perfectly fine. Quit worrying," the man who wiped his car down with a cloth diaper said. "I'll be there in a minute."

That was Jack in a nutshell: no fuss when it mattered. Catherine packed away Glorianne's diary and moved toward the bank of windows beside the door to wait. Unable to help herself, her fingers reverently touched the hand-carved linenfold paneling. Would Nick remember to arrange a tour of that Elizabethan manor? Even if he didn't, she wanted to see him again.

CHAPTER TWO

"Is every train in London running late?" Sally's greeting assaulted Theodosia's ears when she entered her elderly cousin's posh Westminster flat. No matter how upper crust her accent, Sally's tone was lethal enough to kill swine.

Sally was right about the trains; every one Theodosia had taken had run behind schedule, which meant Sally's cook had left for the day and her night nurse was due in an hour. Though she always tried to avoid it, Theodosia was alone with her eighty-two-year-old cousin.

Theodosia Stanhope, aka Lady Hadley, sighed as she hung her raincoat on the elaborate hall tree. The blustery spring day had rearranged Theodosia's sleek bob into something that would do Ed Sheeran's hairdresser proud. Before she answered Sally, she shook her blonde hair into place and tugged at her plunging neckline.

"How are you today?" Theodosia asked, entering the overwarm lounge. Afternoon tea waited on the mahogany table.

"Terribly annoyed," Sally huffed, her multiple chins wiggling. "I'll be dead before I inherit anything from this ancient piece of nonsense."

The Sèvres china, with its exquisitely painted roses, shone under myriad overhead crystals, and a well-worn Christie's catalog lay on the damask tablecloth beside today's mail.

Theodosia had no idea what Sally was grumbling about. At a guess, it had something to do with the opened envelope beside her elbow from their family's legal firm.

Sitting across the table from her cousin, Theodosia sighed again. Visiting Sally was tiresome on a good day. On a bad one, it was all she could do not to strangle her. For the last four of her thirty-six years, she had put up with Sally's abuse in the hope of inheriting her wealth.

Theodosia filled the dainty, old-fashioned cups. "One scone or two?"

Sally ignored her. "I can't believe after all this time my solicitor cannot prove without probable doubt that some little heiress didn't produce off-spring almost three centuries ago. Because of that, millions of pounds sit in a vault collecting interest."

Millions of pounds? Theodosia stopped in the act of placing two scones on Sally's plate. "What are you talking about?"

"Have you never heard of the Countess's Trust?" Sally clanked her cup onto its saucer, sloshing tea.

"I don't believe so." Theodosia added sugar to the Darjeeling and stirred.

"The Earl of Rivendon manages the trust. You work for him. This shouldn't be news to you."

"Rivendon's financials are strictly hush-hush. He keeps his paperwork under lock and key," Theodosia said.

"Millions go to the Church of England if I die before time is up on that trust," Sally explained as though Theodosia were unintelligent.

"Why is that?"

"Stupid girl. If I die before October, the Church of England will benefit from its millions. Total rubbish." Sally thumped her hand on the tablecloth, rattling the china.

Her tirade could not be doing her heart any good, but Theodosia knew better than to interrupt.

"After two and a half centuries, no direct female descendants of the third earl's second wife have surfaced. If none are found, the trust reverts to the present earl's female relatives." Sally picked up a scone and slathered it with clotted cream.

"Surely a trust that old would pass down through the male line. Primogeniture has only been challenged the last decade."

"Not if a woman was wealthy in her own right and took care to do it up legally. Which the third Earl of Rivendon's second wife did." Sally's old eyes gleamed.

Theodosia raised her brow.

Sally nodded. "Most unusual, I admit, but it has been known to happen from time to time. In this case, the contents of the Countess's Trust should be mine. I'm Rivendon's only living female relation. And I have plans for those funds." Sally stroked the Christie's catalog with a pudgy hand.

Theodosia squirmed in her seat as she absorbed the news. She too was a relative, though a distant one. If the trust went to Rivendon's female relations, surely she qualified.

She trembled with excitement at the news. Her financial worries could be over. She looked down at her hands. Her flawless diamond rings sparkled under the light of the chandelier. Perhaps she did not need to sell them after all. She looked up to find Sally's shrewd eyes resting on her.

"If you are harboring thoughts of claiming a portion of the Countess's Trust, give them up." Sally's mind was sharper than most twenty-year-olds' and every bit as quick.

"Why should I?" Theodosia shrugged nonchalantly.

"You don't qualify," Sally taunted with obvious pleasure.

"I might not be Rivendon's first cousin, but I am related," Theodosia said through her teeth.

Sally cackled, her jowls jiggling and her eyes disappearing into folds of wrinkles. She looked more like a pug than a human, but pugs had kinder hearts.

"I visited your parents when you were christened." Sally's smile widened.

"Meaning?" Theodosia took a sip of her beverage.

"You were adopted."

Theodosia sputtered on her tea. Making an attempt to regain her composure, she placed her cup on its saucer. "I don't believe you."

"Your parents had just finalized the adoption when I attended your christening. I even took a family snapshot of the occasion." With the assistance of her cane, Sally hobbled to the piano and selected a framed picture off the top.

Theodosia watched in fascinated horror. A duplicate black-and-white photo sat on her nightstand. Her father, in his vicar's garb, stood beside her mother, holding Theodosia in a white, trailing christening gown.

All her life, Mother had called Theodosia their little miracle. A chill rippled across her skin. Could Sally's words be true? With shaky fingers, Theodosia picked up her teacup for something to hold.

"Adoption disqualifies your inheriting. The trust stipulates bloodline only," Sally said.

"Who else knows about this?" Theodosia tightened her grip on the handle of the teacup.

"Only myself since your parents have passed. I assume this is news to you?" Sally tapped her cane on the rug.

"You know it is." Theodosia's stomach churned, and she thought she would be sick. It cost her, but she kept her voice steady. "You appear to take great pleasure informing me."

"Of course. I have enjoyed our visits over the years, Theodosia, but I was never fooled as to why you came. You want a byline in my will. However, I have no intension of accommodating you. You aren't family." Sally leaned on her cane where she stood by the piano.

A throb started in Theodosia's ears, increasing in volume until it resembled the roar of her neighbor's Harley Davidson. Black spots danced in front of her eyes. *All these years wasted.*

"You are a patient girl. I admire that, which is why I tossed you in front of Hadley. Even though he was twice your age, I knew you would snap him up for that title of his. No doubt he married you for that enhanced figure and those lovely doe eyes." The malicious mouth turned up at the corner. "Men are always attracted to tarts."

Something primitive bubbled deep inside Theodosia.

"Too bad Hadley died so soon after your marriage. It was a shame he didn't have time to change his will in your favor." Sally returned the picture to the top of the piano.

"How dare you." A vein pulsed below Theodosia's left eye. Despite the age difference between them and, yes, her desire for a title and fine things, she had been fond of Hadley.

Fury rose like poisonous bile, erupting like a pot too long on the boil. Not taking her eyes from her tormentor, Theodosia pushed back her chair and rose. She rounded the tea table like a cat stalking its prey. Fear flickered across the vicious old face, giving Theodosia an odd sort of pleasure.

Sally scuttled to put the table between them, her cane soundless on the Aubusson rug.

Theodosia reached her easily. With great deliberation, she kicked the cane out of her cousin's gnarled fingers. The loss of support thrust Sally forward. Her arms flailed. She dropped like a stone, unable to stop herself.

Sally's head struck the heavy base of the table, making a hollow thud. She lay still on the priceless rug. Her eyes stared without blinking.

Everything inside Theodosia froze. Her hands flew to her cheeks. She sucked in short gasps of air. Shaking like a leaf, she knelt beside Sally and touched her warm neck. Through its folds of wrinkles, she checked for a pulse.

"No. No. No." Theodosia squeezed her eyes shut.

Nausea roiled in the pit of her stomach. She ran for the loo. Placing her shaking hands on the cold porcelain commode, she vomited.

Afterward, she rinsed her mouth and returned to the lounge. Sitting weakly at the table, she refused to look at the body sprawled at her feet. She had to think. This was bad. She could go to prison.

Theodosia glanced at her cousin and shuddered, then wiped her sweaty palms on her dress. *Think, Theodosia. Think.* There must be a way out of this mess.

Ah. It was simple. So utterly simple. Her stomach, which had begun to roil again, settled. She'd tell the truth, just not all of it. Picking up Sally's landline, she punched 999 for emergency services.

A voice came on the line.

"There's been a dreadful accident," Theodosia said.

CHAPTER THREE

CATHERINE TRAILED BEHIND JACK AS he wheeled her suitcases up the walkway to his rented thatched cottage. The iron-studded door opened with an ear-splitting screech, reminding Catherine of her favorite horror movie.

She removed her muddy boots on the threshold and followed her brother inside. After a short glance around the cottage, she inwardly cringed. A monk's cell had more personality. The only piece of furniture in the room, a massive oak drafting table, stood in the corner. An old wooden box on the floor contained several blueprint tubes. Jack's TV and stereo system sat on top of a plastic crate with loose wires dangling.

"Your bedroom's up here," Jack called over his shoulder and grabbed her cases.

Her trained eye took in the Tudor architecture, and the waves of tiredness disappeared as she followed her brother. At the base of the stairs, she hesitated, her foot on the bottom step. She had once read a story about a "crooked man who walked a crooked mile." The crooked man's stairwell had taken up residence inside Jack's cottage. The walls leaned at crazy angles, and she had to tilt her head to avoid banging it against the ceiling on the fourth step.

Upstairs, Jack deposited her suitcases inside a bright bedroom. An air mattress lay deflated on the floor beside a folded stack of bedding with price tags from Marks and Spencer. Southern hospitality this was not.

Jack scratched his head. "Sorry about the bed. It didn't come with a blower. I figured you'd have a hair dryer in your suitcase. The outlets are different here, so I bought you some power adapters."

"Thanks."

The white-washed walls were airy with their open beam work and dormer windows. Frilly white curtains covered in poppies hung at the windows. They must have come with the house. She couldn't imagine her brother purchasing something so feminine.

Catherine crossed the room and pulled the poppy covered fabric to the side. Below, a moss-covered garage stood at the end of the garden, backing to the alley. Bulbs poked their vibrant heads through beds cluttered in last year's leaves. The place had potential, and her fingers itched to bring it to life.

She turned back from the window, moving carefully to inspect the closet.

"What's wrong with your leg?" Jack frowned. "Do I need to take you to the surgery?"

"Why would I need surgery?" she asked. "It's just a bumped knee. I bruised it on the steering column when we went into the ditch."

"The 'surgery' is a doctor's office."

She shrugged. "A hot bath will work out the stiffness."

Jack looked unconvinced.

"Trust me. I'm fine. After twelve years at the ballet academy, I know when I'm injured." She'd forgotten how overprotective he could be.

"Okay, if you're sure. Are you hungry?" Jack assessed her.

At her nod, he started down the stairs for the kitchen. Catherine peeked into his room before she followed him. A lone mattress lay on the floor, alongside two open suitcases holding his clothes. Calling this a bachelor pad would be a disservice. It was more in line with a homeless shelter.

"Give me a sec will you?" Jack said when she reached the kitchen. "I've got a deadline and need to check my calculations before I send it in. I'll make dinner when I'm done."

"No thanks. I've tasted your cooking and would rather pass." Running her hand across the smooth surface of the antique farmhouse table, Catherine looked around the kitchen in surprise. When Jack put his mind to it, he had fabulous taste.

"I was thinking takeaway or PB and J with crisps," Jack said from the living room as he retrieved a set of blueprints from the wooden box.

He returned and unfurled the plans on top of the table.

"Takeout sounds more appealing."

"Mmmm." With architectural ruler in hand, Jack double-checked a measurement.

Catherine's stomach rumbled, ricocheting off the back of her ribs. She folded her arms. Jack had slipped into design mode. She had reason to know it made him deaf, dumb, and blind to everything around him.

She tried anyway. "I want to introduce you to Marcus Johnston. He owns the local pub."

No response.

"It might be a good place for you to unwind after you get off work."

"Uh-huh." Jack didn't look at her.

"Did you know Marcus put arsenic in my hot chocolate?"

"Mmmm-hmmm."

Crinkling her nose, she went in for the kill. "I sold your car to Charlie for 1,200 bucks. He'll be by later tonight to pick it up."

"You what?" Jack blinked and looked up.

"You never could pay attention to anything unless a car was involved." Catherine reached over and mussed his hair.

"Sorry, Catherine. My department is waiting on this." He made one final adjustment and straightened. "It's done. Now we can talk."

"You do that a lot, don't you?" She nodded toward his drawings. "Bring work home?"

He shrugged and gathered his things.

"Would you be offended if I made this place a little more comfortable?" Her heart ached for him. Of all her brothers, Jack was the most devoted to family, yet he lived far from home in an empty house, working long hours.

"What's wrong with it?" Jack glanced around.

"Are you serious? You don't even have a couch. Your mattress is on the floor, and you are living out of your suitcase."

"I don't need much."

"You make an excellent salary in a profession you love. It's okay to purchase a dresser, a couch, and a TV stand."

"It's fine," Jack said.

"I don't think so. Tomorrow, we are going—"

"If you want to spruce the place up, fine," Jack cut her off. "I have plenty in the bank. Just don't go overboard. I'm not here that often."

"I know." A sigh escaped her. "You work late so you don't have to think about Mom."

A shadow crossed Jack's face. He turned abruptly, taking his blueprints and depositing them inside their box.

"If you ever want to talk about it . . ." Her voice trailed off when she caught a glimpse of his hurt-mule expression, the same one he'd worn at Mom's funeral. Discussion over.

He stood in the middle of the living area, as though noticing it for the first time. "You're right. This place could use some stuff."

"The Tudor architecture is charming, but your place has serious structural issues." Catherine came up beside him.

"The locals call these black-and-whites," Jack informed her. "Believe it or not, Hawthorne Cottage was built this way over five-hundred years ago."

"I've heard of black and whites before, Jack, but I've never heard of someone purposely building a crooked house." Jack was having one on her. Not once had her master's program covered this in grad school, but, then, her focus was seventeenth century forward.

"No joke. People selected trees of similar height and shape for buildings. They didn't plane the wood like we do today but used the timber as it was."

"Where did you learn that?" she asked.

"A local craftsman did a few repairs on the cottage when I first moved in."

"Okay, Mr. Smarty-Pants. I know the thatch is made of water reed, but why is chicken wire covering it up?"

"To keep out the birds."

"How did you find this place anyway? Aren't they hard to come by?" Catherine examined the blackened fireplace.

"Bishop Watson knew someone at church."

"So what do you do for fun around Bascombe?"

"I have absolutely no idea." Jack avoided her eyes.

"You're a mess. You'll be my first project." She patted his arm.

"Don't get carried away. And no girlie stuff." Jack narrowed his eyes.

"Fine." Her stomach growled. "Why don't we go to the Slurping Monkey for dinner?"

"It sounds disgusting. I never eat there."

"Their hot chocolate is delicious." Catherine picked the car keys off the table, dangling them from her fingers. "I'm going to the pub before I starve to death. Do you want to drive? Or would you like me to?"

"There's only one answer to that question." Jack grabbed the keys from her hand.

Relief filled her. After this afternoon's mishap, she had no intention of driving in the UK again. Satisfied with her brother's response, she headed for the door, but Jack's voice stopped her cold.

"For tomorrow's driving lesson, we're taking the M4."

CHAPTER FOUR

THE MANTEL CLOCK CHIMED THE hour on the marble chimneypiece above the library fire. Theodosia tapped her mechanical pencil against the appointment book and glanced at the Earl of Rivendon. He sat like an emperor in his leather chair, his thick, snowy mane shining under the massive ironworks chandelier. He was her current employer and her father's third cousin.

Why won't that silly old fool go take his nap?

She tapped her pencil again, harder this time. The doctor had given Rivendon specific instructions after his heart attack, one of them being a daily lie down.

If the earl did not nap, she wouldn't have time to search the room's safe for the Countess's Trust. If she had done her math correctly, the Earls of Rivendon had been custodians of the trust for nearly two and a half centuries. After going through his lock box at the bank, she had determined the document must be here, inside his London townhouse.

"My dark-blue suit needs altering before the Dashwood's benefit Saturday next." Rivendon fiddled with his loose-fitting jacket. His arduous recovery had taken a toll on his physique. He paused, breathing hard while she jotted down the assignment. His breathing deepened, and the top of his head began to bob. He woke himself with a snort and looked at her sharply.

She kept her face impassive.

"I think I'll have a lie down." He rose from his dark-leather chair with the aid of his brass-handled cane.

"Yes, my lord." Theodosia knew better than to accompany him.

She listened to Rivendon's shuffling progress as he made his way down the hall. His door closed with a snick of the latch. Heaving a sigh of relief, she shut the library door.

It had been two weeks since Sally's death had been ruled accidental, and it had taken an additional week to locate the combination to Rivendon's wall safe. She needed to read the trust and assure herself that she would inherit.

A wild rush of adrenaline pumped through her as she placed a step stool under the Renoir hiding the wall safe. Wiping her sweaty palms on her trousers, she climbed onto the wooden riser and began to work the combination.

The library door opened with a quiet rush of air and closed behind her with a click. She froze in place, her hand on the lock and her stomach near her toes.

"Lady Hadley, you asked me to come when the old gentleman took his rest," the heavily accented tones of Ari, Rivendon's driver, said.

The pent-up breath she'd held whooshed out like a popped balloon. For a moment, she thought Mr. Scott, the butler, had caught her.

Ari was a different kettle of fish. Glancing over her shoulder, she said, "I need your help."

He came into the room, stopping at the base of her stool. His mouth twitched. Ari was a handsome lad of Sicilian descent, with dark, shoulder-length hair and soul-melting eyes. They had begun dating recently.

Theodosia studied the twenty-two-year-old driver through lowered lashes. The disparity between their ages did not bother her. Ari had an air of command and a worldliness about him that more than made up for his lack of years. She touched his face with a vermillion nail. "Will you keep watch outside the library door?"

"Of course." Ari's eyes brightened.

"I don't want to be caught searching for misplaced papers."

Not for a minute did he buy her excuse, but he nodded agreeably.

"Thank you." She watched him leave the room, knowing he believed himself in love with her. The door closed behind him.

The wall safe gave a soft clack on the last turn of the dial. Theodosia opened the door and removed a stack of files, her fingers flying through bank statements and deeds. Tucked inside a manila envelope was a yellowed document.

A ripple of excitement coursed through her as she opened the envelope. Smoothing the parchment on her thigh, she saw that someone had taken the time to type the legal jargon onto separate sheets of paper. She scanned the contents of the first page and noted the trust expired this October. From what she gathered, Catherine, Countess of Rivendon, had set up the trust on behalf of her daughter. If her daughter died with issue, the trust dispersed among the direct-line female heirs. If said daughter died without female issue . . .

The envelope also contained detailed pages of research. It appeared Rivendon's law firm conducted an investigation to locate the Countess of Rivendon's descendants every decade. The search was still pending.

She continued to peruse the document. Skipping over another dash of legalese, she located the line of succession: Sally Davidson, sole inheritor. Upon her death, the trust was to go to Theodosia Davidson Stanhope. If neither woman was living, the Church of England received the funds.

Sally had lied! Theodosia was to inherit. Relief whooshed through her body. She sat on the top of the stool, her heart lighter than air. How like Sally to torment her about a fictitious adoption.

Out of curiosity, her eyes slid down the document and read the name of the heiress who was going to make her rich: Glorianne.

* * *

Seated at a table inside Bascombe's only pub, Catherine watched the band tune up their instruments for the evening's entertainment. She imagined they were the reason the parking lot had filled to capacity and lined both sides of the road.

With a nod to his band members, the lead vocalist started into a ballad, with the others joining in the chorus. Their voices blended on the five-part harmony, wrapping Catherine in a cocoon of pleasure.

"They're amazing. I can't believe you haven't been here before," she said, leaning in her brother's direction so he could hear her over the noise.

"The thought of eating out alone night after night didn't hold any appeal."

Three men in business attire entered the pub and hung up their hats. The tall one seemed familiar, but she couldn't get a good look at him in the dim lighting. He and another gentleman carried briefcases. The third, a wiry man with a bald spot on top of his head shaped like a yarmulke held an architectural tube.

The tall one's close-cropped dark hair hugged his well-shaped head. Even in the hazy room, she knew his suit was Savile Row. He shook hands with people and nodded greetings to a number of others. His profile, with its square jaw, strong chin, and Greek nose, appealed to her. She continued to watch the man out of the corner of her eye, perplexed that she couldn't place him. Maybe she'd seen him at Heathrow that morning or he was some kind of celebrity . . .

Once the businessmen located a table, they made themselves comfortable. After consulting with his companions, Mr. Savile Row went to the counter to place their order, then stayed on to chat with Marcus, sipping a water bottle from time to time. He threw his head back and laughed, exposing the strong column of his throat.

How, after years of no one capturing her interest, had she come across two such men in the space of eight hours?

Above the pickup counter, red lights flashed Jack's ticket number.

"I'll be right back." Jack scooted his chair back and went to get their order.

Waves of exhaustion rolled over Catherine. She rubbed her eyes to relieve their dryness and longed for the oblivion of sleep.

Jack returned, carrying a tray with two steaming mugs of hot chocolate and dual servings of pie.

"What are those?" Catherine asked.

"Meat pasties." Jack plunked the tray on the table.

"Sounds interesting." Catherine picked at the crust with her fork to discover the contents of her meal. Minced beef, onion, and potato chunks filled the crust.

"The English aren't renowned for their culinary skills. But pasties are filling, and I'm starving."

Catherine bowed her head and silently blessed her food while her brother did the same. Cutting into the crust, she took a tentative nibble. The dough was heavy and flavored in a unique-tasting gravy.

Finishing his pasty in a dozen bites, Jack leaned back in his chair and gave the patrons a once-over. "Going places with you will be an experience."

"Pleasant or disagreeable?" Catherine paused with her fork midway to her mouth.

"Neither. I'll be too busy playing the tough, ugly brother." His lip curled. "If I'm reading signals correctly, the local big fish is checking you out."

Catherine blushed and hoped no one at the nearby tables had overheard his comment.

"He's glanced over here half a dozen times."

Catherine looked where her brother indicated, her eyes connecting with Mr. Savile Row's. He smiled, and recognition hit. She drew in a breath. "That's the *farmer* who pulled us out of the ditch. I didn't recognize him without his hat and overalls."

Jack did a double-take. "Viscount Ainsley's as much a farmer as I am. I only know of him by his title. He runs Ashford Priory and is heir to an earldom."

"The Elizabethan manor?"

"Yeah. The one you were drooling over instead of watching the road."

Unable to contain her curiosity, Catherine watched Nick rejoin his colleagues. Once more, his gaze connected with hers and this time held fast. She forgot to breathe as a jolt of electricity raced down her spine.

His eyes were bright blue, dark lashed, and truly beautiful. Blushing furiously, Catherine dipped her head and hid behind her cascade of curls.

The fact that Nick had assured her that he knew someone who could arrange a tour of the Elizabethan priory made her lips tremble with suppressed laughter. Evidently, he had the same evil sense of humor as her brothers.

"Yeah, you've *definitely* caught someone's attention."

Feeling like a stalker, she peeked across the room and met Nick's knowing grin. She turned away, her heart banging like a kettle drum.

"You always did have expensive taste," Jack said.

Catherine ignored the dig and took another sip of hot chocolate.

"The priory was a disaster when Ainsley took it on. Despite being one of your Oxbridge boys, he turned it around in under four years. He's a venture capitalist and provides jobs for the locals." Jack leaned back in his chair, idly watching the band change out instruments.

"How do you know all this?" Catherine asked.

"A guy from Davis Racing plays on the village cricket team with him."

The fiddler struck up a tune that soon had Catherine's feet tapping. She smiled in delight as several people pushed their tables aside and began dancing in the aisles.

Underneath the table, Jack kicked her foot.

Marcus approached with two steaming mugs. At his side walked Viscount Ainsley, a smile lifting the corners of his mouth.

Her heart thumped double-time, and her stomach flipped at his nearness.

"For the newcomers," Marcus said, setting the mugs on the scarred oak surface. "It's good to see you again, miss. How are you enjoying the entertainment this evening?"

"Very much." She longed to speak to Nick but couldn't think of anything to say. Indicating her brother with a sweep of her hand, she said, "Marcus, this is my brother Jack."

Jack stood and shook hands with Marcus, who was called back to the kitchen almost immediately. Nodding to Nick, Jack said, "Good to see you again, *Lord Ainsley*."

Nick grimaced. "I much prefer Nick. Titles are archaic."

"You know my sister." Jack glanced at Catherine, who had remained in her seat.

"A pleasure to see you again, Miss Pressley-Coombes." Nick's blue eyes twinkled.

She couldn't resist the tug of attraction and found herself smiling in response. "Would you care to join us?"

"I can't stay long. This is a working dinner, and my associates will be missing me." Nick pulled up a chair beside her.

"I noticed the blueprints. Are you building something?" Catherine asked.

"We're updating the priory's east wing," Nick said.

"Historic Grade I and Grade II restrictions must make repairs a challenge."

"You know our codes?" Nick asked.

"Only by theory. I'm certainly no expert. Seventeenth century forward is my specialty."

His eyes sharpened on her, penetrating through her protective wall of reserve. In that moment, she knew he saw her. The real her. The person she kept hidden away from everyone, even her brothers. She trembled. Exposed.

"What historic listing would Ashford Priory or the Slurping Monkey fall into?" Nick's dark brows rose, challenging her.

So this was a test, was it? A little thrill of anticipation sang through her veins. She lifted her chin. "At a glance, I'd say this pub is a Grade I listing. It appears authentic Tudor." At Nick's nod of approval, she continued. "As for the priory, regardless of the state of its interior, its Elizabethan architecture would place it in the same category."

His eyes were intensely blue when he smiled his approval. An enormous tug of attraction pulsed between them, as though it were a living, breathing entity.

Jack's cell phone buzzed, pulling her back to reality.

He checked it and rose abruptly. "We've got to go. My boss wants one more alteration on my design. Thanks again for the tow, Ainsley."

"I was wondering if you were both free for dinner at the priory tomorrow evening?" Nick pulled Catherine's chair out for her.

His deep, cultured accent sent shivers down Catherine's spine.

"Thank you. We'd enjoy that." She answered before Jack could refuse.

* * *

On the drive home, Jack was quiet. He parked on the street and fidgeted with his keys instead of climbing out of the MGB. After rubbing an invisible smudge off the dashboard, he cleared his throat. "Be careful around Lord Ainsley."

"He seems like a nice guy." She tucked a curl behind her ear.

"I'm sure he is." Jack scratched his head. "The ultrarich move in different circles. They have dissimilar governing values. I doubt he's a member of the Church. I don't want you getting your heart broken on my watch."

Her defenses went up. Guy-girl relationship discussions were strictly taboo with her brothers. She had a hard enough time sharing her feelings about common things. No way was she going to discuss this.

"Don't give me the silent treatment. You know I'm right."

"It's just a dinner invitation." A little spurt of anger had her tightening her jaw. Couldn't she enjoy a private attraction without Jack bursting her bubble? Honestly, it had been so long since she'd experienced this sensation, she'd forgotten what it felt like.

"You're right." Jack climbed out of the car, waiting for her so he could lock it. He slung his arm around her shoulder. "Sorry, sis. It's hard playing the overprotective big brother. I'm going to need lots of home-cooked meals to sustain me."

"You are such a dork." She nudged him in the side.

"That's why you love me."

"Must be, because there's no other explanation for it."

CHAPTER FIVE

GRAVEL CRUNCHED UNDER NICK'S BROGUES as he took the fishing-stream path on the priory grounds. His brown-and-white English springer spaniel whined.

Nick picked up a stick and tossed it. "Fetch, Harpo."

The spaniel took off, startling a nuthatch into the air. Star, Nick's golden retriever, remained at his side. Harpo dashed back, circling Nick, the stick hanging from his drooling mouth.

"No more, boy." Nick thrust his hands into his jeans pockets and picked up his pace. When he reached the serpentine-shaped lake, he stopped at the water's edge and stared at the glassy surface.

He knew next to nothing about Catherine Pressley-Coombes, but he couldn't get her out of his mind. Something had happened last night at the pub. He had read once that eyes were windows to the soul. He'd never believed it until he'd looked into Catherine's. Light and goodness had reached out from hers and had drawn him in as effectively as any siren's song. He couldn't shake it, and he didn't want to. He pulled his water bottle out of his back pocket and chugged.

He turned toward the priory and whistled up the dogs. Harpo bounded ahead with the tireless energy of his breed, while Star trotted obediently at his side. Harpo let out a whine and stopped at the base of a larch. He circled the trunk, then jumped against its column, barking for all he was worth.

Curious, Nick strode over, looking up into the boughs to see what had set the dog off. He expected a squirrel, but instead, a pair of gray eyes peered down at him fifteen feet off the ground.

"Nutters! How did he know I was up here?" The branches rustled, and Sammy Benson, the six-year-old grandson of the priory's head groundskeeper, poked his face through the leaves.

"Very little gets past Harpo." How on earth had the boy climbed so high? Better yet, how was he going to get down without a tumble? "Harpo appears to have taken a fancy to you." Nick rubbed the back of his neck and hoped his rusty tree-climbing skills would not be required.

"We're great friends." Sammy shimmied down the main trunk as though he had suction cups for hands.

In case the boy lost his grip, Nick placed himself directly below the child. "I hear you are staying with your grandparents this summer."

Sammy's grandparents, Gavin and Alice Benson, lived in the first-floor flat of the priory's stable block. Alice, Nick's cook, was preparing tonight's meal for his guests. The little devil must have slipped out while she was occupied.

"Dad's been shipped off to the Middle East, and Mum needed a break." Sammy bent over Harpo, who bathed his face in slobber, emitting happy-doggy moans.

"Fancy that." Nick wasn't fooled by Sammy's cherubic smile. He knew the boy would be up to his neck in mischief at the first opportunity. He was Harry Benson's son, after all. Nick remembered the scrapes he and Harry had gotten into as children.

He glanced at his watch and headed for the house, eager to shower before company arrived. Noticing how the child struggled to keep up, Nick slowed his steps to accommodate the lad's shorter stride.

"Gran's making a pudding for dessert. I have to eat smoked eel before I get any. I hate smoked eel. I forgot. Gran sent me to tell you Lady Hadley arrived and is staying for supper," Sammy said without the least pause. "She said you're having a regular dinner party, what with Lady Hadley and those Americans from the village. But Gran is feeding that driver in the kitchen, the one who talks funny. She said she was going to watch him in case he tried to steal the silver."

The boy's a veritable repository of information.

"I suppose I'd better put on a tie with my dinner jacket now that Lady Hadley is here." Nick made a face. Grandfather had offered Lady Hadley, his third cousin, a job when her husband had passed.

So much for an intimate meal. He doubted Catherine would be forthcoming in her conversation with Theodosia in attendance. Nick cleared his throat. "I have a proposal for you, Sammy."

"What's a proposal?" Sammy asked, completely at sea.

"An opportunity for both of us to get something we want." Nick whispered as though sharing a secret. "If you return Harpo to his kennel, I'll see that Alice gives you a double helping of pudding for dessert."

"Cracking!" Sammy's eyes shone with delight, and he took off running for the kennels.

* * *

Theodosia stood alongside Ainsley in the priory's paneled entry, waiting to receive his American friends. She had arrived unannounced an hour ago to pick up several items for Rivendon only to find Ainsley had dinner guests.

For the last quarter hour, she'd been at him to cut down the lime trees lining the drive. During the last century, one of the Earls of Rivendon had planted them cheek-by-jowl down the drive's entire length. The narrow road between limestone hillside and six-foot-wide trunks made her claustrophobic every time she came up the switchbacks.

"Where did you find your latest strays, Ainsley?"

Not by the slightest twitch did Ainsley reveal his thoughts. Theodosia gave him points for that and wished she could perfect his talent. Ainsley's love for commoners irritated his family. He was heir to an earldom, and it was high time he started to behave like an aristocrat.

Ainsley had shown real promise just after university. Theodosia couldn't open the Society pages without seeing his face plastered alongside some socialite's. But four years ago, he'd decamped to the priory and turned into a complete bore.

Fellowes, Ainsley's butler, a tall, spare man of perfect carriage, opened the door to Ainsley's guests. A man stepped forward, blocking his companion from view. He greeted Nick and shook Theodosia's hand when they were introduced.

Jack Pressley-Coombes had a tall, rangy build that looked good in formal attire. Theodosia found his short brown hair, warm chocolate-brown eyes, and angular facial bones utterly dishy. Maybe dinner wouldn't be so tedious after all. He bore no resemblance to typical American tourists, with their loud voices, perennial trainers, and crass manners. In fact, Theodosia doubted he had hopped on or off a Routemaster bus.

Mr. Pressley-Coombes moved aside to introduce his sister. Theodosia hated the girl on sight.

When Theodosia had come downstairs that evening, she'd had a good opinion of herself. Women knew when they were attractive. But this girl, with her golden-brown curls spilling halfway down her back and dark-lashed aquamarine eyes, was exquisite despite her unfortunate lack of curves.

Ainsley led the way into the blue salon and seated their guests. Theodosia sauntered over to the bar to pour out drinks. Both siblings declined. Not the least disturbed, the ever-thoughtful Ainsley pulled chilled water bottles from an ice bucket.

Eyeing the Americans, Theodosia took a sip from her wine glass, not surprised Ainsley had also opted for water, his drink of choice. The man still had a hang-up about his late father's alcoholism. Theodosia wondered briefly if their guests were teetotalers like their host or belonged to some sort of religious sect.

"Mr. Pressley-Coombes, when will Davis release their newest prototype?" Ainsley unscrewed the cap of his water bottle.

"If testing goes as planned, Davis's FW37 should hit the racing circuit by March of next year," Jack said.

"You work for Davis?" Interested, Theodosia sat on the sofa beside Jack. Jack nodded.

"Both Mr. and Miss Pressley-Coombes are designers in their respective fields," Ainsley elaborated.

"And what do you happen to design, Miss Pressley-Coombes?" It was a good thing the girl had a pretty face, Theodosia thought, because her conversation left much to be desired.

"Home interiors." Her voice was soft and well-modulated.

"How do you find Ashford Priory?" Theodosia took another sip of wine.

"Its historic elements are stunning and exceptionally well preserved," Catherine said.

"If you'd like, I'll give you that promised tour after supper, then you can determine if this is a Grade I listed property." A look passed between Ainsley and Catherine that Theodosia could not discern.

"Dinner is served, my lord," Fellowes announced from the doorway.

"Brilliant. Thank you, Fellowes," Nick said.

Fellowes bowed and quit the room.

"Lady Hadley." Ainsley offered Theodosia his arm.

Lord Ainsley led Theodosia into the breakfast room, the Americans following in their wake. When she entered, Theodosia looked around in surprise. The space had undergone a transformation for the evening meal. As usual, the large bank of windows overlooking the grounds was framed by double-hung Norwich lace and gold Dupioni silk draperies. But her eyes were drawn to the center of the room. The round elm-wood table was covered in white linen. Meissen china and glassware glinted under the lights of Austrian crystals. An elegantly trailing centerpiece of exotic flowers added a burst of vivid purples, greens, and orange.

Theodosia admitted the Americans had impeccable manners, but neither was what she'd call a pushover. For all her soft-spoken ways, Catherine had a militant glint in her eye when Theodosia grew too flirtatious with her brother.

"Will you be staying in the village for some time, Miss Pressley-Coombes?" Theodosia cut a slice of beef cheek.

"Until September."

"That seems an extraordinarily long holiday. What will you do with yourself?" Theodosia asked.

"That won't be a problem. She's on a quest." Jack popped a sea scallop in his mouth.

Catherine shifted in her seat and gave her brother a sour look.

"I sense a story. Do tell," Theodosia said.

"I'm trying to locate an ancestor who originated from this area." Catherine lowered her fork.

"From Oxfordshire or Bascombe?" Ainsley perked up.

"Bascombe." Catherine dabbed her lips with her napkin.

"Our family has hired professionals on several occasions, but no one has been able to locate the girl." Jack bit into his smoked eel and chewed.

"What time frame are we speaking of?" Ainsley tilted his head, looking interested.

"Late eighteenth century. Seventeen seventies," Catherine said.

"Does this girl have a name?" Theodosia asked, taking a sip of wine.

"Her given name is Glorianne. We don't know her surname," Catherine said.

A strange ball of dread began to form in Theodosia's stomach. "Locating her is bound to be like looking for the proverbial needle in a haystack."

"Perhaps." Catherine shrugged. "Her name is uncommon. That might help narrow the search."

"I could introduce you to the vicar," Ainsley offered. "There's a collection of ancient registers at St. Sebastian's that date back to the fifteenth century. I'm sure he'd let you look them over."

"That would be great. Thank you. Just last night, I came across the name Ashford Priory in her diary." Catherine's aquamarine eyes sparkled.

"It only took her ten hours to decipher six words," Jack said into his water goblet.

What if this woman was an actual descendant of the eighteenth-century Countess of Rivendon? It didn't bear thinking. Theodosia had gone through too much to inherit those funds.

Any moment now, Ainsley would remember the archive room. Before he offered Catherine carte blanche to estate records, Theodosia had to get downstairs.

Spearing a slice of eel, she popped it into her mouth and chewed, an idea taking root. Holding her breath as long as she could, Theodosia coughed. And gasped. And then coughed some more.

Ainsley rounded the table and hit her between the shoulder blades. Catherine offered her water goblet. Shaking her head, Theodosia excused herself from the table.

In the outer hall, she glanced around for Fellowes. All clear. With her heart pounding hard, she slipped out of her five-inch heels and ran for the basement stairs.

The bookshelves she had recently organized during the Earl of Rivendon's convalescence, with their varied records by century and decade, covered three aisles. Hoping she would not slip on the Spanish tiles, she rushed down two rows before she found the correct time frame. She selected two volumes,1760–1786 and 1786–1800, and placed them on the library table. Several bookcases had loose back panels in need of repair. One was in the nineteenth-century section.

She moved an entire row of volumes from a neighboring shelf and stacked them in chronological order for their immediate return. Lifting a thick account book of the Countess of Rivendon's expenditures from the nineteenth century, she hammered the back panel with her fist until it gave way on one side. She checked the gap between the back of the bookcase and wall. It was deep enough to slide both volumes into the space.

She pushed the books through. They hit the floor behind the case with a thud. With frantic fingers, she tugged the corner of the panel as close as she could get to its original position.

Hurry. Hurry. Hurry. Her fingers, clumsy from stress, dropped several books from her stack onto the tiles. The sound reverberated through the room. Praying to any god who would listen, she hoped no one had heard the commotion.

In quick succession, she reorganized the volumes on the shelves in chronological order. After she finished her task, she snapped off the light.

Quick as a hare, she bounded back up the stairs in her stockinged feet, only stopping in front of the pier glass to smooth her hair and slip on her shoes. Satisfied with her reflection, she turned and sauntered down the hall, her heels clicking on the marble tiles.

When Theodosia reached the breakfast room, she encountered Fellowes carrying in the dessert.

"All better, Lady Hadley?" he asked.

"Yes. Thank you, Fellowes."

As she entered the room, she heard Ainsley's deep voice say, "I believe the priory's archive room might prove helpful in your search, Catherine. I don't know why I didn't think of it earlier."

Ainsley and Jack rose when they saw Theodosia. Reveling in their attention, she threw her shoulders back and sashayed to her seat.

"Are you quite all right, Lady Hadley?" Ainsley asked.

"Never better." Turning to the Americans, she said, "I am dreadfully sorry. So stupid of me. What did I miss while I was indisposed?"

* * *

Bubbles of effervescent excitement sang through Catherine's veins. She wanted to kick off her shoes and dance barefoot across the priory's dew-laden grass. When she and Jack had said their good-byes, Nick had held her hand a second longer than necessary. Not by one word or expression had he given himself away the entire evening, but she knew down to the bottom of her toes he was interested.

She had never been overly attracted to anyone longer than a few days. She'd started to think something was wrong with her until she'd realized her siblings were equally unattached. Why was that? Was there something wrong with her family? Why didn't they fall in love?

Her soaring spirits took a sudden nosedive. She had never dated a member of another faith. Nick was such a good person. If given the chance, she wondered if he would be open to investigating her religion.

A nightingale's liquid trill rent the air, sending her spirits soaring again. She wanted to pinch herself to make sure she wasn't asleep. Instead, she took her brother's arm as they crossed the graveled drive in order to keep her feet anchored to the ground.

Jack opened the MGB's passenger door, and she climbed in, slipping off her heels. "That feels good."

"Interesting night."

Catherine could hear the fatigue in his voice. Their five-course meal and tour of the priory had taken some time. Her favorite room was the medieval dining hall, with its cavernous vaulted ceiling and mounted stag heads.

"Lady Hadley can be very charming when she chooses," she said, thinking of Lady Hadley's attention to her brother.

"So can Lord Ainsley." The engine snarled to life, and Jack flipped on the headlights.

"Can you believe Nick is letting me use the priory's archive room?"

"He seemed anxious to help."

"He's an incredibly nice person."

"Don't mistake manners and polish for kindness," Jack warned as he backed up the car.

Catherine leaned into the bucket seat and closed her eyes, reliving the moment when Nick had held her hand. She smiled to herself in the dark. Jack was wrong about Nick. She knew it.

CHAPTER SIX

THE TREES DRIPPED WITH DEW on both sides of the river as Catherine jogged over the medieval arched bridge. The bell tower from St. Sebastian's pealed seven, and a cyclist shouted hello from across the village green. Barely glancing in his direction, she waved. One of the shop owners wiping down a plate-glass window nodded to her.

What a friendly place, Catherine thought, fighting discomfort. She had downed thirty-two ounces of electrolytes right before her run. By the time she turned onto Jack's tree-lined street, reaching the "loo" was her main objective.

One of Jack's neighbors headed her way with a dog of indeterminate pedigree. She was tiny, with inquisitive eyes and iron-gray hair covered in a bright-green scarf. Avid curiosity was written all over her face.

Catherine groaned inwardly, but years of her mother's training reasserted itself. She stopped and bent to pet the canine. "Hello. What kind of dog is he?"

"As far as I can tell, he's a mutt. Poor thing was a bag of bones when I found him. He's a faithful chap. Never leaves my side." The woman assessed her.

The dog sat, tilted his head, and held out a paw.

"How adorable. Does he know any more tricks?" Catherine shook the paw.

"Yes, he does. Don't you, Buggles?"

Buggles barked and thumped his tail.

"Are you living with Mr. Pressley-Coombes?" The woman cocked her head to the side.

She didn't beat around the bush when she wanted information.

"For a while. I'm his sister."

"A sister." Relief sounded in her words. "And you've come from the States?"

"Yes. I'm here doing research this summer."

"Your brother's a fine man. Handsome too. I was hoping to introduce him to my granddaughter. I've come by several times, but he's never home."

"His job keeps him busy."

"Amelia Hopkins. I'm next door but one." Amelia stuck out her hand for a shake, reminding Catherine of Buggles.

"Catherine Pressley-Coombes."

"What does your brother do for a living?" Amelia continued her interrogation.

"He works at Davis." Catherine crossed her legs, hoping the "interview" would conclude.

"Race cars. Fancy that."

"He puts in long hours." Catherine shifted positions, wondering how many questions Amelia had left in her arsenal.

"That won't do for my Sarah. She needs attention." Amelia eyed her curiously. "How are you enjoying Bascombe?"

"It's very charming." Catherine uncrossed her legs, shifting her weight to the other foot.

"Well, luv, it will be nice having a new neighbor. Can you come to tea tomorrow?"

Catherine was about to decline when the least little something in the woman's expression changed her mind. "Yes. Thank you. That would be nice." *Note to self: bring herbal tea.*

She shifted again.

"It's not nice of me at all. I'm a prying old woman who wants to hear all about life in America. Tea's at four. Cheers." Amelia Hopkins tugged on the leash. "Come, Buggles."

"Bye," Catherine said and dashed inside the cottage.

* * *

Theodosia had a kink in her neck, the result of being on the phone all morning in her London office. While she was put on hold yet again, she attempted to stretch the painful spot and winced. Ari removed himself from the corner of her desk. His hands came down on her neck and began to massage the painful area.

"That feels good." She closed her eyes.

A voice came on the line.

Theodosia straightened and explained to yet another employee, "This is the Earl of Rivendon's personal assistant. Do you happen to know if the alterations he requested have been completed?" There was a pause, and then Theodosia leaned back and mouthed to Ari, "She's checking."

He continued to work the knot in her neck. After a few minutes, the receptionist gave her the answer she'd been waiting for.

"I'll send the driver to collect them before close. Ta," Theodosia said into the receiver. Setting the phone back on its cradle, she added the tailor's address to her list. Ari's hands dropped from her neck when she swiveled her chair to face him. "I have a list of errands I need you to run this afternoon. Can you complete them by half three?"

"I would be happy to," Ari replied in his heavy accent.

A rap sounded on the door.

"Come," Theodosia responded.

"Lady Hadley, a policeman is here to see you," Mr. Scott, the butler, said from the door.

"A policeman? Whatever for?" Theodosia dropped her pen. Did they know about Sally?

"There was a break-in next door. The detective chief inspector is interviewing everyone on the street to see if they noticed anything out of the ordinary."

Relief whooshed through her body, leaving her weak-kneed. "Very well. Show him in." She smoothed her dress, wiping her sweaty palms on her skirt. Out of the corner of her eye, she noticed Ari step behind a large potted palm and inch his way to the opposite exit.

Scott ushered the policeman into her office. He was middle-aged, with a sagging chin and serious brown eyes.

Extending her hand, Theodosia crossed the room, a smile of welcome on her lips. "Won't you come in and take a seat?"

"DCI Hunnicut." The officer shook her hand but remained standing.

"Lady Hadley." Theodosia noticed Ari slip unobtrusively out the side door. *Interesting.*

CHAPTER SEVEN

Nick parked his bicycle inside the Pressley-Coombes gate. He removed his helmet and ran his fingers through his hair. It was seven fifteen in the morning. No one stopped for a chat at this hour. What was he doing? He stared across the garden at the cottage door. *I've gone barking mad.*

When he'd pedaled around the corner on Market Street during his ride and noticed the long, golden-brown ponytail swinging behind the slender runner, he had known immediately who those riotous curls belonged to. He'd shouted a greeting across the village green, but Catherine had only glanced in his general direction, waved, and kept going. He doubted she'd recognized him. Finishing the two remaining miles of his workout, he'd doubled back to her cottage.

Everyone in the village knew where the Americans lived. They were Bascombe's only newcomers in over a decade. Most of the residents had lived here for generations.

Nick told himself he was seven kinds of a fool for following this impulse. But he'd never backed away from a challenge in his life, and he wasn't about to start now. Jogging up the steps, he rapped on the metal-studded wood.

He grinned when Catherine pulled back the kitchen curtain to see who was there. A second later, the front door opened with a shriek of rusty hinges. Still dressed in running gear, Catherine stood on the doorstep, holding a packaged can of electrolytes. Nick shifted, trying to think of something clever to say but came up empty. For the first time in a dozen years, a female had him tongue-tied.

"Nick." She looked at him with questions in her eyes.

"Good morning. I saw you running on the village green just now." He smiled at her, feeling a little self-conscious in his bicycle gear.

"That was you?" Catherine looked past him to his bike propped inside the gate.

He nodded, glancing at the electrolyte drink in her hand. She looked flushed.

"I dehydrate if I don't have one of these after a run. Would you like something to drink?"

"No, thanks. I have a Camelbak." He turned so she could see the water bag strapped to his back.

"That looks serious. How far do you go?"

"Three twenty-five-mile circuits a week and weights on my off days." He took in her running attire. "Are you a marathoner?"

"No. I run strictly for exercise. Dancing's more my thing. But I also play a mean game of American baseball."

That surprised him. With her graceful ways, she didn't strike him as the sporty type.

"I didn't have much of a choice, growing up with three older brothers," Catherine continued. "They wouldn't be caught dead playing dolls or wearing a tutu unless it involved decapitating one or lighting the other on fire. I took up sports to save my Barbies."

Nick laughed. Her brothers must have been something else.

"Is there anything I can do for you?" she asked after an awkward pause.

"I'll let you know when I think of something." Stymied, he looked down, trying to figure out what to say. Catherine's feet were bare and laced with scars. He wondered what had caused such damage. Mentally shaking himself, he said, "After our conversation at dinner last night, I thought you might be interested in meeting the vicar. If you have any spare time today, I could take you to St. Sebastian's and introduce you. The parish has a number of old registers I'm sure Reverend Brown would let you peruse."

"I'd love to." Catherine gave him her wide-flashing smile.

"Would one o'clock do?"

"Absolutely." Her eyes sparkled.

"Brilliant. I'll swing by to collect you at five of one."

"I'll be ready."

He jogged down the steps to his bike. When he pushed off, he took one last look at her standing in the doorway. One o'clock couldn't come soon enough.

* * *

Catherine's footsteps echoed on the stone floor as she wandered the bisecting transept of St. Sebastian's Parish Church. The clerestory windows flooded the building with light. Stopping to marvel at the arches and elaborately painted high-vaulted ceiling, she shivered. Several parishioners sat scattered among the pews with lowered heads.

The porch door opened, and she heard Nick's voice. "She's over here, Reverend Mr. Brown."

Catherine watched the two men approach. Nick did not lower his voice as he passed through the chapel, where a number of parishioners prayed. His disregard for their worship struck her oddly. Nick wasn't a rude man . . . exactly the opposite. Why did he show such a lack of respect?

The vicar's pink cheeks, spectacles, and rotund belly reminded Catherine of Santa Claus, but his cool demeanor matched the chapel's arctic temperature. His brown eyes assessed her. "I understand your people hail from Bascombe, Miss Pressley-Coombes."

"They do."

"Since Lord Ainsley is a patron of St. Sebastian's, I have agreed to allow you access to our registers. Due to their age and historic value, we keep them under lock and key." Reverend Brown shoved his myopic glasses up his nose. Motioning toward the east transept, he said, "This way."

She shivered again and wondered if Nick had put the little vicar's nose out of joint.

"Chilled?" Nick came up beside her.

"It's a little cool in here."

His eyes laughed down at her, clearly aware of her double entendre. "I don't have a jacket; I hope this'll do." Throwing his arm around her, he pulled her close. Leaning into his side, she inhaled his freshly laundered shirt and aftershave. Goose bumps of a different sort broke out along Catherine's skin, and her heart took off at a gallop.

Nick caught her staring.

Attraction simmered between them. She blushed but found it hard to look away.

"Better?" he asked.

She nodded and tucked a curl behind her ear.

"This way, please," the vicar's voice interrupted, making them both jump.

Nick's chest rumbled with suppressed laughter. Upsetting the reverend didn't appear to bother him in the least. Did he have a problem with Reverend Brown or church in general?

Reverend Brown opened a door in the paneling along the chapel wall. A switch clicked, and fluorescent light bathed the musty windowless chamber.

"The registers are located in this section." Reverend Brown indicated a series of locked glass-fronted cabinets. He gave them two pairs of white gloves for handling the volumes. "What era are you researching?"

"Late seventeen hundreds," Catherine tugged on her gloves.

"I'll check your progress within the hour," the vicar said, unlocking a bookcase.

To make it easier for her, Nick stacked the registers on top of a sturdy oak table in the center of the room.

"What year was your ancestor born?" Nick asked.

"About 1760. Her name was Glorianne."

The registers smelled better than Glorianne's diary, but not by much. Catherine turned to the first entry on the brittle parchment.

With the two of them working in tandem, it didn't take long to cover the records. Catherine bit her bottom lip, obviously fighting back disappointment at the large gaps between entries.

At the end of the allotted hour, Reverend Brown returned.

"There seem to be decades missing from the registers. Have any been lost?" Nick asked.

"St. Sebastian's has retained all its original registers." Reverend Brown puffed out his chest.

"Surely the bishops kept transcripts of the christenings." Nick gave Catherine a sympathetic glance.

"Until England passed the civil registration law, clergy were not required to maintain records. Obviously, some vicars did not see the need." Light bounced off Reverend Brown's glasses.

Catherine restacked the registers, and Nick handed them back to the vicar. Thanking him, they left the chapel.

"I can't thank you enough for your help," Catherine said. While his kindness touched her, she wondered if it wouldn't be best to leave their future meetings to chance.

"If Glorianne lived in Bascombe, perhaps she'll be referred to in the priory's archives. You are welcome to make use of the archive room. Our records go back at least four hundred years. Come early, and stay as late as you'd like. No one will bother you, and you can dig through as many musty old tomes as you wish. If you need a break, you're welcome to wander the grounds."

His words had a soothing effect on her skittering senses, erasing some of her earlier doubts about him. Her mother's request had been even more difficult than she had imagined. The priory's archive room might prove a blessing. She needed to exhaust every option available to her. "Would tomorrow be too soon to start?"

"Not at all. I'd be delighted to have you." Nick pressed his key fob, unlocking the SUV, and opened her door.

After she was situated, he climbed behind the driver's wheel, fired up the ignition, and pulled out of the lot. Catherine glanced at him as he drove through the village. She told herself to be practical. No matter how much she liked him, nothing could come of this attraction.

His lack of reverence inside the chapel had underscored how different their Christian belief systems were. No matter how wonderful Nick seemed, she couldn't allow her feelings to grow. Temple marriage had always been her goal, especially after her mother's passing. The covenants her parents had made in the house of the Lord had brought solace to their family, knowing they would be together after this life.

Nick turned down her tree-lined street. After today's trip to St. Sebastian's, a seed of doubt had entered her heart about his capacity for spirituality. Would he listen if she tried to share her beliefs with him? She sighed. Living the gospel had been so easy when her heart had remained unentangled.

CHAPTER EIGHT

THE FOLLOWING DAY, AFTER SEARCHING the archive shelves all morning, Catherine gave up trying to locate household volumes during Glorianne's time in Bascombe. They simply didn't exist. It reminded her of the gaps in St. Sebastian's registers all over again. She began to wonder if her brothers were right about this quest.

Upon her arrival at the priory that morning, Nick had greeted her. He'd obviously been working. Instead of showing her the archive room and leaving her to her research, he had helped set up her computer, moving the table closer to an outlet, then staying to explain the priory's filing system.

Returning to her seat at the table, Catherine opened her computer and logged on to the Church's family history website and pulled up her family tree. She clicked on Glorianne's name and reviewed what little information they had.

The only real piece of documentation was her passage from Bristol on the merchant ship *The Golden Goose*. Glorianne's last name was illegible, and some might question its validity, but two factors had assured a degreed genealogist this was the correct individual: Glorianne's name was unusual for that era, and the family knew approximately where and when she had arrived in Virginia.

Alexander Douglas, a patriot and distant cousin of Glorianne's Scottish grandfather, had collected fifteen-year-old Glorianne at the Yorktown dock shortly after listening to Patrick Henry's impassioned speech. This placed her arrival in March 1775, mere weeks before the War for Independence broke out. Glorianne married her cousin Alexander. The couple had one child, a daughter named Catherine. Glorianne's tombstone and diary were proof she had lived.

With careful fingers, Catherine opened the baggie containing Glorianne's diary. The tan ink on the darkened parchment had faded. Only a word or two were visible, even by magnifying glass in natural light. She bit her bottom lip.

After an unproductive hour, Catherine returned the diary to its baggie. All she needed was an English christening record or a Virginia marriage certificate to obtain Glorianne's surname. Unfortunately, the courthouse in Virginia had burned during the American Civil War. With gaps in the local parish registers, Glorianne's diary or undiscovered records were her only options.

Catherine entered her notations of the day's findings on her electronic research log, then rubbed her temples. How could she read an invisible diary?

"Any luck digging through ancient dust mites?"

She looked up, startled.

Nick leaned against the door frame of the archive room, holding a water bottle. He looked handsome in his plaid button-up shirt and chinos.

"Not yet, but that means I'm closer to a discovery." Her mood lifted at his presence.

"What are you doing?" He came up behind her, looking over her shoulder at the spreadsheet.

"Entering my research notes. That way I won't repeat myself."

"Would you like a break? I'm going for a walk." His hand came down on her shoulder, shooting a zing of awareness through her body.

"Absolutely." She reached for her lightweight jacket, but Nick beat her to it, assisting her into it.

"Thanks."

They clattered up the stairwell.

"I usually bring the dogs. Would you mind if we stopped by the kennel to collect Harpo? Star's waiting by the door. You aren't allergic, are you?"

"Not at all."

When they reached the vestibule, a golden retriever rose, wagging her tail and gazing at them with soft, brown eyes. She brushed up against Nick and whined. He scratched under Star's ear.

Nick donned an anorak and held out a pair of Wellington boots. "These will prove handy. We don't always stay to the trails."

Catherine relieved him of the rubber boots while Star sniffed at her pant leg. She gave her a pat. "You are a sweetheart."

They headed toward the kennels, a small stone building inside a walled enclave housing a group of farm buildings. Star trotted at Nick's side.

"Watch out." he cautioned as he unlatched the gate. "Harpo's a bit hyper, even for an English springer spaniel, but he's a brilliant hunting dog. He can scare up more birds than I could possibly shoot."

A spotted brown-and-white dog barreled out the opening like a ballistic missile off a launchpad. He performed a configuration of circles at break-neck speed that made Catherine stare in wonder. When Harpo's initial burst of energy slowed to a happy gallop, he let out a series of excited yips and doubled back to greet Nick.

"Harpo's an unusual name for a dog." Catherine let the exuberant animal sniff her hand.

"Yes. Well . . . Harpo's personality is rather reminiscent of a particular Marx Brother." Nick's cheeks reddened.

"Jack likes them too."

Nick looked relieved but made no further comment.

Leaving the kennel, they followed a path along the walled enclosure until they reached a gate. A freckle-faced boy no older than six swung on it with a pair of opera glasses dangling from a chain around his neck.

"Hiya, Nick. Are you taking the dogs for a walk?" the little boy asked.

"Sammy." Nick nodded to the boy. "Does Gavin know you're up here?"

The boy shrugged.

"Have you met Miss Catherine?" Nick asked.

"No." The boy turned his gray eyes on her.

"Sammy, this is Miss Catherine."

"I saw you come in a red car this morning." The little boy looked at her with open curiosity.

"You did?" Catherine asked.

The boy's sandy head bobbed up and down. "You're pretty. Gran said you're here to look for dead people. Do you see ghosts?"

Catherine bit back a smile. "No. I'm trying to find their names in books."

"Oh." Sammy's face fell. Obviously, books were not as interesting as ghosts. Sammy held up the small binoculars. "I'm going to be a detective when I grow up. Gran loaned me her opera glasses so I can practice."

"Have you seen anything unusual today?" Catherine played along.

"No."

Nick whistled at Harpo, who was causing an uproar by the chicken coop. The dog came running, speeding through the narrow opening in the gate where Sammy hung.

"Miss Catherine and I are going for a walk. Would you be a gentleman and hold the gate wide?"

Sammy jumped off and pushed back the gate, smiling shyly at her.

"Thank you, Sammy. It's nice to meet you." Catherine lowered her voice conspiratorially. "Try not to let the bad guys see you when you spy on them."

"I won't." The boy blinked. Catherine could see ideas beginning to formulate inside his head.

Leaving Sammy behind, they took the graveled path that cut diagonally across the west lawn. An occasional gust whipped the air, making Catherine grateful for her jacket and boots. She stopped on the edge of the grassy knoll, gazing in open admiration.

At the base of the west lawn, a meandering stream with a series of waterfalls fed into a serpentine lake. Outcroppings of variegated plantings and specimen trees added texture and shape to the panorama.

Nick stood beside her, a faint smile lifting the corners of his mouth.

"Eden couldn't be more beautiful," Catherine said.

"I feel much the same. Regardless of the season, this view stuns my senses." Nick picked up her hand and gave it a squeeze.

"It looks so natural. Is it?" Catherine was having a hard time focusing on anything but her hand in Nick's. How could he look so casual when 100,000 electric currents were rocking her system?

"Capability Brown redesigned the grounds in 1756. He created the lake by damming up the fishing stream and removing the formal gardens."

Star had wandered across the bridge, uniting the property with the vast acreage of lawn and mature plantings on the opposite bank. Harpo emitted an occasional bark and dashed about, flushing birds from the undergrowth.

With interlaced fingers, they continued in companionable silence across the bridge to the far side of the lake. Catherine's body had settled into a happy sizzle, and she wondered how she could be so content with someone she barely knew.

Humming a lilting tune, Nick veered off the graveled path with her in tow. An enormous tree in the distance appeared to be their destination. This must be Nick's regular route, she mused, spying the golden retriever curled under the leafy canopy.

When they reached the tree, Catherine dropped Nick's hand and circled the trunk. "Why is your tree covered in graffiti?"

"It's a Davidson family tradition."

"Your tradition involves carving up trees?" Catherine fingered two sets of initials cut into the trunk.

"It's a long story," he warned with a wary expression.

"I have time." This tree obviously meant a great deal to him.

"This is a three-hundred-year-old sweet chestnut. The fourth Earl of Rivendon selected it when it was hardly more than a sapling. He wanted to leave his personal mark on the place after his death."

"So he started a graffiti campaign?" she teased.

Nick paced, rubbing the back of his neck. He stopped beside the massive trunk and faced her. Catherine located a large, protruding root sticking out of the ground and sat on it.

"My seventh great-grandfather, the fourth earl, inherited the title while still in his teens. In his day, aristocratic marriages were arranged to increase one's wealth and power.

"Up until that time, the Earls of Rivendon did not enjoy successful unions. When the title shifted to our branch of the family, the fourth earl vowed to make his wife as happy as he was able. He wooed her after their marriage. Sometime later, they fell in love and carved their initials on this tree together."

Nick fingered a set of initials on the main trunk. A slight breeze ruffled his hair and rustled the leaves overhead. "They chose the chestnut for its longevity, a symbol of their enduring love. In his will, the fourth earl encouraged his descendants and their spouses to carve their initials in this tree if their unions were love matches. This tree is proof of our family's devotion to the institution of marriage."

"That's quite a tradition."

"Since that time, happy Davidson couples have been chiseling away at this tree." Nick gazed up into the boughs.

"What a wonderful story. The fourth earl sounds very romantic."

"His marriage was arranged, like those before him. But he and his wife engraved their initials less than a year after their nuptials took place."

"It couldn't have been easy climbing in long skirts. Some of those boughs are really high." Every branch Catherine could see from where she stood on the ground bore initials.

"It boggles the mind how they managed without breaking their necks. But the will stipulated both parties had to carve their own name."

"There must be over a hundred sets." Catherine started to count.

"One hundred and eight, to be exact," Nick replied.

"How do you know?"

"As a small boy, I had a lot of time on my hands. I copied their initials and made a game of locating the couples in the portrait gallery. Many were siblings of the successive heirs." Nick looked off into the distance, and Catherine had the distinct impression he'd been lonely.

"Aristocrats didn't marry for love?"

"Rarely. The fourth earl was raised by his maternal uncle, the local vicar. He'd planned to take up religious orders. A distant cousin passed without male issue, and he came into the title. Through him, the family understood marriage took attention, devotion, and time."

"I'm beyond impressed. With his wealth, he could have done as he pleased." Catherine made a sweeping gesture, taking in the priory and its surroundings.

"The fourth earl fascinated me as a child. He was a likable man and quite determined to lead by example."

"Did he succeed?"

He shook his head. "Not with his contemporaries. But I'd say he made a lasting impression on his family."

"Did all his posterity climb this tree?" she asked, voicing her thoughts.

"The odd one here and there didn't, but the vast majority took on the challenge." Nick's expression changed. Catherine could have sworn a wall went up.

Catherine wanted to kick herself. It was obviously a tender subject. Had his parents divorced? She forced herself to say lightly, "I presume one day you'll climb these branches looking for a spot to wield your knife?"

"Most definitely." His answering smile made her think she'd imagined the moment of emotional distance. "At age seven, I selected the perfect location." He pointed quite a way up the tree.

"You're sure she'd be willing to climb that high?" Catherine shaded her eyes to view the branch.

"Definitely." His eyes twinkled, and he said sotto voce, "At seven, I came up with the perfect bribe."

"Oh, you did, did you?"

"I determined to feed my bride chocolate every day and let her ride my pony if she would climb up there with me."

"If someone offered her such devoted tokens of affection, how could she resist?"

"Exactly so." His eyes were very blue.

Her heart fluttered as an invisible cord stretched taut between them. If only he were a Church member, she could follow through with the emotions stirring in her breast. She looked away and said in a brisk tone, "This has provided a much-needed break."

"I must confess, I had an ulterior motive."

"You did?" she asked with equal parts excitement and dread.

"I needed to clear my head, and the dogs needed the exercise."

"Do you always multitask?"

"Guilty as charged." He held up both hands as though under arrest. "Why expend energy on just one thing when you can accomplish several at the same time?"

"Remind me never to challenge you to a game of chess."

"Oh, I don't know. I think you would make a formidable opponent," he said with a rueful expression.

"Hmmm," she said, unconvinced, as he pulled her to her feet.

By unspoken agreement, they started back toward the priory in companionable silence. Nick whistled up the dogs. They came bounding, with Star taking up her position by Nick's side. Harpo darted ahead, circling back from time to time.

When they reached the priory, Catherine thanked Nick.

"Join us any time you wish. We walk at half ten, wet days or dry."

"I'll remember." Catherine removed the wellies and left them in the vestibule. Locating her shoes, she retired to the basement, more confused than ever about her growing emotions.

CHAPTER NINE

WITH HIS HAND AT THE small of her back, Nick led Catherine across the pub to their table for tonight's cèilidh. He never brought his dates to Bascombe. That gauntlet had smacked too much of bringing a young lady home to meet the parents. Until now.

Even though he'd only known Catherine two weeks, he wanted to show her off, win his clannish village's approval, and keep her all to himself. How to go about it, he did not know. No doubt he'd hit on something as the evening progressed.

Marcus rushed by with a harried expression as one of the speakers filled the room with ear-splitting static. Catherine leaned back in her chair and watched the band tune up their instruments. The Irish Celts were playing. It would be a full house. He touched Catherine's hand to gain her attention and kept his hand there.

"Are you hungry? May I get you something?" Nick indicated the menu suspended from the ceiling above the worktop.

"I'd love a hot chocolate."

"Nothing to eat?"

"I already ate." Pink suffused her face. "Americans eat earlier than the English."

"One hot chocolate it is. I'll be right back." Nick pushed back from the table.

At the counter, he placed his order. Before he could turn around, Mitch Colburn, a member of the village council, slapped him on the back.

"Ainsley. I see you've brought a lady friend."

Turning, he gave Mitch a smile. "Miss Pressley-Coombes and her brother are new to the village. He works for Davis."

"The Americans." There it was, the underlying barrier.

"With deep British roots. Miss Pressley-Coombes is here to research her family tree," Nick said.

"Is her family from Oxfordshire?"

"Bascombe."

"How did you meet her?"

"I pulled her out of my ditch." Nick found it difficult not to squirm under the steely gaze.

"If you had a pound for every person who ran into that ditch, you could afford a better farmhand than Charlie." Mitch laughed.

"Charlie's not so bad." That was it? No further questions about Catherine? The tension knotting Nick's shoulders eased. He'd made it over one of Bascombe's hardest hurdles. Evidently, Catherine's ancestral village roots had swayed one of Bascombe's leading citizens to lay off hostilities toward her and her brother.

The manager plunked Nick's order on the counter.

Picking up his meal, he prepared to return to his table.

Mitch tapped him on the shoulder, motioning with his chin toward Catherine. "That's a bonnie lass. Introduce her around."

"Another time, Mitch." Nick didn't mind an inquisition. Not in the village. But tonight was for Catherine and Catherine alone.

Mitch studied him for a second, then slapped him on the back again. "All right, laddie. Tonight's yours. We expect introductions the next time you bring her."

"Of course." Nick headed back to his table with a sense of relief. He placed Catherine's steaming mug in front of her with a flourish. "Your hot chocolate, my lady, with an extra dash of whipped cream."

"Marcus has the best recipe." She took a sip and placed her mug on the table. "Is everything okay?"

"Yes. Why do you ask?" Nick sat at the table and dug into his meal.

"You carry a water bottle wherever you go, but you left yours on the counter."

He turned around to look. Sure enough, a lone water bottle sat on the worktop.

"I think that man frustrated you." Catherine glanced at Mitch.

How the devil did she figure that out? Nick rose from his chair and looked down at her. "Do you read minds?"

"What?" Catherine sputtered on her hot chocolate.

"I'm not used to being so easily read."

"It's a survival trick I learned at the feet of three older brothers."

"I'd say it had more to do with being perceptive." He squeezed her shoulder. "I'll be right back."

Music swept through the room as the band broke into their first song of the night. When Nick returned, Catherine had tears in her eyes.

"Why are Celtic songs so tragic?" She ducked her head, and a curtain of curls swept forward, hiding her flushed face.

She's embarrassed? Nick reached over and took her hand. It was small and fine boned. With a cautious finger, he tucked a golden-brown ringlet behind her ear. She looked at him through her eyelashes, then glanced away.

"Catherine?" He squeezed her hand. Their eyes collided and held. "Celts have a tragic history. The songwriter intended to pluck our heartstrings. I'd wonder if the music didn't affect you the first time or two."

The pub, with its boisterous occupants and lively band, faded into the background. A tremulous smile came and went on her lips. Nick would have pulled her into his arms if they hadn't been surrounded by half the population of Bascombe. Because in the depth of her eyes was the answer he so desperately sought. She cared for him.

A sense of relief washed over him. Years ago, he'd asked Grandfather why love was hard to recognize. Grandfather assured him he would identify the commodity when it arrived. Being a Davidson, Nick knew the chances were strong he would love and serve one woman all his life. Gazing at Catherine, he began to believe his blood ran true. He was fairly certain what he felt for her was no counterfeit.

* * *

Catherine watched the fiddler pick up the mic.

"I'm taking requests," he called out.

People shouted a variety of song titles. The man who had spoken to Nick at the counter glanced across the room, a mischievous expression on his face. Nick shook his head, but the man cupped his hands around his mouth and yelled, "We want Ainsley."

The room took up the chant.

Nick's mouth dented in at the corner, and he sighed. Squeezing her hand, he stood up. "This shouldn't take long."

The pub erupted in cheers as he crossed the ancient plank floor and jumped onto the modular stage.

A moment ago, when he had looked into her eyes, Catherine had seen something that had broken her heart. Nick didn't quite believe anyone could love him. The real Nick, not the celebrated aristocrat. He must long to have the kind of relationship his ancestors had with their spouses. No one seemed aware of it but herself. It made her want to weep.

He took the mic in his hand. "Any requests?"

An elderly lady, hunched with age, waved to get his attention.

"Rose, what'll it be?" Nick called out to her.

"Anything you feel like singing, luv, as long as it's a ballad," she replied.

With a nod, Nick said something to the fiddler. He opened the song in a velvety baritone that made Catherine's toes curl. She watched in amusement as a few old ladies gave audible sighs.

Hamming it up, Nick sang a ballad for old Rose, pretending she was the love of his life. Rose was delighted, and her rusty laugh carried across the room.

Catherine's heart swelled at Nick's generosity of spirit. She'd always admired those who could sing without affectation. And here was Nick, not the least embarrassed to share the talent God had blessed him with.

His next number was a Scottish ballad about Bonnie Prince Charlie escaping to the Isle of Skye. As Nick sang, his voice wrapped itself around her heart, turning it to mush.

Few things in Catherine's life were absolutes. She knew Heavenly Father loved her. She knew the Lord's gospel had been restored to the earth. Her mother's request had resonated with something deep in her heart, propelling her to England. And lastly, never in her life had she experienced such a strong emotional pull toward a man.

If Heavenly Father didn't mean for her and Nick to meet, why had He thrown them together? After spending the last couple weeks in his company, she wanted nothing more than to accept Nick fully into her life.

Up on the stage, he had turned his back to the audience and conversed with the band. The fiddler's eyebrows disappeared into his hairline, and he shot a glance in Catherine's direction. Nodding to Nick, he struck up a lively tune.

Clapping with the crowd, Catherine sat back to enjoy herself. Nick sang to the room with a mischievous twinkle in his eye, never once looking in her direction. It dawned on her slowly that he must be adding something of his own to the song because the villagers kept glancing her way.

The sly looks continued. He and the villagers were in on a secret, and she had no clue what it was. Marcus appeared at her elbow, singing the chorus with the rest of the crowd.

"Why is everyone looking at me?"

"Nick has just let the town in on a wee secret." Marcus patted her shoulder.

"Which is?"

"A minor lyric change of hair color. I'd say yours is a nice gold-brown, wouldn't you? It's much prettier than the nut-brown in the original version."

Heat suffused her face when she realized the enormity of what Nick had done. She covered her mouth with her hand. Despite her embarrassment at his cheeky cleverness, a sappy smile formed on her lips. She took a sip of her lukewarm chocolate.

Nick finished the song and replaced the mic in its stand. All eyes followed him as he hopped off the stage and took his seat at her side. Placing an arm across the back of her chair, he leaned in and whispered, "Are they still watching?"

"What do you think after a performance like that?" she whispered back.

"Are you terribly bothered?"

"What made you do such a thing?" She glanced at the patrons from under her lashes.

"Would you believe I was carried away by a random spark of wickedness?" His eyes rounded with innocence.

"I think that random naughtiness is very much a part of you, Lord Ainsley."

"'Her very frowns are fairer far / Than smiles of other maidens are,'" he quoted.

"And which poet did you just malign with your comparisons?"

"Coleridge."

She laughed in spite of herself. "I seem to remember your telling me you never do just one thing when several could be accomplished at the same time. Your little shenanigan on stage had an ulterior motive. When I figure out what it is, I'll let you know if I'm bothered or not."

A commotion by the door caught Nick's attention. His jaw hardened.

Catherine turned to see what had upset such an affable man. Her stomach dropped in disbelief as she watched the newcomer make his way to their table. Heat burned up her neck, filling her face.

"Time to go, Catherine." Jack pulled out her chair.

CHAPTER TEN

THE SMELL OF SCORCHED EGGS and burnt bacon greeted Catherine's nose as she entered the cottage kitchen the next morning, still sweating from her morning run. Her brother was hunkered down over a plate heaped with food. A salt shaker and a bottle of ketchup sat at his elbow.

"Want some?" Jack smiled at her proudly.

"There should be a law against letting you inside a kitchen."

"Why?"

Why? "Just trust me."

Jack picked up the ketchup bottle and squirted a quarter cup of it onto his eggs. Trying not to gag, Catherine cranked open the kitchen windows and turned to assess the room.

Grease splatters covered the wall. A red light glowed on the stove. Jack had left the burner on. Catherine turned off the heat and placed the skillet inside the stainless basin. If ever a man needed someone to take care of him, it was Jack.

"I'm sorry I embarrassed you last night."

"You're sorry? That's it?"

She plugged the sink and filled it with hot water and a dollop of soap. The temper she had held in check since last night's humiliation flared like gas poured on an open fire. This morning's run had done nothing to dispel it.

Did Jack really think a simple sorry would clear the air? The memory of him barging into the pub in the middle of her date topped every embarrassing moment. Even Nick, who was as smooth tempered as they came, had a bite in his words last night. If she could have crawled under a rock, she would have.

"My timing stank." He took another bite of crunchy, ketchup eggs.

"I agree, and right now, I don't want to agree with anything you say or do." Catherine took a dishrag and scrubbed the back of the stove with extra vigor. "You were a missionary for two years. Didn't you teach your investigators about agency?"

"You're turning our disagreement into a gospel discussion?" Jack's fork clattered on the table.

"I'm making a point."

"I'm all ears."

"Last night, you removed my agency. Where do you get off interrupting my date?" Catherine asked in a quiet voice.

"Dating a guy like him is a bad idea. He's all wrong for you."

"So that justifies what you did? FYI, Jack, you don't need to come charging in to protect me. I'm a grown-up."

"What if you're just another one of the women in Ainsley's life?" Jack leaned forward, his brown eyes hard.

"What did you do, Google him? The internet is filled with fallacies." Catherine rinsed out her rag at the sink and started on the counters.

"Let's assume for a moment that he's interested in marriage. Is Nick a member? Can he take you to the temple?"

"Jack, it was one date." Taking a deep breath, she reined in her frustration. "I know you love me, but there are a couple of things we need to agree on."

Jack took another bite.

"First, I'm not sure what's going on with Nick and me, but it's not your place to make that call."

"Dad called last night right after you left. When he asked where you were, I told him." His fingers drummed the tabletop. "You know Dad. He drilled me and found out Ainsley wasn't a member. He got all quiet, like he does when he's upset."

"So you played hero, barged down to the pub, and removed me from the big, bad clutches of Viscount Ainsley?" Her throat constricted, and she rasped out, "I was not only ashamed of your behavior but embarrassed beyond belief. How dare you treat me like that in public."

"Do you honestly think spending so much time with Ainsley will lead to anything but heartache or, at best, a civil marriage?"

"*If* Nick and I go out again, you are not to interrupt. Mom drilled good manners into all of us, and you are going to use them."

"*If* you go on another date? Get real. You should see the way that guy looks at you." Jack picked up a piece of bacon and bit into it.

Catherine wouldn't be surprised if it broke a tooth. She hung up the dishrag. "How does he look at me?"

Jack shoveled another bite of egg into his mouth. As far as delay tactics went, it was a crummy one. Catherine waited. She wanted the answer to her question and, if she had to, would sit there all day to get it.

"I hate it when you do that," Jack said, breaking the silence.

"Do what?" Catherine gave him her sweetest smile.

"Wait. It drives me crazy."

"How does Nick look at me?"

Jack took a huge gulp of milk.

"Has he been disrespectful?" Catherine checked her fingernails to see if they needed to be filed.

Jack thumped his glass on the farmhouse table. "He's nuts about you, okay? There. I said it. Are you happy? You're headed for a train wreck. But don't worry; I won't say another word about it. Just don't come running to me when he breaks your heart."

Jack tucked into his breakfast with gusto, obviously determined to say no more.

In silence, Catherine pulled an electrolyte drink out of the fridge. Jack would keep his word. He always did.

She took a sip of her drink and headed upstairs to shower. She turned on the water, and the hot spray filled the bathroom with steam as she stuck her head under the water. Her disagreement with Jack filled her with disquiet.

Growing up as a Latter-day Saint, her dreams were simple. She would marry a returned missionary in the temple and live near her family in a modest home where her children would grow up playing with their cousins.

Nothing had turned out as planned. Her mother was dead. Her father was a workaholic. The twins were expanding Coombes Enterprises in the Midwest, and Jack was established in the UK. And not one of them was married.

Catherine dumped a handful of shampoo on her head and worked up a lather. What was up with her family? Going over their pedigree charts, she realized quite a few of them had never married. At twenty-four, she worried about becoming a family statistic.

The shower spray grew cooler as she rinsed her hair and worked in the conditioner. She had never anticipated dating a man who could not take her to the temple, nor did she understand a thing about Nick's religious beliefs.

Sharing her thoughts, let alone her innermost convictions, had never come easily. An internal wall kept her from opening up and sharing her worries. The rising dichotomy inside had no outlet.

Why did her heart respond to him and no one else? What did it mean?

She put her head under the nozzle to rinse out the conditioner, and the water went cold.

CHAPTER ELEVEN

"BACK AGAIN, LORD AINSLEY?" ALICE Benson greeted him as he entered the priory kitchen. Her hands were busy kneading dough, but her blue eyes were merry as she contemplated him over the rim of her glasses.

"I can't seem to focus." Nick rubbed the back of his neck.

"I did gather something of the kind. You've turned up in my kitchen today more times than I see you in a week." Alice hustled over to the sink, turned on the tap, and washed her hands.

Nick sniffed the air. "Do you have anything I can taste test? Perhaps something you're putting in that hamper?"

Picking up a spoon, he lifted the lid off a pot on top of the range cooker. Alice came up behind him, snatching the spoon from his hand. The top of her gray head barely reached his chin. "No, you don't, Master Nicky."

"You can't blame me for trying. It smells delicious."

"You've always been a flatterer where my cooking is concerned." Alice placed the lid back on her simmering pot.

A breeze ruffled the lace curtains at the window. "Did you pack the china and stemware?"

"Shoo." Alice gave him a gentle nudge. "I won't forget your fancy crockery."

"I could place that basket on the worktop for you."

Alice, who'd known him all his life, swatted his hands away. "Leave me in peace, Nicky. I'll never be done filling this basket if you don't." She pursed her lips, a sure sign that she was in good humor.

"Just a taste, Alice. I'm falling apart here. I missed breakfast."

"A taste, then." Alice pulled out a brick of cheese from the fridge and cut him a wedge, serving it with a slice of cold mutton.

"No one cooks like our Alice." Nick grabbed a fork and speared a bite. He popped the mutton and cheese inside his mouth and chewed.

"You fancy this American?" Alice folded her arms and leveled him with a look.

Leaning against the worktop, Nick crossed his legs at the ankles and swallowed. "More than I ever dreamed possible."

"That makes two of my boys who've fallen for her."

Nick raised an eyebrow.

"Sammy. He's forever talking about her." Alice shook her head.

Relief washed over him. *Her boys.* Nick had been Alice's boy since the moment she had found him huddled inside a cupboard, crying after his mother left. Alice had taken him home to the stable block and tucked him into the Benson's spare bedroom. He'd stayed a week before his father had sobered up enough to notice he'd gone missing. By then, Nick was an entrenched member of the Benson household.

"Are you going to introduce her to Rivendon?" Alice looked at him over the top of her spectacles.

"Eventually . . ."

"He'll throw a fit if he catches wind of it before you let him know."

"I had planned to introduce her when things were more settled between us. But you're right—if he hears about her before I tell him, he's liable to have another stroke." The corner of his mouth went up. "Her brother isn't keen on me."

"I gathered that when I saw he turned up at the cèilidh."

"Is it wrong of me to want to keep the world from creeping in on us just yet?"

"You blew that to pieces last night with your song." Alice clicked her tongue.

"I did, didn't I? I couldn't seem to help myself." He slipped a glance at his watch. "There's a charity event in London at the Italian Embassy. I could introduce her to Grandfather then." He took another bite of mutton, chewing thoughtfully before he swallowed.

"It's a good plan as long as the papers don't find out about the two of you first. Where is this grand picnic of yours taking place? I need to send one of Gavin's lads out to the site." Alice tucked two bottles of water into the basket.

"The fishing hole at the south end of the lake."

"You're taking her fishing? Is that your idea of romancing a young lady?" Alice scrunched her face in distaste. "You'd best ring your old mate, Harry, and have him give you a few pointers."

"Catherine is someone I want in my life. I'd like to see how she handles herself doing something as mundane as fishing. It's part of who I am away from all this." He indicated the priory with a sweep of one arm. "In future, I sincerely hope she would expect the same from me. Besides, it's a pretty spot and will keep us from prying eyes and cameras."

"Fishing is not romantic, Nicky. It smells and keeps your hands otherwise occupied."

"Alice Benson, what are you telling me to occupy my hands with?"

Alice blushed to the roots of her hair. "I'm sure your lady-friend wouldn't mind a cuddle or two."

"Catherine is very old-fashioned."

"Then the earl will adore her."

He doubted it. Grandfather was old-school Britannia. Nick covertly glanced at the face of his watch.

"You can't make time move any faster by checking your watch every few seconds," Alice said.

"Now, there you are wrong. When I reach the archive room, Catherine will be putting away her dusty books." He nodded toward the basket on the worktop. "And you will still have a hamper to pack."

"I'll have this hamper packed before you reach the basement stairwell and out to your fishing hole long before you arrive. Now, go find your lady-friend."

Nick saluted her and went.

* * *

"No dogs today?" Catherine asked as Nick led her outside onto the priory grounds.

"The dogs would spoil the activity I have planned."

Whatever they were doing, it had put an extra spring in his step. She found it hard not to smile at the picture he made, with his tall, well-muscled frame mixed judiciously with the eager boyish expression.

They traversed along a dappled glen beside the priory's fishing stream, passing a series of short waterfalls, until they reached the lake. By the water's edge, a stand of cattails swayed in the breeze on their long slender necks.

Nick left the path and stopped on a section of grass. Leaning against a rotting log were two fishing rods, a net, a creel, and a tackle box. One of the estate workers must have brought them out on Nick's orders.

Fishing? Catherine bit her lip. She spied a picnic basket and blanket under a nearby tree and let out a pent-up breath. At least their entire afternoon wouldn't be taken up with trout.

"It's a perfect day for a spot of fishing." Nick pounced on the tackle box.

She hung back. "I wouldn't know. I've never tried."

"You've never gone fishing?" Nick looked at her as though she'd grown two heads.

"I've never seen the point in killing something I didn't plan to eat."

"I'll let you in on a little secret." Nick winked at her. "I don't much care for lake trout myself. The local butcher and I have an agreement. He sells my fish for a profit and sends me home with a few prime pieces of meat."

"Why does that not surprise me?" Catherine muttered under her breath as she knelt beside him on the grass. "How do I get this fishing line in the water?"

"I'll show you." Nick attached a lure on the end of her line, then stood. Taking the pole to the shoreline, he demonstrated how to cast.

Catherine watched with interest. It looked simple.

"Your turn." He placed the pole in her hands.

Following his instructions, she cast off. Her first attempt landed on the grassy slope a good five feet from the water.

Nick performed a few more exhibitions. "Got it?"

"I think so." His nearness made her self-conscious. She swung her pole back and cast. This time, she caught the cattails.

"Use a little more force," Nick encouraged as she reeled in the line.

Her third cast made it into the water. Barely.

Not many would interpret the small indentation at the left corner of Nick's mouth as disappointment, but Catherine was learning to read him. The least little crease was a dead giveaway. She hated being its cause.

"Again." Nick folded his arms across his broad chest. "I'm going to make a first-class angler of you yet." After several more casts, he was satisfied. "I think you're ready. Bait your hook and give it a go."

An airtight container marked "bait" sat on the grass beside the tackle box. Opening the lid, she expected to see fish eggs or cheese. Instead she found big, red, juicy maggots. They wriggled and writhed like cicada larvae but smelled a hundred times worse.

Just what every girl needs: a date with Mr. Wonderful and a cup full of maggots.

At her elbow, watching, stood said Mr. Wonderful with a face devoid of expression. *Men.* Why was it the ones she associated with expected her to enjoy their disgusting activities?

Reminding herself she had put up with a whole lot worse, she reached inside the container, pulled out two maggots and impaled them on the end of her hook.

"They aren't secure. They'll fall off when you cast."

Catherine heard the smile in his voice. Nick was enjoying this.

Scrunching her nose, she looked at the red blob on the end of her line. It was cold. It was slimy. And it was the texture of the twins' loogies.

She glanced at Nick from the corner of her eye to see if he was serious. He was. *Great. Fine. Fantastic.* Biting her lip, she secured the slimy maggots onto her hook.

Nick beamed at her as though she'd climbed Everest. "What do you say to a friendly competition?"

"This *friendly* competition wouldn't happen to be rigged in your favor, would it?" She narrowed her eyes. "You've probably been fishing since you were younger than Sammy."

"I'll catch two for every one of yours," he wheedled.

"Not good enough, Lord Ainsley. Since I'm a novice, be a gentleman and give me extra points if I catch the biggest fish."

"I think you drive a hard bargain, Miss Pressley-Coombes." His blue eyes sparkled with admiration.

With arms akimbo, Catherine waited.

"Agreed. If you catch the biggest fish, you get three extra points. Plus, I have to catch two to your one." Nick picked up his pole. "We don't want to cross our lines, so I'll move down the shore about twenty yards."

"You know where the best fishing holes are."

"Okay, you go downstream, and I'll stay here." Nick shrugged.

"Not on your life, buster. I'm staying beside you. That'll keep you honest." Catherine wasn't about to be bested. She hadn't grown up with a houseful of men for nothing.

"If you say so." Without the slightest sign of offense, Nick baited his hook and cast off with perfect precision. The hook made a plop when it entered the water and sank out of sight.

"You didn't say, 'On your mark. Get set. Go.'"

"On your mark. Get set. Go." The innocent expression he gave her was not convincing.

"You devil." Catherine fought back a giggle at his blatant disregard for what she considered fair play. "What happened to ladies first? Or having us both cast off at the same time?"

"I never said we had to start at the same time. Besides, I've already had a nibble." Sure enough, the tip of his pole dipped.

This spurred Catherine to action. Hurriedly, she opened her reel, held the line with her finger, swung back her rod, and cast with a great deal of frenetic energy. Her fishing line flew straight in the air, glanced off an overhanging branch, whipped three times around the limb's circumference and immobilized Catherine's pole in an upright position.

"Don't move, Catherine. Not. One. Inch." Nick yelled.

Catherine froze, wondering if she'd crossed his line. If one of the groundskeepers came along and saw her "catch of the day," she'd die of embarrassment.

Nick's grunts didn't give her any assurance. She began imagining all kinds of reasons why he'd told her not to move. What if she had hooked a wild beehive? Or strangled a squirrel in the tree?

She couldn't handle the suspense. Opening the metal thingamajig, she let out a length of line before flipping it back in place. With the extra length of line, her pole loosened, and she laid it on the ground.

Turning, she found the elegant Lord Ainsley sitting on the grass, holding his nose. Blood trickled from between his fingers. Realizing what had happened, Catherine walked over to examine her handiwork.

Squatting in front of him, she removed Nick's hands and leaned back on her heels. She wanted to die on the spot. A stream of blood dripped off Nick's chin. He lifted his hand and fingered his right nostril where the fish hook had entered. She felt bad. Really bad. But something inside her twisted. She averted her eyes and blinked twice. Her nostrils flared. Giving up, she double over and laughed.

Nick watched her quietly.

Sobering, she wiped the tears from her eyes. Digging inside her pocket, she located a packet of tissues and handed them over.

"Thanks." Nick stared at her as he mopped his face.

"May I?"

"Only if you plan to be helpful."

Catherine tipped Nick's head back and looked up his nose to see where the hook had embedded itself. Thankfully, her bait had flown off before entering his nasal cavity. Upon closer inspection, she found the metal had dug into the central interior of his skin.

She tilted her head to the side, their eyes mere inches apart. "I caught the biggest fish. Should I be merciful and let him go?"

"I'm not real big on catch and release," Nick said with a wicked gleam in his eye. Taking hold of her hand in a firm clasp, he continued. "If you hook one that size, I think you'd better keep him."

Catherine swallowed hard. She was in over her head and didn't know what to do. Hastily, she pulled her hands free and shoved them inside her pockets as a blush started up her neck.

Sure enough, the left corner of Nick's mouth dented in. Using the tissue, he dabbed at the blood on his chin.

After an awkward minute, she recovered her equilibrium and said, "I can get this out, but it's going to hurt."

"It couldn't hurt much more than my pride right now."

Catherine bit back a smile. "Okay. On three. One."

She felt Nick tense, readying for the inevitable tearing of flesh. "Two."

He shut his eyes, hardening his jaw muscles.

Instead of finishing the count, Catherine pushed the hook backward and tore a small amount of internal skin and freed Nick from the line.

"Ugh," he grunted as blood gushed from the wound. He looked at her as though she'd betrayed him. "What happened to three?"

"Math was never my specialty." She took out a tissue and tried to staunch the flow before it stained his shirt.

He looked at her as though trying to align the mental picture he had with who she really was. "I used to feel sorry that you'd grown up with such rotten brothers. I have come to the conclusion you and your siblings are evenly matched."

Shaking his head, he went to the water's edge and washed his face. When he finished, Catherine handed him two more tissues. He rolled them up and shoved them inside his nostril.

"After such an amusing interlude, shall we get on with our competition? You won't mind terribly if I insist on some distance between our poles?" He cocked an eyebrow at her.

She had assumed they would return to the priory, but it seemed nothing kept Nick from his fish. Still fighting back embarrassment at her behavior, she nodded in agreement. She didn't dare mention his need for disinfectant.

While Nick put a new hook on her fishing line, she rinsed her hands off, then dried them on her jeans. Skewering a few more maggots, she marched fifty feet or so from Nick and cast off.

Nick reeled in three trout in quick succession and had looped them through a stringer before she got her first bite. The tip of her pole dipped. She stared, not believing what was happening. It dipped again. She squealed so hard Nick dropped his pole and came running.

"What do I do?" she asked, laughing with excitement.

"Normally, you set the hook," he said dryly. "I believe you've already done that by accident. You've definitely got a fish on the end of that line. Reel it in."

Winding in her first fish, Catherine was as jubilant as any five-year-old. When it cleared the water, she deflated. The fish was four inches long.

"Anyone would have thought you'd caught Moby Dick by all the racket you made," Nick said as he examined her miniscule fish. "This one goes back if we can get the hook out."

"I thought you weren't big on catch and release, Lord Ainsley," she said, feeling just the least bit naughty.

He'd been fiddling with the fish, but his hands stilled. "My dear Miss Pressley-Coombes, might you be flirting with me?"

She shrugged.

"I was referring to another variety of fish entirely," his deep voice rumbled.

"Would that be a trophy fish?" Catherine asked, emboldened. "Because if that's what you are so elegantly referring to, Lord Ainsley, I'll have you know that particular fish looks pretty weird with two saturated tissues sticking out of its nose."

"It does, does it?" Nick freed Moby Dick and tossed it back into the lake.

At her nod, he yanked the offending tissues from his nostril and pulled a perfectly laundered handkerchief from the pocket of his jeans. He dabbed his nose to see if the bleeding had stopped. It had.

Without warning, he lunged. His shoulder hit her in the stomach while his arms grasped her legs. She was over his shoulder before she could do more than gasp. He spun her in circles until she squealed to be put down.

When her feet touched the grass, he didn't let go. His eyes fastened on her lips. What remaining breath she had left in her lungs whooshed out. He placed his hands on her waist and reeled her in.

Catherine swallowed. She liked him so much but was not ready to obligate herself to a man with differing beliefs. If she kissed him, it would only muddy things between them. She stiffened in his arms, but her galloping heart had other ideas.

Leaves rustled, and footsteps sounded on the path. Nick groaned, and they turned in unison to see Sammy and Gavin Benson coming their way.

"Hiya, Nick," Sammy said.

"Lord Ainsley, to you." Gavin lowered his brows.

"Lord Ainsley, did you catch any fish?"

"Hello, Sammy. Gavin," Nick said without enthusiasm.

Gavin nodded in acknowledgment, his eyes sympathetic. "Alice sent me to make sure Charlie deposited your picnic in the right place."

"It's here. Please thank Alice for putting it together."

"Have you caught any trout?" Sammy was more interested in the fish.

"Lord Ainsley reeled in several good ones," Catherine said.

"Miss Pressley-Coombes hooked the biggest." Nick's eyes sparkled with wicked humor.

"I want to see." Sammy bounced over to the shoreline where Nick had secured the fish.

"Those are Lord Ainsley's fish." Catherine choked back a laugh. "He's teasing you, Sammy. I caught the smallest one. He tossed it back a second ago."

"That's okay, Miss Catherine. One day, it will be a big granddaddy fish, and you can catch it again," Sammy said philosophically.

"Come on, Sammy." Gavin ruffled the boy's hair. "We're done here. Let's leave these two to their *fishing*."

"I want to stay. They're having a jolly good time," Sammy whined.

"Yes, they are, but I doubt it would continue with you underfoot. Come along." Gavin took Sammy's arm in a firm grip and started back the way they came.

"But I want . . ."

CHAPTER TWELVE

PATCHES OF MIST SNAKED ACROSS the priory grounds, spitting on everything in the greenish-gray light. Catherine's shoulders drooped as she trudged toward the MGB. Another day spent digging through records without any leads. Today, it had been receipts, fascinating in historical value but no help in her search.

Not willing to admit the main cause of her discouragement had nothing to do with her search and everything to do with not seeing Nick since Sammy and Gavin had interrupted them at the fishing hole, she wiped a bead of moisture off her face.

Nick had texted earlier that morning to let her know he'd be in Bristol most of the day and competing in a darts tournament tonight at the pub. He doubted he would return in time to see her during the interim.

Reaching the MGB, she pulled Jack's keys out of her tote and slipped the right one into the lock, then she realized the car door had not shut properly. Strange. She always locked up, no matter where she went.

The rapid crunch of gravel reached her ears before a deep, cultured voice hailed. "Catherine. Wait."

Smiling broadly, Catherine spun on her heel as Nick rounded the corner of the priory. Looking handsome in business attire, minus the tie, Nick jogged over, carrying a brown, leather briefcase.

"I was positive I'd missed you." His smile burst through the gloom.

Catherine's pulse took off, banging away like a jackhammer. She wanted to hug him but held back, her emotions seesawing. Nick took the decision out of her hands. Dropping his briefcase, he swooped her up in an enormous hug, her toes lifting off the ground.

"Instead of going straight on to the pub for the tournament, I stopped by on the off chance you were still here." He put her down, resting his forehead against hers. "Lucky for me I did."

"What time is the competition?" Catherine asked, stepping back.

"It starts in less than an hour. Are you off to feed that starving brother of yours?"

"That's the plan we agreed on when I came to visit."

"I believe he got the better end of the deal." Nick pulled his wadded-up tie from his suit pocket and stuffed it into his briefcase. "Do you mind dropping me off at the pub? The lot was full when I passed just now. I'd like to wring every moment I can with you."

"Of course. Hop in."

Nick settled her in the driver's seat, then climbed into the passenger's side.

She turned the key in the ignition. At first, the engine didn't engage.

"It sounds like Jack needs a new battery," Nick said.

The door had been open, so Catherine mentally agreed. The engine hiccupped, then sputtered and roared to life. Relieved, she circled the fountain, with its soaring spray splashing into the reflecting pool, and headed toward the first switchback.

The priory drive, a narrow lane originally built for carriages, had been dynamited from the limestone hillside. A series of four switchbacks crisscrossed the knoll on thirty-degree angles.

Catherine flipped on the fog lamps under the ancient limes as they approached the first turn. Her foot tapped the brakes and met no resistance. In disbelief, she pumped the pedal twice more.

There was nothing. Nothing at all.

Her stomach flipped. A voice she did not recognize as her own said flatly, "No brakes."

Nick glanced at her, then reached for the handbrake. The car slowed but not enough to stop their descent. The MGB picked up speed. Nick yanked hard on the brake this time. The car swung wildly to the right, then rotated to the left in a whip-lash of motion. The rock wall on the nearside of the lane loomed through the windshield not six feet in front them.

Catherine bit her lip and fought the steering wheel. In desperation, she gunned the engine. It was an old trick her brothers had taught her. The car responded, pulling out of the fishtail.

"Sorry," Nick grunted.

Catherine didn't respond, her sole focus on the road. She cranked the wheel, and a spray of gravel shot out from under the rear wheels as they swept around the first bend.

"What do I do?" Flutters of panic quivered inside her. By supreme effort, she forced it back, keeping her eyes on the road.

"Shifting to a lower gear will slow us a bit," Nick said calmly as their speed increased. "We don't want to burn out the handbrake. I'll apply it sparingly. When I brake, try to engage a lower gear."

Trees and rocks flashed by in a blur. Patches of mist swirled as high as the hood and then receded through the trees. Part of her mind refused to accept the situation.

"Now." Nick laid on the handbrake.

Catherine grasped the gearstick with shaky fingers. The transmission ground and clanged in a cacophony of metallic sounds before accepting the lower gear.

On this stretch of drive between the first and second switchbacks, the trees ran against the edge of the lane. As they neared the second curve, Nick applied the handbrake in rapid, short bursts. If she erred at this speed, they would plaster themselves on the rock wall or wrap themselves around one of the trees.

She chewed her lip, her heart pounding like a drumline. She could not give in to the panic that made her want to let go of the wheel. Their chance of survival was slim to none if she did not drive better than she ever had before.

Heading down a hillside at break-neck speed was not the best time for an epiphany. But it came to her then, in a flash of insight. What she felt for Nick was not infatuation. It was deep. It was strong. And it was abiding.

Narrowing her eyes, she tried to make out the road through the bands of mist. Moisture collected on the windshield. Her white-knuckled hands refused to let go of the steering wheel long enough to flick the wipers. Turning the wheel with rigid fingers, she prayed.

The tires shrieked, and gravel spewed as they swooped around the second hairpin turn. Golden glow from their headlights cut through the fog. The tree line leaped out like ghosts of long-dead sentries.

The stench of burning rubber and oil filled the interior as they careened onto the stretch between the second and third switchbacks. Catherine's fears escalated with the worst kind of dread. She could feel the panic rising, bubbling, fighting to be free and wondered if she could stay focused.

"Halfway there," Nick said in that calm, maddening voice.

How could he remain so collected? They were on the razor's edge of disaster.

The descent was steeper on the third segment of the crisscross, and Nick made every brake application count. The car responded and slowed. They took the one-hundred-eighty-degree curve at no more than double the needed speed.

Catherine inhaled the first full breath since she'd discovered the brakes didn't work.

"Brilliant. You handled that well." Approval laced through Nick's voice.

The brief reprieve left her weak and shaky. She took in deep gulps of air, flexing one hand, then the other in order to restore blood flow in her fingers.

As they entered the downhill ramp toward the final bend, the car began to pick up speed. Nick braked but didn't get much response. He took the brake as far as it would go while Catherine waited for the opportunity to downshift. The acrid stench of burning intensified, but the car did not respond.

Nick muttered something under his breath, then said in that calm voice, "Our handbrake's gone."

The MGB hurtled down the hillside as though the hellhound of Hades nipped at its wheels. A wall of ghostly trees leapt out of the mist, adding to the fantasy. Her arms had gone numb. She fought the wheel, refusing to give up. Nick mattered too much.

The MGB skidded. The right side of the car went up and over the embankment and continued down the lane at a precarious angle. Tilted as they were, the MGB began to slide ever closer to the trees.

A desperate prayer rose in her heart. *Help us, Father. Please, please, please . . .*

On the embankment under the trees, ancient, gnarled roots protruded. The right-side wheels ran over them, the impact snapping Catherine's head forward, smacking it against the steering wheel. The distorted tubers slowed the slide.

The wheels gripped for a few precious seconds, and Catherine managed to put them back on the road with a couple inches to spare. Her heart had frozen on the second curve, yet her pulse continued to pound in her ears.

Situated as they were, she could make the gate without mishap. She took a deep cleansing breath. Their flight down the hillside was coming to an end.

"There's a good deal of traffic on the main road tonight because of the darts tournament," Nick said in a conversational tone. "It's quite possible we'll hit someone as we exit the gate. However, there is a narrow gap in the tree line just before the pillars. If you can manage to angle the car, we might pass through it into the pasture."

"Got it," she said and chewed her lip some more. So much for home free. She couldn't miss that gap. Most of the cars would be coming from the north—Nick's side of the vehicle. In such a small vehicle, he wouldn't stand a chance.

This had to work.

The muscles in her arms shook as she crashed and ground the gears in a futile effort to slow their speed. The car thundered down the lane like an out-of-control bobsled in search of Olympic gold.

"The gap is coming up on your right," Nick said quietly.

Catherine squinted ahead through the mist, trying to make out the breach in the trees.

"Now," Nick said.

The space was so narrow she was sure the car would not fit. With no viable options, she turned the wheel. Almost sobbing in frustration, she aimed for the gap. The tires shrieked, and gravel peppered the trunk of an ancient lime like the sound of machine-gun fire. They swooped toward the opening, heading straight for a wall of mist.

* * *

The motorcar catapulted into the mist-laden pasture. Metal crunched. Glass shattered. Blinded by thick, swirling fog, Nick felt the MGB bounce and jostle over the invisible terrain. He hoped the ewes and their young would have enough sense to get out of the way.

The car hit a dip with a mind-jarring bounce. He bit his tongue and swallowed blood. The red sports car rocked to a standstill as the mist slithered away, revealing a hillside of indignant inhabitants. Their protests rent the air outside the motorcar windows.

The roaring in his ears made it difficult to think. He shut his eyes and tried to slow his racing heart.

That had been entirely too close. When they had gone over the embankment, he was sure they were history. But Catherine had used those roots to her advantage, propelling the automobile back onto the drive. Not once had she lost control of the wheel.

The roaring in his ears receded, and a sense of giddy well-being took its place. He stared out the windscreen as his spirits rocketed skyward. Adrenalin junkies had nothing over that wild ride.

"How are you doing over there?" he asked, still staring out the windscreen.

"Fine. You?" Catherine's voice quavered on the words.

Turning, he studied her face. Her lips were raw, and the white knuckles clamped to the steering wheel would take a crowbar to pry loose.

"Brilliant." He managed to say. "That was an adventure I'd not like to repeat anytime soon."

"I agree."

To his horror, tears began to stream down her face. Her shoulders shook, but she made no sound.

Tenderness welled up inside him. Nine women out of ten would have fallen to pieces before they'd made it around the first hairpin turn. Catherine hadn't. Not until after they were safe.

He pried her death grip from the steering wheel, scooted his seat back, and pulled her across the central console onto his lap. To his surprise, she didn't resist but burrowed in, wrapping her arms around his waist.

"It's all right." He smoothed her hair and rested his chin on top of the soft curls. "You were brilliant. Davis Racing is always on the lookout for new talent. I think you should apply."

A deformed chuckle escaped her. "I don't know what I would have done if you hadn't been here."

He rubbed her back and mumbled meaningless nothings into her hair. *Poor darling.* He would give anything to have saved her from that. A thought came and went in the back of his mind, then persisted. "Didn't your brother recently restore this motorcar?"

"Yes."

The mist swirled and subsided outside the window like a lost soul searching blindly for redemption.

Catherine shivered in his arms and snuggled deeper. For days, he'd been dying to kiss her. Now she was right where he wanted, and he couldn't take advantage of her weakened state.

Sighing at the irony, Nick loosened his grip on her and took out his mobile. Checking his contacts, he pressed speed dial. He kissed the top of her head and pulled her close as another set of tremors racked her body.

His groundskeeper answered on the second ring. "Gavin. Nick here. There's been a bit of an accident. Could you bring the tractor and chains round to the sheep pasture?"

"Are you all right, my lord?" Gavin asked.

"We're in one piece. Catherine's brakes gave way on the switchbacks. I think Catherine could do with a rug and a thermos of hot chocolate."

He wiped an errant tear off her face. Another tear glistened on the end of her lashes. Reverently, he touched it with his finger, absorbing the moisture. Their eyes locked and held. Gavin said something he didn't catch. "Could you repeat that, Gavin?"

A slight dimple appeared in the center of Catherine's cheek. He'd never noticed it before. Mentally shaking himself, he glanced at his watch. "I'd nearly forgot. Yes, send the car round as well. Thanks."

He pocketed his mobile. "Gavin will tow your brother's vehicle to Taylor's Garage. He reminded me just now about the darts tournament. Alice will give you a lift home after she drops me at the pub."

"You're still going?" Catherine's eyes widened. "Won't this throw off your game?"

"I'm no worse off than after riding the Smiler at Alton Towers." At her puzzled expression, he added, "It's a fourteen-loop roller coaster."

"You wouldn't admit it even if you were."

No, he wouldn't, but that was beside the point. Pushing a few strands of hair away from her face, he kissed the tip of her nose and was pleased when she didn't pull away. "I was so worried about you, I didn't think about anything else."

"I thought I was going to kill you," she said with a catch in her voice.

"You were brilliant." Still filled with a sense of euphoria, he ran both thumbs across her cheek bones. Her gemstone eyes were aware and receptive.

The realization washed over him. He loved her. He loved everything about her. While her looks had first captured his attention, this feeling had crept up on him unaware. When she had yanked that fish hook out of his nose yesterday, he'd suspected. Now he was certain.

His title and wealth meant nothing to her. She saw him: Nicholas Davidson, the man. Underneath Catherine's shy, feminine grace and competitive nature was a woman of strength and character.

Careful not to spook her, Nick leaned in to see if she would retreat. Catherine's eyelids fluttered shut as he touched his lips to hers. Her mouth was as soft as rose petals. His lips tenderly caressed hers until he couldn't bear it any longer, and then he crushed her to him. Her arms crept around his shoulders.

Nick thought he would explode with joy. Exultation coursed through his body. His Davidson blood ran true. It seared through him, branding his heart and mind to hers. At long last, he had found her, the woman his grandfather had assured him existed.

The question Nick feared to ask slithered into his mind. Did Catherine feel it too? He pulled back to gauge her reaction.

Her lips were swollen from his kisses, and that adorable blush had started up her neck. She tried to turn away, but he wouldn't let her. Placing his finger under her chin, he lifted her face, with her downcast eyes. After what seemed an age, her dark lashes lifted. Glowing in their aquamarine depths was what he'd sought his entire life.

He bent his head for another kiss, but the sound of a powerful engine met his ears. Sheep scattered as the tractor came over the rise and started across the pasture. Nick groaned in frustration.

Catherine let loose a nervous gurgle of laughter.

"The cavalry has arrived," he said, resting his forehead on hers. "I wish they had not been so immediate in their response." After one last quick kiss, he grabbed the keys from the ignition and opened the door.

* * *

Catherine self-consciously climbed out of Jack's car. Sammy, seated on Gavin's lap, waved at them from inside the glass-enclosed cab. His snaggle-toothed grin made Catherine smile in response.

The sheep didn't like the tractor any more than the MGB. Their bleats filled the air and covered the drone of the tractor's powerful motor. Gavin cut the engine. Sammy scampered down the ladder.

Nick caught him as he dropped to the ground. "Hey, Sammy."

"Did you see me drive the tractor, Nick?" Sammy asked.

"Lord Ainsley," Gavin corrected.

"Sorry, Granddad." The boy appeared unrepentant. "Lord Ainsley, did you see me drive your New Holland tractor?"

"I did." Nick ruffled his hair. "Charlie better take care, or I'll be hiring myself a new plow boy."

"Catherine, I came to rescue you." Sammy bounced over to her.

"Neanderthals start young," Nick said to her over the top of Sammy's head.

This remark had Catherine biting the inside of her cheek to keep from laughing.

As Sammy bubbled with enthusiasm, Catherine overheard Nick say to Gavin in that cool tone he'd used as they'd raced down the hillside, "Could you have William check the brake lines? I'm curious as to why they failed."

"Do you think they were tampered with?" Gavin's brows drew together.

"I find it hard to believe a newly restored motorcar would have such an issue," he said.

A horn sounded from the drive.

"There's Alice." Nick tossed the keys to Gavin and turned to her. "Catherine, are you ready?"

With an internal pucker of worry, Catherine reached behind the driver's seat for her tote and paused. If she had left the car door open all day, the battery would have been dead. After a few tries, the engine had started.

Had someone tampered with her brakes? Before she had time to voice her concerns, Nick took her firmly by the hand and propelled her toward the gap in the trees.

CHAPTER THIRTEEN

THEODOSIA SAT AT THE DAINTY Regency desk, weak afternoon sunlight filtering through the office windows, as she finished the earl's correspondence. She sealed the heavy cream envelope with the Rivendon coat of arms while an aria from *Turandot* played softly in the background over the stereo—full-on Puccini at his best.

Normally, *Nessun Dorma* settled her jangling nerves, but Ari had slipped up the back stairs during his shift and refused to leave. However tempting, Theodosia could not afford to lose her job while that stupid American searched the priory for information. She needed to know what was happening in Bascombe. Listening in on Ainsley's daily calls to his grandfather kept her apprised of the situation.

During her covert visit to the priory, she had put the motorcar skills her father had taught her to good use. Despite her best efforts, Catherine Pressley-Coombes had survived.

Theodosia needed an accomplice. Ari's recent game of least-in-sight with the MET Police had roused her curiosity. Two nights ago when he'd been in class, she had searched his room, locating two passports under his mattress bearing his photo with different identities.

Paulo Delgado and Ari Falcone were one and the same. The Delgado name stirred memories of last year's international headlines. Luigi Delgado, head of the Sicilian Delgado crime family, had passed. Ari bore a strong resemblance to the deceased. This information would provide all the leverage Theodosia needed to secure Ari's aid if he should prove difficult.

Over the last few decades, the *Mafiosi* had switched their focus to big-business extortion and human trafficking. Some of Ari's contacts were bound to prove useful.

Under her lashes, Theodosia watched Ari as she slipped her legs, in their thigh-hugging skirt, out from under the desk and crossed them. He unabashedly stared. Perhaps he would be more amenable if his mind were not wholly fixed on her request.

Ari came to the front of her chair and kissed the spot between her brows. "Have you finished the earl's letters?"

"That was the last one." Rising, she placed the envelope in the tray of outgoing mail. Mr. Scott, the butler, would post them later.

"Good." Ari pulled her into his arms.

She responded mechanically while her mind grappled with how to approach her topic. Despite Ari's link to the Mafiosi, Theodosia wasn't 100 percent sure of him.

"Ari, I have a difficult situation." She bit her lips to stop their trembling. "Everything is such a mess."

Ari all but preened, reminding her of a strutting peacock.

"I'm terribly in debt and have held off my creditors under the premise that I'm to inherit a considerable sum in a matter of months. A recent problem has arisen. An American with a closer claim to inherit is snooping for information." She pouted her lips.

"What do you need?"

Theodosia licked her lips and whispered, "I need her to disappear."

"You mean you want me to kill her." Ari removed himself from her arms, his dark eyes inscrutable. Anger poured off him in waves.

Her mouth went dry, and she began to tremble. She clenched her hands together in real fear. She had not anticipated this response.

"By taking the life of an innocent person, you would curse me for eternity."

"I would not wish that upon you, Ari." Terrified he would expose her, Theodosia's eyes flooded with tears.

"That is what you implied."

She stepped backward in an effort to distance herself from his wrath. "It is so hard not having a home of my own, working for a pittance, and not participating in the social life I deserve. I have debts, Ari. My husband was to have taken care of them, but he died before only the most pressing ones were paid."

"You would send the man who loves you to perdition? For debts?" His dark eyes glittered.

"I will be in very great trouble if . . ."

"Why would you assume I would kill someone?" He shook his shoulder length hair out of his eyes. "I am not a killer!"

Theodosia's legs refused to support her. She stumbled to her chair, wondering how she had so miscalculated his willingness to help her. He was part of a crime family. Didn't they remove people who got in their way? Despite his age, she knew Ari had sampled the world's offerings with a great amount of pleasure. Something in his religious upbringing must have stuck. What if he went to the authorities? Cousin Sally's death would be dredged up. Once the police started digging, she would be sent to Her Majesty's Pleasure. Theodosia buried her face in her hands and burst into tears.

After several interminable minutes, Ari's hand touched the back of her head, then proceeded to stroke her hair. "I have an idea." He squatted on the floor in front of her and pulled her hands away from her face.

Black eye makeup covered her fingers. For once in her life, she didn't care.

"I will not kill for you, *amore mia*, but I will help your American disappear."

Her heart skipped a beat. "After what I asked of you, you'll help me?"

"Yes." His eyes were solemn. "My cousins transport people."

Human trafficking? Her heart gave an odd little kick.

Ari did not move but watched her with hooded eyes. The boy was much more intelligent than she had formerly assumed.

"This is acceptable?" Ari asked after several moments.

"I believe it meets with my approval." She said primly as a huge weight lifted from her shoulders.

"They will not murder."

It appeared Ari's hard and fast rule stopped and started with manslaughter. "Would your cousins transport my problem far away—where she would never be found?"

"Yes." White teeth flashed in his swarthy face.

Theodosia's heart flipped and banged in quick, painful jabs. She had never noticed his resemblance to a pirate before. "How shall we go about this procedure?"

"Leave it to me. I will arrange it."

A little thrill zinged down her spine. Though it was implied rather than said, Ari had worked with his cousins before.

He turned to her with his back to the windows; the afternoon light bathed him in its golden glow. The finale to *Turandot* began to play.

With the crashing of cymbals, amusement flashed in Ari's eyes. "Now, shall we talk price?"

CHAPTER FOURTEEN

NICK TOOK NOTE OF THE well-tended garden as he let himself inside Jack's cottage gate. Catherine's touch had extended to the newly planted flowerbeds. The telly blared through the open window. A sportscaster shouted. Whistles blew. Jack was watching the championship football game. Maybe he could get a recap on what he had missed in the last few minutes.

He rapped on the cottage door and plastered a smile on his face. If it killed him, he would be pleasant. The door swung open on its rusty hinges.

"Catherine isn't here." Jack's eyes bored into his.

"As it happens, it's you I came to see."

"Why?"

"This is about your motorcar."

Jack opened the door to let him pass. "Come in." He led him into the lounge.

Leather furniture offered comfortable seating in a room Nick remembered being devoid of furnishings. An industrial configuration of welded pipes and repurposed wood housed electronics where Bromley fans shouted on the telly.

"What's the score?" Nick nodded at the screen.

"Two to one Bromley. You follow football?" Jack looked surprised.

"A bit." Of course he followed football. Who didn't?

Both men were momentarily distracted as Caruso made a goal and tied the score.

"What's this about my car?"

"Taylor's Garage rang this afternoon."

"Why would the garage contact you?" Jack appeared affronted.

"I asked them to if they found anything suspicious during your repairs." That pulled Jack's attention away from the telly.

Nick cleared his throat. "It seems your brake lines were tampered with."

"What?" Jack's brow furrowed.

"I found it rather odd your brakes failed after you had so recently restored your motorcar." Nick looked him in the eye. "I took it upon myself to ask William Taylor to see if my assumption was correct. He confirmed it just now."

Jack's eyes bored into his for a long moment. Nick waited him out until the hostility began to thaw from his expression.

"Do you have any idea who's behind this?" Jack questioned.

"I don't. That's why I'm here." Nick ran a hand through his hair. "Everyone in the village knows Catherine drives your vehicle. My decision to catch a ride with her was purely spur-of-the-moment. Whoever cut those lines knew the brakes would fail on the priory's switchbacks. A car crash on that drive . . ."

"Why would someone want to harm Catherine?" Jack interrupted.

"I was hoping you would know. Has she done anything unusual since her arrival in England?"

Jack shook his head. "Not that I'm aware of. Occasionally, she goes sightseeing, but more often than not, she's researching. Catherine's a homebody."

Nick looked down at his hands, utterly flummoxed.

"Maybe it was one of your jealous ex-girlfriends," Jack suggested.

It was a low dig. Nick's hand tightened into a fist. "She'd have an elephant of a memory. I haven't seen anyone regularly in four years."

"But I thought—" Jack stopped.

"You've been reading tabloids." Nick gave him an icy stare.

"I. Uh." Red splotches dotted Jack's face.

"Which is your favorite? *The Kensington Press*, where I fathered not one but two children with different women in the same week? Or the *Tattler's* article, where I broke off my secret engagement with Princess Charise of Luxembourg?"

Jack looked incapable of a response.

"Whenever I go to London, it's always the same. The press follows." Nick pushed on. "If I take a date to a formal affair, the next morning's papers have a story about our relationship. The wealthy and titled are the paparazzi's bread and butter. None of the stories are true. I'm a farmer at heart and lead a fairly boring existence."

"I thought you were going to take a swing at me." Jack grinned. It was the same wide-flashing smile as his sister's and every bit as disarming.

"I considered it." Nick returned to the topic of his visit. "I'm going to question estate workers to see if they noticed anyone near your vehicle the day of the accident."

"Why haven't you contacted the police?"

"I plan to now that I have William Taylor's report. Our detective chief inspector is overworked and understaffed. Our car crash will be buried under a mountain of paperwork. I'll report it all the same."

"Does Catherine know about this?"

"No. I don't want her upset. She had a bad fright."

"She won't thank you for keeping her out of the loop, Ainsley." Jack shook his head.

"I'll take my chances."

"Don't say I didn't warn you."

By unspoken agreement, both men headed for the door.

"The new lines could have been faulty," Jack offered.

Nick wanted to believe Catherine's brother, but the situation worried at him like an out-of-reach itch. "Does anyone at your church have an issue with Catherine?"

"Maybe her Primary class," Jack drawled.

"Should I get the DCI involved? He could question them."

"About them not liking her peanut butter cookies as much as her chocolate chip ones?"

"How old is her class?" He'd stumbled right into that one.

"Three." Jack held out his hand. "I appreciate your concern, but Catherine will be fine."

Nick shook the proffered hand, hoping Jack was right, but that niggle of doubt still itched. "Cheers."

CHAPTER FIFTEEN

Fourteen minutes after leaving Jack's cottage, Nick entered the steel-and-glass Upper Valley Police Station. With a multitude of closings, the three Cotswold villages of the upper valley were lucky their station remained open even though the police force had been cut by half.

A stout woman in her late forties looked up from the inquiry desk. "Bless my soul, if it isn't Lord Ainsley."

"How are you, Mrs. Farrus?" Nick stopped beside her desk to chat. "It's been awhile since I saw you last."

"We were on holiday in France, then stopped off to see Rachel's newest babe in Dover. She's a darling but the image of her father, poor mite."

"I thought all grandmothers had perfect grandchildren?"

"Don't you believe it." Mrs. Farrus chuckled, jiggling her jowls. "Rachel's two oldest are absolute horrors, and her new babe has inherited her father's nose."

While Mrs. Farrus's son-in-law was no Cyrano De Bergerac, his nose was undeniably large. "A word of advice." Nick leaned forward and whispered. "Start saving for her rhinoplasty."

She let out a belly laugh as DCI Barnes, a tall man with a decided paunch and penetrating hazel eyes, joined them.

"Lord Ainsley. It's a little early to be collecting for St. Sebastian's, isn't it?"

"Actually, I'm here to report a crime."

* * *

Nick lowered the Range Rover's sun visor to block the glare and flipped the blinker to change lanes. Not a single cloud adorned the sky. Catherine sat beside him in the passenger seat.

Switching off the sound system, he punched a contact on his Bluetooth-enabled mobile and listened as the phone rang. A man's voice answered.

"Ainsley here. We're about ten minutes." He paused, listening to instructions. "See you then. Cheers."

"This must be some surprise," Catherine said after he disconnected.

"I hope so." Nick took the motorway exit via the slip road. Reaching over, he took her hand and gave it a squeeze.

Her eyes lit up. "Do you know we never would have met if it hadn't been for my mother?"

"How so?" He didn't see the connection. Her mother had passed eighteen months ago.

"Right before she got sick, Mom found my ancestor's diary. She was positive it holds key information that will help us locate our family. When she realized she wasn't going to recover, I promised her I would come to England and search." Catherine toyed with his fingers. "If I could just read that diary, I think a lot of questions would be answered, but the writing is so faded I can't decipher it."

A recent article from his alumni magazine came to mind. "There are experts at the University of Oxford who specialize in reading old manuscripts by using infrared, photography, and chemicals. If you're interested, I could put you in touch with them."

The fingers that had been making little circles on the back of his hand froze. Nick took his eyes off the road and glanced at her. She stared at him as though he had discovered the cure for cancer.

His heart gave an odd thump, then a few more for good measure. He squeezed her hand and let go. Turning on the blinker, they entered the gates to the park.

"We're here," he said, not wanting to break the spell between them.

She tilted her head, her brow furrowing; she was no doubt trying to figure out what he had planned.

He gave an inward chuckle. She would know soon enough, but for now, two hedgerows and playing fields stood between them and their destination.

He parked and retrieved an orange scarf from the glove box. "This is to ensure you don't peek."

"You don't trust me?"

"That is a redundant question." Looping the fabric around her head, he tied the blindfold snugly in place. He slipped his arm around her waist and guided her across the soggy fields, their shoes squelching on the grass.

The top of the hot-air balloon peeked over the last hedgerow's canopy of trees. A flock of meadow pipits took flight with a flash of brown and white wings.

"Are you Lord Ainsley?" A short, burly man with close-set eyes approached. The embroidered name on his shirt read Tom.

Nick put his finger to his lips. "This is a surprise."

"We're ready," Tom said.

A set of long pressurized tanks let off a loud hiss.

Catherine jumped and tried to tug off the blindfold. "What's that?"

"No questions," Nick told her.

The tanks let off another hiss, sounding like dark-caped monsters on steroids. Nick guided Catherine the last few yards, then scooped her into his arms. She squeaked in surprise as he deposited her inside the balloon's basket. He climbed in, tipping it and throwing Catherine off balance. Grabbing her around the waist, he placed her hand on the railing to steady her.

Tom came aboard while his partner untethered the lead lines. He tossed the anchor ropes over the side to his partner, then applied the burner. A loud whoosh filled the air, and they lifted off.

"Are you ready?" Nick asked Catherine.

At her nod, he untied the scarf.

Catherine's lips made a perfect O. She looked up into the cavity of the balloon, her thick, long curls spilling over his arm, smelling of coconut and lime.

Without warning, she faced him and arched up for a kiss. Her lips were soft and melded to his. They tasted like a pool of pure water. He pulled her close and drank her in. A feeling of coming home swept over him. He closed his eyes and absorbed the foreign sensation as a warmth he had never experienced before enveloped his body.

They turned as one, his arms encircling her, his chin on top of her curls. His heart raced with unchartered emotion, and he was filled with wonder at what had just occurred. He took a deep breath and waited for his pulse to steady.

The balloon rose higher, and he pointed out the University of Oxford, with its numerous steepled colleges, the domed lid of the Bodleian Library, Magdalen Bridge, and the River Cherwell.

Out of the corner of his eye, he caught Tom snapping their photo with his mobile. Nick put up a hand. "This is a private, contracted flight."

"We don't get your kind often. I want to show my friends," Tom excused.

"No photos, and no social media. That was agreed upon before I paid."
Nick wanted to grab Tom's mobile and toss it over the side of the basket.

"Sorry."

The thought of their photos making the papers filled Nick with disquiet.
Turning his back on Tom, he stared at the patchwork fields. He doubted the
man's integrity.

"Are you all right?" Catherine placed a hand on his arm.

"Brilliant." He gave her a forced smile.

They watched the scenery in silence. The wind shifted, sending them in
a northwesterly direction. Bascombe came into view. The picturesque village,
parish church with its Norman tower, and the River Rue winding through
the main thoroughfare always moved him.

"There's Bascombe." Nick nodded to the village.

"It's so beautiful here. How could my ancestors have left?"

"I have no idea, but I'm glad this particular descendant chose to return."
Nick kissed her jaw.

Catherine tilted her head in that way she did while deep in thought.
"Being up here makes me realize how insignificant man really is." Her arm
made one of those fluid motions he loved. "God created this vast world, yet
He watches over each of His children and is intimately involved in our lives."

Nick straightened, letting her go. He could well imagine God watching
over someone like Catherine. She radiated goodness and purity. But for
some unfathomable reason, God hadn't responded to him.

He must have done something terrible for his mother and God to have
abandoned a seven-year-old child. He had begged God to forgive him for
driving his mother away and had pled with Him to send her home. God
had ignored him, just like his father had. Nick hadn't called on Him since.

The villagers had opened their homes to him until Grandfather had
swooped in, taking charge of his life. In an effort to repay the villagers many
kindnesses, Nick created jobs and donated generously to support the local
parish. But the fact remained, the people who should have cared for him
had not.

For the first time since childhood, standing next to Catherine, he felt
whole. The gaping wound inside him closed. Catherine cared for *him*, Nick
Davidson, the man. And Nick was not about to let her go if he could help it.

He came back from his musings to find her gemstone eyes resting on
him, expecting a response. With an effort, he recalled her comment and

attempted to shift the conversation. "It's no stretch of the imagination God would take extra care watching over you."

"God loves all His children. When the . . ."

He felt whole, but that didn't mean God cared about him. Nick closed his ears, trying to block out her words. He pretended to listen so as not to hurt her feelings. But he was very far away.

* * *

Theodosia entered her office, a cup of tea in hand. Placing it on top of her desk, she opened the draperies to let in the morning light. She'd arrived early to settle one of her outstanding accounts before the earl began another day of dictation and correspondence.

The phone rang. She glanced at the familiar number. What was Ainsley doing calling so early in the day? Surely, he realized the earl was not yet up.

She lifted the handle from its cradle. "Rivendon House, Lady Hadley speaking."

"Hallo, Lady Hadley. Nick here."

"Would you like me to patch you through to your grandfather, Lord Ainsley?"

"That won't be necessary. It's you I've called to speak with."

She hesitated. Lord Ainsley, though always polite, rarely spoke to her. "How may I help you?"

"Would it be possible to schedule an appointment with Professor McKellan at Oxford University for Miss Pressley-Coombes?"

"Of course. What is this in regards to?"

"I behaved badly and want to surprise Catherine to make it up to her. I've meetings today, or I would arrange it myself. Catherine has a diary belonging to her ancestor that needs the print raised. Professor McKellan is an expert in this field. Give him my regards when you schedule the appointment, will you?"

"Of course. I'll call this morning." Theodosia's mind raced. This must be a diary belonging to Glorianne. The last thing she wanted was for Miss Pressley-Coombes to further her research.

"Thank you."

"My pleasure." Theodosia heard the click of the line and slammed the handle onto its cradle. She had to get her hands on that diary.

CHAPTER SIXTEEN

FOUR STORIES OF CRENELLATED, ICONIC stone dominated the courtyard outside Oxford University's Bodleian Library. Catherine paused in front of the door to gawk.

A purple-haired, multipierced man bumped into her.

"Sorry." She pulled herself together and entered the hallowed portal in his wake.

The very air in the Bod smelled of history. Catherine waited in queue for security. True to his word, Nick had arranged a meeting for her with one of the dons.

She inhaled deeply and sneezed. It was the kind of sneeze that couldn't be ignored. The kind that stung the nose and watered the eyes and echoed off the vaulted chamber's walls. Students and researchers sitting at tables forty feet away turned and glared. With heated cheeks, she dug inside her tote for a tissue and blew her nose, causing another minor distraction.

"No bags beyond this point," the Bod's crotchety gatekeeper snapped. He shoved a lockbox at Catherine and held out a hand for her reader card.

Catherine handed the card over, removed Glorianne's diary and her cell phone and shoved her tote inside the lockbox. She met the gatekeeper's eyes. "I have an appointment with Professor McKellan. Do you know where his office is located?"

"To your right, around the corner from Duke Humphrey's library." The gatekeeper stared at her phone. "No picture taking."

Catherine powered off her phone and, with head held high, hurried in search of her destination. After several false turns, she located a brass plaque. *Dugal McKellan, Director of Study, Medieval and Modern Languages*

A thin, bowed man with a shock of white hair combed across the top of his pate answered her knock.

"Professor McKellan?"

"Yes?" His rich, booming voice was a contradiction to his feeble frame.

"Catherine Pressley-Coombes. I have an appointment." She held out her hand.

Professor McKellan shook it. "This way please."

He ushered her into a darkened room that resembled a science lab. Black-out material covered the windows. Rows of tables with specialized lamps filled the center space. At one of the tables, a man hunched over a roll of parchment. Setting aside his work, he made his way through the obstacle course to join them beside an enormous desk buried under stacks of paper.

"After our conversation, Miss Pressley-Coombes, I brought in one of our staff experts." He indicated the young man. "Professor Martin Giles works in an innovative field that uses photography and chemicals to raise print on faded script."

Martin Giles couldn't be much older than Nick. Due to his fair coloring and boyish features, she had mistaken him for a student.

"I hope my diary meets your criteria." Catherine handed Professor McKellan the baggie containing Glorianne's record.

"When working with old manuscripts and papers," Professor McKellan took the baggie with obvious displeasure, "it is always best to keep them in a dark and controlled climate. Compounds in ink have the ability to chemically change over time. Some iron-based inks can actually rust away." He put on a pair of white gloves. Taking the diary, he moved to a workstation and tugged a chain on one of the many lamps; the diary was bathed in "natural" light.

Professor Giles joined him at the table, where they examined the cover, binding, and pages of the decomposing diary.

"The workmanship appears Georgian; the pages are of the finest vellum." Professor McKellan lifted his head. "We should be able to expose the print if lead pencil or high-pigmented ink was utilized."

"How do you expose it?" Catherine's curiosity made her ask.

"Silverpoint, or true lead-pencil writings, can be enhanced by converting them into a black lead sulphide," Professor Giles explained. "Basically, the chemical treatment enhances readability."

"It sounds costly. Is it?" Catherine asked.

"Somewhat." Professor McKellan named an amount well beyond what she had anticipated. "This process will take some time. The diarist undoubtedly used several types of writing instruments. If proper ink was utilized, Martin can manipulate the pigments."

"Do you believe this diary can be manipulated enough to read?"

"No doubt about it." Both men responded in unison.

A spurt of excitement pulsed through her. This was the first positive she had encountered in her search.

"I need to call my father and give him the details. He has final say."

"Of course." Professor Giles nodded.

Checking the wall clock, Catherine did a mental calculation. It was 6:00 a.m. in Virginia. She powered on her phone and hit speed dial, hoping her father hadn't already left for work. On the third ring, he picked up.

"Dad." She sighed with relief. "I'm so glad I caught you."

"Good morning, sweetheart."

"Do you have a minute?"

"I sure do, honey. Is everything all right?" His drawl reached across the Atlantic and enveloped her like a warm summer day.

"I think I figured a way around our issue with Glorianne's missing records," she said in a rush.

"How'd you manage that?"

She relayed the information, then swallowed hard. "This research comes with a large price tag."

"What are we looking at?"

"Approximately £12,000."

Silence hummed through the line. Catherine glanced over her shoulder where the two professors idled, pretending not to listen.

"From the outset, we knew this wouldn't be an easy undertaking."

"It's an exorbitant price, Dad." She lowered her voice and whispered, "I could purchase a small car for what they're asking."

"Let me check this quarter's financials. Hang on, honey."

She heard the click of computer keys. Richard Pressley-Coombes was a self-made man. He'd built Coombes Enterprises from the ground up into a multimillion-dollar construction company. Despite his success, he ran a tight ship.

"How positive is this print raising?"

This was not a light question. Catherine knew her dad was crunching numbers and juggling work bonuses.

"Very positive. It will depend on what writing medium Glorianne used."

Dead silence.

Catherine knew better than to interrupt her father while he crunched numbers. Pacing past the row of tables, she fiddled with a lamp chain, watching it swing like a pendulum.

Richard broke the silence. "This was weighing heavily on your mother's mind before she passed."

Another long pause.

Catherine offered a silent prayer as she sensed her father's vacillation.

"I'll fund it."

"Really?" Her voice squeaked. "Thanks, Dad. I wish Mom were here. She'd be so excited. I miss you."

"Miss you too, Catherine."

"I'll call you soon."

"You do that. I love you."

"Love you too." She pressed the red icon on her phone. She couldn't wipe the silly grin off her face as she faced the professors. Both gentlemen looked at her expectantly. "Let's do it."

CHAPTER SEVENTEEN

CATHERINE WATCHED FOUR YOUNG SINGLE adults surround her brother in the chapel foyer as she made her way down the hall. Three of them were female. Jack tugged at his tie and cast a furtive glance toward the exit. Catherine bit back a giggle.

One of the women, a tiny blonde hair-tosser, did everything but stand on her head to gain his attention. The other two were more subtle.

The only other male, a fair-haired man with boyish features, turned in Catherine's direction when she approached.

Catherine stared at him while she greeted her brother. "Sorry to keep you waiting, Jack. The lesson went overtime in Relief Society. Professor Giles. I didn't know you were a Latter-day Saint."

Martin Giles's face had not changed expression, but his eyes laughed.

"Catherine, how do you know Martin?" Jack's head pinged back and forth between them.

"We met last week at Oxford University. He's deciphering Glorianne's diary."

"Good luck with that." Jack slapped Martin's back.

Martin blinked but didn't respond to Jack's sarcasm.

"They're trying to recruit me to the singles branch." Jack indicated the group of singles.

"I didn't know we had one in the area." Catherine raised a brow at her brother.

"I like family wards." Jack splayed his fingers, palms up.

Catherine narrowed her eyes as a thought occurred to her. "Is there an Institute program here?"

Jack flinched.

"Yes, of course. A missionary couple runs it," Martin said, obviously enjoying Jack's discomfort.

Catherine stared at her brother.

"You know I work late. I'm rarely able to make it home before Institute starts." Jack threw both hands in the air.

"Unfortunately, he's telling the truth." Catherine sighed.

"That doesn't stop you from attending, does it?" One of the women, a thin brunette with soft eyes, asked Catherine.

"Catherine, if you'd like to attend Institute, I can offer you a lift," Martin said quietly.

Jack grinned knowingly and wiggled his eyebrows behind Martin's back.

"That's very nice of you, Martin," Catherine responded in a hurried tone, trying to keep him from noticing Jack's behavior. "I'd like that, if it's not too much trouble."

"None at all," Martin said.

"I'll save you a seat when you can make it." The blonde hair-tosser placed her hand on Jack's arm.

"We've got to go. See you guys around." Jack pulled out of her grasp and tugged Catherine's elbow.

Catherine's face burned at her brother's rude behavior. She left the chapel convinced her parents had adopted him.

* * *

Whoever had come up with Oxford's silly rituals should have been sent to the Tower centuries ago. Theodosia looked ridiculous in the short black skirt, black tights, white blouse, and black velvet ribbon tied about her neck. To pass herself off as a university student, she was entering the Bodleian Library dressed in the ridiculous sub fusc required by the university on test days.

Ari had taken her disguise a step further by buttoning her blouse to her chin, scrubbing off her eye makeup, and providing a black wig with fringe to wear. She might look the part, but she lacked an essential piece of information to pull it off.

According to Ari, the simplest things could botch a job. Who would have thought a flower could blow her cover? Why did the university use different colored carnations to represent various exams? She couldn't brazen out an appointment with Professor McKellan wearing the wrong bloom. An Oxford don would spot that first off. Inside her skirt pocket, a trio of artificial flowers wired with camera feed awaited her selection: white for first, red for finals, and pink for everything in between.

She needed to locate a bona fide uni student. Fast.

She tapped her foot as she waited in queue to present her reading card. Sweat broke out on her upper lip. Ari had assured her the wires that ran from the earpiece under her wig into her clothes, would not set off the metal detector. When Theodosia had asked him where he'd gotten her fake ID, he'd kissed her and said he was no amateur. Their reversal in roles had leveled the playing field between them.

She handed the gatekeeper her reading card, who nodded and let her through.

Theodosia let out a jittery sigh and glanced around the cavernous chamber, with its carved beams and bookcases, for someone who could assist her. Pitching her voice a few notes higher than normal, she asked the nearest patron if he could direct her to Professor McKellan's office.

After two wrong turns, she happened across a gangly student in sub fusc, covered in spots and wearing a pink carnation. He shyly pointed her in the right direction.

Removing the matching flower from her pocket, she gave him a flirtatious smile and sauntered down the hall, pinning the blossom to her blouse. If she swiveled her hips more than usual, who was to know?

Ari's voice spoke in her ear, making her jump. "Is my Theodosia teasing university students?"

"Just a little." She smirked. Ari knew her far too well.

"I hope I don't need to punch that boy in the nose." He chuckled in her ear.

Theodosia glanced over her shoulder. The gangly youth stood transfixed. She smiled at him and wiggled her fingers goodbye. "He doesn't hold a candle to you."

"That is good."

Theodosia continued down the hall until she spotted a brass plaque. She read it twice to make sure. *Dugal McKellan, Director of Study, Medieval and Modern Languages.*

"I've arrived," she whispered.

Before turning on the camera, she removed the black ribbon around her neck and unfastened a number of buttons on her blouse, checking her pendant. If she was to succeed, she needed every distraction in her arsenal. She rapped on the door.

"Come," a loud voice called.

Pasting a vapid expression on her face, she entered the cluttered office, hesitating just inside the door. The skinny old man, with his thinning white hair, surprised her. She'd expected a more vigorous specimen to match that booming voice.

No matter. Throwing back her shoulders, she sashayed across the room to his desk. But her award-winning performance was wasted. Professor McKellan hadn't looked up since the initial "Come."

Not used to being ignored by men, Theodosia leaned over the professor's desk from the opposite side. And waited.

Professor McKellan lifted his head, coughed, and said gruffly, "Sit down."

Theodosia sat on one of the two chairs facing his desk.

"What do you want?" he asked.

"I'd heard about your huge success on medieval manuscripts and wondered if you'd ever considered working on something less historic, such as a journal or diary?" she said in a rush of girlish excitement.

"Depending on my workload, I have been known to take on the occasional journal."

"I hope you'll consider ours." Theodosia darted out her tongue and wet her lips.

The professor's eyes flickered. "I need to see your journal to make an assessment."

"Mum wouldn't let me bring it without speaking to you first. It's terribly old and crumbly." She fiddled with the pendant. "Mummy doesn't want it damaged by the weather."

Professor McKellan cleared his throat. "Very wise."

"Our journal is from Cromwell's protectorate. Mum's longing to know what it says. She thinks it might be of historic significance."

"I assure you our department would be most interested in your journal." Professor McKellan all but rubbed his hands together in anticipation.

"That's marvelous." Theodosia rose and bent over his desk, her pendant swinging free. She lowered her voice. "I'm afraid Mum won't let the journal out of the house until I can assure her you've worked on a similar type of project."

The professor watched her pendant, turned pink, and hastily straightened a sheaf of loose papers in front of him.

"You know what humidity and light can do to old parchment. Mum's extremely protective of our family heirlooms. She wants actual proof before she sends the journal in." Theodosia sat on the edge of his desk and crossed her legs.

Professor McKellan covertly watched the swing of her legs. "Marvelous coincidence—I'm working just now on an old diary with similar issues."

"What does it say?" Theodosia demanded, forgetting her role.

"It's early days yet."

Theodosia rubbed her ankle.

The professor tore his eyes away from her legs. "I'd need to examine the parchment to determine which writing materials were utilized before I could hazard a guess."

"If you could show me an example, I could tell Mum you've worked on something similar." Theodosia beamed at him.

Professor McKellan hesitated. "As head of this department, I honor the privacy of our clients."

"You aren't giving away the identity of your client. Their privacy is still intact." Theodosia rounded her eyes.

The professor pinched his nose.

Theodosia gazed at him and batted her eyelashes.

Withdrawing a set of keys from his desk drawer, Professor McKellan rose from his chair and crossed the room, stopping in front of a tall, padlocked cabinet against the wall.

She hopped off the corner of the desk and made sure Ari had a view of the cabinet and its vicinity to the outer windows. While he unlocked the doors, the professor grumbled about improper labeling as he dug through several drawers.

"Here it is." He removed a small box from a drawer near the bottom.

Theodosia hastily sat back on top of the professor's desk.

Professor McKellan returned and placed the archive box on a pile of papers. He lifted the lid. Inside was an envelope no bigger than eleven inches square. Donning a pair of white cotton gloves, he opened the envelope and removed a petite leather-bound volume that smelled like a medieval midden. Theodosia's fingers curled, itching to snatch the journal from the professor. Instead, she cooed over it as though it were the newest royal baby.

With a smile of invitation, the professor motioned her to join him on his side of the desk. "Mind you, old writing is not easy to read. It can be

tedious and time-consuming to decipher. However, the first few pages have been recorded."

Theodosia sidled around the desk and stood beside him to see what he referred to. What she wanted most was a glimpse of the owner's return address. Sure enough, the contact information was on the outside of the envelope. Hawthorne Cottage, Bascombe, Oxford. She didn't need a name.

"I believe that is all the proof you need, miss." Professor McKellan picked up the diary and placed it back inside the archival envelope.

"I can't thank you enough. Mum will be so pleased." Theodosia crossed the room. At the door, she turned and gave Professor McKellan her brightest smile. "I promise I'll return soon."

CHAPTER EIGHTEEN

No MUSE SPOKE AS CATHERINE wandered the Bicester Village outlets. Nick had asked her to the gala weeks ago, and she had yet to find *the dress*. In the slate-paved courtyard between the rows of shops, she spied an open table and sat. No one could jump-start her creative juices quicker than Gillian Buchanan, her best friend and former college roommate.

She pulled out her cell phone and texted. *Gala at Italian Embassy in two weeks. Want to come?*

Gillian responded almost immediately. *Of course. What's the dress?*

White tie.

Stag? Or are you playing matchmaker?

Catherine leaned against the back of the chair as an idea began to formulate. For years, she'd been dying to introduce Gillian to her brother. Mom's funeral hadn't counted. Jack had been too cut up to notice her then.

He had been trying to worm his way out of attending the gala since the invitations had arrived. If he had a date, he would be obligated to attend. It was the perfect way for him to meet Gillian. Catherine typed, *My brother needs a date.*

The yummy one?

Jack?

Definitely yummy.

Are you on heavy meds?

Nope. He's hot. I have the perfect dress.

I don't. Been looking all day.

Have you tried vintage formal wear?

Didn't think of that. Are they any good?

Top designers. Checking right now.

Born and raised in the States, Gillian held dual citizenship due to her British mother. In exchange for room and board, Gillian helped her ailing Scottish grandparents while she completed her master's degree at the University of Edinburgh.

Gillian shot back another text. *Boteak Weddings has five stars. Is your bro any better since the funeral?*

I think so.

Good. I can't wait to dress up.

I'll send you details when I get home.

Catherine typed Boteak Weddings into her GPS and discovered it was a dozen blocks away. Looking at her heels, she groaned.

By the time she reached Market Street, her heels had caught several times between the pavers, once so deeply that she'd stepped right out of her shoe.

With a sense of relief, she entered the two-story building with large plate-glass windows. Chamber music played softly over the sound system. The honey oak floors and Corinthian columns supported a lofty ceiling dripping with crystal chandeliers.

Catherine relaxed as she took in the high-end formal attire. Overwhelmed by the massive selection, she approached the sales clerk, a tiny, fairy-like creature with lavender hair and a nose ring. "I'm attending a white-tie event in a few weeks and need something fabulous."

"What's your budget?" The shop clerk asked, looking up from her paperwork.

"£2000.00."

"I have a number of dresses in your range. Do you know your size?"

Catherine made a face. "Sorry. I have no idea how sizes run in the UK."

"Let's get your measurements, shall we?"

The shop clerk took Catherine into a dressing room, where an ornate chandelier hung over a carpeted dais centered in front of a wall of angled mirrors. Brass numbers hung on each cream and gold-leafed dressing room door opposite the angled mirrors.

The clerk took her measurements and grabbed a short metal rack on wheels. "I can select some gowns, or you can find your own and hang them on the trolley."

"If you don't mind, I'd love some help," Catherine said.

The clerk looked her up and down and hustled across the dress shop, pulling the trolley behind her. Before Catherine caught up to her, the shop clerk had pulled half a dozen formals from the rack. Several stole Catherine's breath. One pale-blush Elie Saab, with its long, sheer, narrow sleeves, fitted bodice, and tasteful smattering of matching appliquéd beadwork, caught her eye. The custom, A-line evening gown cinched at the waist and eased out into a floating organza skirt.

After forty-five minutes in the dressing room, Catherine had narrowed her choices to a pleated vintage Fortuny in peacock hues and the Elie Saab. She liked them both for different reasons but couldn't make up her mind.

The clerk poked her head inside the dressing room to check on her. "How's it going, ducks?"

"I've got it narrowed down to two. I love them both."

"Such a dilemma." The clerk laughed.

"Do you mind if I call my friend?"

"Not at all."

Removing her cell phone, Catherine left the dressing room and pressed speed dial. While she waited for Gillian to pick up, she glanced out the window and caught sight of a dark-haired man standing across the street, staring at the shop.

Gillian answered on the second ring. "Did you find something?"

"Yes and no. I need your help choosing between two gowns." Catherine turned away from the window.

"Which has the best back-side view?"

"Gillian Buchanan!" Catherine exclaimed in shocked surprise.

"Well," Gillian said in a practical tone. "People see as much of your back side as the front. Don't you want the dress to look smashing from all angles? Shoot me a video. I want to see how they move when you walk."

A little embarrassed, Catherine asked the shop attendant to record her. By the time they finished, she and the clerk, Shelly, were on a first-name basis.

Shelly handed Catherine back her phone. "I guess you learn something new every day. Record the backside." The doorbell chimed, and Shelly moved off to greet the new customer.

After texting Gillian the videos, Catherine browsed the shop's accessories, bypassing a bizarre collection of fascinators. The British certainly loved their head gear. Instead, she selected several packages of jeweled hairpins.

Her phone beeped. In typical Gillian style, she started to chat without a greeting. "As much as I like the Fortuny, the Elie Saab is totally you."

"The back's pretty low. That's why I hesitated." Catherine perused the evening bags.

"Ask if they can sew in a flesh-colored inset. You'll be modest, and it won't ruin the line of the dress."

"That's a great idea." Picking a clutch in palest blush with a gold clasp, Catherine compared the hue to the gown. Perfect.

"Catherine?"

"Hmmm?" Idly, Catherine thumbed through costume jewelry, but she had already decided to wear the set of aquamarines her father had given her for graduation.

"Who's your date? You haven't said one word about him. I assume he's the one responsible for the invitations?"

Gillian's question caught her off guard. Catherine hesitated. She had never discussed guys with Gillian for the simple fact that no man had touched her elusive chord while they'd been in college. "It's a guy I met in Bascombe. We've been seeing each other."

"Does this guy have a name?" Catherine heard the smile in Gillian's voice.

"Nick Davidson."

"Sounds familiar."

Catherine chose not to go into Nick's celebrity on the phone. To her, Nick was a hardworking man who loved small-town life.

"How'd you meet him?"

"I ran Jack's car into his ditch. Nick gave us a tow."

"Wow." Gillian sucked in a breath. "And you were going to tell me when?"

"It's all happened so fast." Catching sight of a section of evening gloves suspended from a rotating stand, Catherine panicked. Did one wear gloves to an embassy ball? She had no idea. To be on the safe side, she rummaged through the selection for a matching pair.

"He must be something to turn *your* head."

"I think so," she said softly. The image of Nick singing to a little old lady came to mind.

"What's he like?"

"He's one of the kindest people I've ever known. And he can sing." Catherine smiled as she rummaged through the gloves.

"He sounds wimpy," Gillian snorted. "I wouldn't have pegged you for a wimpy-guy liker."

"Wait and see," Catherine said with a hint of mystery as she thought of Nick's large frame and bulging muscles.

"Have you told your brother he's got a hot date for the gala? I'm dying to hear his reaction."

"I'll tell him when I get home tonight and let you know what he says. I think you two will hit it off."

"Because I like to talk and he doesn't?" Gillian's infectious laughter burst through the earpiece.

"Maybe. Thanks for saying yes." A small pair of elbow-length gloves in white satin stood out among the rest. They were boring, utilitarian, and safe. She could stuff them inside her clutch and pull them out if needed. Draping them over her arm, she gave the shop another once-over.

"I'll have a good time regardless. Parties are for dressing up and showing off. You know how I love to do both," Gillian informed her.

Gillian was the only person Catherine knew who could show up at a party not knowing a soul and leave behind a roomful of friends two hours later.

"If my loquacious date is tongue-tied," Gillian said, "I can stare at his pretty face."

"Gillian, I've missed you."

"Of course you have."

Catherine laughed gaily. "See you in two weeks."

"Ta."

Taking matters into her own hands, Catherine Googled *white tie dress*. After scanning the list of approved attire, she sighed happily and returned the gloves she wasn't buying to their rack.

When she went to make her purchases, Shelly assured her Boteak Weddings would take care of the flesh-colored inset. After a few more measurements in the dressing room, Catherine headed out the door to locate the last item on her list.

Her feet were killing her when she reached London Road, so she found a bench under a large hanging basket of flowers and eased her feet out of her heels. The problem with her feet, she mused, were her ballet scars. She wanted a strappy pair of heels to cover the worst of them. Using the English version of Yelp, she discovered a highly recommended shoe store down a narrow street a few blocks away.

With a silent moan, Catherine slipped her heels back on and headed for the shop. It was ten minutes to closing when she arrived. Luckily, she found a nude pair of Gianvito Rossi sling-back pumps with ankle straps. They were elegant and covered the worst of her scars. She purchased them, thanked the proprietor, and placed her receipt inside her wallet.

She started up the deserted street. Visions of a hot bath filled her mind. She hadn't gone fifty meters before a prickle of awareness crept up her spine.

Glancing casually over her shoulder, she didn't see anything to cause her disquiet. The uneasy sensation persisted though. Catherine stepped up her pace, anxious to reach the main road where pedestrians milled about. A slight sound behind her made the hair on the back of her arms rise. She tightened her tote against her body and started to run. The blisters on the back of her heels screamed in protest.

A vice-like grip clamped down on her arm, yanking her to a halt. Catherine gasped in surprise as something sharp pressed at her side.

"Quiet. This way," a man's heavily accented voice said.

Her heart skipped a beat. She twisted in his grasp to get a look at her captor. Dark eyes glittered behind a black ski mask. He pressed the blade a little harder, nicking her side.

Pain shot through her, and she sucked in air through her mouth. Warm blood trickled down her skin. Everything inside her froze. She opened her mouth to scream, but no sound escaped. Her knees trembled and threatened to buckle. This couldn't be happening.

The man jerked her arm, almost pulling it from the socket. Spinning her around on her nerveless legs, he shoved her in the direction of a narrow alley. A dark sedan with tinted windows stood at the curb, its motor running.

Catherine knew if she reached that car, horrible things would happen. The knowledge spurred her sluggish brain into action. Her legs moved jerkily. With her body's spastic betrayal, she doubted she could knee her kidnapper in the groin or use her heels to advantage.

She refused to go without a fight. Her heart raced like a runaway train on a downhill slope. Her only course of action was surprise. Willing her body to go limp, she sagged, her weight pulling her captor off balance and causing him to drop her arm.

Straightening, Catherine swung her bag, hitting him in the chest. Pivoting on the balls of her feet, she turned and ran.

One heel didn't get the memo. It sank into a crack between the pavers, and the momentum of her body threw her out of kilter. Flapping her arms in a frantic attempt to regain her balance, she lost her footing and fell backward onto the kidnapper's knife.

CHAPTER NINETEEN

THE SMELL OF FRESH VOMIT assaulted Theodosia's nostrils. Trying not to gag, she zipped through Bicester's maze of side streets before the police arrived.

Ari moaned from the passenger seat, his head tucked between his knees.

The steering wheel bit into her fingers. That stupid, stupid boy had panicked and left Miss Pressley-Coombes bleeding on the pavement. Theodosia wanted to scream.

Ari emitted another moan and heaved onto his shoes. Theodosia rolled her eyes. The girl was not worth ruining a pair of Berluti's. She was just an American. A nobody.

Theodosia spared Ari a glance. The boy was positively green. For the briefest moment, she allowed herself a smidge of sympathy. Not long ago, she had reacted in a similar manner. Digging through her handbag while navigating the narrow streets, Theodosia pulled out a packet of tissues and handed them over.

Ari had stabbed the American. So what? It wasn't his fault. The ridiculous woman had lost her balance and fallen onto the knife. She squelched a sigh. It was going to be a long night. But she had done it and rarely had nightmares anymore.

As she entered the M-40 toward London, questions buzzed inside her head, swarming like angry bees. How badly had the girl been injured? Did she bleed out? Where was the knife? Had Ari worn his gloves? Were his fingerprints on file with INTERPOL?

Getting information out of him would be difficult. But she would. It was essential she know the facts.

* * *

Upon their return from Bicester, Ari showered, then immediately burned his clothes in the incinerator on the back terrace. The moment they reached the safety of the garage office, with its gray painted walls, his pacing began. It was driving Theodosia mad.

"She fell on the knife," Theodosia said in an effort to calm him.

"I think I killed her!" Ari's dark eyes flashed.

"Where is the knife, Ari?"

"Gone."

"You didn't leave it . . ." Theodosia paused. She couldn't think of a tactful way of asking, "Inside her?"

Ari cringed at her words. "I'm not an idiot."

"Of course you aren't. I'm simply worried. If the police locate the knife and find your fingerprints . . ." She let it hang in the air. "Could they identify you?"

"I did not mean to kill her," Ari insisted.

"I never thought you did." But she could hope, couldn't she? "What I am asking is, Are you on INTERPOL's records?"

"INTERPOL has no record of me."

She drew her first full breath since their escape from Bicester. She had wondered, especially with his links to the Mafiosi.

Ari continued his pacing, throwing his arms wide and muttering in Italian.

As for the girl, Theodosia couldn't bring herself to care. If the American bled out, so much the better. However, Theodosia had no intention of sharing those particular thoughts with Ari. Instead, she pulled him into her arms and rubbed his back, murmuring words of comfort. "I know you did not mean to hurt her. It's all right." She soothed him much as she would a small child. "I'll call the hospitals to find out. Would you like that?"

"You would do that for me?"

"Of course I will. We meant her no physical harm," Theodosia managed to say in a shocked voice.

Ari buried his face in her neck; hot tears trickled down her blouse. The stupid boy was crying? *Brilliant.* Where was a real man when she needed one?

CHAPTER TWENTY

Nick burst through the Emergency Assessment Unit doors at John Radcliffe Hospital. After circling the hospital more than a dozen times for a parking place, the temptation to leave his Range Rover in front of the main entrance had almost won out.

Children whimpered in their mother's arms; a few adults slept with their heads propped against the wall. Others stared blindly at the telly mounted to the ceiling. The place reeked of pain and despair.

Nick's stomach sank when he caught sight of two police officers standing in the corner. He had a bad feeling as to why they were there. When Jack had called earlier, he'd been rather cryptic.

Queuing at the information desk, Nick replayed their phone conversation while trying to hold back the impulse to push his way to the front. Catherine had been injured and was at hospital. When Jack mentioned he was donating blood for her transfusion, Nick had grabbed his keys and headed out the priory door.

He fought back the panic bubbling inside. Whatever had happened to Catherine could be laid directly at his doorstep. His gut had told him she was in danger, and he'd done nothing to ensure her protection.

In such a short time, Catherine had become the most necessary part of his life. He couldn't bear it if she died.

If God really listened, Nick would ask for help, but he had tried that route once. It hadn't worked. So the prayer that swelled and tugged at his heart stayed firmly tethered, bruising him with its yearnings.

After an interminable amount of time, he reached the front of the queue. "My girlfriend was brought in a while ago."

"What's her name?" the female receptionist asked.

"Catherine." Nick tapped his fingers on the worktop. "Catherine Pressley-Coombes."

The receptionist's eyes flicked to his, then back to her computer screen. Nick had the distinct impression Catherine's case had brought a bit of drama to the bustling EAU. This did nothing to allay his fears.

"May I see her?" Nick asked, clenching his jaw at the further delay.

"I'm checking." The receptionist clicked a few more keys. "Miss Pressley-Coombes is in assessment area four."

"Thanks." Nick followed the signs through a set of double doors to the assessment area. The long corridor of beige-colored tiles smelled strongly of ammonia and less appreciable odors. His brogues echoed as he made his way to triage under the impersonal glare of florescent lights.

What kind of man would leave Catherine at risk? Certainly not the kind who loved her. She wouldn't be hurt if he had hired minders. The guilt almost choked him.

He continued down the corridor until he noticed a man in business attire standing in the hall, talking to someone through the open curtain inside assessment area four. Nothing about his dress proclaimed it, but the man's demeanor screamed of clergy. Nick's heart sputtered. He couldn't be there for last rites.

Two nurses exited Catherine's curtained partition and moved down the corridor in the opposite direction. The suited man entered Catherine's partition and closed the curtain behind him. Nick stopped outside the assessment area and covered both eyes for a second, breathing deeply.

Guilt pressed him down, pinning him as effectively as an iron beam. He couldn't bring himself to open the curtain. Once he did, he'd know if Catherine's life had been altered by his inaction.

He rubbed the back of his neck until the skin grew irritated from the abuse. *Keep it together, Ainsley.* The rumble of men's voices reached him through the curtain. He recognized Jack's as the two men conversed.

Jack's tone changed. Gentled. Slowed. His words were deliberate and thoughtful, not the usual speech pattern Nick associated with Catherine's brother. Nick could make out only bits and pieces of what he said, but the words filled him with peace.

Without being aware, Nick rose and parted the drapes. He stopped cold. Jack and the other man had their hands on Catherine's head, away from the bandage, and were performing some sort of religious rite. They closed in the name of Christ.

Both men glanced in his direction.

"Ainsley," Jack said with obvious relief.

Nick glanced from one man to the other, totally confused. Why had Jack behaved like a priest? He worked for Davis. Too miserable for words and not knowing what to say, he remained silent, desperately wishing they would move out of his way so he could see Catherine. Yet he dreaded seeing her. Refusing to give in to panic, Nick acknowledged Jack with a nod.

"I'll keep my mobile close in case you need me." The man in the suit squeezed Jack's arm.

"Thanks, Bishop. I'm grateful you were able to get here so quickly," Jack said.

Bishop? So his assessment had been correct. The man was clergy, even though he didn't wear a robe and collar.

"We'll keep Catherine in our prayers. Ring me for anything," the bishop said.

Jack nodded, and the bishop let himself out.

If the bishop was the leader of a congregation, was Jack a part-time minister? Though Nick was terrified to ask about Catherine, the question burst out of him. "How is she?"

"Stable."

The blood pressure machine beeped. Nick approached Catherine's side and grabbed a chair, placing it next to her and sitting before his knees gave out. With trembling fingers, he picked up her free hand. It was cold. He massaged it gently.

If Catherine's face were any paler, it would match the hospital sheets. Her curls were matted in dried blood. Gauze wrapped her upper arm, and another bandage circled her forehead. The blood pressure machine continued to beep.

"I should have listened to you, Ainsley. You warned me." Jack stood at the foot of Catherine's bed, staring at his sister.

"I should have hired someone to mind her." Without taking his eyes off her face, he asked, "What happened?"

"Someone tried to abduct her when she left a shoe store. Catherine left her purchase on the counter. The proprietor went outside to hail her and witnessed the incident." Jack ran his hands through his brown hair. "Catherine almost got away, but her shoe tripped her up. She fell on the knife."

Nick's hand clenched.

"The guy had a car nearby and got away. Good thing the shopkeeper knew something about first aid because the knife shaved an artery in her arm. She would have bled out before the ambulance arrived."

For the first time since he'd walked into the room, Nick studied Catherine's brother. Jack had a cotton ball taped to the inside of his elbow. His hands gripping the bed rest were taught, and a vein ticked under one eye. He was not as cool as he let on. That made two of them.

"Did they give her a sedative?"

"No. She hit her head on the pavement. The doctor is more worried about that than her arm." Jack's mobile rang. He left the room to take the call.

Nick overheard the initial part of Jack's conversation. "Hey, Ben. Yeah, I talked to Dad. She's stable. The doctor's concerned about her concussion."

With a shaky breath, Nick kissed the inside of Catherine's palm and closed his eyes. They'd almost lost her. Except for one other time in his life, he'd never felt so helpless.

Who was behind these incidents? And how could he protect her from a faceless enemy?

* * *

The incessant beeping made Catherine's head throb. She tried to open her eyes, then wished she hadn't. Light sliced through her pupils and speared her brain. She slammed her lids shut.

"She's coming round."

Nick. What was he doing in her bedroom? Catherine attempted to open her eyes a second time and failed.

"Catherine, can you hear me?" Why did Nick sound so worried?

She squeezed his hand. Answering took too much effort.

"The hospital's going to keep you for a while." Nick rubbed her cold fingers.

Keep me? Keep me where? She opened her eyes the merest slit. That wasn't so bad.

Nick's face was up close and personal. His breath smelled. Black, day-old beard covered the lower half of his face. His dark hair stood on end. He looked terrible.

Jack appeared at the foot of her bed, speaking into his cell phone. "She's awake, Dad. I'll call you when the doctor gives us an update. The police want an interview."

Nick moved away to turn off the overhead lights and close the blinds.

She gave him a grateful smile. The beeping continued. She turned her head. Kettle drums erupted inside her brain. Her stomach lurched; she clamped her lips tight, refusing to throw up.

Her arm burned, and she glanced at it. *Why is there an IV in my arm?* The last thing she remembered was the pair of Gianvito Rossi sling backs.

"Where are my shoes?" Her voice croaked.

Nick laughed, the sound echoing inside her skull. He was instantly contrite. "Sorry. Your head must hurt like the very devil. But who wakes up in hospital to ask about shoes?"

"It's the last thing I remember." Catherine closed her eyes. Everything was starting to come back to her. The man with the knife. The waiting sedan. The incredible fear. Her heart-monitor alarm went off.

* * *

The smell of flowers woke her. Catherine squinted against the late afternoon sunlight that filtered through the hospital blinds. To her amazement, every available surface was covered in roses. Red ones, pink ones, white ones, blush ones, and a bouquet of yellow roses in a milk-glass vase graced the cart beside her.

Jack snored in a chair across the room, his mouth hanging open. He held a fluffy white teddy bear with an attached balloon. She wanted to snap a picture and send it to Gillian captioned, "Your yummy date."

Catherine tried to read the card on the bouquet by the bed, but the letters looked like black squiggles. A nurse with a spiked pixie cut bustled in to check her vitals.

"You've decided to wake up, have you? Doctor Olson was beginning to fret," she said, the Irish evident in her voice.

Catherine wondered how long she'd been out, but it took too much effort to ask.

The nurse moved a vase out of the way as she dug through the top drawer of a cabinet. "You gave that fancy boyfriend of yours a scare. He must have bought out an entire flower shop."

The heat of a blush started up Catherine's neck. Would she get used to the idea that she and Nick were a couple?

"Oh, there's nothing to be embarrassed about. What woman doesn't enjoy a bit of spoiling, especially from the likes of Lord Ainsley. I recognized him right off. High Society. And that one," the nurse nodded to Jack, who was blinking owlishly at them from his chair, "is mighty fit as well. If all girls could be so lucky."

The doctor entered on a blaze of good cheer. "Sleeping Beauty has revived. How's the head?"

"Still attached," Catherine whispered.

"And you're wishing it weren't?" Dr. Olson's voice boomed.

"Something like that." Catherine wished he'd tone it down.

"Well, let's have a look, shall we?" He pulled a silver light from his pocket and shone it into her eyes, making her long for oblivion. Her eyes watered, and cymbals crashed inside her head. "I know it hurts. The nurse put meds in your IV just now. That should take the edge off. You were very lucky. That laceration shaved an artery. You're a bit concussed and will need a few weeks of quiet so your brain can heal."

A warm, floaty sensation washed through Catherine's body. Tentatively, she turned her head. No nausea. No banging. No pain.

Dr. Olson's lips twitched as he worked on her bandages. When his nose flared, Catherine stifled the urge to giggle. His mannerisms reminded her of a rabbit. The nurse moved about the room, restocking drawers with supplies, shoes squeaking on the linoleum tiles, sounding like a mouse. Catherine tried again not to laugh. She really did. She couldn't help herself.

"How are you feeling?" The doctor continued his examination with an amused grin.

"Wonderful."

Dr. Olson frowned over her chart while the nurse redressed her injury. "Your blood pressure isn't where I'd like it to be. Between the transfusion and head trauma, we'll keep you an extra night to be safe. However, your arm is doing better than expected, and it doesn't appear the scar will pucker. I'll come by on my rounds in the morning. If there is improvement, we'll fill out your discharge papers." He finished his notations on her chart and recapped the pen.

When Dr. Olson and the nurse left, Jack handed her the teddy bear. "Ainsley dropped this by."

"Are you sure you don't want to keep him? You looked like you were enjoying his company." Catherine giggled.

"Are you okay?" Jack's forehead wrinkled.

"I'm good." She rubbed her nose. "I have a big surprise for you, Jack-in-the-Box." A string from her bandage tickled her nose. She blew at it.

"What kind of surprise?" Jack's mouth pursed like he'd bit into a lemon.

"A surprise, surprise. But even though it's a good surprise, you won't like it."

The corner of Jack's mouth quivered. "You're flying pretty high right now, aren't you, sis?"

"I feel great."

"Yeah. I think that nurse put a little too much happy juice in your IV bag."

"Nah." She tried to focus, but Jack kept swaying. "Stop moving. I have to tell you something."

"All right. Tell me about your surprise, surprise."

"You like pretty girls, right?" Catherine's monitor beeped.

"No, I like ugly ones." Jack rolled his eyes.

"Then I did it wrong." Catherine wrinkled her nose. "'Cause I picked a pretty one."

"For what?" he asked, starting to sound wary.

"If I'd known you liked ugly girls, I wouldn't have asked her. But it's too late. You have to take her."

"Take who, where?" Jack frowned at her.

"Take a pretty girl to the gala."

"What did you do?" Jack's voice thundered through the haze of her medication.

Catherine winced. "Shhh."

"Catherine?" Jack looked like a splotchy tomato.

"I asked Gillian Buchanan to be your date for the gala."

"I didn't want to go!"

"Oops." She snickered. "Too late."

"Unbelievable." Jack executed a quick turn, almost knocking over a bouquet of white roses. He grabbed the vase before it crashed onto the tiles.

"I'm really, really, really sorry that she's pretty."

Jack opened his mouth to respond, but someone rapped on the door. Two men dressed in dark suits entered.

"Catherine Pressley-Coombes?" the older one asked.

"That's me." Catherine's bandage slipped, covering part of her eye. She pushed it up with her good hand, but it slipped even farther. She laughed and pointed to her eye. "I have an eye-patch. I'm going to save it for Halloween."

"She's on some pretty heavy meds. I don't know if she can answer your questions," Jack warned.

"We can't postpone this indefinitely," the older one said.

Jack shrugged. "Suit yourself."

The older man stepped forward. "I'm Detective Inspector Gillette, and this is Detective Sergeant Maynard."

"Hi, officers." Catherine waved at them.

Maynard cleared his throat.

Jack did another eye roll and retreated to his chair.

DI Gillette pulled an electronic tablet. "Miss Pressley-Coombes, do you remember what happened when you left the shoe store last evening?"

"Are you playing good cop/bad cop?" Catherine looked back and forth between the two officers. "Who's the good cop? Can I guess?"

"Catherine." Jack made a choking sound.

"Don't they do that in England?" Catherine asked.

Gillette and Maynard shared a glance.

"Perhaps it would be best if we came back after her medication wears off," DI Gillette said.

"Great idea, gentlemen." Jack had the decency to wait until the police were down the hall before erupting into shouts of laughter. "The twins are gonna love this."

"Don't they want to play good cop, bad cop?" Catherine asked, confused.

"You scared them off," Jack choked out, laughing until tears ran down his face.

Nick walked in carrying yet another bouquet and set the vase on the chair. "I seem to have missed all the fun."

"The detectives didn't play good cop, bad cop." Catherine peeked at him from under her bandage.

Nick gave her a funny look and turned to Jack. "Was she able to remember anything?"

"The detectives decided to save it for later," Jack said.

"They didn't ask me about the man." Catherine pulled the gauze bandage on her head lower and sniffed it.

"What man?" Nick came over to the bed and removed her hand from the bandage.

"The man with the accident. No, that's not right . . ." Catherine blew at the frayed threads hanging off the gauze. "Accent. The man with the accent."

Nick's eyes sharpened on her. "Catherine, you are behaving rather oddly."

"That's because she's high, Ainsley. They drugged her for the pain." Jack said with a snicker.

Catherine tried to focus on Nick around the edge of her blindfold. "I assure you, Lord Ainsley, I am perfectly fine."

* * *

Nick excused himself from Catherine's hospital room. He jogged to the bank of elevators and caught up with the detectives. "Detective?"

Both men turned to face him in the empty hall. The elevator door clanged open.

"I believe a separate incident might be related to Miss Pressley-Coombes's near kidnapping. I realize the occurrence took place outside your jurisdiction but thought the information might prove pertinent to the investigation," Nick said, trying to catch his breath.

The elder detective motioned to his partner holding the lift. The younger officer removed his hand, letting the door slide shut. The elevator dinged and chugged its way to the next floor.

"By all means, let's hear it." The senior detective pointed to a group of chairs in a foyer at the end of the hall.

As succinctly as possible, Nick shared his and Catherine's near tragedy on the switchbacks.

"You say the local mechanic believes the brake lines were cut?" the senior detective asked.

"Yes, sir."

"I happen to know DCI Barnes." The detective's nostrils flared.

Everyone knew Barnes was counting months to retirement.

"Given the particulars of this case and the possibility of both incidents being related, I'm contacting Scotland Yard. They'll know who to send," the older one said.

Nick hoped this pair wouldn't brush off the incidents like Barnes had done in Bascombe.

"If not handled properly, this situation could become political dynamite. I considered contacting Scotland Yard last evening when we realized where the near abduction had taken place," the senior detective said.

"Why is that?" Nick wanted to know.

"An Oxford uni student went missing a few months back. Her body was recently recovered in Morocco. She'd been trafficked." The senior detective met his eyes.

"The American Consulate would come down on our heads if Miss Pressley-Coombes were to disappear. With her stunning looks and connection to you, the press would have a field day on both sides of the pond after she leaves hospital. Don't you agree, Lord Ainsley?" The younger detective's eyes glinted.

"Undoubtedly." Nick shifted and glanced away.

"INTERPOL handles high-profile cases dealing with abduction. I have no issue turning this over to them." The senior detective collected their recording equipment.

CHAPTER TWENTY-ONE

"WAKE UP, CATHERINE." JACK SHOOK her shoulder.

Catherine came awake slowly, much like a scuba diver ascending from the depths. The last few days had passed in a blurred kaleidoscope of fractured images. She sat up on the sofa pretzel style, tucking her bare feet from view.

Two men faced her across the room; both were shorter than Jack. One wore a dress shirt and tie. His eyes and hair were flint gray, and he looked as tough as granite. "William Butler, INTERPOL Human Trafficking and Child Exploitation Unit."

The other appeared no older than her own twenty-four. He stood perhaps five feet ten inches with nondescript, dirty-blond hair and hazel eyes. He wore jeans, loafers, and a battered anorak. His shoes were scuffed, and his hair was a trifle too long.

"Peter Davenport, your minder."

She gave Agent Davenport a tentative smile. Over the last few weeks, she had become accustomed to British expressions, but this one threw her. "Minder?"

"Protection officer." Davenport elaborated.

"Won't you please sit?" she said, remembering her manners.

Davenport plunked himself on the love seat, while Butler commandeered the recliner.

"These men are here about your case." Jack took the far end of the sofa Catherine sat on.

Catherine's eyes slid back to Davenport. She had the fleeting impression he was more than he seemed.

A rap on the door had Jack jumping to answer. "This will be Ainsley."

She braced herself for the shriek of hinges, but the nail-studded door opened without a sound. Someone had oiled it.

Nick entered wearing a pair of jeans, a button-up collar shirt, and brogues. He'd also slung a lightweight jacket over his shoulder. His gaze zoomed in on her before taking in the other occupants of the room.

Nick shook both gentlemen's hands as Jack made the introductions. With the formalities over, Nick sat beside her and took her hand.

Butler looked right at their intertwined fingers and glanced at Davenport.

Agent Davenport appeared to study the framed blueprints, but Catherine had the impression he too had not missed a thing.

"Miss Pressley-Coombes," Butler addressed her. "Before we get started, have you reported this crime to the United States Embassy? They need to know a U.S. citizen was assaulted on foreign soil."

"No. I haven't."

"It's always best to apprise your embassy when something occurs. Might I suggest you do so as soon as possible. However, you will follow the same investigative procedures as a British citizen," Davenport said.

"All right," Catherine said.

With the niceties over, Agent Butler jumped in with both feet. "We believe your incident in Bicester is part of a trafficking operation in the shires. Since this crime falls under international law, a multitude of strategies on numerous levels are necessary in order to address the issue."

"In other words, it takes a bunch of your agents working in conjunction with other agencies throughout the world to capture these criminals." Jack rolled his eyes.

Butler inclined his head. "I assure you this abduction is under thorough investigation. CCTV cameras picked up Miss Pressley-Coombes's fall and the unknown subject's flight. We located a dark sedan on several cameras prior to the incident. Incidentally, the motorcar was a rental obtained with false identification.

"To insure your safety, Agent Davenport has rented rooms next door due to the lack of space inside Hawthorne Cottage." Agent Butler continued. "Surveillance equipment has been set up around the perimeter of your home. It feeds directly into his computer."

Agent Davenport gave out his cell number, and Catherine, Nick, and Jack entered it into their contacts.

"William Taylor of Taylor's Garage corroborates your story, Lord Ainsley. The brake lines on Mr. Pressley-Coombes's 1966 MGB were most definitely sliced," Butler said.

Her suspicions were valid. Someone had broken into Jack's car. The pounding in Catherine's head increased and made it hard for her to focus.

"If Miss Pressley-Coombes has been targeted, our surveillance cameras will pick up any suspicious activity around the property. Davenport will monitor the feed and accompany Miss Pressley-Coombes whenever Lord Ainsley or Mr. Pressley-Coombes cannot."

Indignant at her loss of privacy, Catherine moved to dissent and jostled her head. Wincing, she closed her eyes and waited for the slicing pain to subside. How could she function with someone watching her every move?

Butler spoke directly to her. "Trafficking is on the rise. We believe it is connected to organized crime but have not tied it as yet to any particular crime family. If we can catch one human shipment en route, we'll learn a great deal on how they transport their cargo and how to better save lives."

Catherine listened while she stared at her and Nick's joined hands. She didn't see how her aborted kidnapping tied to the MGB incident and wondered if Butler was seeing things that didn't exist.

"It's very nice of your agency to protect me, but I don't think this is a trafficking issue." She met Agent Butler's eyes. "For whatever reason, I believe these attacks are personal."

"Why do you think that?" For the first time, Agent Davenport joined the conversation.

"The switchback incident was surely intended to kill. By a miracle, Nick and I were spared. The second attack could be completely unrelated."

Davenport opened his mouth to reply, but Catherine held up her hand. "Why do you assume this is a trafficking issue?"

Agent Davenport lifted one shoulder when he and Butler exchanged glances, as if to say, "Over to you."

Butler studied her with flinty eyes. The clock's second hand ticked in the otherwise silent room. "With its colleges and shopping, Oxford is a predators' paradise. A number of young women, teens, and children have been abducted in that location over the last few years. Parents get distracted; unwatched children disappear.

"Oxford appears to be one of their bases. Last year, a uni student was snatched in Bicester. Her body was found in Morocco a few weeks ago, a victim of human trafficking."

"My attacks don't have to be related, do they? The last one was enough to contact your unit." Catherine felt the blood leave her face.

"Yes. Though the first crime is worrisome, I'll admit." Butler's brow furrowed.

"What kind of time frame are we looking at before she's safe?" Jack hooked his ankle across his opposite knee.

"There's no way to know." Butler splayed his hands in front of him. "A few weeks, perhaps months."

Nick's eyes narrowed on Butler. "You want them to strike again. You're hoping Catherine will draw them out. That's why you're here."

Butler's eyebrows twitched. Jack leaned back on the brown leather sofa, his foot twitching back and forth at high speed. Nick glanced at Jack and shook his head.

Catherine's mind spun with the truth.

"It would be much easier to capture these traffickers if they made another attempt on Miss Pressley-Coombes," Butler said.

"You have no right to use my sister as bait." Jack jumped off the sofa.

Catherine's mouth went dry. She swallowed convulsively, remembering the mind-numbing fear of her near-abduction.

"What kind of desensitized monsters are you?" Nick burst into the conversation with all the aplomb of a nuclear blast. "You're asking an injured woman to lay herself open to capture by an organized crime ring in the hope of proving your theory? What if you can't protect her?" He glared first at Butler, then Davenport.

"That is a risk only Miss Pressley-Coombes can decide," Davenport said in his mild way, but Catherine saw his eyes flicker. So did Nick. He stopped his tirade and stared at the agent.

"I assure you, Lord Ainsley, I have no intention of Miss Pressley-Coombes running the risk of capture," Agent Davenport said.

Catherine cleared her throat. All four men turned as one in her direction. She could refuse, and no one would blame her.

Nick's eyes begged her not to place herself at risk. Jack likewise. Agent Butler stared at her as though she were a specimen. It was Agent Davenport whose steady gaze read her fear and interpreted her decision. With real warmth, he gave her a nod of approval, letting her see the human underneath his ambiguous shell.

This was no longer just about her. This was about all the women and children who went missing each year, whose families never heard from them again, like the girl from Oxford University. This was for them.

"What do I need to do?" she asked.

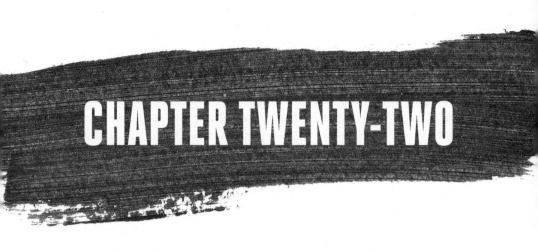

CHAPTER TWENTY-TWO

"Lady Hadley!" The bellow erupted from Rivendon's library.

Theodosia put down the fashion magazine she had been reading. Rising from her office desk, she smoothed the wrinkles from her cream suit and entered the library through the adjoining door.

"Yes, my lord?" Her heels sank into the dense brown-and-gold Axminster carpet. Under the lights of the massive ironworks chandelier, Rivendon's face looked purple.

"Are you quite all right?" Theodosia felt a moment's concern.

"What is this?" Rivendon stabbed a long, thin finger at the front page of Oxford's leading newspaper.

She glanced at the paper. "Most unfortunate, that."

"Unfortunate? The boy has landed himself on the front page!" Knowing Rivendon's propensity to keep the family name from the press, Theodosia had placed the newspaper on his desk where he was sure to find it.

She came around the earl's chair, glancing at the newspaper over his shoulder. The entire front page was dedicated to Rivendon's grandson. The caption read, "Sorry, ladies. He's taken!" The grainy photo, obviously shot with a telephoto lens, showed Lord Ainsley in an embrace with a beautiful young woman.

"I assume Ainsley was unaware," Theodosia murmured.

"Yes. Yes." Rivendon waved his hand in an impatient gesture. "But who is she? Why have I never heard of her? Is she the reason my grandson has neglected his family?"

Clearing a stack of week-old newspapers early this morning, Theodosia had come across the Oxford article. Until that moment, she'd had no notion Ainsley was romantically involved with the American. Theodosia had discerned no particular interest on his part toward Miss Pressley-Coombes at Ainsley's dinner party.

His sudden cessation of phone calls had begun the day of the stabbing. For more than a week, Rivendon had grumbled about his grandson's neglect. Now Theodosia knew why. Ainsley was entangled with that American. And Theodosia needed to know the extent of the woman's injuries. The hospitals had refused information due to patient confidentiality.

Local gossip ran rife in a village the size of Bascombe. If she could incite Rivendon, nothing would keep him away from the priory to interrogate Ainsley. As Rivendon's personal assistant, she would accompany him when Ari drove him to Bascombe. Once they arrived, Ari could mingle with locals at the pub and find out the extent of Miss Pressley-Coombes's injuries.

Theodosia spared another glance at the newsprint and couldn't keep the curl of distaste from her voice. "Her name is Catherine Pressley-Coombes. She is visiting her brother from the States. I met her at the priory during my last visit."

"An American, you say?" Rivendon's voice was void of all expression.

"Yes, my lord." She waited while he dithered with his decision.

"Have Scott pack my bags at once. My grandson has much to answer for." Rivendon glared at the photo.

"Yes, my lord." Theodosia walked sedately out of the room.

* * *

Nick's stomach churned as he watched Fellowes lead his grandfather upstairs to the earl's suite. During his brief conversation with Rivendon in the entrance hall, Nick had deduced the culprit behind Grandfather's sudden and ill-advised visit to Bascombe. Despite his precarious state of health, Lady Hadley had deliberately stirred him up.

Her behavior confused him. She needed her job. If she caused Rivendon's death, Lady Hadley must know that Nick would see to it personally she was put out of the London townhouse, regardless of their distant family connection.

With his brow furrowed in concentration, he entered the library and closed the door softly behind him. CAD drawings of the ironworks stairwell he was working on lit up his computer screen. The desk lamp burned, casting a soft glow over Catherine's sleeping form on the sofa. At least she had not been disrupted by his grandfather's unexpected arrival.

Catherine had not moved, not even the slightest shift in position since he had left. Leaving her to visit with Grandfather had made him nervous, regardless of the protection officer patrolling the grounds.

Nick told himself Catherine would be safer at Ashford Priory than down in the village. That was a fairy story, and he knew it. The brake lines on the MGB had been cut on priory grounds. There were more places to hide on the estate and less people to notice if something occurred.

Whoever was behind these attacks on Catherine had taken great risks during daylight hours. Even with Agent Davenport scouring the estate, someone could get past his guard. The constant worry for her safety had Nick on edge.

He moved about the library, his footsteps silenced by the thick Turkish rug. The clock ticked. His computer hummed. He stopped in front of the sofa where Catherine lay fast asleep. A scatter cushion had fallen onto the floor. He picked it up and caught a whiff of perfume that wasn't Catherine's scent.

Frowning, he placed the pillow back on the sofa, out of range of Catherine's feet. How had she kicked that cushion onto the floor? Starting back to his desk, he stopped, still as a prized pointer. Turning sharply, he stared at Catherine. Was she breathing?

In two steps, he knelt by her side. With fear tearing at his heartstrings, he touched her skin. It was warm. He lifted her wrist and checked her pulse. It beat.

His legs turned to jelly. He sat on the floor. Hard. Burying his head in his hands, Nick began to shake. For the briefest moment, he thought someone had gotten past Davenport and taken her life.

Was he going mad?

CHAPTER TWENTY-THREE

Nine days later

THEODOSIA SAT ON HER BED and slipped out of her heels. Her throbbing feet seemed a small price to pay for what a good pair of stilettos could do for a woman. She lay back on her mattress, and the citrine-colored duvet nestled around her like a cocoon. Closing her eyes, she sighed.

The phone rang on her nightstand. She groaned, debating with herself whether the effort to move was worth listening in. Lately, things hadn't gone according to plan. She and Ari had broken into Professor McKellan's office to search for the diary. It hadn't been there, which meant Miss Pressley-Coombes must have it in her possession.

Another ring pierced the air. She ignored it. Thus far, her eavesdropping hadn't reaped any rewards regarding the American.

The third ring ended abruptly. Against her judgment, curiosity got the best of her. Propping herself on her elbow, she hit the mute button and lifted the phone off its cradle.

Ainsley's deep tones asked Mr. Scott to patch him through to the garage. Theodosia checked her nails while she waited for Ari to answer.

A click sounded. "Ari."

"Ainsley here. I need you to collect Miss Pressley-Coombes from the Gascoyne in Mayfair at seven and deliver her to Davidson House."

"Yes, my lord."

"Thanks, Ari." Nick rang off.

A second click indicated Ari had disconnected, leaving Theodosia holding the dead line. She replaced the receiver in its cradle and pulled her knees up to her chin. An idea began to formulate. Before it solidified, her mobile buzzed inside her handbag.

She dug it out. The screen flashed Ari's name. "Hello, darling. I was thinking about you."

"I thought so."

Theodosia scooted back against the upholstered headboard. With Ari, she never had to pretend. He knew she had listened in.

"Maybe we should postpone our dinner this evening," Ari said.

"What do you have in mind?" Theodosia felt her pulse begin to race.

"An opportunity to snatch the American has come our way." Ari chuckled.

"I agree, but what do we tell Ainsley? You're supposed to pick her up. What excuse can we offer? The time line is shorter than I would like."

"We will collect the American as arranged and take her to the docks. I have a buyer."

"Won't Ainsley be suspicious if you turn up late without her?" She rose from the bed and examined her reflection in the mirror above the camphor desk. *Not bad.*

"We will tell him that we waited, but she did not show up where we were to collect her."

The simplicity of Ari's plan appealed to her. If he called Ainsley after they dropped the girl at the docks, their conversation would serve two purposes: it would throw Ainsley off their scent and provide the needed time to return.

She glanced up at the gilded ceiling with its meticulous plasterwork. "Let's do it."

CHAPTER TWENTY-FOUR

ENSCONCED IN THE BOUTIQUE MAYFAIR hotel, Catherine pinned the last curl in place and examined her creation in the double vanity mirror. "Gillian, do you think this up-do will last four hours?"

Gillian dabbed concealer under her eyes and spoke to Catherine's reflection. "I doubt your hair could move in a stiff breeze. You sprayed half a can of lacquer on it."

"You sound like Jack." The tension clenching inside her stomach eased.

"I sincerely hope not." Sarcasm dripped, but the added sparkle in Gillian's eyes belied her words. "I spent the better part of the day dragging him around London. You should have heard the grumbles he made in Madame Tussauds. Does your brother live under a rock? He didn't have a clue who Colin Firth was."

"Jack's sole interest with celebrities begins and ends with Hollywood car chases. If Madame Tussauds had wax effigies of a Shelby or Lotus, you couldn't drag him away." Catherine checked her hair one last time in the mirror. She had a Goliath to slay before the gala. With Rivendon's dislike of all things American, she wanted to make a good impression. Hence, the unusual amount of time on her hair. "Should I leave my hair up or wear it down? Truth."

Gillian scrutinized her. "I like the half-up do. It's a little formal, which suits the occasion. But I'm glad you didn't put all of it up. It would be a sin to hide those fat, shiny curls. What time is Nick coming for you?"

Catherine squirmed in her chair. The time had come to fill Gillian in about her British boyfriend. "His driver will pick me up in the lobby at seven."

"Driver?"

Catherine nodded and waited. Gillian couldn't resist a puzzle. Catherine had learned over the years to let her connect the dots. After a minute, Gillian's eyes widened, and her darkened lashes flew up and met her eyebrows.

"Nick Davidson. I knew his name sounded familiar." Gillian's eyes narrowed. "Isn't he COE?"

"Yes. He's Church of England." Catherine's stomach pitched, but she met Gillian's eyes squarely.

"He's the one who pulled you out of the ditch?" Gillian returned her makeup to her cosmetic bag.

"And scheduled appointments with his contacts so I can research my family and coached me down the hillside when the brakes were cut." Catherine worried her lip as she waited for Gillian's verdict.

"Do you love him?" Gillian smiled, but it didn't reach her eyes.

Still biting her lower lip, Catherine nodded.

"Then I will too." Careful not to muss her, Gillian gave her a hug.

The unexpectedness of Gillian's support made Catherine's eyes sting. Catherine fanned her face to keep her tears from ruining her makeup.

Stepping back, Gillian changed the subject. "What's the itinerary for the evening? Jack wasn't exactly verbose."

With a hurried glance at the clock, Catherine opened the closet and removed her evening gown. Laying it on the bed, she slipped out of her robe. "The earl's driver is coming in ten minutes to take me to Davidson House. Nick's business meeting went long, so he'll meet me there. In the meantime, Jack made dinner reservations at Chez Cobaire for the two of you. The driver will pick you up at the restaurant and transport everyone to the gala."

With Gillian's help, Catherine slid into her dress and fastened the belt. As she secured the clasp of her aquamarine necklace, she said, "I almost forgot. Your tickets to the gala are in my clutch."

Gillian picked up Catherine's purse and removed the tickets, placing them on the counter.

Sliding into her sling-back heels, Catherine began to worry. "Are you sure you're okay going with Jack?" She tossed her lipstick inside her clutch and looked around for her cell phone.

"Of course. Quit worrying. I can handle Jack if he gets surly."

A knock sounded on the door. Catherine looked through the peep hole and identified Agent Davenport dressed in formal attire. She swung about for one last glance in the mirror.

Her abs clenched, and she wondered how she would keep down her dinner, let alone carry on an intelligent conversation with Nick's grand-father. She would probably spill something on her gown. Why had she accepted Nick's invitation?

"He won't be able to resist you." Gillian patted her arm.

"Nick or his grandfather?"

"Either one." Gillian blew her a kiss and shoved her out the door.

* * *

Nick checked his watch as he climbed out of the cab in front of The Gascoyne Hotel. 6:55 p.m. He was in luck; Grandfather's driver had not yet arrived.

Giving the doorman a nod, he entered the lobby, with its rock-wall fountain, horizontal reveals, and trendy lighting. The boutique hotel's Mayfair location must have come with an exorbitant price tag. Nick wondered, not for the first time, if the Pressley-Coombes family was comfortably placed. He had originally assumed, by their hard-work ethics that they were middle class. But that, he thought, heading toward the reception desk, was an erroneous conjecture.

The concierge, a middle-aged woman in a logoed navy suit, gave him Catherine's room number. Before he reached the lift, its doors clanged shut, and the elevator started its climb. Rather than wait, Nick started for the stairs and ran into Jack.

"Ainsley." Jack looked him over. "Aren't you a little underdressed?"

"My meetings ran late. I swung by on the off chance Catherine was . . ." Movement on the stairs caught his attention.

Catherine entered the landing alongside Agent Davenport. The two conversed softly as they started down the last flight of steps. The blush mate-rial of her dress floated out from her cinched-in waist and bead-encrusted belt. Matching crystals sewn into the fitted bodice and long narrow sleeves sparkled under the lights with her every move. She had done something sophisticated to the front of her hair, and a waterfall of curls spilled down her back. She looked more royal than a Windsor.

Nick stood transfixed, trying to catch his breath.

Glimpsing Jack and him, Catherine flashed her wide smile.

Jack let out a low whistle and elbowed Nick in the ribs. "Lookin' good, Catherine."

Like a magnet, Nick stepped forward, his eyes never leaving her face. He waited at the bottom step and said the only thing that came to mind, "'She walks in beauty, like the night. / Of cloudless climes and starry skies.'"

"Lord Byron," she whispered, appearing much moved.

"You actually know that stuff?" her clueless brother asked, shattering the moment.

"There are times brothers should be muzzled," Catherine said under her breath to Nick as Jack started up the stairs to his room.

"I could have him kenneled for the night," Nick offered. He nodded to Agent Davenport and took Catherine's arm, guiding her toward the exit.

"Hey now." Jack stopped on the landing, turning to object.

"Tempting, isn't it?" Catherine's eyes held a mischievous gleam.

"Very," Nick said, staring at her.

Catherine caught the double entendre and blushed.

The doorman stood at attention. Nick thanked the man and passed him a tip as they came out onto the pavement, followed by Davenport. Nick glanced around, looking for Grandfather's sedan. Catching sight of the motorcar, Nick steered their group in that direction.

Rivendon's driver climbed out of the black sedan, his eyes wide. When Catherine and Nick reached the car, Ari opened the door smartly.

Lady Hadley sat in the backseat, looking put out. Nick's brow furrowed. He'd been quite explicit about what time he needed the car. It was unlike Lady Hadley to infringe on family activities. She must have run into unexpected traffic.

Nick turned to Agent Davenport, "Why don't you sit up front with the driver."

At Davenport's nod, Nick assisted Catherine into the sedan, making sure not to step on her gown. With a slam of the door, they started for Davidson House.

CHAPTER TWENTY-FIVE

AT THE EARL'S INSISTENCE, THE gentlemen retired to Rivendon's library for after-dinner drinks and cigars, leaving Catherine to amuse herself in the gold salon.

Nick spared a glance for Agent Davenport, who paced the far end of the room, obviously uncomfortable leaving Catherine untended. Nick gave the minder a nod, and the man unobtrusively slipped out the door. Since Grandfather desired to hash this out, he doubted Agent Davenport's absence would meet with objections.

"Well, Nicholas?" Rivendon lit up his cigar and took a seat on the tufted leather chair near the fire.

"I wanted you to meet her." Nick fingered the book bindings with their faded gold-leaf lettering on the closest shelf.

"She's a pretty piece. I'll give you that." Rivendon took a drag on his cigar and blew smoke into the air.

Nick waited him out. He didn't take long.

"The girl's an American! A Yankee upstart," Rivendon erupted.

"Southerners do not take well to that label. Catherine comes from a blue-blooded Virginia family whose ancestors originated in Bascombe."

"She's no blue-blood if her family's from Bascombe."

"She's more a lady than the aristocrats I've dated."

"Harrumph." Rivendon took a final puff on his Havana, then stabbed it out in the art deco ashtray. "How did you meet her?"

"I pulled her motorcar out of a ditch." Nick sat on the chair facing Rivendon.

"Playing farmer?"

"I happen to be a farmer."

"Some of the time. You're also a venture capitalist and entrepreneur," Rivendon said with pride. He fiddled with the dead cigar. "How old is she?"

"Twenty-four. She finished her graduate studies this spring. Would you like an accounting of her pedigree as well?" Nick couldn't quite keep the bite from his words. They'd covered all this at dinner, after which the earl had focused on his meal while the clock had ticked away.

"I already know her pedigree. It's mongrel." The earl picked up his high ball glass and glared at him over its rim. "I want more for you, Nicholas. There are any number of titled girls who'd come running if you so much as crooked a finger in their direction."

Nick leaned back in his chair and smiled delightedly. It always put Grandfather on edge.

"What are you smiling at?"

"You are doing so much better."

"No thanks to you. It's been almost two months since I last laid eyes on you."

"You stopped in at the priory not ten days ago, waving that newspaper clipping. Three weeks ago, I stopped over on my way home from Italy." Nick took a sip from his water bottle.

A gleam appeared in Rivendon's eye when he mentioned Italy. "How's that going?"

"Brilliant. I have more orders than I can keep up with. I'll soon need a second warehouse. In fact, I'm meeting a potential investor at the gala."

Rivendon's lips twitched, and he took another sip of his drink.

"Give Catherine a chance," Nick said in a quiet tone, sensing a softening. "She's very old-fashioned and quite special."

Grandfather stared at him while Nick clenched and unclenched his toes, a habit he'd acquired over the years while waiting for Grandfather's verdict on any given subject.

By now, Catherine must have had enough of her own company. He was done waiting and started for the door.

"Why did you bring her?"

Nick stopped, turning to face his grandfather. They had already covered this, but if his grandfather chose to revisit the subject, he'd play. "I originally planned to introduce you this weekend. It was unfortunate you saw the paper first. But the fact remains, Catherine is very dear to me."

"You've been bowled over by arm candy."

Nick's temper flared white-hot. He locked his jaw to halt the angry words until he gained control of himself. "She's so much more than that. Talk to her. Get to know her."

In silence, Nick waited until Grandfather rose from his chair with the help of his cane and accompanied him back to the gold salon.

Catherine stood under a German landscape with her head tilted to the side, studying the oil on canvas by von Eckenbrecher. She greeted them with her wide-flashing smile. "I've been admiring your artwork, Lord Rivendon."

Rivendon thumped across the room and seated himself in a nearby chair, resting his cane against his leg.

Catherine sipped from her water goblet. It appeared Scott had seen to her and Agent Davenport's needs while Nick had been holed up with his grandfather.

"Nicholas tells me you've finished your graduate studies." Rivendon eyed her candidly.

"I have. This September, I start with an architectural firm."

"Do you know anything about art?" Rivendon indicated the paintings lining the salon walls as though it were a test.

"I'm no great connoisseur, but I've always found art fascinating." Catherine took another sip of water.

"Hmmm," Rivendon grunted.

Nick clenched his fists inside his pockets as Grandfather assessed her with a cold-eyed stare. Why didn't Catherine show off a little? He knew her undergrad success in art history and design had opened doors for a specialty in historic homes.

Nick took a step closer to her side. His grandfather had a tendency to bully, and he had promised to jump in if things got too rough.

"I understand London is your primary residence," she said.

"I have always found Bascombe rather dull." Rivendon raised his gray brows at her switch in topic.

Nick swiveled his head back to Catherine, noting the militant gleam in her eye.

"Then you don't enjoy estate management?" Catherine brushed back a curl.

"Not in the least," Rivendon all but snapped. "I leave the farming to Nicholas. He has a penchant for playing in the dirt and common associations."

The remark was a slap in the face. Catherine blinked several times. Nick bit the inside of his cheek, fighting back angry words. He took her hand, preparing to lead Catherine from the room.

Before Nick could make his excuses, Rivendon jumped back into the role of interrogator. "What do your people do in the States?"

"They build things," Catherine said airily.

Her answer spiked Nick's interest. She had never spoken about her father's vocation, only her family associations.

"They work in construction, do they?" Rivendon looked down his nose at her.

Catherine smiled almost coquettishly at the earl. Nick had seen that look a time or two when Jack had pushed her buttons. He shut his eyes, groaning internally. This was not going well. When provoked, Catherine had a way of leveling a person without them seeing it coming.

"If you like." Catherine shrugged.

Fascinated despite himself, Nick waited to see how things would play out.

Grandfather wasn't born yesterday, and her answers were not concrete enough to satisfy him. "So your father pounds nails for a living?" Rivendon cast a superior glance in Nick's direction.

It seemed a tough question, and Catherine appeared to consider it carefully. "Probably as much as Nick enjoys playing in the dirt."

"What does your father do, exactly? Build homes?" The earl's eyes narrowed.

"He's constructed a few of them on request." Catherine's eyes twinkled as she took another sip from her water goblet. "Mostly, he constructs hospitals, shopping malls, and resorts."

"You led me right into that." Rivendon closed his eyes. When he opened them, unholy amusement sparkled in their depths.

Nick heaved an internal sigh of relief.

"You very much deserved it, my lord." Catherine smiled sweetly.

Agent Davenport chuckled under his breath.

"I beg your pardon, Miss Pressley-Coombes." Rivendon cast Nick a glare. "Why didn't you warn me about her?"

"When you cornered her, the temptation was too strong to resist," Nick said.

Catherine opened her mouth to protest.

"When I cornered her? I walked right into her trap, my boy. She annihilated me."

"The car is here, Lord Ainsley," Mr. Scott said from the doorway.

"Thank you, Scott," Nick said.

Rivendon offered Catherine his arm and walked her out. "My dear, I believe I shall like you immensely. I daresay you'll give Nicholas quite a challenge. And between the two of us, he needs one."

CHAPTER TWENTY-SIX

"THIS IS A DISASTER." THEODOSIA paced about Rivendon's London garage like a caged animal. "Ainsley was to meet Miss Pressley-Coombes at Davidson House. Why did he show up at her hotel?"

"I am more concerned with the other man."

Ari's quiet words halted Theodosia midpace. She looked at him.

"He wore a holster under his tuxedo."

"A gun?" A shiver rippled across her skin. "What is Ainsley doing with a man who carries a gun?"

"That is my question." Ari ran a hand over his dark, shoulder-length hair.

"The man is most likely a business associate of Ainsley's."

"He watches." Ari shook his head.

"A protection officer?" Panic began to bubble inside her. Her voice sounded shrill even to her own ears. "Time is running out. Only a few months are left on that trust. If we can't get rid of Miss Pressley-Coombes, I'll be incarcerated for delinquency on my loans."

Ari pulled out his mobile and scrolled through his contacts, pressing one. She could hear it ringing in the silence. A man's voice answered in a foreign tongue. Their exchange was brief.

Ari hung up and pulled her into his arms. "There are always setbacks. Patience. Mistakes happen when we get anxious. We have time. My contact is on standby. People get lazy. When they do, we will get her. We almost got her tonight."

"But we didn't."

"Wait and see," Ari said with such assurance that Theodosia chose to believe him.

* * *

Catherine fidgeted with the clasp on her evening bag as Rivendon's driver pulled the earl's sedan into the embassy queue. Every few seconds, the flash of cameras lit the ground floor of the building. The paparazzi were out in force, buzzing behind the barricades like bees in a beehive.

She wondered how Nick could appear so calm. Right now, a troop of elephants was stampeding inside her stomach. As one of Britain's most eligible bachelors, Nick's entrance would land them on BBC news.

Nick squeezed her hand. "Smile for the cameras and follow my lead. It will be over before you know it."

Gillian let out a squeal from the front middle seat, interrupting Catherine's cloud of worry. She leaned across Jack, all but pasting her nose to the window. "Oh. My. Gosh. Pinch me. That's George Hoffman!" She stabbed the spotless glass, pointing to one of England's top footballers.

Catherine waited for her brother to say something rude. He didn't disappoint.

"Quit drooling. I doubt George Hoffman will be the only celebrity tonight."

Gillian ignored him. She patted her heart and mouthed over her shoulder to Catherine, "George Hoffman."

The back row, comprised of Agent Davenport, Catherine, and Nick, erupted in laughter.

"I doubt this little ol' heart of mine can handle it," Gillian said theatrically.

Davenport spoke for the first time since entering the car. "We might need to pick up some old-fashioned smelling salts for Miss Buchanan. I've spotted Dame Agatha Hilton."

Everyone looked out the window at the glamorous middle-aged woman. Ms. Hilton smiled and posed for the cameras on the shallow flight of stone steps sandwiched between the double set of pillars.

"She's so much smaller than I imagined," Gillian said.

Eyeing the movie star's chic attire, Catherine wondered for the hundredth time if her Elie Saab gown would stand up against the heavy-hitting runway collection inside the embassy. She pulled her long curls over her shoulder, making sure they hadn't frizzed. In the process of giving the driver instructions, Nick stopped midsentence, watching her. The intensity of his gaze darkened his eyes. A current of electricity zipped through her body and stole her breath.

Nick blinked, breaking the spell. Giving her a brief smile, he turned back to complete his instructions. Catherine took a deep breath and let it out slowly as the sedan pulled to the curb.

Jack climbed out and assisted Gillian from the vehicle with more care than Catherine thought him capable of. Gillian looked fantastic in her black-satin mermaid gown and wrap. Her spiked heels gave her curvy figure added elegance.

Agent Davenport exited next, closing his door behind him.

Nick gave Catherine's hand one last squeeze. "Tabloid pictures are the paparazzo's livelihood. They have to eat too. Give them your best smile and look delighted, but don't answer questions. Your every word will be misconstrued."

Catherine took a deep breath. This was it. Showtime.

The cool night air rushed inside the sedan when Nick opened the door and stepped out. A low roar erupted from the crowd. Cameras flashed, and reporters shouted questions. He stood outside her door and waved. Bending at the waist, he reached inside the car and took her hand.

When Catherine slipped out of the back seat and joined Nick, the crowd went crazy. With her insides wobbling like Jell-O, she lifted her head and gave the media her brightest smile. In a protective gesture, Nick's arm slipped around her waist, gently pulling her alongside him.

Glancing at Nick to gauge how she was doing, Catherine caught the same expression he'd given her in the car. Everything inside her went soft, and she smiled up at him. Without a word, he took her hand and led her inside.

* * *

The gala was well underway when their party entered the reception line to greet the Italian ambassador. Catherine blinked at the shifting mass of humanity adorned in an array of glittering jewels and designer labels. Politicians, celebrities, and minor royalty spilled from the ballroom, through the open French doors, and out onto the loggia and the fairy-lit garden beyond.

With the formalities behind them, they entered the massive, two-story ballroom, with its cream-colored walls, gilded molding, and inlaid marble floor. A bevy of potted plants and hot-house flowers softened the corners and lighted wall niches.

After the girls checked their bags, Catherine caught Jack eyeing a chair under a gilded still life. Gillian, however, had other plans. Dragging him in her wake, they entered the sparkling throng.

Agent Davenport scanned the room and moved off to find a good vantage point.

"There are a few people I'd like you to meet before Lord Cavendish corners me with investors. And . . ." Nick nodded toward an elderly gentleman. "He's the best of the lot and uncle to our esteemed prime minister."

Nick guided her toward the man for introductions, pausing to grab two club sodas off a passing waiter's tray. He handed her one. "It helps having something to hold."

He introduced Catherine to Sir Richard Wolthorpe, a short, spare man with a full head of shock-white hair and piercing blue eyes.

"American?" Wolthorpe asked after introductions were made.

"I am, but I promise I left my six-shooter at home." Catherine offered him a smile that wobbled around the edges.

Nick snorted and choked on his sip of club soda.

Wolthorpe's mouth quirked up at the corner.

"It's bad form to laugh at a foreigner, Lord Ainsley," Catherine stage-whispered for Sir Richard's benefit.

"I assure you, Miss Pressley-Coombes, I would never laugh at you to your face or otherwise," Nick said, still sputtering. "She's full of surprises, Sir Richard. I'd advise you to watch yourself."

"Indubitably." Wolthorpe's smile faded, and he asked in a more serious tone, "How is Rivendon?"

"Much improved and growing more cantankerous," Nick said. "He's refusing surgery."

"At his age, I can hardly blame him." Sir Richard swirled his drink. "Tell him I shall pay a visit soon." The old gentleman turned to Catherine and bowed. "It was a pleasure, Miss Pressley-Coombes."

In Nick's world, where money dripped like icicles in a spring thaw, there was something steady about Wolthorpe. She gave him her first genuine smile since entering the embassy.

Sir Richard paused. "Ainsley, if you don't snap that one up, you will without doubt be the world's stupidest fish."

Nick looked amused.

"If I were twenty years younger, I'd cast a lure in her direction." The old gentleman winked at Catherine.

Wolthorpe was giving her huge marks.

"And I would take the bait, Sir Richard," she boldly replied.

"Remember what I said." Wolthorpe tapped Nick on the arm, then bowed and moved off.

"Sir Richard's one of the most decent men I know. A wise man always takes his advice."

Nick's reference to Wolthorpe's parting shot filled Catherine with unease. Of late, Nick's flirting held serious undertones. She knew he expected their relationship to progress, and in her heart of hearts, she wanted nothing more than to accommodate him. Her feelings for him were powerful, but so were her religious convictions. Whenever she brought up God, Nick avoided or changed the subject. It troubled her. Deeply. And her natural reserve made discussing anything close to her heart next to impossible.

Gillian approached, looking as though someone had popped her balloon. "George Hoffman is a narcissistic jerk. He cut in on Jack's dance and tried to feel up my backside." She speared a shrimp off a passing waiter's tray. Holding her shrimp aloft, Gillian said, "I put my heels to good use."

Catherine laughed, and several females cast speculative glances her way. Even among the top echelon of Society, women were not impervious to Nick's appeal. Oblivious or simply choosing to ignore them, Nick watched the crowd, his hand never leaving her waist.

Jack sauntered over, munching an hors d'oeuvre.

"Where did you find those?" Gillian asked.

"In the alcove. I would have gotten you some, but you were so busy drooling over that puffed-up peacock, I didn't think you'd be interested." Gillian pulled Jack's face down to hers. "If you show me where those yummies are, I won't make you dance for an hour."

A calculating gleam came and went in her brother's eyes.

"Come on." Gillian took Jack's hand in hers.

While Catherine watched them go, the lead violinist started into a waltz.

Nick's blue eyes twinkled down at her. The strong jaw line and angular planes of his face stood out against the crisp white collar. Under the chandeliers, his dark hair shone.

"Miss Pressley Coombes, would you honor me with a dance?"

She placed her drink on a waiter's tray, and Nick swept her into a waltz. The skirt of her gown belled out, flowing and ebbing around them as they turned. The whirl of lights, the glitter of jewels, and the images of faces she had seen only on the cover of magazines flashed past.

She couldn't imagine a more romantic setting, but violins had been playing in her heart for weeks. They had soared while she'd tromped the priory grounds in muddy rubber boots, fished in the lake beside Nick, with tissues stuck up his nose, and listened to him serenade an old woman in a smoke-filled pub.

She knew her heart was in her eyes and saw Nick take it in. The intensity of his gaze caressed every portion of her face, melting her bones. The corner of his mouth lifted, then widened into a smile. Her throat tightened in response, launching her heart skyward.

The flash of a camera sent her soaring spirits crashing to the earth. She turned her head away and worried her lip. Their poignant moment would be smeared across the nation, tainting and crumbling it to dust.

A small indentation appeared beside Nick's mouth, a sure sign of frustration. Letting go of her waist, he took her by the hand and led her off the dance floor not far from where Jack stood. "I'm sorry, Catherine. My appointment has arrived."

A blond man in his thirties approached. Nick flashed his party smile. "Cavendish. I had almost given you up."

Nick made the introductions. Lord Cavendish gave her a wolfish grin and a lengthy once-over. Catherine felt her smile slip and wished she really did carry a six-shooter.

Beside her, Nick's hand went rigid. "Catherine, will you excuse us?" Taking Lord Cavendish firmly by the arm, Nick propelled him to a distant corner where they could converse.

Tired of the raised brows, side-long glances, and overheated ballroom, Catherine left her brother and slipped through the french doors onto the loggia.

Agent Davenport stood three steps away smoking a cigarette in the shadows of a gnarled wisteria vine. She glanced over her shoulder through the french doors. From Agent Davenport's position, he could see the entire ballroom. She nodded to him and continued into the garden.

The cool air, splashing fountain, and fairy lights provided the perfect reprieve to sort through her thoughts. Sitting on the edge of the basin, she gazed up at the waxing moon.

In her heart, she knew Nick was ready to move into a more serious relationship. To be honest with herself, she was so far down that particular rabbit hole, she wasn't sure she could stop the freefall. But worries still consumed her.

In Britain, class mattered. The aristocracy was a separate entity beyond wealth, education, and manners. Though he lived quietly in the country, Nick belonged to that world. She did not.

Even if he offered her the fairy tale, Nick couldn't provide the one thing that mattered most—a temple marriage. Due to the Davidson's four-hundred-year religious affiliation with the local parish, she doubted Nick would accept the gospel message.

Her doubts swarmed like a plague of midges. It boiled down to class and religion, the age-old dividers. Wars had started for less. And yet, her heart yearned for the impossible.

CHAPTER TWENTY-SEVEN

THE BEDROOM LAMP CAST A golden halo onto the page of Theodosia's book. She scratched her scalp under the Dutch-girl wig and touched her pocket where the small handgun Hadley had given her rested. Turning the page, she attempted to resume where she had left off.

A soft knock rapped on her door. Ari poked his head inside. Black stubble covered his jaw. His face looked pinched with exhaustion. He had just returned Ainsley's party to their hotel. Half two in the morning was no time to persuade a tired man to spend the remainder of the night doing something illegal.

"Why are you dressed like that?" Ari eyed her black outfit suspiciously.

"I had an idea." Theodosia knew she had better explain fast, or he would refuse.

"Do you never sleep?" Ari entered her room, shutting the door behind him. He rubbed his face with both hands and leaned against the wall.

"I cannot afford to. With the trust hanging over me, I must tie up loose ends. No one is in Bascombe. Who is to stop us from visiting their place tonight and getting the diary?"

"My job?" he said, yawning.

She waved her hand inconsequentially. "Call in sick. Mr. Scott can cover for you. Besides, Rivendon doesn't rise until eight. We can be there and back by then."

"Theodosia, this is what I warned you about. Your idea is not planned out."

"The cottage is empty right now, and Bascombe is a two-hour drive at best. We'll arrive just before dawn," she argued.

"Where? Do you have any idea?" He crossed his arms, a scowl marring his face.

"I have their address. Rivendon had me check them out." She rose from her chair, placing both hands on his shoulders.

Ari shut his eyes. "Vehicle? We cannot take Rivendon's motorcar."

"I rented something."

His eyes opened, glinting with amusement. "Good. You can drive. I'll sleep."

At her nod, he grabbed her around the waist. "You are a persistent lady."

* * *

Pushing through dripping, waist-high shrubbery, Theodosia joined Ari under the Pressley-Coombes's front-facing window. Birds in all their varieties opened their noisy little beaks, filling the air with a cacophony of sound as purple tinged the horizon. Theodosia stifled a yawn. Mud squelched under her boots. She blew at the itchy fringe of her wig.

A door slammed. Ari tackled her, throwing her to the ground. Her eye socket connected with the hedge, and pain ricocheted through her head. The maligned eye began to pour like a leaky tap as she sank into the soft mud beneath the bushes, trying not to howl.

Holding her breath, Theodosia watched an elderly woman in a bright-green head scarf attach a lead to her dog's collar. The dog sniffed the air and gave a woof in their direction, but the woman was having none of it.

"Come, Buggles." The old lady tugged on the leash.

Woman and beast set off in the opposite direction; Theodosia heaved a sigh of relief. She wiped her runny eye with her shirt sleeve and hoisted herself to her feet.

"Is she gone?" At her nod, Ari informed her, "I cannot reach the window. Let me stand on your back."

"I will not kneel in that." She pointed at the goop underfoot.

"Then you wish to climb through the window instead?"

Theodosia measured the height of the sill and folded her arms. "Fine. Go ahead." With a drippy eye and covered in mud, Theodosia knelt on all fours in the black, mucky mess and tried not to gag.

Ari's combat boots dug into her spine.

"Ouch!" Craning her neck to see if he had been able to pry open the window, the boxwood scratched her face. She inhaled sharply.

Breaking in had seemed so simple. This morning, however, she was having second thoughts. Ari's weight shifted, and her hands sank another inch. She doubted her black, Givenchy trousers would ever be the same.

Another door slammed. Did all of Bascombe rise with the birds? Ari lost his balance and fell on top of her, knocking the air from her lungs.

Theodosia lay on her face, gasping for air.

"Shhh." Ari pressed a grimy finger to her lips.

At that moment, she didn't care about anything except getting air into her lungs. After a few frightened moments, where she knew she would die, her passageway opened, and she sucked in a full breath.

A motorcar roared to life at the curb, its headlamps sweeping across the Pressley-Coombes's garden as it made a U-turn. Ari pushed her head down. She tasted mud.

"Stop it," she protested, spitting.

"Sorry. Stay put." Ari peeked over the hedge and zipped soundlessly around the right side of the cottage.

Theodosia sat up and wiped her grimy hands on her ruined £1200.00 trousers. She coughed, trying to muffle the sound from her position behind the shrubbery. A low growl emitted from the opposite side of the wall from where she crouched. Theodosia eyed the five-foot barricade and hoped it would keep Fido contained.

"Nice doggy," she whispered.

Fido snarled and threw himself against the wall in a convincing display of savage fury. Other dogs on the street took up the bark. First one, then another, and another, until half a dozen canines drowned out the aviary chorus.

Several porch lights went on down the street. Fido's owner opened a window and yelled, "Shut yer trap, Daisy."

Daisy? That monster dog's name is Daisy?

Daisy let out a whimper and subsided, emitting an occasional growl.

Theodosia left her hiding place and slipped around the corner of the cottage to see what was keeping Ari.

He stood against the back of the house and placed a small tool with suction cups on the window pane closest to the door and etched a circle on the glass. The suction cups didn't hold, and the glass fell inside the house with a tinkle of shards as it hit the floor.

Ari reached inside the circular hole and unlocked the dead bolt. Flashing his pirate's grin, he slipped inside, motioning for her to follow. "Take off your shoes."

"You can't be serious." She glanced at her muddy boots, then back at him. He waited. "Very well." She sat on the damp stone step and gingerly unlaced the ties on her filthy boots.

Ari tossed her a pair of gloves. "Put those on, and mind the glass," he said, stepping over the shards that lay strewn across the floor. "I disconnected the monitors in the yard." Ari reached up over the door inside the butler's pantry and snipped several wires. "And inside."

They split up. She took one side of the ground floor; he took the other.

In the adjoining room, a lone desk topped with computer paraphernalia sat under a chandelier. Theodosia rifled through the drawers but only found a ream of paper, a few writing pens, and a discarded chewing-gum wrapper.

The living room made her laugh. If this was an example of Miss Pressley-Coombes's design work, Theodosia was doing Ainsley a favor. A cowhide covered the plank floor. Beat up, rough-hewn lumber and plumbing pipes served as occasional tables and the telly holder. A wooden box filled with various large-sized plastic tubes stood beside an oak architect's desk in the corner. Framed F1 blueprints served for artwork.

Theodosia curled her nose and blew the itchy fringe on her black wig. That diary had to be here somewhere. She pulled off the scatter cushions to check but came up empty. Squatting on the cowhide rug, she checked under the furniture. Not even a dust bunny met her searching eyes.

Where could it be?

Ari came out of the kitchen empty-handed.

She sighed heavily and looked for the stairs. The crooked stairwell brought back nostalgic childhood memories of the old Tudor rectory where she had grown up.

Ari touched her arm. He stood with his head cocked to the side. His eyes flashed a warning. Then she heard it, the unmistakable scrape of a key in the lock. Someone was at the front door. Her mind whirled, looking for a way to escape. They had to run through the kitchen to reach the butler's pantry. The kitchen was only steps from the front door. They were trapped.

In a blind panic, Theodosia raced up the stairs with Ari at her heels. In the upper hall, she stopped to catch her breath. Her heart thundered; her eye throbbed, the swollen lid affecting her vision.

The front door opened.

Glancing at Ari for guidance, she forgot to breathe. A half smile lit his features. The twit was enjoying this.

"Stay, Buggles," a voice said.

Theodosia recognized the name of the dog. It was the woman with the green scarf.

"Stay. We don't want to dirty Miss Catherine's clean floors." The neighbor continued. "Mumsy's going to water the plants."

Ari touched Theodosia's arm, motioning for her to step back from the top of the stairs. A floorboard creaked underfoot. Buggles growled. Theodosia closed her eyes. This could not be happening.

"Is anyone there?" The older woman's voice quavered.

Ari placed his finger on her lips.

Theodosia rolled her eyes. She had no intention of making a sound. If that old lady came upstairs to investigate, she would deal with her. The very thought hardened her resolve. Her hand slid inside her trouser pocket and touched Hadley's gun. Nothing and no one would stand in her way.

A tap turned on in the kitchen. The old woman must have passed off the sound as the old house settling.

The water shut off. Footsteps moved toward the butler's pantry, where she and Ari had let themselves in—and where broken glass lay strewn across the tiles.

"Oh! My goodness!"

They heard the crunch of glass. If the old lady opened the back door and found Theodosia's boots, she would know someone was inside. Theodosia's heart thundered, and her fingers closed around the gun.

Mercifully, the woman beat a hasty retreat to the front of the house. Theodosia could practically feel her panic as she let herself out the front gate, letting it crash behind her.

Ari whispered. "We have ten minutes before the police arrive. Search the bedrooms. We will leave by the back garden."

She and Ari searched, but there was no sign of the diary she had seen in Professor McKellan's office. If the diary wasn't at Oxford University or in the cottage, where could it be?

The thin wail of sirens in the distance broke into her thoughts. Her pulse accelerated, heightening her senses.

"Time to go." Ari flashed his teeth.

Theodosia recognized the expression for what it was. To Ari's twenty-two years, this was no more than a game, an adrenalin rush. If she were completely honest, she enjoyed the added thrill of danger as well.

They ran down the stairs, through the kitchen and across the glass-strewn tiles. Theodosia gasped as a shard plunged into her heel. There was no time to pull it out.

The wail of sirens drew closer. Banging the door shut behind her, she grabbed her boots and followed Ari to the back wall. She watched as he effortlessly vaulted over the top.

She tossed her boots after him and heard a muttered curse. Grasping a hand hold, she attempted to follow his example, but her foot had saturated its stocking. She slipped, smearing the stonework with her DNA.

Ari peeked at her over the wall. "Come. Come."

"I can't."

Ari stared at her, the seconds lengthening. He would abandon her. She swallowed hard as an odd sort of pang struck somewhere near her heart.

Nimble as a rabbit, Ari hopped the wall and knelt at her feet. He cupped his hands. "Hurry."

She placed her foot in his hands and shot over the stone wall as though she were a champion vaulter. Unable to catch herself, she flapped helplessly. She landed flat on her rump in a puddle, bruising her tail bone. Could this day get any worse?

Ari rejoined her, pulling her to her feet. Bleeding, bruised, and covered in mud, she hobbled alongside her erstwhile companion as they made their way up the alley. The sirens drew closer. Her heart beat a crazy tattoo. She wanted to hide. In this light, anyone looking out their garden window would notice two ragtag indigents making their way toward the road. When the police questioned the neighbors, someone would remember them.

"I shall wait for you at the top of the alley." She pulled the keys from her pocket and handed them to Ari.

"You want me to get the vehicle?"

At her nod, he took the keys and jogged up the alley without a backward glance.

With her foot bleeding like a stuck pig, Theodosia secreted herself behind a double set of trash bins. The neighborhood dogs, which had piped down earlier, started into a howl-le-lu-jah chorus.

A boxer jumped its garden wall. Sighting her, the dog growled, baring its teeth, and approached in a semicrouched position with ears pinned to its skull.

"Nice doggy."

The boxer growled deep in its throat and crept forward, red lights glinting in its eyes. The set of bins would be no protection. Too frightened to move, she closed her eyes and waited for the inevitable.

The rev of an engine and rattle of loose stones preceded Ari's arrival in their car hire. He leaned across the passenger seat and opened the nearside door. Theodosia hobble-ran the few yards separating her and freedom. The dog charged in pursuit.

She dove for the front seat as the dog lunged. Grabbing her trouser leg with his canines, he shook it with appalling strength. The fabric tore. Her Givenchys were rubbish.

Ari threw the handbrake, leaving the engine to idle, and jumped out of the motorcar. Windmilling her boots by the laces, he rushed the dog. One heel connected with the boxer's muzzle, loosening the beast's grip. Theodosia pulled herself in the rest of the way and slammed the door.

With ruffled fur, the dog jumped against her window, growling and baring its fangs. Ari hopped back inside the motorcar and slammed the door. He started down the street, making for the A-417 with the dog giving chase.

Ari tossed her boots in the back seat and dug a packet of tissues from his pocket.

Theodosia took them gratefully and applied them to her bleeding heel. The glass shard was deeply imbedded. She'd need tweezers to remove it. Leaning back in her seat, she closed her eyes.

They had not located the diary. Her trousers were in tatters. She would be hard pressed to explain away a black eye and limp when she returned to London.

But a smile lifted the corners of her lips. Ari had not abandoned her.

CHAPTER TWENTY-EIGHT

EVERYTHING WAS GRAY: THE SKY, the street, and the Uber car that met Catherine and her party the next morning at the Bascombe train station. She wondered if Cinderella had experienced the same letdown after the ball. Nick had flown to Italy just hours after the gala, leaving her more confused than ever.

Rain clattered down the drainpipe beside her. She moved to stand beside Agent Davenport under the station roof and booted up her cell while Jack loaded their cases inside the back of the Uber SUV.

Once they were headed for the cottage, Catherine's phone lit up with half a dozen texts. She briefly scrolled through, but none was from Nick. She opened Gillian's.

At my gate. Had a fantastic time. Thanks for the invite. Two weeks until our trip to the Highlands. Can't wait.

Catherine dropped her cell back into her tote, planning to read the rest of her texts later.

"Who was that?" her brother asked.

"Gillian."

"Did she make her flight?" Jack turned halfway in his seat to meet her eyes.

She nodded just as their driver slammed on the brakes.

"Sorry about that," the driver said.

Looking out her window, she saw the reason for their driver's quick stop. A barricade of cones blocked their street. Two police cars were parked in front of the cottage. Apprehension knotted inside Catherine's stomach.

Agent Davenport rolled down his window, a frown puckering his forehead as he surveyed the crowd huddled under an array of umbrellas outside their garden gate.

"I can't take you any closer," the driver said. "You'll have to walk."

With dread knotting her stomach, Catherine climbed out of the car. Maybe it was something normal, like a leaky gas line or a broken water main. But she had a niggling suspicion that was not the case.

Jack retrieved their luggage. Catherine pulled up her hood, and the three of them rolled their cases down the sidewalk with the ever-alert Agent Davenport at her side.

Amelia caught sight of them and broke away from their group of neighbors. The absence of Buggles told its own story. "Where have you been? The police want to talk to Jack. I didn't have his mobile number, so I called yours."

Catherine's dread deepened.

"What's all the fuss about?" Jack let go of his luggage.

"You were robbed." Amelia flapped her hands.

Catherine stiffened. This was one too many incidents.

"I went to water your plants this morning and found the butler's pantry window broken," Amelia said quietly.

"The glass panes were loose," Jack said.

"Glass doesn't cut itself in a perfect circle and fall to the floor." Amelia's mouth twisted.

A low buzzing started in Catherine's ears. Enough was enough. She was sick of being a victim. Tossing up her chin, she started forward, proverbially rolling up her sleeves.

"Not any closer until I confer with the DCI and have a look around," Agent Davenport said under his breath.

Catherine scowled at him, silently seething. Davenport's mild eyes held hers.

"Okay." She huffed in frustration.

One of the policemen approached. DCI Barnes introduced himself, and Agent Davenport flashed his badge. The men turned aside, conversing away from civilian ears. Whatever passed between them left Davenport less than happy. He pulled out his cell and punched in a number.

"We tried contacting your sister an hour ago," Barnes said to Jack.

"I turned my phone off on the train," Catherine interjected in her defense.

"Your home was vandalized. We need you to determine what's missing," Barnes said, not the least assuaged.

They followed Barnes inside the cottage, leaving their suitcases by the door.

Catherine glanced quickly around the living room, but other than an off-centered pillow on the sofa, nothing looked out of place. Jack zeroed in on his TV and high-tech stereo equipment. Both were intact. She wandered the main floor, pausing in the dining room, where Jack's computer and her laptop sat where they had left them.

A chill went down her spine when she saw the perfectly cut circle on the pane of glass in the butler's pantry. Broken shards lay scattered across the floor, and the dead bolt was unlocked. She had personally secured it before they'd left.

A sense of violation intermixed with fury swamped her. Jack had been silent since entering. Not unusual for him. By the set expression on his face, she could tell he felt much the same.

Upstairs, the condition of the bedrooms offered a different story. Catherine's suitcase was in disarray, along with her mattress and bedding. The clothes inside her closet were on the floor.

With her heart beating hard and fast, she checked the outside pocket of her suitcase for her jewelry. She had several nice pieces: a strand of Mikimoto pearls her parents had given her on her eighteenth birthday, a pair of diamond and pearl earrings, several gold chains of varying widths and lengths and a few semiprecious pendants.

She opened the black velvet bags with unsteady fingers and thumbed through their contents. The tightness in her shoulders eased, and she heaved a sigh of relief. Nothing was missing.

This *burglary* didn't make sense, she thought as she watched rivulets of water stream down her window. What kind of thief bypassed jewelry and state-of-the-art electronics? Jack's sound system alone could sell for thousands of pounds on the street. Why would a thief break into a home if he weren't after something he could pawn?

Catherine peeked inside Jack's room. It resembled hers. He looked up at her from where he knelt on the floor, still wearing that grim expression.

"Nothing's missing as far as I can tell. You?" she asked.

"Same here. Weird." Jack shook his head.

She went back to her bedroom, trying to figure out the target of their raid. The stack of books she normally kept on the window seat lay on the floor. Absently, she picked them up, straightening a few wrinkled pages. The soft leather of her scriptures comforted her as she put them back in place. The faint scent of leather triggered the image of Glorianne's tattered diary. Transfixed, she stared sightlessly out the dormer window. Martin had it. The diary was the only thing she had brought to England that was not inside the cottage.

When she had asked Martin for an update on his progress, he'd blushed and admitted he had fallen behind. Professor McKellan's office had been vandalized, and they were still putting it to rights. The diary was safe though. Martin had taken it home with him the night of the incident.

Looking into the back garden, the pieces fit together with perfect clarity. Someone wanted the diary. But why?

When Mom had found it, she'd had the strongest feeling it would help them find their family. After weeks of research, Catherine had to agree. Other than the diary, tombstone, and ship's passenger list, no documentation existed, digital or otherwise, on Glorianne.

Was it too big a stretch to think the vandals might be behind her other incidents?

Catherine went downstairs to find Jack, passing Davenport arguing with someone on his cell phone. Whatever their conversation, Davenport did not appear pleased. She found Jack in the butler's pantry, where the redheaded Thackey, Barnes's DS, was bagging evidence from the shattered glass on the floor.

"The unsub cut himself on a piece of his own handiwork." Thackey held up a sealed container.

"What's an unsub?" Catherine asked.

"An unidentified subject," Thackey said.

"If they are in the system, this DNA sample will identify our burglar. We've dusted for prints. The thieves wore gloves." Barnes pushed himself off the floor, his knees creaking loudly.

"They, as in plural?" Catherine asked.

"We found two sets of footprints underneath the kitchen window," Barnes stated with a rueful grimace. "Unfortunately, the soupy mud kept us from getting a good print. They also cut your surveillance feed lines."

"How long will it take to get DNA results?" Jack questioned.

"It depends on how backed up the lab is. Weeks. Months." Barnes lifted a shoulder. "This isn't telly, you know. Real-life police work takes time."

Catherine watched Jack's jaw clench. She knew he was counting and wondered idly how high the number would climb before his temper subsided. Personally, she'd like nothing better than seeing Barnes taken down a notch. His attitude grated.

Davenport glanced at Catherine and said into the mouthpiece of his phone, "She's here. You tell her." By the unhappy expression on his face when he handed Catherine his phone, she had a good idea what was coming.

"Miss Pressley-Coombes?"

"Yes?"

"Agent Butler here."

"What can I do for you?" Catherine watched Thackey pack up his DNA samples and store them inside a containment bag.

"Due to this morning's event, my department no longer believes your situation is a trafficking issue. With budget restraints what they are, Agent Davenport has been reassigned to London."

"This is the third attack," she protested into the phone.

"The unsub does not fit our unit's scenario. With this latest turn of events, we believe your near abduction to be a piece of random misfortune."

"What if this case is all tied together?"

"That will be for your local constabulary to determine."

Before Catherine could protest further, Butler hung up. She stared at Davenport's cell phone until the screen went dark. Jack placed a hand on her shoulder. She handed Davenport his phone, not meeting his eyes. If Barnes was the only thing between her and the unsub, she was better off on her own.

She rubbed her temples, trying to ease the throb.

"For what it's worth," Agent Davenport broke the silence, "I'm most dreadfully sorry, Miss Pressley-Coombes."

"It's not your fault, Agent Davenport." She dropped her hands and gave him a forced smile. "Thank you for all your help."

Davenport turned, picked up his suitcase inside the entry, and opened the front door. For a moment, he stood silhouetted against the rain before closing the door behind him. The finality of Scotland Yard's decision stung and left her feeling vulnerable.

Jack wrapped his arm around her. For a second, she weakened and leaned into his side, savoring his support. Her brothers might tease her mercilessly, but when it mattered, they stood together.

She took a deep breath and moved away from Jack. He wasn't going to like what she had to say. In fact, she knew he would hate it. "I think I know what the vandal was after."

CHAPTER TWENTY-NINE

NICK LANDED MIDMORNING AT LONDON's Stansted Airport and took the express train to the city. All too soon, he pulled into Tottenham Hale and transferred to the Underground. The peculiar odor of metal and exhaust in an enclosed space greeted him when he exited at South Kensington and made his way to Davidson House to meet Grandfather.

He had an appointment at Coutts before twelve and another at Garrard shortly thereafter. Since the night of the gala, Nick could think of little else. But first, he wanted his grandfather's blessing. One thing was certain: no matter how Rivendon responded, Nick's mind was made up.

Nick ran up the cement steps, passing the large urns spilling their profusion of blooms, and rapped with the brass knocker.

"It's good to see you again, my lord." Mr. Scott opened the door with a bow.

"Good morning, Mr. Scott." Nick handed the butler his jacket. "Where might I find my grandfather?"

"He's expecting you in the library."

Why did Rivendon keep the place so blazing hot? Nick loosened his tie and followed Scott to his grandfather's inner sanctum. He passed Lady Hadley in the hall. She wore sunglasses and limped slightly.

"Hallo, Lady Hadley. Nice to see you."

She nodded as she passed but did not linger. Puzzled, Nick glanced over his shoulder at her. She had been unfriendly of late.

Scott knocked on the door.

"Come," Rivendon barked.

"Lord Ainsley," Scott announced.

Grandfather sat behind his massive desk, a wreath of smoke curling past his left ear. Nick felt his chest tighten. Rivendon was deliberately disobeying doctors' orders to leave off the cigars.

"Nicholas, I must say it's a pleasure to see you so soon after your last visit." Rivendon watched him under heavy gray brows.

"I thought the doctor told you to quit smoking those?" Nick took the leather chair facing Rivendon's desk, watching the smoke rise toward the ceiling.

"I plan to once I finish this box of Havanas." Rivendon blew out another stream.

Nick leaned back in his chair, taking in the dark-wood shelves lined with books. He had always loved this room. It was not a showpiece like the rest of the townhouse but comfortable and well worn, the leather chairs and couches soft from use, the book bindings colorful with faded gilding.

He had spent many a rainy day prone on the rug, reading adventure stories during school holidays while Grandfather conducted business calls. At first Rivendon's conversations were background noise. After a time, Nick had started to understand the intricacies of investing.

"Sir Richard was here earlier." The earl took another drag on his cigar and half closed his eyes as he exhaled. "He mentioned seeing you at the gala."

"I introduced Catherine to him."

"Sir Richard was quite charmed. He thought she would keep you on your toes." After one last puff, Rivendon stabbed out his cigar. "I know why you're here, Nicholas."

"I must say, that makes this conversation much easier." Nick wiggled his toes inside his shoes, his body tense. He had learned the value of not rushing his fences with Rivendon. Too much hung in the balance. The clock ticked, its second hand filling the pregnant pause in conversation.

Rivendon cleared his throat. "I think she'll do."

The rigid muscles in Nick's neck and back loosened, and he heaved an internal sigh of relief.

"You had already made up your mind, hadn't you?" Grandfather's eyes twinkled.

"I hoped for your blessing, but, yes, I do plan to marry Catherine with or without it."

The earl's mouth twitched as he tried to suppress a smile. He failed horribly and chuckled like a skinny Santa. "Nicholas, our family has a strong propensity to love deeply only once. When you introduced Miss Pressley-Coombes to me, I knew you were done looking. I must say, it took you long enough."

"You must admit, I did give it a go, especially after University." Nick ran a hand along his jaw. He needed a shave.

"If showing up regularly in the *London Tattler* is what you would term 'giving it a go.'"

Nick's taste in females had improved dramatically since college.

"Mind you, I don't like Americans in general," Rivendon said, clearly preparing to make a point. "Miss Pressley-Coombes possesses beauty and intelligence, certainly, but she also has backbone. When the corporate businessman in you takes over, you ever so nicely steamroll everyone in your path. Miss Pressley-Coombes will demand her time, and you had better listen when she does."

"Or?" Nick steepled his fingers under his chin, imitating his grandfather's favorite pose.

"Or that little wisp of a thing will make you regret it."

They both burst into laughter.

"That she will." Relieved with his good fortune, Nick checked his watch, trying to suppress his excitement. He could spare a few more minutes before he left for Coutts.

Grandfather picked up the telephone on his desk and pressed an extension. "Ari, could you bring round the Bentley? Nicholas and I are going to the bank at quarter past," he said and hung up.

"How did you know about my appointment?" Nick asked in surprise.

"The Coutts manager called Davidson House yesterday to confirm your appointment. He had his wires crossed, and I did not inform him otherwise."

Nick searched Rivendon's face. He supposed he should thank the manager for the mix-up. It had given Grandfather time to consider the ramifications of Nick's appointment.

"Do you mind if I tag along?" Rivendon asked. "This is rather a momentous occasion. I thought perhaps you might consider a few of the Davidson pieces in the vault."

"I should like it above all things." If Grandfather wanted him to look over the family heirlooms, Nick would humor him. Who knew? Maybe something in the vault would suit Catherine and appease Rivendon at the same time.

They made their way to the foyer.

While they waited for the car, Nick put forth the question that had troubled him most of his life. "Did my father love my mother?"

"Very much." Rivendon sighed heavily. "I worried when Arthur fell in love. He was so much older than your mother. Margaret was barely out of finishing school and more excited about the title and tiara than your father. It crushed Arthur when she left."

That explained it. Father had inherited the Davidson curse, a brittle heart that gave itself once. Unfortunately, he had bestowed his affections on a young and frivolous girl.

Nick rubbed the back of his neck. Mummy's abandonment had devastated them all. Until a woman with aquamarine eyes had landed in his ditch, Nick had never thought the emptiness inside him would abate.

Rivendon coughed several times before he said gruffly, "You have chosen more wisely than your father. Miss Pressley-Coombes gives herself away with every glance. She loves you deeply."

CHAPTER THIRTY

NICK DROVE ACROSS THE RIVER Rue. Afternoon sunlight glinted off the water, creating a dazzling sparkle under the blue sky. He wanted to see Catherine but didn't trust himself to behave normally.

Sleep had eluded him last night, and he doubted he would get much more until Garrard delivered Catherine's ring by private courier on Tuesday. The stone he had settled on, an oval multifaceted, four-carat diamond, came from a hideous brooch Catherine of Braganza had bestowed upon one of his upteenth great-grandmothers. The new setting would be a vast improvement.

Downshifting, he turned onto High Street, navigating alongside the village green. A group of small boys clustered, watching two adults playing an odd game of ball.

Recognizing the long golden-brown ponytail, Nick pulled over to the curb and eyed Catherine longingly. His ironwork company's electronic gate and balcony installations in Italy had run into a few snags and had taken longer than expected, forcing him to tack another day on to his business trip. He had missed Catherine terribly.

He watched Catherine toss a ball toward her brother. Over and over, Jack hit it with a bat. One of the lads jumped and caught the ball. A chorus of cheers went up from his friends.

Using the bat, Jack pointed to the green behind Catherine. The children broke into a run, jostling each other and spreading out across the grass. He had watched the game a time or two on the telly but had never seen American baseball played in person.

Sammy Benson tossed Catherine the ball. She caught it in her mitt with a deft move born of practice. Facing her brother, she wound up for a pitch, letting loose an impressive fastball. Jack swung, and the resounding thwack of wood connecting with ball reached his ears across the street.

"Catch it. Throw it to me! Throw it to me!" Catherine hollered instructions as the ball sailed over her head.

The ball bounced once, and a sturdy lad picked it up and relayed it back to her. She sprinted over the green like the attendant devils of Satan were after her.

"Don't try it," Jack yelled as Catherine zipped across the grass on a collision course with her brother. She ignored Jack's warning and, if possible, increased her speed. The siblings converged on the base from two different angles, with Catherine in the lead. Jack used his momentum and went down into a slide, attempting to avoid her tag. With her leather mitt outstretched, Catherine bent over and smacked Jack.

"Out. Out. Out." She shouted in her brother's face. Gleeful as a child, she danced on top of the base. "I can take you any day of the week, buddy." She reached down a hand and helped her brother up.

When Jack was vertical, he rubbed his mitt on top of her head, messing up her ponytail.

Seeing Catherine give her brother sass superimposed itself over the elegant sophisticate that had accompanied Nick to the gala. One made him want to kneel at her feet and worship, while the other, with her dancing eyes, laughing lips, and competitive nature made him want to tickle her until she squealed. He adored her.

"Come here, Sammy. I'll show you how to hit a ball." Catherine motioned for the boy to join her.

"I'll do it," Jack said.

"Oh, no you don't. It's your turn to pitch." Catherine pointed at her brother, stabbing the air for emphasis.

In the act of wiping dirt off his clothes, Jack caught sight of Nick's Range Rover. Nick placed a finger to his lips. He didn't want Catherine to know he was there. If she did, it would make her self-conscious and most likely break up the game.

Taking the bat, Catherine positioned Sammy's hands and showed him how to swing. Jack pitched a slow ball. Sammy swung. Missed.

Sammy kicked the ground, looking discouraged.

"That's okay," she consoled.

Sammy hit a pop fly on the second pitch, but Jack caught it.

"You're out."

Sammy didn't seem to care. He'd hit the ball.

Up next, Catherine took a couple practice swings before nodding to her brother. She crouched over the base with the bat high, her eyes intent.

Jack pitched a fastball, and Catherine swung and missed.

"Strike! That's one," Jack taunted.

Jack pitched another. It came in hard and fast. The Pressley-Coombes siblings, it appeared, gave no quarter. Catherine had said she'd had to work hard to play with her brothers.

Catherine swung and missed again.

"You've gone soft, sis."

Catherine didn't respond. Nick watched as she anchored her back leg and wondered what kind of torque she could produce if her bat connected with the ball. The intensity of her focus made him sit up, sensing it was now or never.

Jack pitched again with amazing accuracy. The ball arced, going fast.

In a graceful movement, Catherine swung, using her back leg to put some muscle into it, and connected. In a blur, the ball whizzed directly over the boys' heads and zipped toward the end of the green.

Nick's mouth fell open in surprise. When Catherine had told him she played a mean game of baseball, she hadn't been putting him on.

Jack whistled. "Glad to see you still know how to play."

By the time the boys relayed the ball to Jack, two runners had scored.

"You should have made it home on that hit," Jack yelled.

Catherine made a face at him from third base.

Another boy marched out onto the field and picked up the bat.

Unable to keep his distance any longer, Nick climbed out of the Range Rover and jogged across the village green, coming up behind Catherine while she stood on base.

Jack pitched a slow ball. The youngster swung and missed. Some of the lads moaned. Nick had never been one to interrupt a game of sport, but seeing Catherine was too great a temptation.

He caught up to her on her sprint toward home plate. She saw him out of the corner of her eye and stutter-stepped. He grabbed her around the waist and hoisted her into the air, flipping her in his arms as though she were a sack of flour.

Catherine let out a startled cry and tossed him a naughty look before her lips curved into the smile he loved. Unable to help himself, Nick dipped his head and kissed her in broad daylight. With a crowd of witnesses.

"Bleh," Sammy complained to a teammate. "He's always kissing her."

She blushed fiery red. Nick set her down, keeping his arm around her waist. He was so happy to see her that he hadn't put together what had been niggling at the back of his mind. "Where the devil is Davenport?"

Catherine bit her lip and glanced at Jack, who trotted in from the pitcher's mound.

"A lot's happened since you left. Come over to the cottage, and we'll fill you in," Jack said quietly.

By the look of things, Nick doubted their news would bring much joy.

Jack tapped Catherine on the shoulder with the ball. "By the way, sis, you're out."

CHAPTER THIRTY-ONE

CATHERINE PULLED INTO THE OXFORD chapel parking lot with ten minutes to spare. Nick had a meeting tonight, or she would have stayed in Bascombe. She had missed him so much while he'd been in Italy, the yearning had nearly consumed her. Yet his trip had had its advantages. The short video clips of the Italian countryside and his texts were filled with romance and humor.

Her phone pinged. It was Nick.

Have a delightful time at Institute.

Touched that he'd remembered her schedule, she texted back. *Thanks. What are we doing tomorrow?*

It's a surprise. I know how you love them.:)

Catherine rolled her eyes and dropped her phone inside her bag.

Pulling her can of mace from her pocket, she glanced around the chapel parking lot to make sure all was clear before she went inside the building. Jack and Nick would have a fit if they knew she'd driven by herself.

A university student sat at the piano, playing prelude music. Catherine greeted their instructor, a CES missionary from Utah, and found a seat. She opened her LDS mobile app to the lesson as a trickle of young single adults came into the classroom. The YSAs were from all over the UK and Europe. Most were uni students.

Martin dropped into the seat beside her. "Sorry I couldn't give you a lift tonight. The seminar ran late."

"It's totally fine," she whispered as the class president called on someone to say the opening prayer.

"I found something in the diary," Martin whispered back.

A stocky, redheaded guy went to the front of the room to offer the invocation, but Martin's words distracted Catherine from the prayer.

"What did you find?" she whispered when the last amen was uttered.

"You have to wait until after class." His eyes twinkled as he opened his cell phone to the Gospel Library.

"That's just wrong." Catherine scowled at him. Martin had given her a lift to Institute the last few weeks. She loosely considered him a friend, despite the exorbitant amount Oxford University was charging her for the diary.

The lesson tonight focused on the new and everlasting covenant of marriage. Catherine wanted to groan. Even though she had never broadcasted her relationship with Nick, she knew at least half the YSAs were aware of it. After the gala, photos of Nick and her had featured heavily in the London papers. She guessed their instructor had received the memo.

Hoping this lesson was not a result of those photographs, she determined not to take it as such. None of the remarks from the singles was pointed or judgmental. By their comments, she realized, many of her contemporaries dated nonmembers due to the small member dating pool available.

One girl seemed more verbal than the rest. She raised her hand in response to a question. "I never set out to fall in love. He was my friend. We hung out a lot. Before I realized it, we were in love, the kind you marry for."

"Why did you allow that to happen in the first place?" the CES missionary asked.

Catherine ducked her head, fiddling with her phone, but her attention was riveted on the girl and her comments. Even in Virginia, the dating pool was larger than Europe's. The instructor had obviously been raised in the western US with a large population of members to choose from.

"When someone has never been in love, they assume they have control over the situation. It took me by complete surprise," the girl answered calmly.

"What did you do?" their instructor asked.

"I realized our relationship involved more than the two of us. Our future children would not be born in the covenant. If anything happened to either of us, we would not be an eternal unit. Therefore, our children would essentially be eternal orphans."

Until now, Catherine had considered only her relationship with Nick as a couple, not as a family unit. At some point, her love for him had her willing to consider marriage. The reality of children born to their union without the sealing ordinance of the temple hit her with unusual force. She envisioned her future offspring, little boys with Nick's bright-blue eyes and bent for mischief and a daughter with her curls. Her children deserved better. They deserved the sealing power.

As those thoughts entered her mind, warmth seeped into her, enveloping her body. Her heart raced high in her chest as she was encircled about with heavenly love.

She had felt the manifestation of the Holy Spirit many times throughout her life, but never had it testified with such power of the importance of this sacred covenant. This was Heavenly Father's plan, and He wanted this for her.

The ramifications overwhelmed her. Her heart split open and broke on the Institute floor. A knot filled the base of her throat, obstructing air.

She argued with herself on Nick's behalf. He attended and donated financially to the local parish. He provided jobs for the community. He helped anyone in need, stranger or friend.

None of the single guys she had dated cared about others the way Nick did. Certainly that stood for something. How could she bring herself to destroy what felt so right? The thought of spending eternity with someone else made her physically ill.

After the benediction, she shoved her cell inside her tote with shaky fingers. The instructor looked her way with a determined expression. Catherine didn't need a personal lecture, not with the knot in her throat threatening to breach the dam of tears. She had to get out of there.

She rose from her seat, but a group of YSAs had congregated at the end of her row, blocking the exit. Turning in the opposite direction, she prepared to squeeze past Martin. The hard knot of grief rose. Her knees wobbled.

"Don't you want to know what I discovered?" Martin touched her arm.

"I've got to get back." Catherine forced a smile. "I'll call you later."

Martin studied her face. At his nod, she slipped out of class and hurried down the hall. She made it to the foyer before the first tear slipped down her face.

CHAPTER THIRTY-TWO

Nick spread the rug on the damp grass beside the wooden picnic hamper. The sun shone brightly and evaporated the last of the morning dew. Overhead, branches of the priory's chestnut tree swayed in the breeze. Ripples of excitement jigged through his stomach like a champion cèilidh dancer, making him wish he hadn't eaten such a hearty breakfast. Even now, five hours later, Nick doubted he could swallow a morsel.

Out of habit, he fingered the carved initials of the fourth earl on the ancient trunk. Smiling, he slipped his hand inside his trouser pocket and touched the ring Garrard's had delivered that morning. Another blast of excitement ripped through him. In a few short months, Catherine would need to call upon her tree-climbing skills.

He hoped he wouldn't bungle the proposal he'd rehearsed and come off like a hasty school boy. His peers would think he had rushed into marriage, but he knew in his bones this was right. He had never felt so strongly about anything.

The sun beat down, and the air stirred, carrying the scent of newly cut hay. Nick savored the moment. This was a day he wanted to remember for the rest of his life.

He glanced at the time and groaned. Only three minutes had passed. At this rate, he would be all to bits before Catherine arrived.

Disgusted with himself, he flipped the lid off the hamper. Despite his and Catherine's nonalcoholic proclivity, he refused to propose without a proper toast. Knowing her American preference for cold beverages, he dumped ice into the engraved bucket and set the sparkling cider to cool.

The breeze kicked up, and low-lying clouds scudded across the sky. By the look of things, there would be rain by late afternoon.

He checked his watch, then shaded his eyes, gazing across the field toward the priory. What was keeping Catherine? This wasn't like her. He began to pace.

Pausing, he picked up a stone and chucked it, watching it bounce across the meadow. He checked his watch again. Where was she? Worry for her well-being set in. With Davenport off the case, anything could have happened. Pulling out his mobile, his finger hovered over her number, but before he could press it, her golden-brown curls, shining like a halo, topped the rise.

He let out a pent-up breath and waved a greeting. Shoving his hands inside his trouser pocket, he touched the ring like a talisman. Its tangible presence steadied him, keeping his nerves at bay. He dropped on his haunches and set out their picnic.

From his peripheral view, he saw Catherine's boots stop a few paces from the edge of the plaid rug. She was quiet so long Nick glanced up. One look at her face and everything inside him froze.

Purple circles stood out like bruises under her eyes. Her cheeks were devoid of color. When he made eye contact with her, she flinched and looked away.

"What's wrong?" He jumped to his feet.

"I can't do this." Catherine's arm made a fluid sweep toward the picnic.

"Come again?" He glanced from her to the picnic in confusion.

"I can't see you romantically." Her shoulders hunched in on herself.

He closed his eyes for a moment, trying to settle the mass of confusion circling inside his mind. Her words made no sense. Even though they had never spoken the words, he knew Catherine loved him.

Obviously, something had upset her. Had another attempt been made on her? It would be just like Catherine to withhold that information to protect him from anything distasteful.

"May I inquire as to what brought this on?" He touched her chin, but Catherine wouldn't meet his eyes. He shoved his hands inside his pockets and balled them into fists.

"We need to stop seeing each other before things get carried away." She turned, staring across the fields.

Her words were a knife thrust to the heart. *Carried away? Brilliant.* He fingered the £40,000 engagement ring in his trouser pocket and stared at her, unable to move or think. The searing pain almost bent him double.

Then he saw the tear. It crept down her face, stopping on her chin, where it hovered, then fell, marking her blouse.

"What brought this on?" he asked with a calm he did not possess. "Do you think this is a summer flirtation?"

Catherine's lips trembled, and she swallowed with a shudder. She shook her head. The wind caught her long, loose curls. With trembling fingers, she tucked the wayward strands behind her ear.

Was she going to make him puzzle it out by himself, or would she take pity on him and explain? Until a moment ago, he had seen them as two halves of the same whole. They completed each other. Something must have frightened her. Nothing else made sense.

"I'll hire a protection officer to keep you safe. I won't let anything happen to you again."

Her curls swung forward, and she hid behind their protective screen. His heart sank; she hadn't done that since the first few days he had known her. A hard and heavy fear began to gnaw at his defenses.

"My decision isn't about my safety or thinking this is a summer romance. It's about the difference in our core beliefs." She bowed her head, pressing her fingers to her temples. She took a deep breath and squared her shoulders as if preparing for battle.

"What core beliefs?" Confusion scattered his thoughts.

"What matters most to me isn't the same for you."

Struggling to maintain control, Nick reached for her hands.

Catherine stepped back.

His hands dropped empty to his side. "Enlighten me," he bit out through gritted teeth.

"Religion."

His stomach plunged somewhere near his knees, and his chest tightened as though a metal vice had clamped around it and squeezed. Catherine had brought up religion more than a few times over the last several months. He had purposely sidestepped her attempts. More fool him.

"Is this about me not spending as much time in church as Latter-day Saints do? We have a paid clergy to minister our church affairs."

Two indentations furrowed above her nose, and the corner of her mouth turned down. Another tear spilled over, running alongside the crevice of her nose. Nick had never been overly fond of tears. Catherine's tears unmanned him, but she wasn't like the women from his past. Never once had she used them for personal gain. If there was any hypocrisy in her, he had yet to discover it. He adored everything about her; there wasn't one thing he would change.

"I love you, Catherine," he whispered. With a reverent finger, he wiped the errant tear.

"I love you too." The tear multiplied into a waterfall, streaming down her cheeks, while her eyes looked dead and hopeless.

"But you are going to end this, aren't you?"

She bent her head, and the wall of curls fell forward.

"If this is about religion, I'll join your church." That decision would cause a bit of an upheaval in the local parish. Four hundred years of Davidsons had supported St. Sebastian's financially, but Catherine was worth any sacrifice.

"I don't want you to join my church to make me happy. Your heart wouldn't be in it."

Then what was she driving at? He had offered to fix the issue, and she had turned him down? He rubbed the back of his neck, utterly confused.

"I don't think you understand what I'm trying to say." Catherine waved her hand in that graceful movement that so fascinated him.

"Then by all means, elucidate." Temper licked through his words. With effort, he squelched it down.

A gust of wind sent a spray of yellowed leaves flying off the chestnut tree. One of them tangled in her curls. Nick plucked it out, his fingers lingering on the silky texture. He longed to bury his face in her hair and pretend this conversation didn't exist.

"Regardless of your weekly church attendance, I don't sense God factoring into the everyday aspects of your life." He closed his eyes, trying to keep a lid on his frustration. When he opened them, she was biting her bottom lip, a sure sign of upset. She was holding something back. Before he could call her on it, she continued. "Our differing religious views would affect how we raise our children and would eventually divide us."

Nick stepped close, the toes of his shoes touching her boots. He needed her to focus on their relationship, not religion. If she could, everything would work out. "I do not understand why you are choosing to walk away from what we have together. I love you more than my own life. It's as if my soul knows yours."

"I believe that too," she whispered. Her countenance brightened, and the light in her eyes burned with hope.

When he had seen the light in her eyes that first night at the pub, everything in his life had snapped into place. Had God thrown them together? He didn't know, nor did he wish to think about it. It was too painful. He needed to focus on Catherine, then sort out the rest. This certainly wasn't the time to delve into his hang-up.

"Ending our relationship makes no sense, Catherine."

The momentary flare of light in her eyes snuffed out. The palpable silence between them lengthened. A gust of wind ruffled her hair. She had never looked more beautiful or unobtainable.

"You are going to walk away from this? From us?" His voice sounded hoarse. This day that had dawned with such happy anticipation had become a nightmare. Catherine found him lacking in an area he could neither fathom nor fix.

"Things can't work the way they stand." Her face twisted with grief, and she sobbed. "You mean the world to me, but God comes first and always will. I'm so desperately sorry, Nick."

"So you are going to flip a switch and walk away? I have news for you, Catherine; what we have is rare." A gust of wind whipped at the edge of the rug. In agony, Nick watched her guardedly as the tears rained down her face. Unable to restrain himself, he pulled her into his arms. Catherine came woodenly.

His lips descended on hers with a ferocity he had always held in check. He let her taste his frustration and longing, pouring all of himself into one brief moment.

She clung to him, returning kiss for kiss. He could feel her shudders and taste the salt of her tears.

"Catherine, please don't do this," he rasped. Nick buried his face in her hair, breathing in her scent, sensing his kisses had changed nothing.

"In my religion, when two people marry in one of our temples, that marriage does not end at death. It continues into the eternities." She eased back, her eyes full of heartbreak.

Nick pulled a handkerchief out of his pocket and wiped her face with unsteady fingers. He watched her inhale the smell of the freshly laundered fabric.

"Even though my mother is no longer living, my parents have that kind of marriage. They have the assurance that their love will endure forever." Her breath hitched. "My heart will always love you, Nicholas Davidson. There will never be anyone for me but you. But my love for you wants a forever after. And my future children deserve a forever family. As much as I love you, this can't work. What I'm asking isn't fair to you, and it isn't fair to me. This has to end before we hurt each other even more than it hurts us now."

Gently, she disengaged herself from his arms and turned, walking away from him across the field.

Nick watched her go until she disappeared over the rise, all the while fingering his damp handkerchief. This was not happening. She would come running over that swale any minute.

But she didn't.

* * *

Locked inside the safety of her room, Catherine climbed under the covers. She stared at the patch of sunlight on the floor. If she lived to be a thousand, she would never forget the look on Nick's face when she'd left him under the chestnut tree.

Nick.

Her heart broke on the word. He was not the only one who had shattered under that tree. Catherine had given him her whole heart. And she knew she would never get it back.

Grief gnawed, relentless and uncaring, tearing at her every breath. The vibrancy of her future had drained like a color portrait washed in sepia.

Catherine shook herself. If there was one thing she loathed, it was self-pity, especially when her misery could be laid squarely on her own shoulders. She should have listened to Jack, but she had fallen in love with Nick before she'd realized how deep it was.

Pressure built behind her eyes. Blinking, she willed herself to hold back the tide. No matter how hard she fought, her tears breached her inner core, cracking its fortifications and pouring down her face.

Wrapping her arms around her knees, great wracking sobs beat against her ribs. She wept until there were no tears left and the dismal, gray light of dawn filtered through her bedroom curtains. Spent at last, she allowed sleep to wrap its tentacles around her and pull her under.

A persistent knocking woke her.

"Catherine, are you all right?" Jack poked his head inside her bedroom door, then flipped on the overhead light.

She glanced in his direction, her swollen eyes squinting from the light. Jack must be on his way to work. She heard him cross the room and felt him touch her shoulder.

"Are you sick?" Her brother's image floated above her bed.

She moaned as another set of knifelike jabs attacked her stomach.

"Catherine?" Jack bent close.

She smelled the minty toothpaste on his breath and turned away, burrowing deeper under the quilt. The movement made the room swing. She splayed one hand against her mattress to steady herself against the motion.

"You're ice cold."

"I'm all right. I'm just a little tired." Her body ached, and sleep beckoned like the comfort of a mother's arms.

"Have you had anything to drink?" Jack jostled her shoulder.

"I don't remember." Her lips stuck to her gums, and her heart fluttered like a trapped bird.

She dozed.

The next thing she knew, Jack was back with a glass and a towel. The mattress dipped under her brother's weight. Placing an arm under her shoulders, Jack lifted her upper torso to a sitting position. The thick quilt she had tucked around her shoulders slipped to her waist. She shivered. The room spun, and spasms stabbed her stomach.

"Drink this. You don't want to dehydrate."

"I'm fine." She closed her eyes and inhaled a jittery breath.

"Don't be ridiculous." Jack pushed a glass against her mouth. "Drink up, or I'll plug your nose."

"Go away." She tried to push the cup aside.

"Nope. Not until you drink the entire thing."

She opened her eyes and stared at him. His jaw had hardened; she knew that look well. Jack wouldn't give up. He was a Pressley-Coombes. They were the most ornery people on earth once they got something inside their stupid heads . . . Like breaking up with the most wonderful man in the world.

The fire-hydrant pressure built behind her stinging eyes, but no tears came. Why wouldn't Jack leave her alone to grieve in private? Hollowed out like an empty drum and too tired to fight her brother, she longed for the sweet oblivion of sleep.

"Bottoms up," he said and tipped the glass.

Unprepared, she choked on the sticky electrolytes. A good bit of it spilled down the front of her neck.

"Sorry." Jack mopped her up with the towel and forced the rest of the orange-flavored contents down her throat.

Finished at last, she curled up under her quilt. The light clicked off, and her brother disappeared, leaving her in blessed peace.

A gentle warmth crept over her, and she drifted to that woozy place just before sleep. The light switch clicked back on. Jack had returned, bearing a heavy quilt. He spread it over her, its added weight pressing her into the mattress. She knew for a fact there were no extra blankets in the cottage.

"Are you sick, or has something upset you?" Jack pushed the hair from her face. His eyes were filled with concern.

Catherine stared at him. If she told Jack she had broken with Nick, he'd voice his satisfaction. She couldn't bear it. Not now. Maybe never.

Rolling over, she closed her eyes and blocked him out.

When next she woke, it was dark and rain poured in rivulets down the window panes. Weakly, she rose on wobbly legs and went to the bathroom. Her head pounded against the inside of her skull like a jackhammer. The room lurched, and her stomach churned. Breaking into a cold sweat, she returned to bed and tugged at the covers, wondering if she was ill.

All she could think about was Nick: his blue eyes twinkling with laughter, the strong lines of his face and square jaw, and the sensitive mouth that curved with easy humor.

She wanted him. She yearned for him. And she could not have him.

A deep wave of grief washed over her, pulling her under. When it receded, she stared, exhausted, at the whitewashed walls and prayed for the nirvana of sleep.

* * *

The concert pianist repeated Tchaikivsky's "Dance of the Clowns" on the grand piano in Madame's ballet studio. Standing in the middle of a trio of dancers, Catherine hung her head. She brushed her toe shoes against the wood floor and waited for the inevitable stream of French from her instructor.

"Mademoiselle Catherine?"

"*Oui*, madame?"

"Have you quite finished daydreaming?"

Catherine swallowed and nodded.

"*Bien*. I want a second position plié with the weight on the front foot between the preparation and the retiré post in that last set of pirouettes en pointe."

"Oui, madame."

The music began, but the piano seemed far away, moving down a long tunnel where she could not follow. Her toe shoes were no longer on her feet but were nailed to the wall of her bedroom, high above her head. She jumped and jumped to reach them but could not. The loss of her dance shoes filled her with despair.

"Wake up. You have to wake up."

Surfacing from the dream, Catherine heard the desperation in her brother's voice and vaguely wondered what had upset him.

"Drink this." Jack held a pitcher of colored liquid.

She'd be lucky to get one swallow down.

Propping her up, Jack tried to pour the foul brew down her throat. She locked her jaw.

"You're running a fever," he said.

Why was Jack making such a big deal about this? So what if she was a little warm. It felt good after freezing all night. She stared at him numbly.

"You need to see a doctor." Jack marched out of the room.

Presently, she heard his voice in the hallway outside her door. "Your website says you make house calls. Jack Pressley-Coombes. We're in Bascombe at Hawthorne Cottage on Welles Road. I think my sister is severely dehydrated."

"No, I'm not a doctor, but she used to pull this stunt when she was a kid." The tread on squeaky boards filled the quiet. Step. Step. Squeak. Step. Step. Squeak. Jack stopped and checked on her through the open doorway.

Catherine closed her eyes and drifted back to sleep.

* * *

A bee stung Catherine's hand, waking her. "Ouch."

"Sorry, dearie." Cool hands picked up her wrist. "Her pulse is erratic."

Catherine squinted at the blurred image above her bed. A stocky woman in a nurse's uniform took her pulse.

"We'll have you right as rain in no time." The nurse beamed at her with a gap between her front teeth.

With complete disinterest, Catherine watched as the nurse hooked the tubing to an IV bag and started a drip line.

* * *

Trills of early-morning birdsong woke Catherine. Dust glittered and danced in the sunlight, streaking through the opening in her bedroom curtains. The nurse had gone, taking her IV with her. The only evidence of her visit was the square bandage taped to the back of Catherine's hand.

Jack lay asleep on the plush carpet, rolled up like a cocoon inside a sheet from his bed.

Swinging her legs over the side of the air mattress, she stood up and made her way to the bathroom, using the wall for support. Turning on the tap, Catherine glanced in the mirror. A cadaver going five rounds with Chuck the Rock had better color.

Leaning against the countertop, she splashed cold water on her face and neck, then toweled dry. Grabbing her toothbrush, she liberally applied it with paste and plunged it into her mouth.

Then she remembered.

She leaned against the sink and stared at the wreck of her former self in the glass. Pain seared through her like she had swallowed battery acid. She didn't know how to go on. She felt dead inside.

Regardless of how bleak her future appeared, she was done crying. Tears solved nothing. She squared her shoulders. She knew healing would come if she forgot herself. There were always people in much more dire circumstances. With a determined lift of her chin, she pulled her tangled mop into a ponytail. Her arms shook from the effort.

Opening the door, she noticed a dark shadow move in the semidarkness. She tried to scream. Her voice wheezed out breathless and frayed. Staggering back, she yanked at the shower rod, hoping to use it as a weapon. It didn't budge.

"It's me!" her bleary-eyed brother bellowed.

"Sheesh, Jack. You scared me to death." Her arms dropped to her sides. With a thud, she sat on the edge of the porcelain bathtub.

"I wanted to make sure you could make it back to bed," Jack said.

"Oh," she croaked, drawing an unsteady breath.

Jack pulled her to her feet and helped her back to her room. She was pretty sure she could make it on her own, but Jack obviously needed to help her.

A lapwing sunned itself on her windowsill, its iridescent green and purple plumage shimmering in the light. Catherine sat on the side of the bed, her eyes on the bird. "I need to change. Can you give me a minute?"

"Sure." Jack closed the door behind him.

The fresh underwear and nightgown smelled of fabric softener and did much to improve her psyche. Trembling, she climbed into bed, dreading Jack's twenty questions.

"I'm decent," she called.

Jack entered, holding an electrolyte drink in his hand. "The nurse says you have to drink five of these a day."

"I'll drown if I do."

He beamed at her as though she'd said something clever. "You were really sick."

"I'm sorry."

"You were out of it for four days."

"Four?" Her voice squeaked.

"As in days. You scared the crud out of me, Catherine." He handed her the drink.

"Sorry. Can we talk later? I'm really tired." Catherine put the drink on the floor beside her mattress. Pulling her blankets up to her chin, she closed her eyes.

She could feel him watching her, but to her relief, he left the room. Opening her eyes, she stared at the now-empty sill; the lapwing had gone.

CHAPTER THIRTY-THREE

CATHERINE FOCUSED ON THE COMPUTER screen, trying to block out her brother's drumming fingers on the pub table. She was well aware that Jack would rather be home watching a ballgame. Instead, he had chosen to accompany her to the pub with the idea of acting as Davenport's replacement while she met with Martin to find out what he had discovered in Glorianne's diary.

"You've always been a beanpole, but a good wind could knock you down," Jack observed, leaning back in his chair.

"Is there a reason for your flattering remark?" Catherine looked up from her laptop.

Jack liked to state facts, but she had to give it to him, he had never once mentioned Nick. There was no way her obtuse brother had missed her lack of attention by Bascombe's local aristocrat.

Since their split and her recovery, her mother's quest had proven a lifeline. Catherine had recently located a collection of online wills through London's National Archives, predating 1858. Her name search had culled one hundred thirty-seven Glorianne's living in Oxfordshire during the last quarter of the eighteenth century. Without a surname, she could only guess, but it gave her focus during the wee hours when sleep often eluded her.

Tonight was her first foray into village society since the breakup. In a town the size of Bascombe, she knew a chance encounter with Nick was likely. She hoped he would not approach her. Catherine doubted she would survive the emotional fallout.

Through the smoky haze of the pub's interior, she saw Martin enter. She shut down her computer and packed it away. Martin's fair coloring and boyish features hid the fact that his hair was starting to thin. His buttoned-up v-neck sweater and plaid collared shirt fairly screamed academia.

He beelined it to their bistro-sized table. Jack removed his coat from the spare seat closest to him and lowered all four legs of his chair. Martin's eyes bugged when he caught sight of her. Never a smooth operator, his mouth hung open, and she could see a breath mint dissolving on his tongue.

Catherine knew she was a pale ghost of herself. Her clothes hung like a sack, and no amount of cosmetics could hide the dark circles under her eyes. Her long, golden-brown curls fell dull and limp down her back.

"Catherine. Jack," Martin greeted, still staring.

"Have a seat, Martin." Jack offered the age-old chin thrust men used to acknowledge one another. With his foot, Jack pushed the farthest chair from Catherine in Martin's direction.

He sat. His poleaxed expression made Catherine turn to her brother with raised brows.

"So, Martin, what are you having tonight?" Laughter sparkled in Jack's warm-brown eyes.

"Ahh." Martin tore his gaze from her. With great deliberation, he considered his options. After making his selection, he and Jack went to the counter to order.

Marcus Johnston caught sight of their party from the grill and accompanied the men back to their table, his round, florid face wreathed in smiles.

"I heard you were sick, Miss Catherine. I'm glad to see you are up and about." Marcus squeezed her shoulder before moving to the next table.

His kindness made Catherine's eyes sting.

Martin might be awkward around females, but he wasn't oblivious. Catherine's continued silence prompted him to carry the conversation while they waited for their food. His topic of choice, a manuscript from the fifteenth century. Jack was doing his level best to appear interested.

While Martin droned on, Catherine had nothing to do but notice the hostile glares cast her way by some of the locals. The village drums had been at work, banging out the news of her breakup with its most famous son.

Ducking her head, she fingered the dings on the battered tabletop. She could hardly blame the villagers for closing ranks.

Their meal number flashed over the pick-up counter, and the men went to retrieve their food. For the next half hour, Catherine pushed her vegetables around her plate in an effort to avoid the judgmental glares.

"How's Glorianne's diary coming along?" Jack finally started the conversation for which they had gathered.

Catherine felt a little spurt of surprise. Since when did Jack care about her quest?

"Slowly. I told you about the break-in at Professor McKellan's office. Most things are sorted and back in place. I've been able to make some headway on the first few entries." Waving his fork for emphasis, Martin leaned forward. "Your ancestress was a most unusual female."

"She must be for someone in our century to be after her diary," Catherine said.

Martin did a double-take. "Who's after it?"

"We don't know, but Professor McKellan's office was ransacked within days after I delivered it to him. Jack's cottage was broken into shortly thereafter." Catherine glanced at her brother.

Jack nodded in agreement.

"When was this?" Martin asked.

"Almost a week ago," Jack said.

"How do you know it wasn't a vandal or thief?" Martin sounded skeptical.

"Nothing was taken from the cottage. A thief could easily have fenced a number of high-end items. None of them was touched. The diary was the only thing I brought to England that wasn't inside the cottage." Catherine supposed questioning her theory was normal for a professor, but it rankled that Martin wasn't more open to the idea.

The pupils inside Martin's eyes dilated a smidge.

"That's when I remembered Professor McKellan's office was trashed a few days after you acquired the diary." Catherine had Martin's full attention.

"Then we're lucky I took it home the night Professor McKellan's office was vandalized." Martin mulled this over before he asked, "You believe the two break-ins are connected?"

"I do. What could be so important about a servant's diary?" Catherine met his eyes squarely.

"Whatever gave you the idea Glorianne was a servant?" Martin accidentally brushed against her hand.

"Why would she have gone to America by herself at fifteen if she weren't some type of indentured servant?" Catherine challenged.

"Several clues contradict your assumption."

"Such as?" Jack straightened, showing interest.

"In the late eighteenth century, most people owned one change of clothing." Martin's eyes lit with passion at his topic. "When they traveled, a carpet bag could hold all their belongings. If they possessed a trunk, it suggested a certain affluence.

"Within the first few pages of Glorianne's diary, she mentions riding to Bristol in her father's carriage, accompanied by her personal maid and several outriders. Their conveyance was followed by a wagon." Martin paused, his finger stroking Catherine's arm.

Alarm bells went off inside Catherine's head. That was the second time Martin had touched her in as many minutes. She moved her arm out of his proximity.

"Only those of high rank kept carriages and servants. The wagon in their entourage contained eight trunks, all filled with her personal belongings." If Martin noticed her withdrawal, he did not show it.

"You're saying Glorianne was . . . ?" Catherine let it hang in the air.

"Not of the servant class." Martin picked up the water carafe and topped off her glass.

With an internal groan, Catherine tried not to frown. What she had viewed as an uncomplicated friendship, Martin appeared to have interpreted differently.

"Have you discovered her surname?" Jack's dimple deepened. He hadn't missed the byplay.

"Not yet. One entry mentioned her father had exiled her to the colonies because she had insulted the young man he intended her to marry. Her behavior ended those negotiations."

"Weren't arranged marriages a common occurrence in the eighteenth century?" Catherine asked.

"Depending on one's social station, yes. The higher the rank, the more common it was. Glorianne's birth places her among the gentry or wealthy merchant class."

"I wonder who she objected to?" Jack chuckled.

"It must have been a powerful alliance to have angered her father enough to banish her across an ocean. Glorianne was quite headstrong for a female of her time." Martin fiddled with a packet of mint sauce inside the condiment tray.

Involved in Martin's tale, Catherine almost fainted when Nick's voice said, "Good evening, Catherine. Jack."

Heat rushed into her face when she met his gaze. There was a strained look around Nick's eyes, as though the skin was drawn tight. His square jaw appeared clenched, and his well-sculpted lips were unsmiling.

"Nick." Jack responded with a nod.

Nick looked pointedly at Martin.

"Martin Giles." Jack made the introductions.

"Professor Giles." Martin stood to shake the proffered hand, correcting Jack with a supercilious tilt of the head.

"Lord Ainsley," Nick said in a cool tone Catherine had never heard him use.

There was an incremental pause on Martin's part before the clasping of hands. Martin returned to his seat with heightened color. Catherine could not have spoken if she'd tried. Jack lounged in his chair, a toothpick stuck between his teeth and an amused expression on his face.

When Nick had appeared, Catherine's eyes had locked on him, refusing to tear away during the introductions. Her soul tugged against its constraints, yearning for what it had lost.

"I heard you were ill, Catherine. I'm happy to see you have recovered." Nick touched her arm tentatively, his features softening when he met her gaze.

"Thank you." She trembled at his touch.

"Whatever bug Catherine picked up must be making the rounds. It appears you had a slight bout with it as well," Jack observed in a subdued tone.

"You would be right." With one lingering look at Catherine, Nick moved off to order his meal. Later, he took up a game of darts with Charlie and a few other men across the room.

When Catherine rose to leave, several people met her eye, offering her sheepish smiles. It dawned on her what Nick's visit to their table had accomplished. Despite her rejection, he had swooped in on his white charger to rescue her from village ostracism.

With a catch in her throat, she let Jack help her on with her jacket. He tossed her backpack with her laptop over his shoulder. Catherine felt Nick's eyes boring into her back as their party left the pub. Everything inside her screamed to take him back. Instead, she went out into the darkness, where the cool night wind blasted down her neck and chilled her skin.

They crossed the graveled lot and came to a halt on the pavement.

"I've a train to catch. I assure you, our office will be vigilant in keeping your diary safe." Martin zipped up his fleece.

"Thank you, Martin." Catherine took her brother's arm, ready to head for the cottage.

Martin's gaze skimmed the lot, then swung back to her. "Catherine, could I offer you a lift to Institute this week?"

"I'll be out of town," she said. After Martin's unwanted attentions, she was thankful her trip to the Highlands with Gillian had arrived.

"I'll be in touch, then." Disappointment flitted across his face. He shook Jack's hand and headed for the train station.

A brisk gust caught Catherine's thin jacket, billowing it out like a stuffed mushroom. She found the physical sensation invigorating. Lifting her face to the night sky, she pushed the strain and the undercurrents of the evening aside and watched the stars flicker overhead.

"I wasn't hallucinating tonight, was I? A few of your comments supported Mom's quest."

"After all my snotty remarks over the years, it is pretty funny, isn't it?" Jack gave her a wry grin.

"More like miraculous. What brought about the change?"

"I think it was Glorianne's eight trunks."

Catherine giggled.

"That and I didn't like having our house broken into. I know you're right about the vandals, which means there's more to that diary than the ramblings of a fifteen-year-old-girl." Jack tucked his chin inside the opening of his sweater.

They walked in silence, accompanied by an occasional gust of wind and the twinkle of a million stars. Letting go of Jack's arm, Catherine gathered her mass of curls and shoved them inside her jacket.

"He looks almost as bad as you do." Her brother didn't identify whom he meant. He didn't need to.

"Not here. Not now."

"I disagree." Jack took her arm and pulled her to a halt, then continued in a gentler tone, "I know I never supported your dating Nick, but last night, Dad shared a few quirky things about Mom's side of the family. I need to ask you a few questions."

"I won't discuss Nick with you."

"You haven't changed much since you were a kid. Do you know that, Catherine? Even when we were little, you never shared anything with me unless I cornered you." Her brother threw his hands in the air.

"This subject is off limits."

"I can't bear to see you like this. That's why I called Dad." Jack leveled his eyes with hers.

"You told Dad?" She gritted her teeth.

He nodded and wrapped his arm around her shoulders in a vicelike grip, propelling her down the sidewalk.

She gulped in air and wondered if counting to a thousand would help, because reaching ten wasn't anywhere close enough to her calming down. Why did Jack think he had a right to meddle in her personal life?

The answer to that was simple. He loved her, and being closer in age, Jack had taken more of an interest in her than the twins. Her bad humor eased marginally.

"According to Dad, Mom's side of the family has a genetic defect. It goes way up her family tree."

Catherine frowned. She'd never heard this before. Maybe she hadn't been paying attention.

"Mom's family starts through life healthy enough, but sometime in their twenties, they develop a heart condition."

Suspicious, she glanced at him out of the corner of her eye.

"They meet someone and fall in love. Really hard. If their affection isn't reciprocated, they don't marry. I assume that's why there are so few of Mom's people left."

"Come on, Jack. That's ridiculous."

"I thought so too until Dad gave a few examples."

Catherine rolled her eyes, but a little tremor of fear settled in the pit of her stomach. What if the hokey thing were true?

"The twins date all the time and have never been in love."

"That's because no girl in her right mind would have either of them," Catherine muttered under her breath.

"True." By the light of the street lamp, she saw Jack's smile flash briefly. "Look, Catherine. I'm really sorry I teased you about your boyfriends when you first arrived. It's hard to believe you don't have a dozen guys after you."

Catherine gave an inelegant snort.

He let out a long sigh.

"No one ever captured my interest before." Talking like this was always awkward between them. Her mind churned, rejecting and assessing his words.

Jack nodded as though she had confirmed something. "I've never seen two people crazier about each other than you and Ainsley."

She and Nick were rarely demonstrative in public.

"I'm not talking PDA." Jack correctly interpreted her expression. "The two of you light up like Christmas trees when you're in the same room."

"We do not."

"It's kind of hard to miss. When Nick visited our table, no one else existed while the two of you made googley eyes at each other. Martin went home pretty disappointed."

The heat of a blush rose up her neck.

"The entire village knows about the split, but Nick made sure everyone knows he bears you no ill will. In another time and place, he would have drawn his sword and shielded you from censure. That's real love, Catherine." Jack glanced at her.

Catherine bit her lip and drew a shaky breath. Nick had told her he loved her more than his own life. That his soul knew hers. She doubted any other man would ever love her like that.

"Why did it end?"

"You are so not asking me that. Who was the one who hounded me about not dating a person not of our faith?" Catherine mimicked his tone. "'He's not a member. He can't take you to the temple.'"

"I did do that, didn't I?" Jack's expression was rueful.

"Yes."

"I'm sorry."

"You're sorry?" Her voice cracked on the words, the anger seeping out through the fissures. They continued toward the cottage as her frustration dissolved.

"You were right." Catherine's sense of fair play got the better of her.

"*You* ended it?"

She nodded.

"Did you ever discuss religion with him?"

"Every time I mentioned it, Nick deflected or changed the subject."

"So you gave up?" Jack didn't bother to hide his surprise. When it came to the gospel, he knew no fear. He'd taught with boldness on his mission, and six years after his return from the Dominican Republic, he still turned in referrals on a regular basis.

"What was I supposed to do? Keep seeing him when every day I loved him more? Do you know what the lesson was in Institute the night before I cut things off? Eternal marriage. I got the message, Jack." Angry tears trickled down her face. She dashed them with the back of her hand. "I love him more than my own life, and I let him go."

Jack wrapped his brotherly arms around her. "I think you gave up on Nick too soon."

"I tried to talk to him about God. It went nowhere."

"How many times?" Jack dropped his arms and gave her a level stare.

"What do you mean, how many times? Come on, Jack. I'm not dense. He didn't want to talk about it."

"Did you ask him why?"

"No." She blinked.

"Is he worth fighting for?"

"He was willing to get baptized just to make me happy. Do you know how tempted I was to accept? Nick's family has been Church of England for four hundred years. He holds to tradition harder than you love race cars. I couldn't ask that of him unless he had a solid conviction that his decision was right."

"So you gave up and walked away."

She stared at him, her chest heaving with the effort it took not to yell. Shouting matches solved nothing.

"If I loved someone that much, I'd do a whole lot more than bring up God a few times. And I sure wouldn't back down when the person I loved didn't take the hint. Love is patient, Catherine. It's also persistent. You ran away."

Catherine clamped her teeth together and stormed through their front gate. Unlocking the door, she let herself in and raced up the stairs, slamming her bedroom door. It was childish. It was stupid. But it made her feel a whole lot better.

Deep inside, she knew Jack was right. She should have fought harder for Nick to listen. And now it was too late.

Jack's words had her tossing and turning in bed for hours.

When her cell phone rang at midnight with Agent Butler's name, she answered immediately.

"Miss Pressley-Coombes, Agent Butler here. Sorry for the late hour."

"Agent Butler." Her chest tightened, and she sat up in the darkened room.

"I believe we have apprehended your would-be abductor tonight. We caught him when he tried to board a plane for Morocco. I thought you'd want to know."

Her heart skipped a beat, stuttered, then pounded at a quicker pace.

His clipped words sounded no different than the first time they'd met. Perhaps he regretted pulling Davenport off protective detail, and this was his way of making it up to her. With Butler, it was impossible to tell.

"How did you find him?" She leaned her head against the wall above the air mattress.

"We've been monitoring a cell just outside of Oxford. His picture set off an alarm in our system."

"I'm so relieved. Thank you for the information."

"Think nothing of it." The phone clicked as he disconnected.

At 2:30 a.m., she gave up on sleep and reached for her cell phone.

CHAPTER THIRTY-FOUR

THEODOSIA'S FINGERS WERE NUMB FROM taking dictation. Just because Rivendon had quit smoking did not give him license to drive everyone mad. The brutal pace he had set to distract himself would tire a man half his age.

With a band of fire burning across her back from hunching over her steno pad, she straightened and asked politely, "Will there be anything else, my lord?"

Rivendon fumbled through a stack of papers. "I believe there are some—"

The peal of his private line interrupted him, and a look of eagerness crossed the wrinkled features as he contemplated the number on the caller ID. Placing a hand on the receiver, he said, "Why don't you take a short break, Lady Hadley. We shall reconvene at the quarter hour."

She did not need to be told twice. Quivering with curiosity, the heels of her Ferragamos sank into the plush pile of Axminster carpet on her way out of the library. Few people had access to Rivendon's private line. Which of them was the cause of such happy anticipation?

"Nicholas." Rivendon's voice boomed through the crack in the door.

Ainsley? Theodosia's antennae went on high alert. Turning, she made a quick survey of the empty foyer. Tiptoeing across the marble tiles, she reached the foyer phone. The red square button of Rivendon's private line flashed like an airport beacon, advertising the conversation taking place in the library.

Careful not to make a sound, she lifted the handle off its cradle and simultaneously hit mute. She glanced upstairs where the hall overlooked the main foyer. All clear.

Moving against the curve of the stairs, she placed her steno pad on the floor and shook out a few loose papers, letting them scatter where they may. Kneeling on the cool, gray-and-white marble, she hugged the phone to her ear. If Scott or one of the maids came along, she could collect her "dropped papers" with little concern of censure.

"How did your follow-up appointment go with Dr. Beauchamp?" Ainsley's baritone vibrated through the line.

"As well as can be expected. You didn't, by chance, tell him about my Havanas?"

Female voices sounded in the upstairs hall. Reluctant to hang up just yet, Theodosia clung to the phone, hoping the women would pass without detecting her.

The housekeeper and a maid stopped above, deep in conversation about which table linens needed pressing. Theodosia rolled her eyes. Table linens? If she was going to be caught eavesdropping, it certainly would not be over something as trivial as table linens.

She made as though to hang up, but the housekeeper concluded her business and moved off. The maid bustled in the opposite direction.

"What did he say?" Ainsley asked.

"To stop smoking them, of course, and lay off cook's creamed lobster bisque."

"Will you?" Ainsley's voice, though polite, sounded distracted, his good-natured bonhomie oddly absent.

"I smoked my last Cuban over a week ago. You were witness. But I warn you, Nicholas, Dr. Beauchamp will not dictate what I shall and shall not eat at this stage in life."

Ainsley made an exasperated sound.

"And what of you, my boy? Has an impending announcement been sent to the papers?" Suppressed excitement rang through Rivendon's words.

Theodosia's interest spiked. What announcement? What had she missed? The pause stretched so long, Theodosia thought the line had gone dead.

"No announcement. I entirely misread the situation," Ainsley said as though he'd held in his response until the words had festered, then spat them out with the force of a lanced wound.

"No, laddie, you did not." Rivendon's voice gentled. "That girl loves you."

"That may be, but not enough to overcome religious differences."

Theodosia's mouth opened in disbelief. Ainsley had proposed? It must be the American. She was the only one he had spent any time with recently.

What woman in her right mind would turn down a catch like Ainsley? He had a title, money, and connections. The American was stupider than Theodosia had imagined.

"Religion?"

"Unfortunately."

Theodosia fiddled with the telephone cord. Part of her was grateful she would not be responsible for destroying her cousin's happiness. Ainsley was a decent sort, and she did not wish him ill. He certainly could do better than Miss Pressley-Coombes.

With Ainsley's broken romance, his calls would no longer sprinkle tidbits of information about the American's movements. Doubtless Ari had a dubious connection or two that could spy on the girl. Idly, she wondered what he would charge. One thing could be said about Ari: he knew how to conduct business.

All things considered, Ainsley's disappointment was good news. With Theodosia's cousin out of the picture and the American's minder recalled to London, kidnapping Miss Pressley-Coombes would be easier than scooping a butterfly up with a net.

Theodosia disconnected the line. A smile lifted her mouth as she gathered her papers off the floor. A trip to Bascombe was long overdue, but this time she needn't stop at the priory.

CHAPTER THIRTY-FIVE

WITH A SHAKY FINGER, CATHERINE pressed speed dial on her cell phone. Her father deserved to hear Agent Butler's news. And she needed parental council, regardless of the five-hour time difference.

In the past, she'd always spoken to her mother about personal issues, but Mom wasn't there, and even if she were, Catherine would have asked to speak to her father anyway. She needed council, not sympathy. Sympathy had a tendency to break her down. What she needed was take-it-on-the-chin advice. For that, she needed her father's no-nonsense, straight talk.

After four rings, Catherine pulled the phone away from her ear to disconnect, when her father answered.

"How's my baby girl?"

"Did I catch you at a bad time?" Catherine wet her dry lips.

Her father's nightly ritual of barricading himself inside his home office until ten o'clock while he ran numbers on multimillion-dollar projects was sacrosanct. Her call had cut into the last half hour of number crunching.

"What's the matter?"

"Can we video chat? I need to see your face." Too much was riding on this conversation.

"This sounds serious."

"It is."

"Give me two minutes." He disconnected.

Catherine got out of bed, ran a brush through her hair, and threw on a robe, cinching it at the waist. Booting up her computer, she propped a pillow against the wall above the air mattress, then settled herself in her nest of blankets to wait for her father's call.

Her computer chimed with an incoming video. She swiped the icon with her finger, and the screen lit up her father's image. Sure enough, he was seated at his desk. The wall behind him displayed the boys' childhood trophies and several pictures of her in pink tutus.

Her dad's warm, chocolate-brown eyes, so similar to Jack's, looked weary. The crows' feet were more deeply etched than she remembered, and his once-dark hair was liberally sprinkled with gray.

"How are you, honey?" He noticeably took in the dark circles under her eyes and the unusual pallor of her skin. He frowned but thankfully didn't comment.

"Really good. INTERPOL's human trafficking unit called tonight." She was still weak with relief. "They apprehended the guy who tried to kidnap me."

The strain in her father's face eased. "That's a relief. I'd been considering asking you to bag the search and come home."

"Then it's a good thing they caught him. How are things at Coombes Enterprises?" Dad chaffed at chitchat, so she did her best to catch up on things first.

"Busy. The twins have landed a large project in Kansas City. I'm think-ing about appointing Ben head of that division and pulling James back to the East Coast. I need his expertise on several ventures I'm pursuing in the mid-Atlantic and overseas."

"What was their reaction to that?" Dad was going to separate the twins? The only time that had occurred was on their missions.

"I haven't spoken to them about it, but the business is growing faster than I can keep up with."

She didn't know how to respond.

"I know what you're thinking, Catherine. They're big boys and can handle the separation. I, for one, think it might help them evaluate their future on a more serious level."

"You could be right." Who was she to say?

"I spoke to Jack last night. Are you calling about that Englishman?" In his typical fashion, Dad got to the point.

That Englishman? Nick was so much more than that. He was her whole world. If Jack was right, did she and Nick stand a chance, or had she blown it? Catherine nodded, not trusting her voice. She didn't want to cry. If Dad probed too hard, she was very much afraid she might.

"Catherine?"

"Yeah?"

"I'm not very good at this sort of thing. I always left the emotional stuff to your mother." Dad glanced away, his distress obvious. He didn't like heavy, emotional conversations any more than she enjoyed baring her soul. But it couldn't be helped.

"I'm sure Jack filled you in about our conversation," he said after a pause.

"His version sounded a little farfetched." Catherine raised her brows, hoping this was a joke.

"I agree, and if I didn't know for a fact it was true, I'd mock it myself."

Dad was the most pragmatic, sane person she knew. If he had bought into the "love-only-once" family story, she was truly doomed.

"What am I going to do?" She smoothed the blanket on her knees.

"Do you love him?"

"Yes."

"Then why did you break up with him without sharing the gospel?" he asked.

"I tried."

"Jack wasn't convinced you had made a strong enough effort." Dad rubbed a hand along his jaw, where the salt-and-pepper stubble was starting to show at the end of a long day.

She felt herself bristle, then tamped it down. This was why she had called in the first place. Getting defensive would not help. "Nick's family has been Church of England for four hundred years. The local parish depends on his financial support."

"When men are violently in love, they want to please their women. Did you ever talk to him about the gospel? Even once?" Dad's expression softened.

"It never got that far."

"There are times men need a stiff knock upside the head to get their attention. By breaking up with him, you accomplished that."

Despite herself, Catherine smiled.

"In the case of your brothers, I'd say the women who gain their attention will need sledge hammers."

Her chuckle turned into a laugh, ringing with genuine mirth.

"At a guess, I'd say you've captured your Englishman's attention." Her father studied her for a minute. "When people marry, they must learn to discuss and work through issues as a team. There is no room for pride or fear in marriage. If two people truly love each another, they will find a way to work things through.

"If you never discussed the Church with this guy, you probably blind-sided him when you broke up. Being a man, he was probably more worried about losing you than why you were dumping him. Most men can't focus on two strong emotional subjects at a time. Each one is all-consuming, especially when the guy is young. Men are natural fixers. You presented him with an impossible task."

"What do I do? I'm not even sure he'll listen to me. I crushed him, Dad."

"Men who are deeply in love don't fall out of it in a few weeks. You'll find a way to reach him."

"You think so?"

"If he loves you, he's still yours."

Her father's words reassured her, but the reason for the break-up still existed. She didn't know how to share the gospel with Nick in a way that he would not feel pressured. Nick might view it as an ultimatum—"Join my church or else." Essentially, that was true. But she viewed this more as a last-ditch effort to save both of them from a lifetime of loneliness.

"It may take some time to patch things up. You need a plan."

"That sounds calculated."

"Sweetheart, do you think your Englishman got ahead in life flying by the seat of his pants? From what I hear, he's a force to be reckoned with. Men like that understand a strong campaign. You are going to need one to get him to focus on religion instead of getting you back."

She didn't agree, and it must have shown on her face.

"Catherine, this is a war, and you are fighting for your future happiness, and his."

For the first time in her life, Catherine realized her father's quintessential business strategies applied to general living conditions.

"Is there anything you can do to soften his heart enough to participate in the discussions?"

"I don't know. I doubt it." The late hour had caught up to her, and her brain was becoming sluggish. She rubbed her face with both hands.

"Don't be a defeatist. If he's worth it, you'll come up with something. Run it past Gillian. Don't you two have a trip to the Highlands planned?"

"Yes. We leave in a few days."

"Don't put things off with Nick too long."

"I won't. I need a day or so to think about it though. My head's a little foggy right now." She smiled at her father's bleary image.

"You're going to be dead on your feet in the morning."

"I'll be fine. Thanks, Dad. You did very well for a man who doesn't do emotional conversations. I love you." She blew him a kiss.

"Love you too. Night."

Her father's image went black. What worried her the most about Nick was that he had an invisible wall when it came to God. What could she possibly do to breach it? And if she did, what if he did not feel inclined to accept?

Regardless of the outcome, she had to try. Nick was worth it. Whatever her campaign, it must come from the heart.

Catherine closed her computer and placed it on the floor beside her bed. Pulling the pillow flat onto the mattress, she snuggled under the covers. How could she share her love of the gospel with a man who did not need God? What could she disclose that would soften his heart enough to wipe away the pain of last week?

CHAPTER THIRTY-SIX

Nick tossed the contract onto his desk, watching as it slid across the surface and came to a halt against a pile of invoices. He had stared at the same paragraph for the last half hour and could not recall a word of it.

Burying his face in his hands, he felt the beginnings of an all too familiar headache. For the first time in his life, he understood why his father had taken to the bottle. Nick had a suspicion nothing could remove the ache around his heart.

His reflection in the pier glass caught his eye when he leaned back in his chair. The sour expression, with its two vertical indentations above his nose, reminded him of his grandfather on a particularly bad day. Disgusted with himself, he turned away, clicking the top of his pen.

Until today, work had provided a much-needed distraction from Catherine's rejection. He had congratulated himself on his ability to function. But twelve hours ago, his last bastion had crumbled when he'd heard the news.

Catherine had left the village.

He had been at the pub playing darts when the story had first circulated. Nick hadn't put much credence into Charlie's tale until he'd seen Jack enter the pub alone. Only hunger would have driven Jack from the cottage.

With a sinking in his gut, Nick realized the gossip was true. Catherine had left Bascombe. He had stood rooted to the spot for several seconds, staring at Jack while the implications sank in.

The curious glances cast his direction had wrenched him out of his trance. Being quizzed by well-meaning locals was not high on his agenda, so he'd left with his composure intact.

He did not remember the drive home or what he'd done afterward. Until this morning, he had felt oddly insulated from the effects of Catherine's departure. But when he'd woken up, the finality of her loss had hit him like a punch to the gut.

He flung his pen aside and wandered over to the window. The gun-metal sky reflected its dismal shade on the serpentine lake. A good spot of fishing would help pull himself together. Brightening, he started toward the vestibule for his Mackintosh and wellies. He made it as far as the stone fireplace before his steps slowed.

What was he thinking? The lake was where he had suspected his strong feelings for Catherine. He couldn't escape her there. Nick rubbed his nose absently and, turning, glared at the room.

Recollections of Catherine washed over him. In his mind's eye, he saw her curled up on the tufted leather sofa with a book across her knees, her golden-brown curls spilling over the arm of the couch like a shimmering waterfall.

Catherine was everywhere. And nowhere. He stirred impatiently.

The tension he had kept so neatly compartmentalized exploded like a canister of dry gunpowder exposed to an open flame. He wanted to hit something. Anything. He didn't care what.

The clock chimed the hour. He glared at it. Time. All he had was time. Time without Catherine. His fingers bunched, and before he could think it through, his fist shot out and punched the carved stonework on the fireplace.

Pain ricocheted up his arm. He grunted and set his jaw. Blood dripped onto the floor. The instantaneous blue staining of skin above his knuckles left him fairly certain he had done some damage. Snatching a handkerchief from his pocket, he gingerly wrapped his hand to staunch the flow.

The physical pain seemed to cancel out his emotional duress, at least for now. Ashamed of himself for his show of weakness, he turned back to the window. Gusts of wind and rain battered the foliage Catherine had once admired. The acrid taste of bitterness filled his mouth.

Bascombe and the priory had become a shrine of all he had lost. The very walls seemed to close in on him. Glancing wearily at his hand, he deter-mined a change of location would be in the best interests of the estate and himself.

Fellowes knocked on the library door, interrupting thoughts best left unexplored.

"Come," Nick responded quietly.

Fellowes entered, carrying a small box bearing Catherine's address, the same box he had attempted to deliver the last three days. "Where shall I put this, my lord?"

"On the library table. Thank you, Fellowes." Nick gave the man marks for persistence. He closed his eyes, fairly certain Catherine was returning things he had given her. There was no way he was opening it.

"Very good, my lord." The butler deposited the box on top of the library table with its barley twisted legs. Instead of leaving, Fellowes cleared his throat.

"Yes?" Nick scowled.

"I wondered if you were sickening and in need of medical aid." Fellowes lowered his eyes to Nick's wrapped hand.

"I only wish I were."

"Opening that package might work wonders on your constitution."

The problem with old family retainers, thought Nick, is they felt entitled to offer advice as they saw fit. His staff had known him since he'd worn nappies, and it was often difficult to maintain the respect due an employer.

Silent-footed, he stalked to the table where the box lay. Unable to accept the rejection of her returned gifts, Nick grabbed the box and lobbed it across the room. It hit the wall and made a satisfying tinkle of broken glass.

Without another word, he shouldered past Fellowes and quit the library. Heartily sick of his own company, he made a spur-of-the-moment decision halfway up the stairwell. Grandfather could use some company, and London could dish up any distraction he desired.

The heavily carpeted runner muffled his footsteps as he made his way through the first-floor gallery. Portraits of his ancestors lined the walls, staring at him as though he were a distasteful object.

If he didn't break loose of the priory, he would go barking mad. After his behavior downstairs, he was fairly certain that had already occurred. He retrieved his cases from the attic and called Gavin on the way to his suite to bring round the Range Rover. Then he rang for the maid.

Never one to stand upon ceremony, he began pulling clothes at random from the closet and dumping them on top of the gold silk bedding.

One of the priory's two maids appeared in the doorway.

"Would you mind packing those items?" He pointed toward the bed.

"Not at all. Will this be an extended trip, my lord, or shall we keep your room aired?" She bustled to the pile of clothes and folded a pair of chinos.

"I shall be away for some time." Nick rubbed a hand along the back of his neck. Saying it out loud made it real.

"Very good, my lord."

As she packed, Nick wandered idly about the room, picking up objects, then slamming them down. Reaching the window, he fingered the thick brocade drapery as he stared out at the summer storm.

If his belonging to her church meant so much to Catherine, why had she opposed his willingness to be baptized? They were both miserable. And now she was gone.

"All finished," the maid said, interrupting his train of thought.

"Thank you." Nick picked up his cases and descended the stairs, retrieving his Mackintosh and wellies in the vestibule. Gavin brought round the Range Rover and helped load his suitcases inside the back, where they joined several rods, creels, and tackle boxes. His bicycle was mounted to the outside rack.

"I thought you might enjoy a spot of fishing in your spare time. God speed, my boy." Gavin looked as though he wanted to say more, but Nick was impatient to be off. Gavin thumped him on the back instead.

Nick nodded and climbed inside the Range Rover, speeding down the switchbacks. On the way out of town, he stopped at the post office to put in a forwarding address. After making every effort at friendliness to his monosyllabic responses, the postmistress retreated in silence while he filled out the necessary form.

The wind gusted once he was back outside, slapping rain into his eyes. Ducking his head against the elements, Nick hopped over a spreading puddle. Hurry. Hurry. Hurry. His pulse beat out the panicky rhythm. He picked up his pace.

Two cars but one from his sport utility vehicle, he ran smack into Jack Pressley-Coombes. *Brilliant.*

"Ainsley." Jack eyed him quietly.

"Jack." He gave a curt nod.

"Going somewhere?" Jack indicated Nick's four by four.

"London."

"You look terrible." There was a pronounced twinkle in Jack's eye.

"Enjoying this?"

"Maybe," Jack said. "Yeah. A little."

The two men stared at each other, neither anxious to respond to the unspoken question pulsing between them.

"I'm not going to ask," Nick finally stated.

"How she's doing, you mean?" Jack had a quick mind behind that lazy Southern drawl. Evidently, Catherine's brother possessed the same gift to read people as his sister.

The rain beat harder. Jack wiped water off his face. Nick's eyes burned a hole in him.

"She's lost a lot of weight and cries buckets when she thinks no one can hear her."

"I told her I'd join your blasted church, but she was having none of it," Nick bit out.

"Lack of sincerity was probably what she had an issue with, mate." The left side of Jack's lip went up.

Nick started for his car, but Jack blocked his path.

"Out of the way, Yank."

"I have something to say, begging your lordship's pardon. I warned Catherine not to spend so much time with you. You weren't of our faith, and she's deeply religious. The two of you were a disaster waiting to happen." Jack flung his hair back, scattering water.

Nick leveled him with an icy stare.

"Then you started dating. From the first, it was obvious the two of you were a matched pair." Jack folded his arms.

Waiting for the punch in Jack's line, Nick held his peace.

"My brothers and I enjoy teasing Catherine out of that natural reserve of hers. When she gets upset, she does one of two things: retaliates in a way we never expect or hides in her room for days." Jack jerked his chin toward Nick's loaded-down sports utility vehicle. "You and Catherine have more in common than I thought."

"Our relationship is none of your business." The man knew how to administer acute discomfort.

"It is when the happiness of my sister is at stake."

"She made her choice." His stomach knotted, and his head began to throb.

"Yes and no." Jack waited a heartbeat. "Did you open her box?"

"I did not."

"Afraid of what's inside?" Jack taunted.

When a man all but called you a coward, only a few responses would do: hit him square on the nose, ignore him, or be willing to consider other options.

Nick clenched his fist, tempted beyond belief. He'd like nothing more than to knock a few of Jack's teeth loose, but he managed to restrain himself, barely.

"Open the box, and when you do, try opening your mind." Jack waved his soggy letters and pushed past him, heading for the post office.

Seething, Nick watched him go. Unable to stop himself, he called after Jack's retreating form. "What's in the box that's so blasted important?"

Jack slowed to a stop and turned to face him in the pouring rain. "Treasure."

CHAPTER THIRTY-SEVEN

NICK DROVE LIKE A MANIAC up the switchbacks in the downpour. Taking the curves twice as fast as he should, his tires skidded on the gravel of each bend, spraying rocks. Reaching the top, he skirted the fountain at a sedate forty kilometers and slammed on his brakes in front of the main entrance.

Bounding from the motorcar, Nick ran inside, leaving the door wide and tracking debris on Mrs. Wilkin's clean floor. She would have his head, he thought, remembering other times he and Harry Benson had messed up her prized surfaces.

He skidded down the hall, slipping on the soles of his grimy, wet brogues. On entering the library, he scanned the room for Catherine's package. The box had magically disappeared. With hands on hips, he wandered about, poking in dark corners. It was no use. The package had vanished.

"Fellowes. Fellowes," he shouted.

The butler did not appear. Nick went to his desk and pressed the button to summon him. When Fellowes arrived, Nick was down on all fours, looking under the sofa.

"You called, my lord?"

"Yes. Do you happen to know what became of Catherine's package?" Nick rose to his knees on the opposite side of the sofa.

"The package Miss Catherine sent? The one you threw across the room and did not wish to open?" Fellowes appeared confused.

Nick swallowed. The butler was having one on him, and he deserved it. He had behaved abominably.

"I'll see if Mrs. Wilkins knows what came of it," Fellowes said.

"Fellowes?" Nick asked, suspicion lacing his voice.

"Yes, my lord?" Fellows tilted his head in deference.

"You know precisely where that box is, don't you?" Nick bit the inside of his cheek to keep a straight face.

"I believe it is inside the liquor cabinet."

"Why would you put it inside the liquor cabinet?"

"Because it would be the last place you would explore, Master Nicholas." Fellowes looked down the length of his long nose as though Nick were exceptionally dim witted.

Nick attempted to mimic one of his grandfather's superior expressions, but his sense of humor got in the way. His butler had just downgraded him from *my lord* to *Master Nicholas* in that top-lofty way Fellowes used when he was displeased. Nick squelched several chuckles rather unsuccessfully before he gained control of himself.

"That would have been quite a hunt," Nick said.

"I thought so."

"Before I lose what dignity I have left, would you mind granting me a few moments of privacy?" Nick asked humbly.

"Yes, my lord." The butler bowed.

Nick was at the liquor cabinet before Fellowes had closed the door. On the bottom shelf was a small cardboard box, no more than twelve inches square. Picking it up as though it were priceless, he shook it gingerly. The sound of tinkling glass met his ears. He had broken something when he'd lobbed it across the room. He hoped it wasn't important.

He carried the box to his desk. Jack's definition had assured him it contained something Catherine valued. Using the letter opener, Nick cut through the packing tape.

Folding back the lid flaps, he found a business envelope with his name in Catherine's elegant script. He reached inside and lifted one corner of the letter, shaking loose several glass shards. His hands were a tad unsteady as he slit open the seal.

Dear Nick,

When I mailed this box, I wasn't sure you would open it, especially after I hurt you the way I did.

When it comes to things that matter most, I don't share. I could blame it on a number of things, but my shyness boils down to pride. I was too self-centered and so self-focused on my own fears that I lost sight of who you are. Your kindness is one of the many things I love about you. Regardless of how well you receive these things, I know you would never ridicule my hoard of treasures.

Instead of approaching you in person, I have mailed this box so you can go at your own pace. It contains my most important belongings, and I want to share them with the most important person in my life. Please read everything I've sent you and give it a chance.

There is an order to the contents, and they are numbered as such.

ONE—Edgehill House: Our home in Virginia. This is where I grew up.

Nick picked up a photo of a white, two-story Southern antebellum, complete with Corinthian columns. The house was beautifully proportioned.

Edgehill House has been in our family since the 1850s. The only reason it wasn't burned in our Civil War was because General Burnside of the Union Army used it for his headquarters. Most of the property was sold, except for the twenty-odd acres directly surrounding the house. It's no Ashford Priory, but I love it.

TWO—Ballet Recital

Nick handled a second photo. The words on the back said, *"Don Quixote, Kitri."*

Ballet came as easily to me as breathing.

Nick studied Catherine's teenage self. The image of her in a red tutu, flying through the air with her leading leg straight out front and her trailing leg level with her waist. She looked like she was doing splits in the air. Her slender arms were poised in a rounded position above her head, while one hand held a closed red fan.

During the academy's end-of-year recitals, the New York Ballet officials flew out to overlook Colette's students. It's an unusual arrangement, but Colette had been one of their principal dancers until she shattered her ankle during a performance.

I was culled from the group at fifteen and offered a contract. My parents turned it down. They believed I was too young and didn't want me living unsupervised so far from home. It caused a huge uproar at the academy. Colette met with my parents to explain what a great honor it was to have their daughter selected at such a young age. She felt I was on my way to becoming a principal dancer.

My parents held firm and eventually removed me from the academy. You can only imagine my reaction.

In Nick's hand was hard proof of Catherine's incredible talent. She could have been a dancing sensation, touring the world many times over the course of her life. Why would her parents have denied such a remarkable gift?

Setting aside his musings, Nick read on.

I was so angry; I didn't speak to anyone for weeks. After several months, I calmed down enough to pray. I wanted to know if God was real and, if He was, why He had allowed this to happen.

Heavenly Father answered.

That was when I knew He loved me and was intimately involved in my life. Once I knew Heavenly Father cared, I wanted to know Him. I read the Bible, then the Book of Mormon. The scriptures comforted me during that dark time. I studied and prayed every night before bed.

One night, I received a confirmation that what I was reading was true. It changed my life, my focus, and my understanding of life's plan. And eventually, I realized my parents had done the right thing.

THREE—The Book of Mormon

Slowly, Nick picked up a well-worn copy of the Book of Mormon, turning it over in his hands. He fanned the pages and was rather shocked to see a rainbow of colors marking particular passages. The Davidson family bible sat on a tabletop, only opened to mark births, deaths, and marriages. He wondered why Catherine had abused holy writ.

It's pretty marked up. I get excited when a certain passage touches me, and I underline and color it by topic so I won't forget where it is.

Well, that explained a lot.

It comforts me to know you have it. I hope this book will come to mean as much to you as it does to me.

FOUR—Us.

The glass had broken on the framed photo when he'd tossed it across the room. Prying the back off the frame, he rescued the newspaper clipping inside. Suspended in the air, he and Catherine were wrapped in one another's arms inside a hot-air balloon. The photo was grainy, obviously taken with a telephoto lens. It had made the Oxfordshire papers.

Nick rushed from the library to find Fellowes.

"Would it be possible to frame this? I'd like to place it on my desk," he asked when he ran the butler to ground.

"How soon do you need it?" Fellowes took the clipping.

"How soon is reasonably acceptable?"

"I shall see to it immediately, my lord."

CHAPTER THIRTY-EIGHT

DAWN NUDGED AT THE INKY sky when Catherine slipped out of Gillian's Highland cottage with her rucksack strapped to her back. Her waterproof boots made little noise as she trudged up the dirt-packed lane. Since Catherine had arrived in the Highlands four days ago, she had headed for the hills each morning, dragging a sleepy Gillian in her wake. Today, she needed her own space and left a note for her friend in case she woke before Catherine returned.

Using her flashlight, she walked the mile of unpaved road to the kirkyard where Balquhidder's most notorious resident, Rob Roy, lay buried beside his wife and sons. From there, she scrambled up the rocky slope to reach Creag an Tuirc's Highland track.

The two-and-a-half-mile trail cut a swath through a sea of old pine forest. Partway up the mountainside, she passed a roaring waterfall that tumbled its way to the loch below. Continuing, she emerged above the tree line.

Moisture beaded on her clothes and hair as she made her way to Creag an Turic's crest. During her climb, the sky had lightened, touching the clouds with lavender, then blazing vermillion and gold.

When she reached the summit, a cairn of piled stone stood tribute to the ancient rallying place of Clan MacLaren, surrounded by prickly gorse and heather. Catherine stopped beside the marker to catch her breath and admire the view.

Propping her rucksack against the cairn, she retrieved her camera and water bottle. Setting her shutter speed, she focused her lens. Mist clung to the low-lying elevations of the Highland glen. The patchwork fields of emerald farmland were surrounded by hedgerows, and small stands of larch dotted the valley floor. Here and there, the dozen cottages comprising Balquhidder peeked through the trees.

Catherine turned to the right and focused her lens yet again. Loch Voil stretched up the glen, a shimmering mirror reflecting the sky and forested hillsides. Loch Doine lay just beyond, connected by a burn, twisting and coiling back on itself like an umbilical cord, forever linking the two mountain lakes. Above the glen rose Ben More, standing over its domain like a reigning monarch.

Snapping shot after shot of the breathtaking views, Catherine hoped one of them would make a nice canvas. Satisfied, she plunked down on an outcropping of rock and retrieved her water bottle and sipped.

For the first time since Gillian had picked her up at Edinburgh airport, she allowed herself to think about Nick. After her conversation with her father, Catherine had realized her heart had run true to its hereditary track and had fused itself to Nick's.

In a last-ditch effort to touch him spiritually, she had mailed her box, opening to him the deepest parts of her soul. He had not responded.

With the beauties of the Trossachs all around her, she accepted his decision and lifted her face to the brightening sky. Four days detached from civilization had gone a long way to restoring her emotional equilibrium. Strike that. Four days in the Highlands with Gillian's effervescent personality had done the trick.

Catherine's battered heart had resonated with the wild munros that towered over the valley floor. In the distance, her eyes fixed on a crag. Rock erupted from the earth like ancient broadswords reaching for the sky. The granite outcropping had stood throughout a millennia of storms. She resolved to do the same.

Her father had taught her the importance of having a plan. This morning's hike was to help her create one. Only a month remained before Catherine took up her job in Virginia; Gillian had convinced her to extend her two-week holiday in Scotland to three so they could spend most of that time together.

Martin would have enough time to finish Glorianne's diary in her absence, and she could decipher the last of the Oxfordshire wills she had downloaded onto her computer during her stay.

The cry of a golden eagle split the air. Grabbing her camera, Catherine snapped a series of pictures on high shutter speed before it disappeared. A pair of red squirrels chattered, chasing each other in the pines below.

Catherine needed a cause when she returned to the States, something to throw herself into that would make a difference. When her parents had pulled her from the ballet academy, she had volunteered at a battered children's center, largely to keep her distance from her parents until she calmed down. As she learned the different children's stories, her own heartbreak became trivial by comparison. Serving them had given her purpose and perspective. This time around, she determined to research charitable options and sign on as a long-term patron.

Placing her camera on the boulder beside her, Catherine wrapped her arms around her knees and inhaled the scent of pine and the softer, more acrid smell of larch. Holiday makers flooded Loch Lomond and the Trossachs every summer, but in sleepy little Balquhidder, with its dirt lanes and hard-to-get-at trails, tourists rarely ventured beyond the kirkyard, where the old stone church stood.

The track to her left ran under the road near Mhor, wove through the glen along the burn, and climbed the slope of Creag an Tuirc, joining a series of interconnecting footpaths through the Trossachs. The trails attracted people from all over the world, from day walkers to advanced mountain climbers.

Catherine didn't hear the hiker until the crunch of boots sounded a few yards away. She turned sharply, her hand instinctively reaching for the closest rock.

A frown marred Gillian's otherwise flawless complexion. Her pale-blonde hair stuck out in every direction. Yesterday's mascara was smudged under one eye. Her pajama collar hung over the top of her fleece jacket, and her boot laces, though tied, were not laced to the top. She took a moment to catch her breath.

"You left without telling me," Gillian said when she could talk.

"I felt bad waking you up, so I let you sleep. I needed time to think."

"You've done nothing but think since we got here. When I picked you up at the airport, you looked like a half-starved zombie. But did I pry?"

Catherine didn't respond. When Gillian was on a rant, there was no stopping her.

"I know how private you are, so I waited. Do you know how hard it is for me not to pry?"

Catherine waited a heartbeat. "Almost impossible?"

"You are not going to make me laugh." Gillian's mouth twisted.

"Of course not," Catherine deadpanned.

"Move over."

Catherine scooted over on the boulder, and Gillian sat next to her.

"I was worried sick until I saw your note." Gillian gave her a corner eye.

An apology formed on Catherine's lips.

"I promised your brother I would watch over you while you were here."

"When did you talk to Jack?" Catherine felt a little jolt of surprise.

"Oh, you know . . . When he found out you were coming, he called and asked me to stay close." Gillian made a restless gesture with her hand.

"Jack's being ridiculous. Agent Butler's unit caught the guy who tried to kidnap me. Is there something going on between you two that I should know about?" Catherine narrowed her eyes at her friend.

"There is absolutely nothing going on between us. Your brother is . . . He's just . . ." Gillian exhaled loudly.

"Girl stupid? Thick-headed? Obtuse?" Catherine wrapped an arm around Gillian's shoulder.

"That's good for starters." Gillian beamed, her good humor restored. "But seriously, I did promise Jack. When I woke up and found you missing, I freaked."

"I'm sorry I upset you. Jack's being overprotective. I came up here to figure out what I am going to do when I go home. This seemed like a good place to work it out."

"There's no chance with Nick?"

"I don't think so." Catherine wrapped her arms around her knees and dropped her chin on top of them, her eyes resting on Loch Voil's reflective surface.

They didn't talk for a time, but Gillian's restlessness finally communicated itself to her.

"What do you want to do today?" Catherine asked.

"How about a picnic at the base of Ben Vane? We can take selfies and check out the verra fit men bagging that munro." Gillian looked stricken the minute the words left her mouth. "Sorry, Catherine. I forgot."

"I'm fine."

"If you want to talk, I'm here."

"There's not much to say. I shared something personal with Nick before I left, but he didn't respond. End of story." She stood and grabbed her rucksack, slipping her arms through the straps.

"You forgot these." Gillian picked up Catherine's camera and water bottle and tucked them inside the top flap.

"Thanks. This is our trip, and we're going to have a blast," she said, taking in one last drink of the view.

"No, you aren't, but you'll be a lot better after three weeks of no outside influences. It's very peaceful and primitive here. There's a lot to be said about no cell or Wi-Fi service. And since it's my turn to call the day's activity, we're hiking over to Ben Vane and checking out some hot-looking Scots."

CHAPTER THIRTY-NINE

THEODOSIA FROWNED AS SHE HANDED Ari his ringing mobile. The number had an Italian area code. They were in Rivendon's London garage office, as it was the only place they could meet unobserved by staff.

"*Pronto*," Ari said into the mobile. He rose to his feet, calm and self-assured as he listened to a blast of Italian from whoever was on the line.

She crossed her legs on the uncomfortable sofa, letting her skirt ride high.

Ari was only half listening now. His dark eyes glittered under the fluorescent lights. He smirked at her and winked.

Drawing a shaky breath, Theodosia gave him a pouty smile. Ari had skill sets she had never dreamed of and had stolen a piece of her heart as surely as he had their neighbors' valuables.

Despite their large age gap, she knew Ari loved her. Strange though it seemed, the more time she spent with him, the more she craved. His presence, his way of command, and even his shady connections gave her a decadent thrill of pleasure.

"You idiot. Why did you do that?" His eyes flashed when he switched to English.

Theodosia felt a moment's sympathy for the person on the receiving end and shifted on the uncomfortable couch.

"I gave you a simple assignment. You did not follow my directions. You will only get half pay for not doing the job I hired you for. I do not need you. I will do it myself." Ari paced away.

The voice on the other end rose.

"Get a jammer. I'll find a motorcar." He disconnected. "I have good and not-so-good news. Which do you want first?" Ari faced her with his hands on his hips.

"Why don't you decide." She swung her leg.

"*Amore mia*, my contact lost the American at Edinburgh airport."

Theodosia clenched her teeth together. Ari knew her displeasure; she saw him take it in with a sweep of those soulful eyes.

"Don't worry. We have her return flight." A boyish smile lit his features, and she briefly recognized the Ari she had first known. "I will do it myself this time. Then there will not be any mistakes. I have secured a place for her until the transport arrives. Agostino is getting me a mobile jammer, and I will 'borrow' a motorcar. The old lady will never miss it."

Ari went to the desk-cum-workbench and withdrew a key from his pocket to unlock the bottom cabinet. Opening the drawer, he removed a long manacled chain and a set of matching handcuffs.

"This is for you. I do not need them." He handed her a set of handcuffs and a key.

"May I watch you capture her?" She took the handcuffs and dropped them into her bag without a thought, her focus on the manacle. Darting out her tongue, she wet her suddenly dry lips.

Ari gazed at her with hooded lids, his expression inscrutable.

She waited, not trying to entice him. Miss Pressley-Coombes's abduction meant far too much for that.

"This is a tricky situation."

The plunge of disappointment stabbed through her.

"I won't make any promises. I will not ever place you in danger. Not ever. Do you understand?" Lifting her chin with his finger, Ari ran his thumb over her cheekbones.

Staring up into his face, she read his desire to protect her and nodded.

"We'll see, okay? I want to please my Theodosia. Your happiness is my happiness. But I want you safe first."

Deep emotion, poignant as a lover's first kiss, built inside her, constricting her throat and making it ache. No one had truly cared for her well-being since she was a child, not even Hadley. Tears trembled on her lashes and trailed unheeded down her face.

Theodosia reached for her bag to grab a tissue, but Ari beat her to it, dabbing her eyes gently with his own handkerchief. As he repocketed the damp fabric, Theodosia felt the last of her heart crumble at his feet.

CHAPTER FORTY

NICK CIRCLED THE BLOCK THREE times before he drummed up enough courage to park. He knew Jack was home; he could see him watching a ball game through the picture window.

The dread he experienced as he walked up the wet pavement with his hat pulled low was akin to waiting in line for school vaccinations. He knew it was going to hurt, and the anticipation about killed him before they plunged the needle into his arm.

Lifting his hand, Nick banged good and hard. Jack answered almost immediately. He didn't say anything, but his eyes bored into Nick, probing, assessing. The telly screen went to halftime. Jack hit a button on the controller, and the screen went blank.

Humble pie had never been Nick's strong suit. Even one forkful had a tendency to make him choke.

"I opened the box." Nick bared his teeth.

"And?" Humor lit Jack's features.

"I have some questions," Nick said, scooping up another bite of humble pie.

"Come in out of the rain, Ainsley." Jack held the door wide enough for him to enter.

Nick glanced about the living room as he toed off his wet brogues. Everything looked the same, except a card was missing from a bunch of dried roses on a side table. The vase was from Estelle's, the florist he'd used the day he had purchased Catherine's engagement ring.

"Have a seat." Jack indicated the sofa.

"I'd like my visit kept strictly confidential. For everyone's sake, I do not wish to raise false hope." He reddened, knowing Jack's gaze had caught him staring at the vase. Nick removed his mobile and opened the note app that contained his questions.

"That sounds fair."

Scrollong to the first item on his list, Nick read, "The Book of Mormon is a record written by Jews who left Jerusalem and colonized the Americas?"

"Yes."

"Joseph Smith found it inside a buried stone box?"

Jack nodded.

"Why do people have a problem with that? The British Museum has a number of ancient metal books that were found in similar stone boxes." Nick had a pragmatic mind. Fact was fact.

"Some believe we have replaced the Bible with the Book of Mormon. They've also been taught or told we are not Christians."

"Are you Christians?" Nick had never considered that they weren't, but it was best to find out up front. Despite his issue with God, he did accept Jesus Christ as his Savior.

"Yes, we are. In fact, the name of our church is The Church of Jesus Christ of Latter-day Saints. If you have more questions, the missionaries can answer them a lot better than I can. I can give them a ring and schedule an appointment for you."

"All right."

* * *

Catherine beached her kayak on Loch Voil's north shore. The shallow water rocked the narrow boat and soaked into her water shoes as she climbed out. Holding the bow grab handle, she pulled the kayak onto the grass and stopped to gaze up at Ben More's peak. Her breath made small white puffs in the crisp morning air. It felt more like fall than late August.

"I wish I could stay longer. I'd like to climb Ben More before we leave the Highlands," Catherine said with a hint of regret.

"You want to 'bag a munro' the day before we leave? Don't you want to go shopping in Glasgow or something? You haven't left the glen once in three weeks."

Gillian needed people like fish needed water. She had driven to Callander several times over the three weeks to visit her aunt's family and restock their groceries. Opting out, Catherine had tossed her some cash and holed up in the cottage until Gillian had returned.

The girls pulled the second kayak out of the water. Between the two of them, they lugged it to the car and strapped it on the rack.

Ben More had beckoned to Catherine since her arrival in the glen.

"Are there hiking trails this side of Ben More, or do we have to drive to the farm and take the trailhead?"

"There's a path where the road dips." Gillian pointed down the dirt-packed lane. "It goes partway up this side but stops at the base of the crags. I'm game for either as long as you don't pull out mountaineering equipment and make me climb the rest of the way with my fingers and toes."

Laughing, the girls hoisted the second kayak on top of the car and tied it down for the short drive back to the whitewashed cottage.

"You look better than when I picked you up at the airport." Gillian searched her face.

"This trip was the perfect medicine. I can't thank you enough for inviting me."

"You did me a favor. I needed a break from school. Even though I don't mind helping with the grandparents, it's been nice getting away.

"When we first arrived, I thought the physical activity would kill me. But my clothes are loose, and . . . That never happens. I can make it up Creag an Tuirc without huffing." Gillian gave Catherine an impish grin.

"You should be proud of yourself." Catherine went to rinse her water shoes in the loch.

"Believe me, I am. I hate hiking. It impairs my ability to giggle, and I like to giggle."

"If you hate it so much, why did you agree to go?"

"Because there is one thing I hate more than hiking, and that's being a party pooper. Besides, something fun might happen." Gillian tossed Catherine her water shoes to rinse.

"We could have done something else."

"I know, but you got such a kick out of the views, and I didn't want you to start moping."

"I'm done moping." For all her chatter, Gillian was perceptive.

"Of course. Who can mope when they're with me?"

"You're impossible." Catherine laughed as she shook out their shoes and put them in a bag.

"It's part of my charm." Gillian pulled the car keys out of her pocket.

"And you're so modest too."

Giggling, they climbed into the car. Gillian fired it up, and they headed down the dirt lane toward the cottage.

"At least at the end of the day, you're too tired to think about Nick."

"Is that why you've agreed to this physical activity?"

"I promised your brother I'd keep an eye on you, and sitting around isn't your thing."

Gillian hit a pot hole and scraped the bottom of the car.

"I'm fine." Catherine gritted her teeth.

"He's worried."

"Jack is ridiculous. He insists they only caught one man and that the second is still at large. I think they were after the diary, and when they didn't find it, they gave up. Nothing has happened in over a month." Catherine rolled her eyes.

"If this is about your diary, why are we wasting time hiking when we should be trying to find information on your ancestor?" Gillian shot through a mud puddle, splashing the car.

"I downloaded some old wills on my computer and have been plugging away at them every night while we watch movies."

"Oh. I thought you were writing in your journal." Gillian turned into their parking space in front of her family's holiday cottage.

Catherine opened her car door. She wasn't ready to write about her break-up with Nick.

CHAPTER FORTY-ONE

"How did your assignment on prayer go last night, Nick?" Elder Peterson asked after Elder Marcinski offered the opening prayer. Nick had met with the missionaries for the last four evenings. On Sunday, he'd attended church with Jack.

"I . . ." Nick tried to think of a legitimate excuse without being dishonest. He took a sip from his water bottle to delay answering.

Things had gone swimmingly until the end of last night's lesson. Nick had retired early. Unwilling to kneel, he'd paced his room. Then he'd remembered the dogs hadn't gone for their evening run, so he'd taken them out on the grounds. Upon coming back into the house, he'd turned on a football game in the library until the wee hours of the morning.

Peterson caught his eye. It was as though the missionary could see right into his brain.

Nick didn't want to admit he had an issue, but he couldn't lie. "Not well."

"What's holding you back? Yesterday when we read in Alma about the seed, you seemed willing to participate in your own experiment." Despite his youth, Peterson's question was straight to the point.

"I read all the scriptures you assigned." Nick knew his response was flimsy, at best.

"But you haven't prayed, Nick, not once since we started teaching you," eighteen-year-old Marcinski pointed out, his Coke-bottle glasses winking in the light.

Nick rubbed the back of his neck and glanced at Jack out of the corner of his eye. He had no desire to discuss his hang-up with God in front of Catherine's brother. The missionaries, yes, if he must. But not Jack. If Jack learned that God didn't care for Nick, he would never let Nick near Catherine again.

The silence stretched. Elder Peterson was playing the American game of chicken. Nick hated to lose. He couldn't come out on top, and Peterson wouldn't let him off.

Jack coughed and excused himself for a drink. His performance wouldn't win him any BAFTAs but proved Jack had more tact than Nick had given him credit for.

"God doesn't listen to my prayers," Nick said under his breath, taking advantage of Jack's absence. "I don't know what I did as a child to cause it, but God has taken me in aversion."

"Why do you believe that?" Marcinski asked.

Nick's throat constricted, but he finally squeezed out, "When my mother left, my father took to the bottle. I prayed with everything in me for God to send my mother back. But she didn't come. Not even once. Eventually, my grandfather took over my guardianship and raised me."

"So you believe God abandoned you like your parents?" Peterson clarified.

Nick's lunch curdled in the pit of his stomach. He glanced toward the kitchen, hoping Jack couldn't hear. "Yes, He did."

"How old were you?" Elder Peterson asked, truly interested.

At Peterson's question, Nick met his eyes. "Seven. A year older than that little scamp, Sammy Benson." Both missionaries had met Sammy before lunch. He'd been dressed as Agent 008, complete with bow tie and spy glasses.

"I'd like you to read this passage from Luke 18:16. Jesus Christ is speaking to His disciples." Peterson picked up his scriptures, turning the pages until he seemed satisfied.

"Suffer the children to come unto me, . . . for of such is the kingdom of heaven," Nick read.

"Try Moroni 8:8." Marcinski passed his set of scriptures to Nick.

"Little children are whole, for they are not capable of committing sin . . ." The words jumped out at him, and his heart slammed inside his chest. "I don't understand. If God feels like this about children, why didn't He answer my prayer?"

"One of God's fundamental laws deals with agency. No one has the right to remove another's freedom to act. Man has the power to choose, but we can't determine the consequences," Marcinski said.

"I'd like you to read one more scripture, Nick. It's in 1 Nephi 21: 15–16." Peterson helped him find the scripture.

"'For can a woman forget her sucking child, that she should not have compassion on the son of her womb? Yea, they may forget, yet will I not forget thee, O house of Israel.'" Nick's voice grew so thick that he could hardly finish the last verse of scripture. "'Behold, I have graven thee upon the palms of my hands; thy walls are continually before me.'"

"Your mom chose to forget you, and your dad chose to abandon you—that was their prerogative in God's plan, their ability to choose for themselves—but God did not forget you," Elder Peterson said softly.

Nick ducked his head and blew out a heavy breath, trying to regain his composure. God hadn't forgotten him. Catherine had told him much the same. He hadn't believed her.

"We testify that He did not. He cannot forget you. Christ lived and died for you, and everything He does is because He loves you. He might not have answered your prayers in the way you wanted, but we promise, He answered your prayers. Sometimes He knows a different answer will be better for our lives. He answered your prayers in His way, not yours, and He will answer them now." Elder Peterson gave his shoulder a squeeze.

God had sent Grandfather and the Bensons, Nick realized. His prayers had been answered in the Lord's own way.

"Do you think you could make an effort to pray, to test Him again? Will you put Him to the test?" Marcinski asked.

"Yes." He nodded. And this time he meant it.

* * *

The next afternoon, Nick headed to the stream with his fishing pole slung over his shoulder. After two nights with little to no sleep, he was starting to wear thin. He laid the rod beside a clump of cattails and sat on a lichen-covered stump.

His scripture reading that morning encompassed the book of Enos. For such a small book of scripture, Enos's powerful words had stayed with him all day, echoing in his mind.

Like Enos, his soul hungered. He too wanted to know if God was there. He wanted to feel His love. He wanted to know if what the missionaries were teaching him was true.

He realized he would never get any sleep until he faced his fears. That meant he had to pray. After yesterday's meeting with the elders, he had determined to try.

Feeling a little foolish, he glanced around to make sure he was alone before he knelt in the dappled sunlight along the edge of the stream. After a few awkward attempts, he poured out his entire soul to God in simple words, asking to know the truth.

And suddenly, that love Catherine had spoken about surrounded Nick, enveloping him in a warmth and acceptance he couldn't deny. Nick struggled against the sudden sting of tears. He hadn't cried since his mother left, but the healing tears persisted and eventually overpowered his senses. After a time, he collected himself enough to voice his questions.

Much, much later, he stumbled to his feet. The summer sun was low on the horizon. Unashamedly, he wiped the moisture from his face. He was exhausted but felt light as air. Walking back to the priory, he texted Catherine, but his message went undelivered. He tried calling, but it went straight to voice mail. He left a message. But she didn't respond. In desperation, he pulled up his email account and searched for Catherine's address, sending her a long note. Still nothing.

He had to tell someone. He texted Jack and asked if they could meet that evening at Hawthorne Cottage with the elders.

* * *

When the missionaries entered Jack's living room that night, Peterson took one look at Nick and said, "You know."

With so much joy burning inside him, all Nick could do was nod.

Peterson slapped him on the back and gave him a man hug.

"Do you have time Saturday to be baptized?" Marcinski pumped his hand enough times to wring it from his arm.

"I'd rather wait another week until Catherine returns."

The missionaries looked at each other, clearly unhappy.

"Have I missed something, gentlemen?" Nick glanced from Peterson to Marcinski.

"Elder Peterson is going home on Tuesday." Marcinski elaborated.

"Why?" Nick asked.

"Missions last two years. My time is up," Peterson said.

The elder's reply felt like a punch to the face. Nick shook his head to clear it. During every discussion, Elder Peterson seemed to know what he was thinking. Peterson explained things in a way he found easy to understand. Nick wanted him at his baptism.

"Are you getting baptized for Catherine or for yourself?" Jack's eyes bored into his.

Nick got up off the sofa and paced Jack's small living room. Stopping under a framed Formula One blueprint, Nick stared at the drawing. He reflected on his experience beside the fishing stream and how he'd felt when he'd read the scriptures.

"I'm doing it for me," he said with quiet conviction.

* * *

The white jumpsuit hit Nick midcalf, exposing his dark, hairy legs. To make matters worse, he couldn't close the last six inches at the top. If he zipped it all the way up, he would sing soprano the rest of his life. Standing inside the men's stall, he wondered what to do.

"How are you doing in there, Nick?" Elder Peterson asked.

"I believe we have a bit of a snag, gentlemen." Nick opened the stall door.

Elder Peterson folded his arms and took in Nick's situation. He kept a straight face, but his eyes gave him away. The lad was enjoying himself.

"I look ridiculous. Don't you have something larger?" Nick glanced back and forth between the elders.

"What do you think, Elder Marcinski?" Elder Peterson asked.

Marcinski shrugged.

Nick doubted the little elder filled out a thirty-four shoulder.

"That's the largest size we have. If you can zip it a little higher, I think it'll be fine. Besides," Peterson assured him, "it will all be done in a few minutes."

"For the first time, I'm grateful Catherine is not here to witness this debacle," Nick muttered under his breath. He tugged the zipper up another notch. It would go no farther.

"This will keep you decent during the service." Peterson draped a towel around his neck.

"Thanks, Yank." Nick said sarcastically.

"My pleasure." Peterson ushered him into the Relief Society room.

Nick's face burned with embarrassment. Jack caught his eye and jerked his chin for him to sit up front, but Nick stayed by the wall. If he sat in this costume, he'd split the backside open.

Despite his discomfort, slowly, a sense of calm filled him, and his embarrassment subsided. Nick took note of the small number of people in attendance.

With so much of his life lived in the public eye, he had requested an intimate service. He didn't want strangers witnessing something so personal to him. This baptism was between himself and Heavenly Father.

The opening song brought a warmth he now recognized as the Spirit. After the talk on baptism, Elder Peterson escorted Nick to the men's washroom and opened an adjoining door into the baptistry. Standing at the top of the tiled steps, waiting to descend into the font, peace washed over him. In the deepest part of his soul, he knew this decision was right.

Over the last few days, he'd reflected on his life and realized the missionaries were right. Heavenly Father had answered his childhood prayer in an unexpected way. When he had begged God to send his mother home, Heavenly Father could not alter her choice.

The Lord, in His infinite wisdom, had sent his grandfather, who had loved him and set rules and expectations. The lack of extra cash had protected him from a good bit of trouble as well. At an early age, he had learned how to work creatively to save the family estates. Heavenly Father had indeed watched over him his entire life, just as Catherine had said.

"Ready?" Elder Peterson interrupted his thoughts.

"Yes." Nerves jangled in his system. He took a fortifying breath.

"Remember, it's like we practiced."

Elder Peterson entered the font first and gave him a slight nod when he reached the bottom of the stairs.

Nick grabbed the font handrail and took the first step toward his new life.

CHAPTER FORTY-TWO

Outside the MGB's passenger window, Catherine watched the closely spaced homes on the outskirts of central London slip by. Their rust-colored shingles, identical elevations, and front yards looked tired and neglected. She missed the bright, clean air of the Highlands already.

"Scotland seems to have agreed with you." The engine roared as Jack pressed down on the accelerator.

"I didn't want to leave." Catherine yawned. She and Gillian had left Balquhidder at 4:00 a.m. to make her flight.

Catherine took note of the dark circles under Jack's eyes. "Back to working late hours?"

"I guess you could call it that. I've been assisting someone on a new project." Jack smirked, flipping the blinker and changing lanes.

At Reading, Jack took the A417 to Knoxham in order to drop off a set of plans at his office. He parked outside the glass and metal structure.

"I'll only be a minute. Lock the doors."

She huffed. Regardless of her abductor's arrest, Jack insisted on playing bodyguard. She had been incident free for over a month, but he remained obdurate. If someone else were after her, he would have struck by now. Jack's precautions were ridiculous.

Leaning against the headrest, she closed her eyes, basking in the sunshine. The warmth soaked into her bones, making her drowsy. The next thing she knew, Jack was banging on the window, motioning for her to unlock his door.

She pulled up the lock. Jack climbed in and backed out of their parking space, entering the main road to Bascombe.

"How was your trip? Were you bored?"

"No one could be bored around Gillian, and the Highlands were a sensory overload."

"Yeah, I'll bet. How'd you enjoy being disconnected from the world?" Jack cocked his head to the side and gave her an I-told-you-so look.

"It was hard at first, then I got used to it. I dragged Gillian all over that glen." She giggled at the memory.

"Gillian doesn't strike me as the outdoorsy type." Jack checked his rearview mirror.

"She's not, but she's a good sport."

They were silent for a while. Catherine gazed out the window, watching the road curve its way past fields, small villages, and hedgerows. She didn't mention Nick, but his name fairly screamed between them.

Caving, Catherine decided to get her brother's input. "There were a lot of texts from Nick when I turned on my phone at the airport."

"What did they say?" Jack's voice was deliberately bland.

"I don't know. I didn't read them." Catherine bit her lip.

"Why not?" Jack flicked a glance in her direction.

"I never heard back from him when I mailed the box. I'm in a really good place right now. If I read his texts or listen to those voice mails, I'll crumble." She fiddled with a strand of curls.

"Why don't you open a few just to see what he has to say. Nick doesn't strike me as the kind of guy to pester you. It might be important. What if he opened your box?" He opened his mouth, hesitated, then closed it again.

"Maybe I'll read them tonight." She chewed on her lip, considering.

"Behind closed doors with the drawbridge pulled up?"

Catherine avoided his gaze and shrugged. Jack knew her too well.

The hedgerows disappeared, opening to wide pastures. The sheep resembled cotton balls scattered over a blanket of emerald green. A church tower rose above a copse of trees in the distance. An ache filled her as she took in the view. In a week, this would be a memory.

"By the way, Martin called. He finished Glorianne's diary." Jack interrupted her thoughts.

"Did he give you any information?"

"No, but he said you were never going to believe what he discovered." Jack swerved to miss a pothole.

Her stomach rumbled.

"Hungry?"

"A little. I thought I'd grab something at the airport, but there wasn't time."

"I think there's a couple eggs in the fridge and some peanut butter." The tinny click of the blinker filled the car when Jack took the exit.

"Let's swing by Tesco and pick up some groceries," Catherine suggested.

"Sorry, that will have to wait. I have to complete some alterations for my boss. If I don't start now, they won't be done by three."

"Let me drop you off at the cottage, and I'll go shopping. It'll take half an hour."

"I'd rather not." Jack rubbed the stubble on his chin.

"You're just being overprotective. Butler's unit arrested my abductor, remember? Even if there were accomplices, they know we don't have the diary. Since we're pretty sure that's what they're after and nothing's happened since the break-in, it's a fair guess that I'm safe."

Her stomach growled again. "You aren't really going to make me starve until three o'clock, are you?"

He frowned. Catherine could tell Jack was uneasy, but her logic made sense.

"All right, but you have thirty minutes."

"Deal."

* * *

The Tesco parking spaces were full when Catherine arrived. She drove around the lot until she gave up and found a place on the side of the building near the loading dock.

She would have been home by now if Amelia Hopkins hadn't stopped her in the dairy isle to ask about her trip. Catherine checked her cell for the time as she wheeled her shopping cart out of the grocery store. Twenty-five minutes. She shoved the phone into her front jeans pocket. If she hurried, she might make it back to the cottage before Jack had a panic attack.

Her mind went back to Nick's numerous texts as she rounded the building. Maybe he had opened the box. The thought tantalized her. Perhaps she'd peek at a few of them before she started lunch.

Transporting groceries had always been a bit of a challenge in Jack's car. To maximize interior space, she filled the cubbies behind the driver and passenger seats, then filled the passenger floor boards, saving the open seat for non-squishables.

Unlocking the door, she propped the black leather chair forward and placed three bags into the cubby. A dark sedan slid into the space beside her. Out of her peripheral vision, she saw the driver glance at her over the top of his partially lowered window and heard him pop the trunk of his car.

"I'll be out of your way in just a minute," Catherine called, grabbing two more bags from the cart beside her and tossing them onto the floorboards. She turned for the last bag, but the man had climbed out of his vehicle and handed it to her.

"Thank you." Catherine took the bag of bread and placed it on the passenger seat.

The olive-complected man wheeled her cart directly behind Jack's MGB. Catherine frowned in confusion, wondering why he would do that. The man stood near the rear bumper between their two cars.

The hair on Catherine's arms rose. No one else was parked on this side of the building.

His dark eyes glittered, triggering a memory of the street in Bicester. Recognition hit her like a blow to the windpipe. She was alone with the man who had stabbed her.

Her pulse accelerated, and her hands went clammy. Grabbing the only thing at hand, Catherine swung her tote at him and screamed to draw attention. Her tote hit him in the shoulder, upending its contents on the asphalt. Improvising, Catherine reached behind her and located the handle of Jack's car door. Her thought was to climb through the passenger side and exit out the driver's door.

The man took two steps forward. He removed a gun-like object from the inside of his jacket and squeezed the trigger. Two spinning barbs imbedded themselves in her body, one at her breast and the other at her ribs, zapping her slender frame like a bolt of lightning.

Pain exploded inside her chest, radiating out to her extremities. Catherine crumpled to the ground, a groaning mass of agony. The world spun in tight circles, and she thought her head was going to fly off her shoulders. She couldn't move.

The man picked her up like a rag doll and dumped her inside the trunk of his car. Yanking her arms behind her back, he zip-tied them together. Hard plastic bit into her flesh. The cloth he shoved in her mouth made her gag and dried her mouth of moisture. A rough hand at her breast yanked the barbed metal prongs from her skin.

Catherine groaned and felt the warm trickle of blood.

He took hold of the second prong in her ribs and tore it loose. Her scream was muffled by the wad of fabric. One of her legs twitched. The shock from his taser had begun to wear off. Fighting against the pain, Catherine kicked out. The electric volts had discombobulated her coordination. She missed, catching her captor in the thigh.

He grunted. His furious dark eyes connected with hers. Reaching inside the trunk, he grabbed a handful of her hair and shook her while a stream of foreign words spewed from his lips. Balling his fist, he slammed it into her jaw. A burst of white light flashed in her head, and everything went dark.

* * *

The clang of metal against metal woke her. Catherine had no idea where she was. Moaning, she tried to open her eyes, but everything was dark.

Slowly, images from the parking lot came back to her. The man with the glittering eyes. The sense of familiarity washed over her. She knew him from somewhere, somewhere besides the incident outside the shoe store, but the incessant pounding made it hard to think.

Her jaw throbbed. She tried to move, but she was trussed up like a turkey on Thanksgiving day. Her feet were bare. And cold. Whatever she lay on poked through her thin blouse and smelled of decomposing organic matter. Wiggling her fingers, she touched the prickly substance. Hay. Her nose tickled, and she sneezed.

Who was that man? More importantly, what did he want from her?

The pounding stopped.

The hay compressed beside her. Gentle fingers touched her jaw and pushed her hair from her face. Something cold and metallic slipped around her neck and locked into place. She began to shake, and her body broke out in clammy sweat.

"Do not move," her captor said in a heavy accent.

Cold metal slipped between her hands, cutting the binding on her wrists. Though freed from their confinement, her arms remained numb. Rolling her onto her side, the man removed the gag and blindfold, finally cutting the restrictions on her ankles.

Needlelike jabs wracked her arms and legs when circulation began to flow. With shaky fingers, she reached for her neck. A large shackle, like those she had seen in torture chambers on castle tours, clamped around it.

She blinked rapidly up at her captor from the pile of rotting hay as her fear morphed into mind-blowing anger. Anger at herself for not listening to Jack. Anger at this man for first hurting, then capturing her. Anger at being denied her freedom.

If she had paid more attention, she wouldn't be in this predicament. Her time in Scotland had lulled her into a false sense of security. Her captor had only been biding his time, waiting until she was vulnerable.

Jack would be out of his mind with worry.

She took in her surroundings; the building looked to be some sort of shed. Its aged clapboards had shrunk, letting in outdoor light. Two broken windows, missing their panes and most of their framing, provided little protection from the elements. She estimated the structure couldn't be more than twenty feet square. Other than the rotting pile of hay, the building was bare.

Her captor made a sudden movement and jostled a half-forgotten memory. She remembered him. The night of the gala, he had taken her first to Davidson House, then on to the Italian embassy. He was the Earl of Rivendon's driver. Ari.

"Why?" She stared at him as she wiggled her sore jaw.

He ignored her and checked the chain he had secured to the support beam.

Through the open door hanging on one rusty hinge, thousands of acres of crops spread across the vista. A bubble of hysteria rose in her chest. He had chosen well. No one would hear her if she screamed.

Ari went outside. She heard the slam of a car door.

Bunching her knees beneath her, she sat up. Had he taken her cell phone after he'd hit her? Her long blouse covered her jeans pockets. She touched her hip and felt the hard plastic of her phone and almost sobbed in relief.

Ari returned from his car with a large bucket, a package of water bottles, and a box of granola bars. He dumped them at her feet. Obviously, he meant to keep her awhile.

"Why am I here?"

He didn't answer but moved to the doorway and pulled his phone from his jacket.

Catherine closed her eyes in relief. There was coverage in this area. Her captor pressed speed dial. He watched her while it rang.

He spoke in a foreign tongue, then listened, nodding several times. Muttering a curse, he shoved his phone inside his jacket. Turning to her, he said, "Lie down."

"No." Catherine's heart pounded in the top of her throat, beating against the manacle.

"You do what I tell you."

Catherine locked her arms around her knees and lifted her chin.

In two long strides, Ari was across the dirt floor. Grabbing her by the hair, he kneed her in the kidneys and shoved her face-first into the straw.

She gasped, stunned and unable to whimper. Pinning her to the floor, he patted her in places she had never been touched. She blushed furiously and struck out at him with her legs.

He was stronger than she had anticipated. When he flipped her onto her back, holding her arms over her head, tears of fury seeped from her eyes. Her hair had fallen forward. She tossed it back and spit in his face.

Wiping the spittle with his sleeve, he glared at her for the space of a dozen heartbeats. With great deliberation, he pulled back his arm and back-handed her. Her ears rang, and she tasted blood.

"Stop. I do not like to hit women."

The heat of his mark burned her cheek, and she quivered with fear.

"Do not fight me." Ari studied the swelling on her face and touched it with gentle fingers.

As he began another systematic search, Catherine thrashed about, trying to get away. It did no good.

With an exclamation, Ari located her cell in the front pocket of her jeans. Her heart sank, and the tears she had kept at bay filled her eyes, spilling down her face.

Manacled as she was, her phone had been her only chance at rescue.

Staring at her as though she were Medusa, Ari removed the phone from her pocket. Rising from his knees, he brushed the hay from his trousers in slow, deliberate swipes, never taking his eyes from her face. With a smile, he dropped her cell to the floor and crushed it under his heel.

CHAPTER FORTY-THREE

NICK CAST THE FISHING LINE into the middle of the stream. It made a satisfactory plop and sank below the surface. Seven nice-sized rainbow trout were attached to his stringer. Today's catch would land him a prime piece of mutton at the local butcher's.

He glanced up at the gray clouds. The wind had kicked up, a sure sign of an incoming storm. The tip of his pole dipped. Yanking the rod, he set the hook.

His mobile rang. Jack's name flashed on the screen. Nick dropped his pole and answered on the first ring.

"Did she get my messages?" he asked, trying not to sound too eager.

"Catherine's gone. They kidnapped her in the freaking parking lot," Jack's voice rasped.

No. Nick couldn't be hearing correctly. The police had arrested her abductor. He rubbed the back of his neck, refusing to accept Jack's words.

"I tried calling her phone; she didn't pick up," Jack continued. "DCI Barnes is going to ping it."

"Where are you?" Nick's stomach plunged to his knees. The police were already there? Abandoning his pole and tackle box, he sprinted for the priory.

"In the Tesco lot."

"Have you called Butler?" Nick charged over the bridge spanning the serpentine lake.

"He's mobilizing his unit as we speak. I offered your place as headquarters. Agent Butler said the first twenty-four hours are critical. We have to find her."

"We will." Nick swallowed hard and prayed his words were true.

* * *

INTERPOL's Human Trafficking and Child Exploitation Unit arrived at the priory via helicopter within two hours of Jack's call, along with overseas FBI Agent Steigler. After Nick escorted Butler through the priory's ground floor, he requisitioned the formal dining hall for their base of operations.

"How far is it to Oxford by motorcar?" Butler asked.

"Less than half an hour," Jack said. "Why?"

Butler and Steigler exchanged a glance. "Could you drive one of my men and Agent Steigler to the Oxford Control Room? They house all CCTV feed for this area. We need to keep the helicopter for search and rescue."

Jack agreed and took off immediately with both agents.

With no way to contribute, Nick watched as the team set up their electronic devices on the dining room table. He unabashedly listened in when Butler took a call, struggling to understand the one-sided conversation.

"The police pinged her mobile," Butler said after he hung up. "No response. It's possible the unknown subject is using a jammer."

"Don't you have software to override a jamming signal?" Nick balled his fists inside his trouser pockets, his short nails digging into his palms.

"Not at this time," Butler said.

Nick paced to the window, turning his back on the room as worry ate at his thoughts, his stomach, and his newfound trust in God. The minutes crawled, each interminable second striking against his heart.

Half an hour later, one of Butler's team announced, "Agent Jorgason has identified a dark sedan exiting the Tesco lot about the time Miss Pressley-Coombes disappeared. He is connecting us to Oxford Control Room feed."

"Excellent." Butler indicated a man seated in front of a large computer screen. "Agent Smith will be scouring CCTV feed to locate the sedan."

"Feed's up," another member of the team said.

Nick rejoined the group and took up position behind Agent Smith's chair. A dark sedan exited the Tesco lot on tape.

"Zoom in on the driver," Butler barked.

Smith, a tall beanpole of a man with goggle eyes and protruding nose, magnified the vehicle.

"Hooded. He's no amateur." Butler blew out a sigh. "All right, men, find that car on every camera it passes."

"Got it," Smith said.

The motorcar turned right, heading out of town on the A417.

"That's a busy road," Nick murmured.

"We should be able to follow his progress easily enough," Smith said, manipulating his computer keys.

Several minutes passed between camera sightings.

"He's turning off and looping back toward Bascombe," Smith commented, playing the computer keyboard like a string instrument, focusing and blowing up every inch of the driver's face. The unsub's features remained obscured.

"That's odd." Butler hopped on the computer beside Agent Smith and pulled up Bascombe's street map.

Silence reigned until Smith picked up the sedan's trail. "He's back on the A417, heading the same direction as before."

Smith switched to the next camera and waited for the car to come into view. Nothing.

"Where's the next camera on that stretch of road?"

"Two kilometers," Smith said.

"Find out if there is anything wrong with that feed," Butler ordered.

A quiet man with gray eyes placed the call. After a short conversation with his teammate in Oxford, the agent hung up. "The camera's working, boss."

"He must have taken a side road." Butler tapped a tattoo on the tabletop.

Nick gripped the back of a Chippendale dining chair, squeezing it until his knuckles went white. "There are no paved roads off that stretch. Most are simple farm tracks."

"Do you happen to know if any of them exit onto major highways?" Butler zoomed in and out on the satellite map.

"A few." Nick stood at his shoulder and pointed out several places.

"McMullen, take the helicopter and see if you can locate that motorcar," Butler said, never taking his eyes off the computer screen.

Agent McMullen glanced out the window. It was getting dark. A crease furrowed his brow, but he left to do his boss's bidding. A sudden gust of wind spattered rain against the glass. The storm had arrived.

"How many farm tracks are on that segment of road?" Butler asked.

"Three." Nick rubbed his forehead as if that would help him remember. "Four at best. One of them belongs to the priory. It's a service entrance for the harvesters."

The sudden throb of the helicopter made talking impossible. Nick twitched back the drapery and watched it take off.

Butler left his chair and paced by the bank of windows facing the terrace. "Smith, connect us to the chopper feed. I need you to direct them to those farm tracks."

Smith donned a headset with an attached mouthpiece. Due to the incoming storm, it was too dark to see, and the helicopter returned after a handful of minutes. The outdoor search was shelved until morning.

Nick uncurled his fingers with effort and popped an antacid from the roll in his pocket. He went to the library, where he paced the remainder of the night.

At 8:00 a.m., Alice wheeled a tea cart loaded with beverages, fruit, scones, and clotted cream into the dining room. Inhaling the scent of freshly brewed coffee almost did Nick in. Certain things about his religion were going to take some getting used to.

Recently returned from the Oxford Control Room, Jack arrived with black circles under his eyes. "What's the latest?"

"The police pinged Catherine's mobile yesterday." Jack's features brightened until Nick added, "They believe her abductor is using a jammer. Did you find anything on those tapes?" Nick snagged a banana off the tea cart, hoping it would settle his stomach.

"No. The Oxford Control Room called out a ground search-and-rescue unit to cover the quadrant south of A417 as we were leaving."

Butler's team and Agent Steigler crowded round the tea cart, slathering scones and pouring coffee.

Steam wafted up from Smith's coffee mug, and Nick took another sniff. Smith took a sip, then jerked forward in his chair, sloshing his beverage. "Unsub on A417 heading toward Knoxham. I think he's going to enter the M4 at junction fifteen."

Smith's hunch proved correct. The sedan entered the M4. Agent Smith placed his mug on the table and followed the vehicle until it approached Reading. "Unsub exiting motorway."

Butler's men and FBI Agent Steigler jumped to their monitors, pulling up satellite images of roadways in Reading close to the M4. Catherine's abductor led them on a merry chase through the west side of the city before parking the stolen sedan at a car hire agency. Ditching the vehicle, the unsub started down the pavement on foot.

"He's still hooded," Smith said.

"This guy's a pro," Jorgason muttered.

Butler picked up his mobile and patched through to Reading's DCI. "Unsub is male, hooded, dark trousers, and under six feet."

Holding a hand over the mouthpiece, Butler said, "Jorgason, ask the controllers in Reading and Oxford to check camera feed for number plate BD52 SMR at all petrol stations and green grocers off the A41 and M4. We might get lucky with a facial if he stopped."

Jorgason didn't need further prompting. He made the calls while Agent Butler continued his conversation with the Reading police.

Nick popped another antacid as he watched the car-hire screen, waiting for the police to arrive. The clock continued to tick as the unknown subject passed several more CCTV cameras. Nick rubbed his neck. Where were the police?

Switching to another feed, Smith followed the kidnapper's route, but just like in Bascombe, the man disappeared between cameras.

"Tracking him is like hunting a ghost." Steigler scratched his head. "He knows where every camera is on any given route."

A police vehicle entered the car-hire lot, where the unsub had dumped the sedan. Bottled tension knotted Nick's shoulders. He took a turn around the room. Butler's unit was doing everything possible to locate Catherine, but he feared it wasn't enough.

Another call sounded on Butler's mobile. He hit speaker so all could listen in. Nick spared a thought for Jack, who had taken position by one of the windows some time ago.

"Controller Elliott, Reading District." The youngish male voice filled the silent room. "We've hit a patch of luck. A petrol station off the M4 has your unsub on film." Nick heard the satisfaction in Elliott's tone. "Sending now."

Within a few minutes, a video feed of the unsub relayed to Smith, who immediately sent it on to INTERPOL.

"Running facial recognition through INTERPOL," Smith said.

After a sleepless night filled with worry, Nick found it hard to converse or keep the negativity at bay. He wondered how Catherine's brother had remained so collected this morning.

Jack stared out the windows, seemingly oblivious to the activity in the room behind him. Nick came up beside him. Jack motioned Nick toward the door. Nick followed him into the hall, where they ran into Fellowes busily dusting the wainscoting not far from the dining room door. The man should at least attempt more covert tactics, Nick thought. Even Sammy was better at subterfuge. He nodded to the butler as they passed and continued to the terrace.

Last night's rain left a white, smoky haze of humidity hanging over the estate.

"How do you manage to stay so calm? I'm on the edge of madness," Nick asked without preamble.

Jack placed a hand on his shoulder. "I've been praying since yesterday. Every time I start to panic and think they won't find Catherine, peace settles over me. I can't explain it any better than that. One thing I do know: Heavenly Father is aware of this situation."

"I didn't see you leave the room to pray." Nick gave him a disgruntled stare.

"If the situation calls for it, you can pray with your eyes open and say it silently in your head. The Lord can hear us, even if we can't verbalize the words."

Never in Nick's life had he felt so close to falling apart. If anyone needed peace, he did. "Do you mind if we pray together?" Nick hesitated. "I haven't had much practice."

"Not at all."

Both men stood on the terrace, facing the lake. They bowed their heads and prayed for Catherine's safety. Nick was astonished that Jack included those working the case to be blessed with inspiration to locate her.

At the conclusion of the prayer, Nick leaned against the balustrade. He took several deep breaths to clear his thoughts. The jittery nerves that had been jangling through him since yesterday began to settle. Bit by bit, that peace Jack had referred to flowed into his soul.

Three weeks ago, he wouldn't have spoken to Jack without hostility, nor would he have bowed his head in supplication to the Lord. He gave an internal shake of the head; Catherine's box had altered his life.

"We should get back," Jack said.

"Have you been able to contact your father?" Nick asked as they reentered the priory.

"James is still trying to reach him. Dad's in the Andes drilling wells in primitive villages. It's his annual humanitarian trip."

When they returned to the dining room, Agent Butler's unit was grouped behind Smith's chair. Each man's gaze was laser-focused on the screen. Their hushed excitement communicated itself to Nick's brain.

"What's going on?" Jack and Nick inserted themselves beside Jorgason.

"See for yourself." Jorgason nodded to Smith's monitor.

A picture of the man appeared. Beside it, the result of INTERPOL's search flashed the words, "Unknown Subject. Not in system."

Nick leaned forward to take a closer look. His mouth went dry, and his heart pounded triple time. "I know this man. He works for my grandfather."

CHAPTER FORTY-FOUR

CATHERINE STARED OUT THE PANELESS window as the sun peeked over the horizon. The vast sea of crops were devoid of human habitation. She chewed the last bite of granola bar and swallowed.

Ari had left yesterday after securing her manacle. She made use of the bucket and tossed the refuse out the broken-hinged door. With any luck, Ari would step in it when he returned.

The skin around her neck was raw from constant chafing. She shifted position. Her fetter jangled. Ari had cleared the shed of anything she could use to pick the lock.

She paced away from the window, the chain clinking behind her. The manacle dug into her neck. She lifted it off her skin. Her lip curled in distaste as she looked at the links stretched across the dirt-packed floor. The long chain gave Catherine full mobility inside the building and then some.

Returning to the window, her fingers touched the splintered wood. The building was low to the ground, limiting her view. If she could reach the roof, perhaps she could signal for help.

She climbed onto the rotted sill. Chunks of wood jabbed her backside as she investigated the eaves. They protruded four inches from the external wall. During last night's rain, she had stayed fairly dry and assumed the lumber overhead was sound enough to hold her weight.

Catherine pulled herself to a stand on the sill. She would have to swing free of her position in order to hoist herself onto the roof. The added weight of the chain could make it tricky, if not downright impossible. If she fell . . . Hopefully after last night's rain, the ground would be soft and wouldn't hurt too much.

Sitting like a good little girl waiting for her captor's return was not on her agenda. Bundling up her chain, she dumped it outside the window. The weight from the manacle caused the metal to cut into her neck. She didn't need the chain pulling her toward the structure as well.

Glancing from the window to the roofline, she measured the distance. To get her leg onto the shingles, she'd need momentum and flexibility. Ballet had given her plenty of the second. Reaching her arms as high onto the roof as possible, she jumped, swinging her legs to the side. Her leg missed the roofline, and she dangled in the air by her forearms, her fingers scrabbling for purchase. The weight of the chain pulled on her neck. She felt herself start to slip. Grabbing for a better hold, her fingers located a ridge in the missing shingles.

Pushing her head forward to fight the weight of the chain, she shifted side to side, swinging her body pendulum style. This gave her right leg enough impetus to catch the edge of the roof on her second attempt. Splinters dug into her ankle. The manacle grated the raw flesh of her throat as she leaned forward, straining to keep her balance. Sweat beaded on her forehead and broke out on her lower back. Clawing and pulling, she inched her body high enough to hoist her torso onto the shingles.

She flopped onto the roof, panting. The weight of the manacle pulled. She sat up, holding the metal off her skin, and scooted back from the edge. Slowly, her breathing settled, and she took in her surroundings.

Behind the storage shed, the land rose steeply, covered in oilseed rape, a crop converted into vegetable oil. When she had first arrived in the UK, their bright yellow blooms had blanketed the Cotswold hillsides. Today, the rapeseed appeared ready for harvest.

Farther up the slope, a group of chimneys clustered. The building was too far to call for help. No one would hear her. In every other direction, crops spread like a blanket across the rolling terrain. A farm track started at the two-lane highway a good mile to the south and wound its way through the fields past the storage shed upon which she sat and continued on toward the distant chimneys.

Since her abduction, Catherine had refused to accept her predicament, fostering a hope of escape. Propping her chin on her knees, she felt the press of tears pushing against the back of her eyelids. After seeing how isolated she was, her hope died. She had exhausted her own resources, so she turned to the Lord once again, offering up what had to be her thousandth prayer for strength and a way to free herself.

She had a sneaking suspicion the diary had something to do with her abduction. Whatever it contained remained a mystery. How she wished she had listened to Martin that night after Institute. Instead, she had run out of the Church building to keep from making a fool of herself. Now she might never know the answer.

From her perch, she heard an engine. A blue car, followed by a box truck entered the farm track from the main road. With joy filling her heart, Catherine rose to her knees on the shingles and waved frantically.

Tension drained from her body as they turned at the fork that led to the shed. Joy spurted and sputtered inside her heart. The lead car stopped, and the driver got out.

It was Ari.

Ari was back. And he had company. Cold sweat broke out on Catherine's body. Her skin rippled as though something slimy slithered over her bare feet. She sat on the roof, hugging her arms around her torso, and waited.

A dark-haired woman with a big floppy hat and oversized sunglasses sat in the passenger seat of the bright-blue car. The box truck parked behind them. Three dark-haired men sat inside the cab.

Ari ignored her. He approached the truck and spoke to the driver. The woman turned her head in Catherine's direction and stared. Gooseflesh stood up on Catherine's arms.

One of the men climbed out of the truck, carrying a large black case, a backpack, camera bag, and a folding metal chair. With a brief glance in her direction, he entered the structure. The woman exited the blue car and followed him inside.

Ari approached the shed. He stopped below her and looked up. "Get down."

Catherine knew she had no option. All he had to do was *yank her chain*, and she would tumble off. Scooting toward the edge, she flipped onto her stomach and swung her lower body over the edge. Ari caught her legs and helped her to the ground. Her knees wanted to buckle.

"No more games." Grasping her by the manacle loop, Ari shoved her toward the window. She tripped. The manacle cut into her flesh. Catherine bit her lip to keep from crying out. He boosted her up and pushed her through the opening, her chain landing on top of her.

From her heap on the ground, she watched the man from the truck setting up video equipment on a tripod and connecting it to a laptop. Catherine rose to her feet on the dirt floor.

Ari entered through the door and asked something in a foreign language. The man grunted.

The dark-haired woman stared at her, never removing her gaze. Something about her made Catherine's flesh crawl.

Ari approached and handed Catherine a sweater that buttoned up the front. "Take off your shirt and put this on."

Catherine blinked. He couldn't mean for her to change in front of them. By the expression on Ari's face, he did. She reached down her leg and tried to gather up the chain, thinking to use it as a weapon.

The ever alert Ari narrowed his eyes and stepped on it. "You change your shirt, or I will help you change it."

Tossing her head, she turned her back and began to unbutton her blouse with shaky fingers. She dropped the filthy piece of clothing on the ground and slipped her arms inside the sweater. Her fingers were too numb with fear to do up her buttons. The woman came over and fastened them, her long red nails scraping the skin on Catherine's chest. She seemed familiar, but Catherine couldn't place her.

When the woman finished, Ari shoved Catherine into the folding chair facing the camera. He jerked her arms behind her back on the outside of the chair and duct taped her wrists.

Catherine glared at all three of her captors. Were they going to send a ransom video to her father?

The woman began to scrub the dirt off Catherine's face with baby wipes, pushing hard on her bruised jaw. Catherine winced and jerked her head away, but the woman yanked on the manacle. Gritting her teeth, Catherine refused to cry out.

Ari inserted a key into her manacle. As the weight dropped away, Catherine took her first deep breath since her abduction. The woman continued to wipe her face and neck, pressing on the raw flesh. Catherine bit her tongue, unwilling to give her satisfaction.

Finished, the woman covered Catherine's facial bruises with makeup. Why were they improving her appearance? If this was an abduction video, wouldn't they want her father to see her battered face?

Standing beside the videographer, Ari watched the proceedings. He turned to the woman. "Fix her hair."

Without a word, the woman removed a large brush and spritzer from her bag and began to work the bristles through Catherine's tangled mane. She was not gentle. Catherine's eyes watered from the abuse.

Ari placed a hand on the woman's arm. The intimate gesture stopped his accomplice midbrush. "Be nice. We don't want her to cry for the camera. We only have ten minutes until the auction starts."

Auction? They were going to sell her? Like a slave. Like . . . Catherine wanted to vomit.

The thing she had not allowed herself to consider burst upon her consciousness. For the better part of two days, she had convinced herself that they were holding her for ransom. This was far, far worse. She was being trafficked.

Reaching forward, the woman unbuttoned the top several fastenings on Catherine's sweater. "The girl has no cleavage. No one will bid on her," she said over her shoulder.

Catherine felt the heat of a blush rise up her neck and flood her face at the woman's vulgar words. Only the sick and depraved purchased women and children. Her stomach quivered, and bile filled her mouth. She hadn't forgotten the Oxford University student whose body had been found in Morocco, nor the hundreds of thousands of children who went missing each year.

Blind fury coursed through her body. These were evil people. People who dealt in human bondage. She wasn't going to make it easy for them. There must be something left she could do.

Furtively, she measured the distance between herself and the camera. Her legs weren't bound, but her arms were pinned behind her. If she tried to escape, she wouldn't make it to the door. She was doomed.

The cameraman tested the lighting, then turned on the video feed. Ari and the woman moved to the doorway. With delighted smiles, they conversed in soft tones. Ari leaned forward and kissed the woman's lips.

Taking advantage of their distraction, Catherine squeezed her arms tight, securing the back of the metal chair between her body and her arms. Rising in a hunched, bent-knee position, she took three steps forward and swung her body to the left. The chair legs made contact with the tripod and light stands, knocking them to the floor amidst what she assumed was foreign swearing. She smacked one leg of the chair in the middle of the laptop keyboard and plunked herself, chair and all, on top of it. The black plastic casing cracked and went dark.

The woman screamed, her high-pitched shriek splitting the air. Ari grabbed a handful of Catherine's hair and pulled her head back, glaring at her with inexpressible fury. In defiance, she smiled up into his face.

Ari doubled his fist and punched her in the stomach. She pitched forward in her chair, gasping, but his hand in her hair pulled her back. He hit her again. This time his fist connected with her sore jaw, and everything went black.

CHAPTER FORTY-FIVE

CATHERINE CAME SLOWLY AWAKE. HER head was muzzy, and her jaw ached. She lay on her side. Her arms were numb and pinned behind her, a dead weight on her shoulders. The rattling overhead echoed inside her brain.

Fractured bits of conversation, real or imagined, floated through her mind.

"Shipment to Reykjavik."

"Transport?"

"Yacht is in Oban."

Memories of the shed came pouring back. Sweat broke out on her body. She wanted to scream. No one knew where she was.

Lifting her head off the metal floorboards in the semidarkness, she realized she was not alone, nor was she inside the shed. More than a dozen bodies lay in heaps around her. She shuddered and closed her eyes, praying they weren't dead.

The truck hit a pothole, bouncing her into the body beside her. Recoiling, she scrabbled away. Then she noticed the rhythmic rise and fall of the person's chest.

Sleeping? Most likely drugged. Anyone else would have woken after a hit like that. Leaning over, she blew the hair out of the child's tear-stained face to get a better look at him. He couldn't be older than ten or eleven.

She glanced at the faces closest to her. Most of them were girls in their early to midteens. Two more were boys about the same size as the child beside her.

Groaning, she sat up and scooted the few feet to the side of the truck. She pressed her shoulders against the interior wall to keep herself upright. The metallic rattling sounded like an out-of-range radio station.

When she had destroyed her captors' equipment, Catherine had hoped to anger them enough to force their hand. Death had seemed a much better alternative than what lay ahead.

While working on her undergrad, she had written a paper on international crime, with a focus on human trafficking. Her research on the survivors had broken her heart. Their once vibrant personalities had altered. Many suffered drug addictions, and others committed suicide.

Her thoughts shifted to her companions inside the truck. None of them stood a chance. Their minds would shatter from the atrocities committed against them. Pressing her face against the cool, reverberating wall, tears slid down her cheeks. Most of these children would die from overdose, abuse, or disease. Those who survived would suffer longer. She shuddered.

Days ago, while sitting on Creag an Tuirc, Catherine had pondered what she could do to make a difference. Finding a cause to champion, she had told herself, would take time. She snorted, the sick humor sour on her tongue. Her cause lay all around her, for however long she lived.

Anger consumed her with a fury so white it devoured personal fear. A desire to protect these children rose in her heart. Wiping her nose on her shoulder, she sat up straighter.

Halfway across the truck, a Middle Eastern girl met her eyes. Catherine tried to smile, but it hurt her jaw. The teenager rose on her haunches and inched her way to Catherine's side, trying not to fall on the other children.

"Don't drink the water," the girl whispered with a heavy accent. "It makes you sleep."

The girl's words confirmed her suspicions. Catherine licked her chapped lips. What an easy way to accomplish a drugging.

"How long have you been on this truck?" Catherine shifted her legs to a more comfortable position.

"Maybe two days. They are collecting." The teenager didn't need to elaborate on what. "I heard them say you were the last."

"I think they plan to ship us to Iceland from a small port in Scotland." Catherine's eyes swept over the children. Like the girl beside her, most of them looked foreign. "Do any of the others speak English?"

"My brother, Diaab." The girl pointed to a small boy.

"We've got to get everyone off this truck before we reach Oban."

"I will help. My parents will grieve if we do not return. Diaab is their only son." Though she did not express it, the girl seemed to understand their predicament.

The truck hit a pothole, jarring Catherine's arms and scraping her skin against a partially imbedded screw. She sucked in her breath. The screw . . . Her pulse quickened, and hope bloomed. Rising to her knees, she located it and sawed at her bindings.

The girl sat forward. "Let me help. I am Afsana."

The girl gently pushed Catherine aside so she had access to her wrists. Taking the tape in her teeth, Afsana began tearing at the snag Catherine had created in the duct tape. The girl was not bound, Catherine noticed, nor were the other children. Ari must have dumped her in the truck *as is* after he'd coldcocked her.

"I'm Catherine. Do any of the men in the cab speak English?"

"I think the driver might. The other two do not."

She and Afsana continued to speak in whispers.

"How come you aren't asleep?" Catherine asked.

"The water tasted bitter. I woke up later, and the light had changed when they opened the door. I realized what they were doing. Since then, I only sip enough to help the body."

"And your brother? He drank the water?"

"Yes. He was very thirsty when the men came last time." Afsana's eyes grew moist, glistening in the dim lighting.

"How do you get away with not drinking?"

"I pretend I am asleep. Diaad was thirsty. He is only eleven." She gave a shrug of her slender shoulders, as if to explain how useless it was to work with small boys. "These men are lazy. Only one comes inside to make us drink. The other stands outside the door."

Afsana touched Catherine's hand. Her lips trembled. "Do not drink too much. One boy did not wake up. They left him on the side of the road."

They had killed a child and tossed him away like refuse? Bile rose in Catherine's throat, and she thought she would vomit.

"There are three of them, aren't there?" Catherine asked when she felt like she could speak evenly. "What about the driver?"

"He stays in the cab." Afsana wet her lips and looked scared. "There is a gun in his trousers."

The tape on Catherine's wrists separated. Afsana tore it from her skin, ripping off hair. Catherine grunted and slumped forward, wiggling her fingers. Her arms felt like blocks of wood attached to her shoulders.

Afsana lifted Catherine's right arm and began to rub it to restore circulation. After a few minutes, the restricted blood began to move, stinging like a handful of hypodermics plunging into her skin. Catherine inhaled sharply through her nose. Needlelike pain shot up her arms.

"I need a weapon." Catherine tried to focus on their next step to freedom instead of the stabbing sensations in her upper extremities.

"There is nothing. I have checked." Doubt clouded Afsana's features. "How can you free all of us? You would have to run for help. How far could you go without shoes before they caught you?" Afsana picked up Catherine's left arm and started to rub.

Failure had never been part of Catherine's vocabulary. She refused to accept it now. Not with so many lives at stake.

The truck hit another bump. The rattling increased. Her head pounded, and the incessant noise wasn't helping. Catherine glared at the metal frame above her head. Her eyes narrowed further. An idea occurred to her.

"Afsana, kneel down. I'm going to see if I can free that rod. I think it's loose," she said urgently.

Without questioning her, the Middle Eastern girl knelt. Catherine stepped onto Afsana's back and inspected the rod. It was half an inch thick and had entirely come away from one of its fastenings. She climbed down.

"Help me move these girls."

Together they shifted teenagers so she could check the other end of the metal rod.

Resuming her investigation, Catherine realized the rods that framed the ceiling had not been welded together. They were connected by couplers. One of the rods had worked itself loose, causing the racket. Corrosion covered the opposite end, freezing the joint.

Catherine groaned. If she had her brother's welding torch, she could free the rod easily. But this . . . This would be like trying to pry open a clam with a pair of false eyelashes.

Her arms shook. Catherine took a break to rest them. Afsana was too short to change places, so it was left to Catherine to find a solution. During her brief respite, Catherine noticed two teens beginning to stir.

"The sleeping drug is wearing off. The men will stop soon. They usually find a private stretch of road for us to relieve ourselves before they make us drink." Afsana explained their transporters' pattern.

The girl seemed incredibly observant. Doubtless, her little brother's safety had brought out a protective streak in her. Whatever it was, Catherine was grateful for her maturity and assistance.

Climbing back up, Catherine twisted the coupler until the skin wore off her fingertips and bled freely on the metal joint. The truck swerved around a tight curve, pitching Catherine off Afsana's back. She grasped the rod to keep from falling and swung free of Afsana's back. The lubricant of blood combined with her added weight snapped the rod free.

Catherine dropped, landing hard on top of three teenage girls. One of them cried out, making enough noise for those in the cab to hear. Holding her thigh, the girl shrieked with all the drama of a Vaudeville act.

The other two girls looked blearily at her through dilated eyes. Catherine stood, pushing her long curls out of her face, grateful she hadn't skewered anyone with her newly acquired weapon. She knelt on the floor beside the squalling girl to see if she had done any real damage. The girl appeared more bruised than hurt.

Putting a finger to her lips, Catherine pointed to the partition dividing the truck from the cab. The injured girl nodded, understanding the need for silence. Unfortunately, it came too late.

The truck pulled to the side of the road, braking hard. She could hear the men speaking to one another in a foreign tongue through the partition. Afsana was signaling frantically for her to lie down. Catherine couldn't do that until she found a hiding place for their weapon. If their transporters caught sight of the metal bar, they would lose it. By now, most of the children were stirring and looking around blearily.

Frantically, Catherine glanced around. The floor was made of systematic grooves, but the metal tube was bigger than the depressions in the floor. They might be able to keep it from view if Afsana and her brother laid on it.

The squeak of the cab door put new panic in Catherine's heart. Waving her arms to get Afsana's attention, Catherine motioned for her to lie on top of the rod. Sliding the tube into the floor groove, Afsana covered it with most of her body.

The unmistakable crunch of gravel reached her ears as the men came around the back of the truck. Catherine searched for a place to lie on the crowded floor. The children had shifted around when they'd woken up. Only one gap by the door was large enough for her.

The padlock rattled, and Catherine jumped over two children and knelt. She pulled her arms behind her back as the door opened. An olive-skinned man with an unkempt beard poked his head inside, narrowing his eyes at her.

With a sickening thud, her heart plunged to her toes. In one hand, he carried a two-liter bottle. There would be no way out of drinking his foul brew.

Muttering something to her in a guttural language, the bearded man climbed inside the truck. Unscrewing the top, he shoved the end of the bottle against her lips. She could taste the bitterness of the drug before the water touched her tongue. She took a small sip, holding it inside her mouth.

He opened his lips and pointed for her to do the same. Catherine glared at him, refusing to comply. Shrugging, he kicked the girl next to Catherine with his steel-toed boot. The girl screamed and bent double, holding her stomach.

Catherine got the message and swallowed the water. The gleam of success shone in his eyes as he moved on to his next victim.

The drug worked almost immediately. Wave after wave of sleepiness washed over her like a rising tide. The second man's dizzy image came into view when she turned her head. He stood behind the truck, playing with his phone. Of the driver there was no sign. Afsana was right, she thought. He must be inside the cab.

As she fought the drug to stay awake, her mind slipped back to the incidents that had led to her abduction. She still had the strongest impression Glorianne's diary played into this somehow. If only she had kept it together long enough to listen to Martin.

Her vision blurred. The last thing Catherine remembered was the rise and fall of the mist blanketing the scenery outside the truck door.

CHAPTER FORTY-SIX

THE DOORBELL RANG, AND THE typical murmur of voices ensued. Believing it to be one of Rivendon's numerous acquaintances, Theodosia continued with her mountain of correspondence. The canary diamond engagement ring Ari had given her last night flashed in the natural light from the window.

A hoarse shout and crash of crockery brought her to her feet. Smoothing her snug, citrine skirt, she went to investigate, her heels clicking on the marble tiles.

A group of men in dark suits filled the entry hall. Two of them had Ari by the arms and were in the process of slapping handcuffs on his wrists. He struggled between them, refusing to glance at her.

Her heart screamed, but she bit back her fear. She must stay calm. Glancing from one face to another, she asked, "What is going on?"

A man stepped forward and handed her his card. His eyes were flint gray and resembled granite. "William Butler, INTERPOL Human Trafficking and Child Exploitation Unit."

Theodosia took it with two fingers, not bothering to read his credentials. "We are here to arrest Ari Falcone."

"Whatever for?" Theodosia placed a hand on her heart as it tried to leap out of her chest.

"Who might you be?" Agent Butler ignored her question.

"Lady Hadley, the Earl of Rivendon's personal assistant." Theodosia looked down her nose at him.

"This young man has been involved in a human trafficking operation."

"I assure you, Ari is above board. The Earl of Rivendon would not have hired him otherwise," she said, trying to stifle the panic mounting inside her.

"That may be, Lady Hadley, but he has been positively identified on CCTV."

Across the hall, Ari started, looking much surprised.

Agent Butler's phone rang. He excused himself, standing on the porch to take the call just as Mr. Scott appeared. It was his day off. One of the maids must have notified him.

"What's all this about?" Scott demanded at his most proper.

Theodosia knew it would be a matter of moments before Ari incriminated her. When she could bear it no longer, she glanced at him across the marbled hall. Their gazes locked. An expression of utter devotion flashed briefly on his face. She had misjudged him.

Her eyes filled with tears. How could she go on without him? He was her happiness. Ari's glittering dark eyes stared into hers, then glanced at the spot where a Chinese umbrella stand lay broken on the floor.

She followed his gaze. On the marble tiles, beside the broken crockery, lay a white business card. Looking back up at Ari, she let him know she had seen it.

"I am not a citizen of this country. You have no right to arrest me." He struck out, trying to break free.

He was immediately surrounded.

Theodosia edged her way around the men and stepped on top of the card. Glancing at Ari through her lashes, she caught his slight nod. Whatever was on that card, Ari wanted her to have the information.

Agent Butler bustled back inside. Without further ado, he rattled off Ari's right to silence. "Ari Falcone, I am arresting you for the kidnapping and human trafficking of Catherine Pressley-Coombes. You do not have to say anything that may harm your defense. If you do not mention when questioned something which you later rely on in court. Anything you do say may be given in evidence."

The right to silence made little sense to British citizens. How Agent Butler expected Ari, an Italian, to comprehend it was beyond Theodosia. But she stood tall, trying not to shatter like the Chinese umbrella stand as Butler's men led Ari out the front door, past the potted urns to a waiting sedan. Inside the vehicle, Ari turned his head, gazing at her through the window with the same adoring expression as the day they had first met.

"Is there a private room where I may question individual members of the household?" Agent Butler asked Mr. Scott.

"I believe the library would be best." Scott closed the front door and led Agent Butler down the hall, leaving Theodosia in the entry. She had to get Ari released. Human trafficking was a fourteen-year sentence. Theodosia picked up the white card, and flipping it over, she read, Donato Delgado, Barrister, Middle Temple Lane, London.

Delgado. That was Ari's name on the second passport. If anyone could release Ari, the Delgado crime family could.

One thought consumed her as she sat at her desk. If Catherine Pressley-Coombes was free, she would pay for this. Theodosia would see to it personally. Ari could not save her this time.

CHAPTER FORTY-SEVEN

NICK POPPED FOUR ASPIRIN AND chased them down with an entire water bottle. The extra stimulus was one of two things that had kept him going during the last thirty hours—aspirin and prayer. But not necessarily in that order.

Only three inhabitants were in the priory's dining room, four counting himself, when he came back from showering. The place smelled like a dozen smelly schoolboys after a cricket match. He opened the sash windows, letting in fresh air.

Jack was sprawled in a chair, his head tipped forward onto his chest, asleep. The American FBI agent worked in tandem with Agent Smith. Nick began to pace, looping the room. The men were exhausted, and Nick had never felt so helpless or emotionally spent.

Butler had recently returned by chopper after arresting Ari. Grandfather and his entire staff had been questioned. The Earl of Rivendon had not been pleased. And Ari was not cooperating.

Nick ran his hands through his hair and took another loop around the room. Agent Smith and FBI Agent Steigler were at their computers going over CCTV feeds like judges for Academy Award–winning Hollywood dramas.

Of the four farm tracks off the A417, three of them lay to the south under a heavy canopy of trees, making it impossible to locate buildings by air. The priory's farmland lay to the north, covered in crops and largely denuded of forest. The small Ground Search and Rescue force opted to scour the property south of the carriageway.

Smith shifted, his body language suddenly alert, his fingers flying over the keyboard. Nick hustled across the room. On the screen, a white lorry travelled on the A417 behind a blue car. The truck did not reappear on the next camera. It had disappeared on the same stretch of motorway as the sedan.

Agent Smith picked up his mobile and dialed the ground unit. "This is Agent Smith. Have any of your men encountered a white lorry on one of the three farm tracks this morning? I'll hold." Smith tipped his head back and gave Nick a shrug. "Might be nothing, but it never hurts to check."

While he waited, Smith manipulated the camera, focusing and magnifying the lorry's number plate. He took a screen shot and sent it to the ground unit. A full five minutes later, their team lead came back on the line.

Smith put him on speaker. "Negative. No white lorry came down these farm tracks this morning."

"Thank you." Smith disconnected.

"The only other track that lorry could have taken is on priory land. Only one outbuilding is in those fields. If that lorry entered priory land, that's where it will be," Nick said.

Smith called Butler. It rang three times before he picked up. "Hey, Chief. I think we found something."

After hanging up, Agent Smith then called the ground teams and relayed Nick's information. "There's a small shed located on the track just across A417 from you. It's part of Ashford Priory. Could you send a few men over to check? I'll stay on the line."

Another agent sauntered in, freshly shaven and smelling of musk cologne. "Any new developments?"

"Just following my nose on something." Smith gave him a shrug and took a sip of cold coffee.

Agent Steigler turned to Nick. "How far off the motorway is that shed?"

"A mile or so. It's quite small and low lying." Nick went to Jack, placed a hand on his shoulder, and gave him a shake.

"Whaaa? I'm awake." Jack rubbed his face. Dark stubble covered his cheeks. He looked like a vagrant and didn't smell much better.

"Smith might have found something," Nick said quietly.

Jack pushed himself out of his chair, an enormous yawn splitting his face. "When did you find time to shower?"

"Sometime around four this morning. Any of the guest suites are at your disposal. Might I suggest you wait for the ground crew's report first."

Jack idly rubbed his chest as another yawn split his face.

Yet again, Nick prayed for Catherine's safety. He was appalled that she might have been detained on his land and scared half out of her wits.

Smith fiddled with his computer keys. His mobile lay on the table with the speaker amplified.

"Entering farm track," Ground Search and Rescue said over the speaker. "Several sets of tire treads since last night's storm."

Smith continued to run through feed while they waited. Without warning, he punched the air. A white lorry reappeared on tape, leaving Bascombe.

"Tracks stop at the shed. We're getting out," a disembodied voice spoke through Smith's mobile speaker.

Nick and Jack assembled between Smith and Steigler's chairs while the rest of Butler's unit straggled in. Silence ensued. Faintly, through the speaker, they could hear orders being issued.

"Clear," someone yelled from the ground team.

More indistinct talking. The team lead's voice came on the line. "Send a forensics unit."

Nick's heart literally stopped. Everything inside him froze. He couldn't think. He couldn't feel. He couldn't speak.

"We have a smashed mobile and broken electronic bits and bobs," the lead added.

Nick sat, exchanging glances with Jack. He shut his eyes and prayed.

"Her cell phone case is bright purple," Jack said quietly to Smith.

Smith locked eyes with Jack and said into his mouthpiece, "By any chance, does that mobile have a bright-purple case?"

"Affirmative."

Jack smacked the tabletop beside Steigler's computer with both palms.

Feeling like a caged bear, Nick got up and took another turn around the room. If Catherine were in the shed, search and rescue would have said. Where was she?

Nick stopped beside Smith's chair. "What time did that lorry leave my property?" In other words, how much of a head start did they have on Butler's unit?

"Almost four hours ago," Smith said.

Agent Butler entered the room, his hair still wet from the shower. "Update."

"We have identified a transport vehicle. A white lorry. Mercedes. Number plate LL63 RQY. Ground Search and Rescue have a tentative identification on Miss Pressley-Coombes's mobile."

"I assume she was nearby?" Butler asked.

"On my land." Nick was nauseated. All this time, she had been a stone's throw away.

"Smith, you and Steigler track that lorry. How much of a head start do they have?" Butler was all business.

"Four hours, sir," Smith said.

Butler grimaced. "Jorgason, get the National Air Police Service on the line."

"Transporters heading north on M6," Agent Smith cut in.

"Get a list of every controller station off that motorway." Butler's words were sharp and focused. "We'll need their help."

Jorgason spoke in clipped tones to the air police and hung up. "The air police asked us to call back when we know the white lorry's approximate location. They're following another situation that should wrap shortly."

Nick marched to the window, fists bunched inside his trouser pockets. In theory, he understood the air police's point. Why take up support aircraft if the ground crew hadn't narrowed the search? The expense would be prohibitive, and other lives could benefit during the interim.

But this was Catherine, not a nameless individual.

The rattle of computer keys reached his ears as Smith manipulated his keyboard, going over old feed on the M6. Agent Butler jumped on the computer next to Agent Smith, blowing up an electronic map. Another team member entered, and Butler set him to messaging an APW to every police precinct.

Jack joined Nick behind Agent Smith's computer screen. He had been quiet for some time, holding his emotions close to his chest.

"What's an APW?" Jack inquired of Agent Butler.

"We circulate a suspect's or vehicle's description to all airports, ports, and railway stations. It helps us apprehend an offender leaving the country."

Nick knew Jack wasn't as calm as he appeared. Ari had refused to cooperate. And time was passing.

One of the agents placed a hand over the mouthpiece of his mobile. "Lorry exited M6 at the border. Controller picked it up on B7076."

"Why would they exit a major motorway? I would think they would head directly for their destination as quickly as possible," Nick remarked.

"Precautionary tactics or a rest stop." Steigler shrugged.

There were fewer CCTV cameras on this secondary road. They needed an eye in the sky. Jorgason patched a call to the air police service. After identifying himself, he passed the phone to Butler.

"Agent Butler, Human Trafficking and Child Exploitation Unit. We have a white lorry, number plate LL63 RQY. Heading north on B7076."

Agent Butler listened to the person on the other end. "I understand you have quite a distance to cover. Sorry we can't give you lot the exact address. With your special equipment, this should be a simple operation. My team is on its way by chopper. We'll be in contact."

Butler disconnected. "Fat lot of country club boys."

"I would be most happy to place a few phone calls after this is over," Nick said dryly.

Butler's stern countenance softened. He gave Nick a smile, the first one he had seen on the man's face. "I believe I shall take you up on that, Lord Ainsley."

"It would be my pleasure."

"Wheels up in ten," Butler addressed his pilot, then turned to FBI Agent Steigler. "Pack your bag. You're coming with us."

Steigler nodded and shut down his computer.

Nick turned to Agent Smith. "Would you text us with updates? We won't be far behind Butler." Grabbing Jack by the arm, he collected jackets and hats in the vestibule on the way out and set off at a jog for the stable block.

"Why are we running a freaking 5K?" Jack muttered under his breath, keeping pace with him.

Ignoring him, Nick opened his mobile and called the municipal airport.

"This is Lord Ainsley. I'd like to charter a flight. We'll arrive in the quarter hour. Two seats. A Learjet if you have one." He made a face. "A chopper will do. Cheers."

"You can't make it to the Kidlington airport in fifteen minutes, Ainsley." Jack's mouth quirked.

Nick smiled and stepped up the pace. On reaching the stable block, he hit his pocket fob, and one of the garage doors opened. Inside, he pulled a sheet off a bright-blue vintage Porsche 964 3.6 Turbo.

"Nice." Jack let out a low whistle.

"You aren't the only one with a taste for vintage cars." Nick climbed behind the wheel and revved the engine.

CHAPTER FORTY-EIGHT

CATHERINE SAT UP, SHAKING HER head to clear her vision. How long had she been asleep? She rubbed the grit from her eyes. Her temples thundered like a truck going over a cattle grid.

She could barely see in the dim light. Afsana sat against the truck wall; her brother, Diaad, leaned against her knee. Both were awake.

A horn blared. The only sound on an otherwise empty stretch of road. The lights of a city faded from the crack around the hinged door. Catherine suspected their transport had passed through either Glasgow or Stirling. If she remembered correctly, Oban was another hour or two north along a circuitous route. One hour, two at best, and she and the children would board ship.

She climbed over the sleeping children to map out her plan with Afsana. As they conferred, Catherine heard Afsana and Diaad's stomachs growl. Withholding food was another tactic the traffickers used to ensure their victims cooperation.

Catherine rubbed her temples. She'd gone too long without liquid. If she didn't drink soon, she would become vilely ill.

"Diaad, I have a very special job for you," Catherine whispered.

Diaad perked up.

"I need you to pretend to be hurt." Catherine glanced at Afsana.

"Diaad loves to play-act," Afsana said.

"That's good. If all goes well, he'll also be a hero." Catherine pressed a hand on the boy's shoulder.

As she presented her plan, doubts assailed her. What made her think a twenty-four-year-old woman and a few children could stand against a hardened trafficking ring? Was she crazy? Considering the alternative, she knew this was their only option.

She glanced at Afsana. The girl watched her with steady eyes, waiting for her signal. Gritting her teeth, Catherine pulled herself together. This had to work.

Picking up the metal rod, she moved to the corner just inside the padlocked door. Diaad clambered over sleeping bodies and settled next to the partitioned wall the trailer shared with the cab. Afsana took up her position on the opposite side of the door.

"Now, Diaad," Catherine whispered.

Diaad didn't need a second invitation. An ear-splitting scream filled the trailer. No girl could have done better. He was at a marvelous age, just before puberty, where boys could sing as high as any girl. The Vienna Boys' Choir was missing a stellar performance.

Exclamations came from inside the cab. Diaad carried on, keeping to his role. The truck began to brake. When they came to a stop, the passenger door squeaked open. A double set of footsteps crunched on the road. The driver's side door didn't open.

Catherine offered a prayer of thanks. The armed driver was her main concern.

Diaad's screams bounced off the thin walls. The padlock rattled, but Catherine's heart hammered so loud it nearly blocked the sound. A solid object dropped to the ground. One of the men cursed.

Bending her arms in batting position, Catherine clung to the rod. Her breath came and went in short gasps.

The door opened. Light from a distant street lamp slipped into the dim interior. The bearded abductor poked his head inside. Diaad sounded as though he were being drawn and quartered. Mr. Beard shouted at him in a guttural tongue.

The boy whimpered, then emitted another scream. Mr. Beard turned on his flashlight and hoisted himself inside the truck. Catherine held her breath, hardly daring to breathe. Her body quivered like a cat ready to pounce on its prey. If the man glanced in her direction, Afsana would distract him.

Focusing his light directly on Diaad, the bearded man went to investigate. Careful not to draw his attention, Catherine tiptoed the few feet she needed to get within swinging range. Choking up on the "bat" the way her brothers had taught her, she swung, giving it all she had.

Metal connected with bone and made a hollow crunching sound. The bearded man collapsed with a groan; two sleeping teens cushioned his fall. Catherine closed her eyes and hoped she hadn't killed him.

Mechanically, almost as if she were on the outside of her body watching things unfold, she returned to her corner, hiding in the darkest shadows. Readying her pole, she tried to think about anything but the man's body lying on the floor.

In all the excitement, Diaad had stopped screaming. He resumed his theatrics. Her ears rang from the sound. Catherine shook her head, trying to stay focused, though everything inside her recoiled.

Through the crack in the door hinge, Catherine saw the second man's cell phone screen changing colors. She shifted her shoulders. He must be gaming. After what seemed an eternity but could have been only seconds, his screen went dark. His feet shuffled as he approached the back of the truck.

Raising her weapon, Catherine waited for the unsuspecting man. A large shadow threw itself across the bed of the truck. Calling to his friend, the man stuck his head inside the door. Straining with all her might, Catherine smacked the pole down on his head. The sound reminded her of thumping melons.

The man plunged facedown onto the floorboards, his upper body sliding backward out the door.

"Afsana, help me pull him the rest of the way inside," Catherine hissed. Afsana rushed over to help. They grabbed him by the shoulders and hoisted his body inside the truck, dumping him beside his partner. He was still breathing.

Relief whooshed through her body. "We need to tie them up in case they regain consciousness," she whispered to Afsana.

Catherine searched the second man for his cell phone. Locating it in his shirt pocket, she pulled it out and pressed the power button. It required a password. Catherine groaned in frustration.

"Diaad, give me your shirt," Afsana said softly.

The boy shucked it off. The two girls hastily tore the fabric into strips and tied their captors' arms.

"Diaad, you've done wonderfully. We need you to keep screaming," Catherine whispered with a worried glance toward the back door.

As Catherine got back into position, she had the distinct impression to leave the truck and secret herself beside the tires. She hesitated. The prompting came again, stronger this time.

Taking her weapon, Catherine whispered to Afsana, "Stay hidden."

Easing over the lip of the bed, Catherine let her weight slowly shift off the truck. On the horizon, the white, orbed moon was on the rise, casting long shadows as it ascended the night sky. Afsana's big, dark eyes were the last thing Catherine saw as she slipped underneath the vehicle and disappeared from view.

The asphalt was cold under her feet. The air nipped, feeling of autumn. A train whistled, and the sound of helicopters rumbled in the distance. Several miles away, the lights of a city glowed.

Crouching, Catherine sidled up against the tires, hoping her shadow would meld with their bulk. She had barely secreted herself when the rusty hinges of the driver's door protested as he let himself out.

Calling to his cohorts, his feet hit the ground. Gravel scraped under the soles of a pair of heavy work boots. Catherine could see the dark slacks of his lower leg and prayed he would not check underneath the vehicle.

Diaad still screamed, but his wails were growing weaker.

That boy should receive an award for his heroic efforts, Catherine thought.

After a few steps, the driver paused. Catherine heard a click and the double swipe of metal in quick succession. She knew that sound. His gun was cocked and ready. The driver was taking no risks.

A convulsive shudder ripped through her body. Sweat broke out on her hands, and her heart beat against her ribs.

A flashlight snapped on. The driver waved it in front of him, lighting the way. When he reached the corner of the vehicle, his pace slowed. When he turned the corner and didn't see his accomplices, he would know something was wrong.

Catherine slipped out from under the truck, her bare feet making no sound. Diaad's screams sounded as though he were in agony. Her body quivered like a tightly strung bow. Readying her pole, she waited for the right moment.

Calling once more to his companions, the driver rounded the corner. His flashlight swept the ground not two feet from her bare toes. Catherine held her breath. The light disappeared as he shone it into the bowels of the trailer.

With her heart beating high in her throat, Catherine took two running steps and came around the opposite corner of the truck, swinging the metal rod. The driver must have seen movement in his peripheral vision. He tacked to the right.

Instead of the pole connecting with his head like with the others, it came down on his left shoulder.

Grunting from the impact, the driver faced her, raising his gun. Fire belched from the small black hole. Catherine felt wind fly past her face.

Before she could take another swing, Afsana, from her place inside the truck, slammed the metal door into the back of the driver's head. Her action both surprised and stunned him. He swayed on his feet, trying to stay upright.

Without waiting to see if he would collapse, Catherine hit his gun arm. The gun dropped from his useless fingers. He doubled over, groaning.

"Afsana, get his gun," Catherine yelled and kicked the firearm away.

Scrambling out of the truck, Afsana picked up the gun and gripped it with shaking hands. She pointed the weapon at the driver. Catherine stood over him, ready to strike again if he so much as twitched.

Noise erupted everywhere. Sirens blared, helicopters throbbed, and a kaleidoscope of colors and lights added to the confusion. One of two choppers overhead blinded them with a searchlight, turning darkness to midday. The second helicopter landed, whipping the air with its blades and plastering Catherine's clothes to her body.

Half a dozen police cars screeched to a halt, surrounding the truck and emptying their occupants of uniformed men. Catherine recognized Agent Butler from the Human Trafficking and Child Exploitation Unit.

It was over.

The driver glared at her. Blood ran down his neck from where the metal door had slammed into him. Two police officers ran forward, weapons drawn, and grasped him by the arm.

Police encircled the open cab, wearing Kevlar vests and holding guns at ready. One of them poked his head inside the back of the truck, then shouted for a medic.

In the middle of this cacophony of sound and motion, Catherine stood like a frightened animal, unable to move. Agent Butler approached her, but she couldn't make out his words. The light and sounds added to her disorientation. The first children were being lifted out of the truck.

Catherine watched as the driver was cuffed, and she heard the murmur of, "I am arresting you for the illegal transportation of . . ."

She heard her name called hoarsely and thought she was hallucinating.

"Miss Pressley-Coombes." Agent Butler touched her shoulder. "I have some questions after the medics check your vitals."

Catherine looked back at the truck. Children were carried to a makeshift triage station on the side of the road beside the blue-and-yellow ambulances.

Taking her solicitously by the arm, Butler led her toward the medics. Before she reached it, strong arms came around her. Jack.

"I told you to stay back," Agent Butler bit out.

Jack ignored him. Catherine laid her head on her brother's shoulder, too tired to speak. But it wasn't Jack's voice she had heard. Over her brother's shoulder, she searched the group of men until she found the one face she most wanted to see.

Nick.

He stood at the perimeter, where the police held him back, his blue eyes serious and his face blanched of color. He was the only solid thing in the chaos of movement.

Catherine tried to reach for him, but the metal rod had fused to her hand. With considerable effort, she opened her fingers and let it fall, where it clanged to the ground and rolled to the side of the road.

CHAPTER FORTY-NINE

Four days later

CATHERINE BIT HER LIP AS she and Nick started across the priory's sloping west lawn. Her insides quivered like jelly. This was the first time they had been alone since their break-up.

Why didn't Nick say something? His silence was killing her. Was he angry with her for not responding to all those messages he had sent? She swallowed carefully, knowing he needed an explanation as to why she had not responded to his calls.

At the bottom of the grassy hillside, the serpentine lake sparkled like diamonds under an azure sky. They took the path toward the newly harvested fields on the opposite side of the bridge. Harpo raced ahead, startling a flock of barn swallows.

Due to court proceedings, Catherine's return to the States had been delayed. Thankfully, her boss was understanding of the situation. Taking a deep breath, she tackled the topic uppermost on her mind. "I didn't see your messages until I reached Edinburgh. I'm afraid I didn't read them."

He glanced at her but didn't respond. Things were awkward, and she didn't know how to improve the situation.

She assumed his texts had something to do with the box but had no way to know until she picked up her new cell phone and could access them.

"I planned to read your messages in the privacy of my room, but . . ." She let it hang, not caring to remember what had happened.

"I opened the box after you went on holiday. When it arrived, I thought you were returning my gifts." His mouth quirked, but there was regret in his eyes. "So I set it aside."

"What made you change your mind?"

"I ran into your brother. During our exchange, he threw out a crumb of hope." Nick opened his mouth to say something else, then whistled to the dogs instead. Harpo was well ahead and ignored him, but Star turned and trotted back. If it had been anyone else, she would think Nick was nervous.

"Your box was like looking inside a window to your soul." His voice sounded hoarse. "Your gifts touched me deeply. Especially your old Book of Mormon. It changed my life."

Her eyes widened in astonishment.

"While you were on holiday, I met with the missionaries." Nick rubbed the back of his neck. "Catherine, what I'm trying to say is . . ." He met her eyes. His countenance glowed, reflecting an inner joy she had never seen in him before.

"While you were gone, the elders taught me the discussions, and I was baptized."

If a bomb had exploded in front of them, it could not have stunned her more. Catherine stopped in the middle of the graveled path, staring mutely at him, too dumbfounded for words.

"My messages were invitations to my baptism. When you didn't respond, I asked Jack for your address. I planned to fly up and tell you in person, but he didn't have your direction."

"You were baptized?" The question burst from her lips.

Nick nodded. "I even learned how to pray."

After several shaky breaths, his words began to sink in. She covered her mouth with a trembling hand.

"I've had a massive amount of practice over the last few days." His smile wobbled around the edges, and he tucked one of her stray curls behind her ear. For such a manly guy, that lip wobble convinced her of his sincerity. Her eyes stung. Her vision distorted with unshed tears. Nick had read the Book of Mormon. He was a member. Elation fizzed, then bubbled, and erupted like a geyser shooting toward the heavens. Jack had been right. She had given up on him too soon.

Even so, the least little doubt niggled.

Nick took both her hands, his thumbs rubbing circles on the back of her palms. "Catherine, I'm sorry I kept turning the conversation when you brought up religion. I had a substantial hang-up to work through. If you hadn't walked away, I doubt I would have read your Book of Mormon or considered listening to the missionaries."

Dad had been right too. He'd said breaking up with Nick had caught his attention.

Star whined and brushed up against Nick's leg. Letting go of Catherine's hands, Nick reached down and scratched behind the golden retriever's ears. "After studying the gospel and its tenets, I'm rather surprised you dated me to begin with. You took a terrible risk, Catherine. I completely understand why you broke things off."

"You sound like Jack."

"Don't hold it against me," he teased, then his expression sobered. "I have no idea what you saw in me. There are much better men in this world than I. You deserve the best."

"You're one of the kindest men I have ever known. Besides," she added with a playful toss of her head, "I like the way you sing."

He chuckled and picked up her hand. "I missed you horribly."

"I missed you back." She looked him in the eye, refusing to hide behind a wall of curls.

"I knew you weren't safe. When Jack told me you were taken, I blamed myself."

"I was positive he was after Glorianne's diary. No one could convince me otherwise. Even now, part of me doesn't accept that her diary didn't play a part in everything that occurred." Catherine touched the raw skin on her neck with her free hand.

"Do you have any evidence?"

"No." She shook her head. "It's just a feeling I have that won't let up. Perhaps Martin will know more. He said he had discovered something."

"Why don't you give him a ring, and we'll discuss it over dinner."

"All of us?"

"Of course. I'm rather attached to this ancestor of yours. If it weren't for her, I would never have met you or joined the Church. Professor Giles seems rather attentive. I'd like to make sure he knows where your loyalties lie." Nick's face darkened.

Nick's possessiveness gave Catherine a little thrill.

Harpo came bounding back with a stick hanging out one side of his mouth. He dropped it at Nick's feet, whining for a toss. Nick picked it up and chucked it end over end down the field. The English springer spaniel was off like a shot.

Nick fell silent again. She wondered what thoughts caused such a serious expression.

"Are there any other reasons for us to remain apart?" he finally asked.

"No." She gulped and stared straight ahead. She had forgotten how direct he could be when pursuing a goal.

"Then is it safe to assume this is now acceptable?" Nick ducked his head and brushed his lips across hers, his touch feather-light.

Catherine closed her eyes, sure her bones would melt. When she could breathe without making a conscious effort, she couldn't help teasing him just a little. "You call that a kiss?"

Confusion swirled in his blue eyes.

She felt a momentary twinge of guilt. "After all I've been through, you'll have to do better than that, Lord Ainsley."

Naked relief flashed on his face for the merest second. He threw his head back and laughed as though a huge weight had dropped from his shoulders. Grabbing her around the waist, he crushed her in a tight hug, pulling her off her feet. He didn't let her down until his lips had mashed hers in a most satisfying way.

"That's much better. You were treating me like I was made of glass." She reached up and touched the well-loved planes of his face.

"All my old haunts held memories of you. I couldn't bear it. I was in the process of moving to London when I ran into your brother." With his free hand, Nick touched her cheekbone. "I'm afraid to think what would have happened if either of us had arrived at the post office one moment later. I'll always be grateful that wasn't the case."

He dipped his head and kissed her, holding her like he'd never let her out of his arms again.

CHAPTER FIFTY

JACK CLATTERED DOWN THE STAIRS, buttoning his plaid shirt as Catherine checked the tablescape one last time. Martin planned to share his discovery from Glorianne's diary over dinner. Catherine could hardly contain her excitement.

Nick's familiar knock sounded on the cottage's nail-studded door. She heard the murmur of masculine voices when Jack let Nick and Martin in. She lit the candles, hoping the flickering glow would hide the worst of her bruises, and went to greet their guests.

Over chicken cordon bleu, Martin broached the subject foremost on everyone's mind. "Do you remember my saying Glorianne was no servant?"

"Yeah. It had something to do with her eight trunks." Jack winked at Catherine.

"In two separate passages, Glorianne refers to her father as being an earl and sitting in the House of Lords." Martin cut a piece of chicken and popped it inside his mouth.

Jack choked on his drink.

"An earl?" Catherine's eyes widened.

Nick, who was seated beside her, reached over and squeezed Catherine's knee.

Martin swallowed and continued. "Glorianne's father's political aspirations were quite lofty. He had drawn up her marriage contract with the Duke of Beaufort's heir."

Nick raised his brows, but Catherine didn't see the significance. He elaborated for her and Jack's benefit. "Other than royal dukes, the Duke of Beaufort is the second highest ranking duke in the United Kingdom."

"Oh, yes. Did I mention Glorianne's last name was Davidson?" Martin said almost as an afterthought. He speared another piece of chicken with his fork.

The room went silent. The glass Catherine had raised froze midair. There was only one earldom in England with the surname of Davidson. Nick's.

"What?" Catherine gasped.

"Come again?" Nick asked.

Jack let out a belly-busting laugh.

"She was the Earl of Rivendon's daughter." Martin's lips curved at the corners, his eyes crinkling. Catherine could tell he was pleased by their reaction.

"Which one?" Nick's eyes were alive with curiosity.

"Glorianne said her father's name was Rudolph, but she never stipulated which Earl of Rivendon. I took it upon myself to do some digging." Martin dabbed his lips with a napkin.

Nick sat back in his chair, clearly aware of Martin's delay tactics.

"Her father was the third Earl of Rivendon." Martin lifted his glass and sipped.

"That's rich. All summer you've been researching Glorianne inside her ancestral home." Jack's shoulders shook.

Catherine spared her brother a dirty look before she addressed Martin's revelation. "You would think something like that would have passed down in our family. There was never any hint of it."

"Catherine's right." Jack crossed his fork and knife over one another on his plate.

"From what I gather, Glorianne married within a year after she reached the colonies. She dropped her title after the ceremony." Martin shrugged. "Her husband, a young Scot, fought on the side of the Americans. The couple had one child together, a daughter named Catherine.

"While you were on holiday, I took the liberty of tracing your ancestors," Martin's voice warmed into what Catherine assumed was lecture mode. "Rudolph Davidson was Glorianne's father. He inherited the title upon the death of his father, Hector, the second Earl of Rivendon. Hector inherited the title from his father, James, a knight who fought with valor. Sir James was made an earl in his twenties by King Charles II when the Stuarts resumed the throne."

Catherine's head swam with the news, and she pressed her fingers to her temples.

"Can't stomach the idea of being related to me?" Nick slipped an arm around her shoulders, his blue eyes alight with suppressed merriment.

"Oh, I don't know." She turned toward him. "I could think of worse things."

"Glorianne was the third earl's only offspring. English primogeniture being what it is, the title passed to a distant cousin after Rudolph died without male issue," Martin said.

"How are we related, Ainsley?" Jack folded his arms across his chest.

"With the family connection so far back, I'll need to hire a professional genealogist to figure it out." Nick wiggled his brows suggestively at Catherine. "But I have it on good authority there are such things as kissing cousins."

CHAPTER FIFTY-ONE

THEODOSIA LOOKED UP FROM HER supper in surprise as Mr. Scott entered Rivendon's dining room with a slender package under his arm. Scott never interrupted meals; it was strictly taboo. Glancing at Rivendon, she said nothing and spooned another swallow of consommé into her mouth.

"What is it, Scott?" Rivendon barked.

"A courier is here for Lady Hadley. He insists on a reply." Scott gave Theodosia a baleful glare.

"Excuse me, my lord." Theodosia made a distasteful expression for Rivendon's behalf as she took the slender packet from Scott.

The Middle Temple address had her hurrying to her office. Why had Donato Delgado sent it? Ripping off the perforated seal, she removed the contents.

Lady Hadley,

Thank you for the document. My firm used it to ship a valuable package overseas.

Inside is a small token of our family's appreciation.

Donato Delgado

The airline ticket to Bali blurred before her eyes. Donato had done it. Ari was safely out of the country. She had couriered Ari's second passport to Delgado's legal firm shortly before the police had returned to search Ari's room.

Tapping the airline ticket with a vermillion nail, Theodosia conjured images of turquoise water, colorful silks, and open-air markets. Best of all, Indonesia did not expedite criminals to the western world. Ari was safe.

Leaving her office, she went to the entry hall. A young man of Italianate visage politely waited, watched over by the basilisk stare of Mr. Scott.

She nodded to him. "Please thank your employer for his kind gesture. I intend to use it."

"Mr. Delgado will be most pleased." The youth tilted his head in a graceful bow.

As Mr. Scott let the courier out, Theodosia turned on her heel, grateful there would be time to tie up one loose end before she left. Her business in Bascombe would not take long, but she looked forward to it with great anticipation.

Entering the dining room, Rivendon narrowed his eyes at her. "I assume these interruptions will not occur a second time while we are at supper?"

"Most decidedly not. I assure you, no one will ever interrupt your suppers on my behalf again." Theodosia spread her napkin on her lap.

Picking up her utensil, she spooned another sampling of consommé. Idly, she wondered if it would be necessary to purchase a third suitcase. Her summer wardrobe would never fit in two.

* * *

Nick's leg muscles strained as he pedaled the steep incline of the priory's switchbacks. The brightest part of the gray morning ride was seeing Catherine out on her morning run. She'd blown him a kiss across the village green. If he hadn't been late meeting his contractor, he would have cycled across the massive field and given her a proper greeting.

After a glance at his sport watch, he pedaled faster. His contractor had arrived early to discuss wood-rot remediation in the east wing. When cash began to flow back into the estate, he had purposely left the east wing closed, knowing it would need the most extensive repairs.

Parking his bike beside the front steps, he raced upstairs, crossing the gallery and entering the disused section of the house. The unheated rooms cooled his overwarm body. Following the sound of hammering, he located his contractor.

He stopped at the bedchamber door and glanced around. The wall of windows faced the fishing stream, where water raced over boulders and tumbled down a short fall. Even the Holland covers draped over the furniture looked in need of repair. Grime caked the few pieces of artwork that had not been stored away.

From the far side of the bed, his contractor looked up from where he knelt examining a wall.

"What have you found, David?" Nick rubbed his neck where the muscles knotted.

"Good news. You're clear of deathwatch beetle." David sat back on his heels.

Nick knew a moment's thankfulness. The cost would have been exorbitant to treat a house this size for wood borers.

"This wall is the worst of the lot." David nodded to the section beside the bed. "I'll need to replace the timbers and redo the plaster. Only this room and the adjoining one are affected."

They negotiated price and talked schedule. Nick had gotten off much lighter than expected. The tension coiling in his shoulders began to ease. Preparing to leave, he scanned the space.

One of the oil paintings had started to curl. He wandered over to take a closer look. By the stiffly arranged subjects and unflattering clothes, he surmised it was from the Georgian era.

An electric shock sang through his veins when his gaze settled on the youngest member of the trio. Her dark hair disappeared into the background, but Nick made out the long, loose curls. The wide-flashing smile and aquamarine eyes were all too familiar. Even the tilt of the girl's head and her nose were carbon copies.

Catherine and this girl could pass for sisters. With curiosity, his eyes shifted to the other subjects in the portrait. The man appeared twice the age of his wife and had a stern countenance and stubborn chin. His blue eyes, dark hair, and strong jawline proclaimed his Davidson lineage.

Long-term unhappiness had settled its mask over the exquisite features the woman shared with her daughter. The protective arm wrapped about her child's waist told its own story.

With great difficulty, Nick read the tarnished plaque attached to the frame. Rudolph Davidson, Third Earl of Rivendon, Catherine, Countess of Rivendon, Lady Glorianne Davidson.

You were here all along. Nick touched the painting as a foggy memory about the countess niggled at the back of his mind. Grandfather had said something about her years ago. What was it?

Filled with elation, Nick began to plan how to surprise Catherine with the portrait. He said to David, "I'll be downstairs in my office. I have some calls to make."

Unable to contain his excitement, Nick texted Catherine. *I discovered something. Are you free to come over?*

What is it?
I can't tell you. It's a surprise.
I HATE surprises!!! Please tell me.
This can only be shared in person.
Coming.
:)

* * *

After his shower, Nick called his grandfather.

"This is a little early for a social call," Grandfather boomed through the speaker.

"I've been up for hours," Nick said, holding the phone away from his ear.

"You've spent too many years farming. An aristocrat does not rise with the chickens."

He could hear the humor in Grandfather's words; Nick must have caught him on a good day. "Do you have a few minutes to chat?"

"What's on your mind, Nicholas?"

"I discovered a painting in the east wing." Nick took a seat on the tufted brown sofa and thrust out his legs.

"Are we speaking famous artwork?"

"Sir Joshua Reynolds." Nick crossed his ankles and looked up at the gilded ceiling. "As it happens, this one's damaged. But it's the subjects I'm curious about."

"Spit it out, my boy. I don't have all day."

"I discovered a family portrait of the third Earl of Rivendon and his family," Nick said.

"I thought the family had destroyed all paintings of him." The earl sounded perplexed. "We were told he murdered or exiled his daughter when she botched his political career."

"One painting survived. Sadly, it needs restoring." Clearing his throat, Nick said, "My call deals with his second wife. Her name was Catherine. I remember you telling me something about her but I can't remember the details."

"A man your age should have perfect recall." The earl snorted.

"I agree."

"You amiable types aren't any fun to argue with."

"Are you stalling because you can't remember?" Nick rose from the sofa, crossed the room, and rested one hip on the edge of his desk.

A bark of laughter erupted through the line. "Are you baiting me?"

"Perhaps." Nick enjoyed the repartee and knew there wouldn't be many years left of this sort of interchange. His phone beeped with an incoming text across the top of his screen. It was from Catherine.

Be there in a few.

Rivendon's tone changed. "Your memory lapse deals with The Countess's Trust. The third earl's second wife set up a trust for her daughter from her private income. The funds went to her daughter, or direct female descendants, upon her death. The trust ensured her daughter's right to independence rather than be manipulated into a marriage not of her liking."

"Why didn't her daughter receive her inheritance?" Nick wanted the entire story before he shared what he knew.

"The girl disappeared. Rumor had it she went to the colonies before they rebelled."

"Why didn't they send an agent over after the war?" Nick fiddled with the stack of ironwork orders on top of his desk.

"By then, the third earl and his wife had passed, and the title and entail came to our branch of the family. The new earl was seventeen years old and didn't know anything about estate administration. By the time he and his trustees had a handle on it, no one knew what had become of the former earl's daughter."

Nick considered the information. "As the Earl of Rivendon, I assume you manage The Countess's Trust?"

"Yes. It's odd you should ask. Within a few months, the trust will revert to the female relatives of the present Earl of Rivendon. If no female relations are found, the money goes to the Church of England."

"Within a few months, you say? Why is that?"

"I don't know exactly. I suppose the countess figured 250-plus years after her death was enough time to find her daughter or her daughter's descendants."

"When exactly does The Countess's Trust come due?"

"October, I believe."

"How many female relations do you have?" A sense of foreboding settled over Nick.

"Since Sally died, just one. Lady Hadley."

"Didn't Sally die from a nasty fall when Lady Hadley was present?" Nick tensed as his mind flashed over the recent incidents Catherine had been subjected to.

"What are you saying?"

"I believe Lady Hadley bears watching." A snippet of conversation came back to him in Sammy's voice. "I saw Lady Hadley kissing Ari . . ."

He rubbed his neck and paced away from the desk. Reaching the window, he twitched the curtain aside, wondering what was keeping Catherine.

"Grandfather, I have reason to believe I have located the legitimate heir to The Countess's Trust."

"Who is it?" Rivendon asked, his voice filled with curiosity.

"Catherine Pressley-Coombes."

CHAPTER FIFTY-TWO

DIGGING FOR HER KEYS, CATHERINE ran down the cottage steps toward the MGB and climbed in. As she rolled down her windows, she noticed a woman dressed in slacks and five-inch heels. Catherine's eyes narrowed with recognition. Lady Hadley strutted down the sidewalk in her direction like a runway model. Catherine waited until the woman drew abreast of the car.

"Is something wrong, Lady Hadley?"

A smile lifted Lady Hadley's red-painted lips but didn't reach her eyes. "Miss Pressley-Coombes. My motorcar has a flat. I'm on my way to Ashford Priory. Would it be too much trouble to give me a lift?"

"Not at all. Hop in." Catherine sighed internally. Would Lady Hadley's unexpected visit interrupt Nick's surprise?

"How supreme. Walking in heels on uneven pavement is dangerous." Lady Hadley's eyes glinted.

Tell me about it.

Lady Hadley let herself in, clutching her Louis Vuitton handbag.

"Would you like me to call Taylor's Garage for you?" Catherine offered.

"That won't be necessary. Lord Ainsley will handle the issue. I would have called him myself, but my mobile is dead."

Catherine pulled onto the road, wishing she didn't dislike this woman so much. They clattered over the medieval bridge spanning the River Rue. Water babbled over the moss-covered stones, and two little boys stood on the bank, chucking rocks.

As the MGB reached the four-way junction on the outskirts of town, Lady Hadley broke the silence. "I'm here to collect a few items on the earl's behalf. He's donating them for a charity auction."

"That was kind of you to make the trip." Catherine didn't know what else to say.

Approaching the pillars marking the entrance to Ashford Priory, Catherine downshifted to second gear. The gate was open, and they started up the steep incline toward the switchbacks. The lime trees enveloped the car under their dark canopy as they wound up the narrow lane against the limestone hillside.

When they reached the top, Lady Hadley pulled a small pearl-handled Browning and Browning from her handbag and pointed it at Catherine.

Catherine's heart seized, and time slowed to a crawl.

"Take the right lane to the outbuildings." The snarl on Lady Hadley's mouth reminded her of the woman at the shed. Ari's helper. Catherine focused on those painted lips. "It was you!"

"Drive." Lady Hadley's gun wobbled in her hand.

Catherine's hands grew clammy, and her heart raced. Praying for time, Catherine shifted gears and stalled. "Sorry. Sorry. That was an accident."

"Shut up." Lady Hadley's large doe-shaped eyes glittered like shards of ice.

Catherine restarted the engine with trembling fingers. Letting up on the clutch too fast, the car bounced forward before it engaged the gear.

Lady Hadley glared at her, her plump painted lips thinning into a straight line. In disbelief, Catherine saw her point the gun at the tree outside the lowered window. The weapon belched fire and let out a deafening roar.

"Stop your nonsense and drive." In the act of crossing her legs, Lady Hadley spilled the contents of her purse onto the floorboards. She bent to return them to her handbag.

Outside the passenger window, a rustle of leaves caught Catherine's attention. Sammy Benson swung into view, hanging by his knees in full spy gear. Her body chilled, and Catherine squeezed the steering wheel until her knuckles went white. Fearing for his life, she placed her finger to her lips and hit the gas, praying the woman had not noticed the child.

The sudden lurch of the car banged Lady Hadley's head against the dashboard. "Are all Americans horrible drivers?"

She took the narrow lane to the walled enclosure of farm buildings. Past the barns and henhouses stood a small stone structure surrounded by trees, its double doors standing wide.

"Pull in there." Lady Hadley motioned toward the open doors.

With the gun trained on her, Catherine did as she was told.

Lady Hadley jumped out of the car and closed the milking parlor doors. "Get out."

Weak kneed, Catherine slid off the seat. How could this be happening to her again?

"You have been a thorn in my side since you arrived in England." The gun wobbled as Lady Hadley removed a pair of handcuffs from her bag.

One glance at the manacles and Catherine's body broke out in a cold sweat. "Why are you doing this?"

"I am protecting my future." She tapped the cuffs against her leg and sneered. "On the eve of my inheriting a substantial fortune, you showed up with a closer claim."

"I have no idea what you're talking about." *Was this woman insane?*

"The Countess's Trust."

"I've never heard of it."

"Removing you resolves my dilemma. As if that weren't enough, your testimony put my Ari in prison." Lady Hadley advanced on her, the cuffs jangling.

Pressing the gun nozzle to Catherine's throat, Lady Hadley slapped a manacle around her wrist. Catherine gasped. Her breath sucked in noisily as Lady Hadley walked her backward to the side of the building.

"If Ari weren't so well connected, he would still be in prison."

Ari was out of jail?

Lady Hadley's large brown eyes gleamed as Catherine absorbed the news. "It's best this way. Ari's too soft hearted for what I have planned."

"Why kill me?"

"Three and a half million pounds is nothing to trifle with."

The rock wall pressed into Catherine's back, halting her retreat. Lady Hadley dug the gun barrel once more into her sore throat. Catherine winced. Quick as a lynx, Lady Hadley pounced, snapping the spare metal cuff around a plumbing line. The drain pipe ran the entire length of wall, its base buried in cement, its top exiting the roof beside a small window.

"Your motorcar has an old exhaust system. Running the engine inside a small, enclosed space might prove hazardous. Don't you agree?" Lady Hadley tossed the blonde hair from her eyes and gave Catherine a saccharine smile.

"Please don't do this. I don't want the money." Catherine's voice shook.

"I don't believe you. Not to worry; you won't feel a thing; you'll simply fall asleep."

Going back to the car, Lady Hadley picked up the abandoned keys and turned on the ignition. She removed a long silk scarf from her handbag. Folding it lengthwise, she approached.

Catherine lifted her chin; her nostrils flared, and her nails dug into her palms. If she was going to die, she wouldn't go meekly.

Lowering her head, Catherine rammed it into Lady Hadley's stomach as hard as she could. Air whooshed out of Lady Hadley's lungs. She bent double, a surprised expression on her face as she gasped for air.

Catherine kicked out, her shoe making contact with the weapon dangling from the woman's hand. The gun flew through the air in a perfect arc. It hit the MGB's fender and went off.

After regaining her breath, Lady Hadley straightened and slapped Catherine's face, knocking her head into the metal pole. Stunned, Catherine slid to the floor in a daze.

CHAPTER FIFTY-THREE

WHERE WAS CATHERINE? NICK WANDERED past the fountain to the edge of the east lawn, squinting through the lime trees for sight of the red motorcar. Catherine had texted forty minutes ago.

Perhaps she'd parked at the stable block and had run into Sammy. The boy had more charm than a box of newborn puppies. Gravel crunched under his feet as he turned in that direction.

At the junction where the lane split, he caught sight of Sammy, his little brow furrowed in concentration. The young spymaster was gouging a hole in one of the priory's specimen trees.

"Why are you digging a hole in my tree?" Nick came up beside the boy, planting his feet wide.

The child looked up, his eyes serious. "I'm collecting evidence."

"What kind of evidence?"

"A bullet."

"Are you sure?" Nick squatted to take a look. Sammy's personality and imagination were so large they were almost two separate entities. Nick fingered the rough bark. Sure enough, a small piece of lead was embedded inside the trunk.

"I wonder how that got there?" The use of firearms was forbidden in this area of the estate. It was too dangerous.

"Lady Hadley shot the tree. She was mad at Miss Catherine's driving."

"Lady Hadley is here? On the estate?" Nick's gut twisted, and cold sweat beaded on his forehead.

Sammy nodded.

"Where is Miss Catherine?"

"She's inside the milking parlor," Sammy said matter-of-factly.

"What is she doing in there?" Nick's heart skittered.

"I dunno. The doors are locked."

Nick pulled out his mobile and punched 999 for emergency services. Holding the phone to his ear, he sprinted for the milking parlor, praying it wasn't too late.

* * *

The low throb of an idling engine greeted Nick's ears when he skidded to a halt in front of the milking parlor. He tried the door. It was locked just as Sammy had said.

"Catherine!" he yelled, throwing his weight against the door. The thick planks wouldn't budge. Nick planted his hands on his knees, panting from exertion. He had to get the door open. The chainsaw was inside the tractor barn several hundred yards away.

The MGB had an original exhaust system. The possibility of carbon monoxide poisoning was very real. How long could she survive? He had no idea when emergency services would arrive. He couldn't take the risk of waiting.

Circling the building, he located the lone window. It was near the rafters and perhaps eighteen inches square. Too small for his bulk. If he could break the glass, it might delay her poisoning.

Where was Lady Hadley? Had she left the vicinity, or was she hiding on the estate? He couldn't worry about her right now. Every second mattered.

Several large trees grew around the perimeter of the building; one of them brushed up against the structure. He started to shimmy up its trunk.

"Whatcha doing, Nick?"

Nick glanced over his shoulder. Sammy Benson had followed him.

He dropped to the ground. "Sammy, if I give you a boost, do you think you could climb up and break that window?" Nick indicated the small square window near the roofline.

"I'm not supposed to break anything. Gran gets mad when I do." The boy's eyes were round as euros.

"It's my window; you won't be in trouble. Can you can reach it?" Nick measured the distance and knew a moment's worry.

Sammy studied the tree and nodded. "Why do you want me to break the glass?"

"There is bad air inside. Miss Catherine needs fresh air."

Hoisting Sammy onto his shoulders, the child caught hold of the lowest branch. Reaching the limb, he scampered up the tree, sure-footed as a monkey, until he reached the window.

Dusting off the glass, Sammy cupped his hands to see inside. "Miss Catherine looks awfully tired. Hey, there's a fireman pole!"

"Is Miss Catherine moving?"

"No." The boy called down to him. "I think she's taking a nap."

Nick had difficulty swallowing from the sudden ache inside his throat. "Take off your shoe and break the glazing. Try not to cut yourself."

Sammy slipped off his footwear and hit the pane. The glass was old and thin and shattered easily.

"I did it, Nick. I like that fire pole." The boy's face lit up.

"Excellent."

"It smells funny." Sammy recoiled and wrinkled his nose.

"Climb down. I'm going to get something to open that door." Nick sprinted to the tractor barn, where his tools were housed, praying Catherine was still alive.

* * *

Nick reached his workshop and stared in dismay. His chain saw lay on the workbench where Charlie had dismantled it. Gritting his teeth in frustration, he grabbed a woodsman's axe and crowbar.

A slight noise behind him made his skin prickle. Glancing over his shoulder, Lady Hadley stood inside the barn door, a gun in her hand.

"Lady Hadley." Holding the axe, Nick turned to face her.

"Hullo, Ainsley. Though I find this scenario rather distasteful, I really cannot allow you to save her."

Nick took in the way she held the gun with the safety partially engaged. She obviously knew nothing about firearms. He estimated his chances were fifty-fifty.

"No questions?" A coy smile lifted her red-painted lips.

"I know the basics."

"You were always clever."

"The police are on their way. You won't get away with this, Theodosia."

"Yes, I will." She took several steps forward, her heels clicking on the concrete. "As I remember, you are rather fond of prose. Star-crossed lovers are rather memorable, aren't they? You'll make headlines, just like always."

Nick moved forward diagonally, forcing her to realign the gun.

"No tricks, Ainsley. Drop that axe, and put your hands up." Using both arms, she steadied the weapon.

In the guise of lowering the axe, he shuffle-stepped forward. Keeping his eyes on hers, Nick measured the distance between them. Thirty inches. Too far. Scooting forward another half step, he saw the determination in her eyes as she lined up the weapon.

With no time to plan, he sprang. His body slammed into hers, pushing her arms up.

The gun discharged with a roar, saturating the air around them with sulfur and smoke. The whine of a ricochet bounced off the tractor and buried itself in the cement floor somewhere to his left.

Lady Hadley's desperation lent her strength. Her fingers locked on the gun. Clapping his hands over hers, Nick turned the gun, bending her wrists backward.

Her lip curled, and she squeezed the trigger. The gun belched fire. Searing pain erupted in his left triceps. The smell of burned flesh filled the air. Lady Hadley grunted and let go of the weapon.

Warm blood dripped down his arm as Nick dragged himself to his feet. Kicking the gun under the tractor, he stared at Lady Hadley. She had curled in on herself like a shrimp doused in cocktail sauce. The bullet had passed through the back of his arm and imbedded itself in her torso.

With his arm burning like fire and his hand slippery with blood, he picked up the axe and left her bleeding on the ground.

Sprinting past the henhouses, he heard the wail of sirens. With a prayer of thankfulness in his heart, he ran up the enclave. The first police car pulled in behind him. DCI Barnes and his sidekick, the red-headed Thackey, were inside.

"Get a medic," Nick yelled.

He rounded the curve in the lane and came to a standstill. The double doors to the milking parlor stood wide.

Six-year-old Sammy Benson swung on the door handle, his cowlick waving in the sunlight like a banner. "That's a cracking fire pole!"

CHAPTER FIFTY-FOUR

Three weeks later

MUCH TO NICK'S DELIGHT, CATHERINE'S departure to the States had been delayed yet again due to police and inheritance proceedings. Last night, he had received a semipanicked call from Catherine. Her father, Richard Pressley-Coombes, and the twins had shown up unannounced at Hawthorne Cottage.

The birthday dinner she had planned for Jack needed a larger space. She had asked to move the party to the priory and use the grounds to play a game of American baseball afterward. Eager to meet her father, he had been delighted to oblige. It would save him a trip to the States. And needless to say, he was more than a little curious about the infamous twins.

After dinner, the Pressley-Coombes siblings started a game of American baseball on the priory's east lawn, with Sammy Benson playing umpire.

Nick went in search of Catherine's father. He found Richard in the library as BBC Business News concluded on the telly. The windows were open, and a slight breeze stirred the air. Richard, an older version of Jack, with graying dark hair and chocolate brown eyes, stood at the window, watching his children.

A picture of Catherine flashed on the telly screen. "DNA test proves American heiress, Catherine Pressley-Coombes, is the sole recipient of a contested two-hundred-fifty-year-old trust set up by her seventh great-grand-mother, Catherine, Countess of Rivendon. The challenging party, Theodosia Stanhope, wife of late MP, Sir Donald Hadley, has been arrested for attempted manslaughter. DNA results prove she is not a member of the Davidson family and has no claim to the inheritance."

"Catherine Pressley-Coombes's name has been linked in recent months to Nicholas Davidson, Viscount Ainsley. The couple is rumored to be engaged."

Nick switched off the telly and joined Richard at the window.

"Sir, with your permission, I'd like to make that last bit of news a reality," Nick said.

"I assume you have a ring burning a hole in your pocket?" Richard's mouth twisted up.

Nick cleared his throat. "Yes, of course."

"Relax, Nick." Richard clapped a hand on his shoulder, jarring Nick's sore arm. His stitches were out, but the gunshot wound had become infected. "Catherine's been yours since the day she ran Jack's car into that ditch."

Out on the lawn, Catherine caught a fly ball and crowed at the top of her lungs, "You are sooo out, Benjamin Pressley-Coombes."

Her antics brought a smile to Nick's face. "You were saying?"

"Our family has a singular track record when it comes to romance."

"I believe that hiccup might have originated from Davidson stock." Nick thought of his own family and their gift for woodcarving.

"Catherine can be a handful when she gets stirred up. You have her brothers to blame for that," Richard warned.

"Thank goodness." Nick hadn't forgotten how she had dealt with the traffickers.

Outside the window, Catherine was up. She took the bat from Ben with a look of grim determination.

"Everybody move in," James yelled. All three brothers erupted in laughter.

Choking up on the bat, Catherine planted her back leg, keeping her eyes on Jack. He tossed a fastball, no slow pitches for his sister. Swinging through, wood and ball connected.

A soft chuckle emitted from Richard as the baseball sailed over James's head.

"Come on, Catherine. Play nice," James groaned, tossing his mitt and running for the ball.

"When have you *ever* played nice with me?" Her laughter pealed like bells.

"Dad should have kept her in ballet. This is embarrassing." Jack readjusted his cap.

Richard slapped Nick on the shoulder, making him wince a second time. "Welcome to the family, son. May I suggest you learn to play baseball?"

* * *

Overheated from the ballgame, Catherine pulled her hair into a ponytail as she watched her family drive toward the priory's first switchback.

Nick waited until she finished, then took her hand. "Do you need to get back right away?"

Thinking about the lineup for the cottage's single shower, Catherine said, "I have time. What do you have in mind?"

"We won't have too many fine evenings left before the weather cools. I thought a walk might do."

She agreed, and they meandered past the fountain, taking the path around the side of the priory to the lake. The panorama of lake, bridge, and fishing stream pressed upon her heart. Soon, she would be gone and all this loveliness a memory.

With the transcription completed on Glorianne's diary, she had fulfilled her mother's request and located her missing family. She wished Mom were here to share the moment. It comforted her to know Jack had changed his opinion about Mom's lineage. The twins too had come around, but she suspected her inheritance had something to do with that.

With her job waiting in Virginia, she couldn't delay her return much longer. Nick hadn't given her a reason to stay. She would have given up her employment if he had, but Mom had drilled Southern manners into her. Women did not propose to men. She was tempted to threaten Nick with her baseball bat if he didn't though.

She knew he loved her, yet he seemed content to leave their relationship status quo. The Countess's Trust meant little to her without the man she loved. She had planned to set up trusts for their children and start a foundation for victims of human trafficking with the rest. With a pang, she realized those future children might never be born. If that was the case, at least her inheritance would provide rehabilitation for those who had been trafficked.

Crossing the bridge over the lake, the sweet chestnut tree loomed in the near distance. It had been some time since she had come this way. The breeze rippled the long grass. A lark called out in the silence.

Nick interrupted her thoughts. "I have something for you at the priory. In all the excitement, I forgot."

"What is it?"

"I discovered a painting in the east wing of Rudolph Davidson; his wife, Catherine; and their daughter, Glorianne." When they reached the chestnut tree, Nick stopped under its boughs.

Catherine's mouth dropped open.

"The painting is by Reynolds and needs restoring. Despite the stylized portraiture, you bear a strong resemblance to Glorianne."

"Really?" She laughed in delight.

"Very much so." Nick brought her hand to his mouth and kissed it, sending shivery thrills through her body.

"I've been thinking." A furrow creased his forehead.

"What about?"

"I really dislike your name."

"What's wrong with my name?" It was so unexpected, she gaped at him.

"It's all wrong for you." With his free hand, he touched her cheek.

Her heart took off like a rocket, leaving her a little light-headed.

"Lady Ainsley sounds rather nice, doesn't it?"

Her throat closed entirely. She couldn't speak.

"I had a ring made from a queen's brooch and a pretty speech to match it. You broke things off before I gave you either. As it happens, I'm quite happy you did." He smiled at her.

"You're glad you didn't propose?" Her heart constricted, and she tugged to free her hand.

He refused to let go. "Thank you for holding true to your ideals."

Her heart began to pound again, slapping against her rib cage.

"Without your box, I would never know this depth of joy."

She tried to swallow, but her throat was so tight she almost strangled.

"I adore you, Catherine." His hands slid to her waist. "I have since that very first day when I found you stuck in my ditch. You smiled at me, and I knew I'd been waiting my entire life for you. I promised myself I'd marry you if you'd have me."

"You didn't know me then. What if I'd been a horrible person like your cousin?"

According to Agent Butler, when Lady Hadley recovered, they had enough evidence to put her away for twenty-five years. Unfortunately, Ari had gotten clean away.

"Impossible." Nick shook his head.

"How so? You weren't to know."

"There was goodness shining in your eyes." He wrapped a strand of her curls around his hand. "I love you, Catherine. I didn't understand what you were talking about the day we parted. But I do now. I too want a forever after. And I want it with you."

Catherine closed her eyes, melting. He could say such pretty things with that accent.

Pulling out of their embrace, Nick knelt at her feet and held out an impossibly large split-shank diamond ring. Catherine's knees bent, and she had to concentrate on breathing. A halo of small diamonds surrounded the oval stone. *Beautiful.*

"Would you do me the very great honor of becoming my wife?"

All she could do was nod.

"Catherine, if I'm to kneel at your feet on this cold, wet ground, I need to hear you say the words."

She touched the chestnut's rough bark for support as Nick and the ring swung in a dizzy arc before her eyes. Her fingers brushed against the carved initials of the fourth earl. The significance of their location did not escape her. She gave him a sassy smile. "I will, if you promise to feed me chocolate every day and let me ride your pony."

"Bargaining, are we?" Nick glanced at the tree, taking in the fourth earl's initials. "Agreed."

"Then, yes, Lord Ainsley. I will marry you."

He rose from his knee and slipped the ring onto her finger.

The stone was huge.

"Which queen did you say?" she asked, gulping.

"Catherine of Braganza, the wife of King Charles II. The four-carat diamond was the centerpiece of a hideous brooch." He held her hand, looking at the ring. "I'll need to purchase another pony; Walter is too old to hold even a feather-weight like you."

"Actually, I'm scared of horses," Catherine said, a blush rising up her neck.

His jaw dropped. "I didn't think you were afraid of anything. It was quite a blow when I didn't save you on either occasion. The worst of it was being beat out by a six-year-old."

"You've saved me from eternal loneliness." She cupped his face.

"That makes two of us," he whispered against her mouth, and kissed her soundly. After a time, he said, "Pick your temple. I don't care which. My baptism anniversary is in ten months and three days. Does that make a reasonable date for a wedding?"

"It's perfect." Catherine glanced up at the spreading boughs with their myriad initials. Once she and Nick were married, she imagined they would return to the temple often. A lot of forever afters depended on them.

With their arms entwined, she and Nick started back toward the priory.

ABOUT THE AUTHOR

BORN AND RAISED IN SOUTHERN California, Paige Edwards is a multi-award-winning author who enjoys clean romances and thrillers. A BYU–I alumna, she went on to graduate summa cum laude from NOVA with a degree in interior design. Her husband's job transferred their family to the mid-Atlantic states, where they have lived ever since. As a member of the Daughters of the American Revolution and former chapter registrar, she has spent a great amount of time researching applicants' genealogical credentials. When she needs a break from writing, you can find her shooing deer out of her garden, biking battlefields, or kayaking on the lake.

Find out about Paige's upcoming projects, research trips, and book recommendations at:

Website: www.authorpaigeedwards.com

Facebook: https://www.facebook.com/authorpaigeedwards/

Instagram: https://www.instagram.com/authorpaigeedwards/